The Economy of Literary Form

The Economy of Literary Form

*English Literature and the
Industrialization of Publishing,
1800-1850*

LEE ERICKSON

THE JOHNS HOPKINS UNIVERSITY PRESS

Baltimore and London

© 1996 The Johns Hopkins University Press
All rights reserved. Published 1996
Printed in the United States of America on acid-free paper
05 04 03 02 01 00 99 98 97 96   5 4 3 2 1

The Johns Hopkins University Press
2715 North Charles Street
Baltimore, Maryland 21218-4319
The Johns Hopkins Press Ltd., London

ISBN 0-8018-5145-9

Library of Congress Cataloging-in-Publication Data will be
found at the end of this book.
A catalog record for this book is available from the British
Library.

Paperback edition, 1999
ISBN 0-8018-6358-9

For Alan Roper

Contents

Preface and Acknowledgments

The late Warren Woodrow "Woody" Wooden asked me in 1982 to give a paper at the Carolinas Symposium on British Studies, for which he was then the program director. In the middle of revising my book on Browning, I wrote a paper that speculated about the reasons for the decline of the early-nineteenth-century poetry market, something that had affected the beginning of Browning's career in the 1830s. I pursued this research further at an NEH Summer Seminar directed by Alvin B. Kernan at Princeton University in 1983. This work developed into an article, "The Poets' Corner," which appeared in *ELH* in 1985 and whose editors have graciously allowed me to reprint it as the first chapter here in a revised and longer form. I subsequently received an NEH Summer Stipend in 1984 to work on the market for the essay, and was later awarded an NEH Fellowship for 1985–86 to work on the complete project. In 1987 I received an ACLS Grant-in-Aid to continue my research. I am grateful to have received these fellowships and grants, which have enabled me to devote more time to my research and writing. During the ACLS grant, I completed an essay on Wordsworth's poetic career, which was first published in the *Journal of English and Germanic Philology* in 1990, and which appears here with the editor's permission in a revised form as the second chapter.

In describing the decline in the market for poetry, I had begun with the easiest part of my study, and, finding myself working in the middle of nineteenth-century publishing history, I discovered that I had much to learn. The expanding markets for the essay and for the novel proved much more difficult to describe and required much more extensive research. In 1990 I published an essay on Jane Austen and the circulating library in *Studies in English Literature, 1500–1900*, which, with the editor's permission, is reprinted here in a revised version as the fifth chapter. Since then, I have been the recipient of a sabbatical year, several grants of release time, and three awards for summer research from Marshall University, for which I am grateful and without which this study would have taken much longer to complete. I also would like to thank the Bayerische Staatsgemälde-sammlungen for its permission to reproduce from the Neue Pinakothek München Carl Spitzweg's *Der arme Poet*; Yale University's British Art Center for permission to reproduce Thomas Malton's print after a drawing by Georgiana Keate of *Hall's Library at Margate*, and the New York Public Library for permission to reproduce a drawing by Daniel Maclise of "The Fraserians." I am especially grateful to Robert De Maria for informing me that a copy of Malton's print was to be found at Yale's British Art Center.

The research for this book has been done primarily at the New York Public Library, whose librarians and staff have aided me over the twelve years of my research. Preliminary work was done both here at the Marshall University Library, with much help from its interlibrary loan librarians, and also, when I was on sabbatical leave in 1991–92, at the Vassar College Library. I have also consulted the Columbia University Library, the New York University Library, the Yale University Library, the Princeton University Library, the Harvard University Library, the Cornell University Library, and the Ohio State University Library. I owe the helpful librarians and staff at all of these institutions my thanks for their assistance. As the paper in many books from the early nineteenth century becomes brittle and as bindings and backs decay, research in this field is becoming more difficult, since many books are literally disappearing. I may have been, for example, the last scholar to see Yale University's copy of Michael Banim's *The Ghost-Hunter and His Family* (1833), which I read in the Preservation Section there in 1991, but which three years later could not be found and of which apparently no record exists other than my notes recording that it was last seen there. Fortunately, a photographic reprint of Yale's copy of Banim's novel had already been made, but scholars will not be so lucky with many other books. Soon, no doubt, the difference between books that were actually published and bibliographical ghosts will in many cases only be the testimony of the readers and cataloguers who once saw them.

Further, since my study concerns long-term economic trends in the early-nineteenth-century marketplace, I have observed with trepidation that many of the first scholarly histories about publishing in the period were written in the late 1920s and early 1930s; A. S. Collins' *Profession of English Letters*, for instance, first appeared in 1929. The appearance of the present work and others like it may well be an unconscious harbinger of financial hard times in the offing. I hope I am wrong, because much of the financial support for humanities research in America, especially that coming from the endowments of the private universities and foundations, now depends directly upon continued corporate growth and upon rising stock markets. Certainly, no one will thank me if I am right in seeing a financial heart of darkness ahead for the scholarly and academic world in this country. Yet, I would point out that we are now attempting to educate about half of our eighteen-year-olds in some version of college (and graduating only about half of those), while no other nation in the world is providing higher education for more than a third of the same age group. Thus, even without some severe financial shock, existing economic pressures to optimize long-term social returns on educational resources seem likely to grow stronger and to lead inevitably to widespread retrenchment in universities, foundations, and research centers.

Perhaps because I have such forebodings, I find the poet of Carl Spitzweg's *Der arme Poet* (1839) an immensely attractive and congenial figure (pg. 2). He is intent upon counting the syllables and accents of his new poem, even as he is forced to burn the manuscripts of his old ones to keep warm, and even as he must protect himself in his bed from the leaks in his garret's roof by placing a torn umbrella above his head. He is cheerful in his artistic obsession, although he obviously has no market for his work, and although, as the hexameters scanned on his wall and the copy of *Gradus ad Parnassum* beside his bed appear to indicate, he seems dedicated to a long-outmoded neoclassical ideal of poetry. Finally, in the loving care that Spitzweg shows for the details of this eccentric German poet's life, down to the creases on his oversized pillows and to his writing on the wall, I have seen a visual correlative of my scholarly concern for the details of the publishing market that affected early-nineteenth-century English writers and their choice of literary forms, details that I hope will make the conditions under which those writers worked come to life for readers today.

To the extent that I have succeeded in making the past live in this study, I owe special thanks to many who have read or commented on my work during its slow evolution. I have gained much from the advice and comments of Alvin B. Kernan, Alan Roper, Kurt Heinzelman, John Sutherland, Alan Liu, Frederick Burwick, Carl Woodring, Alistair Duckworth, and Robert L. Patten. This book is dedicated to Alan Roper, Professor Emeritus of UCLA, who directed me toward literary history, and whose belief that literature best records the spirit of its time and place has informed every page of the present work. Although I am grateful to Robert Kinsman for reasons that do not bear on this study, I should say that he once remarked to me in passing that the darkest secrets of nineteenth-century literature must lie in its publishing history, a statement that I then attributed to his bibliographical interests as an editor of Sir Thomas Elyot's *Book of the Governor,* but which I now know to have been more right than he perhaps realized or guessed. To John Teel and Julia Thomas go my thanks for their friendship and conversation over the years at Marshall. And I am particularly grateful to my colleagues at Marshall who took the time to read my work. My thanks go to Richard Badenhausen, who helped me sort out the introduction, and especially to Michele Schiavone, who has saved me from making many errors that I would have otherwise never seen. Finally, I must thank my wife, Ellen Martin, who for years has listened to me talk about my work and its difficulties, has provided long-distance emergency assistance when Marshall's library could not immediately provide answers to my bibliographical questions, and has long endured my scattered papers that have often threatened to submerge her New York apartment during the summers and that are now gathered together here.

The Economy of Literary Form

Carl Spitzweg, *Der arme Poet* (1839). Oil on canvas.
Reproduced courtesy of the Bayerische Staatsgemäldesammlungen from the Neue
Pinakothek München, Inv. Nr. 7751.

The Marginal Utility of Literary Form

In these days, ten ordinary Histories of Kings and Courtiers were well exchanged against the tenth part of one good History of Booksellers.

—Carlyle, "Boswell's Life of Johnson" (1832)

I became interested in the subject of this study while writing a book on Robert Browning and wondering why, in the 1830s and 1840s, Edward Moxon was virtually the only publisher of contemporary poetry, but that in the days of Scott and Byron many publishers had welcomed the manuscripts of new poets. I was also rereading Marshall McLuhan's *Gutenberg Galaxy* (1962) and thought that perhaps some change in printing comparable to the invention of moveable type had occurred in the early nineteenth century and that it had somehow affected the publishing of poetry. This hypothesis led me to discover what many bibliographers and publishing historians have long known but have insufficiently emphasized, namely, that publishing became industrialized in the early nineteenth century. But why this should have affected poetry in the way it did was not immediately clear. There seemed to be a need for an exploration of the economic connections between the publication of literary forms and market conditions. The decline in the market for poetry reflected by the publishers' lack of enthusiasm for verse manuscripts in the 1830s seemed to suggest that there existed some kind of economy of readers' demands and authors' productions represented and made evident by literary form and that an investigation into the publishing market and its mechanisms would help to explain the relations in the early nineteenth century among genres in the literary marketplace.

It would seem reasonable to suppose that as writing became more lucrative and more professional in the nineteenth century, authors shifted from literary forms suited for the pursuit of patronage to forms that would in themselves be productive property, from forms that economically exhibited the literary excellence appreciated by cultivated patrons to forms that excited voracious young readers.[1] But as publishing historians have shown, the history of copyright reflects more the interests of publishers than of authors, especially since long-lived profitable copyrights were rare.[2] In the early-nineteenth-century literary marketplace, the increasing competition that periodicals offered against books gradually made publishers happy to let authors retain copyright and so bear more of the initial economic risk in producing books. In studying historical publishing trends it seemed to me that the general shift of talented authors from writing in one form to another needed to be explained within the framework of an economy of literary forms; the literary forms needed to be viewed as patterns articulated by the intersection of readers' desires and authors' aspirations; and such a hermeneutic of aesthetic response and production had to be grounded in a historical study of the early-nineteenth-century English literary marketplace.

Since I have tried to understand the context in which the work of canonical authors was formed, I have confined my study to poetry, the essay, and the novel. Further, in my discussion I concentrate on relatively well known authors and works. This focus reflects my general attempt to explain to literary critics and historians the significance of the publishing market. It also underlines the financial importance of appealing to the fashionable taste in the publishing marketplace during the period. Because early-nineteenth-century readers found that books were still expensive luxuries, publishers made more money and assumed less risk by selling fashionable literature to the few who were well off than by catering to the undeveloped tastes of many who were newly literate. Two thousand copies of a three-decker novel by, say, Bulwer-Lytton, costing thirty-one shillings sixpence, would bring his publisher £300; in contrast, 200,000 copies of a number of G. W. M. Reynolds' *Mysteries of London* (1845–46) costing a penny would produce a profit of only £83. Cheap literary publications would have had to have been bought by many more people to have been as profitable.

1. Ian Watt observes that "poetry is peculiarly suited to a system of patronage, if only because many patrons may be presumed to be even more chary of their time than of their money" ("Publishers and Sinners," 12).
2. For the history of copyright in this period, see J. J. Barnes, *Authors, Publishers, and Politicians.* See also John Feather, "Publishers and Politicians," parts 1 and 2.

Publishing and social historians, however, have traditionally been interested in sociological questions concerning the scale of publication and the distribution of books rather than their literary qualities or their profitability. This growing body of publishing history is valuable, but it has inevitably concerned itself with counting or listing works that almost no one has been willing to read for a long time and that only a few scholars today are even willing to read about. To make the importance of publishing and literary history clear to scholars and critics who focus on the major nineteenth-century English authors in their teaching and research, my study explores the interrelations between literary quality and profitability in order to arrive at an understanding of the nineteenth-century publishing market and its effects upon literature. Thus, I concern myself primarily with the effects on literary forms resulting from the changes of scale in publishing made possible by technological and economic developments in early-nineteenth-century England, and I investigate how the economic implications of those changes affected those forms in the literary marketplace.

In presenting a classical free-market economic analysis of the early-nineteenth-century English literary market, I attempt to describe the relative cultural status of poetry, the essay, and the novel after the developments of the Fourdrinier papermaking machine, stereotyping, and the power press had industrialized printing, thus making economies of scale possible in publishing and so allowing more readers to read than ever before. Further, I consider briefly a few of the aesthetic effects created by writers' attempts to reach larger audiences. Many aesthetic issues in early-nineteenth-century English literature revolve around the pressures that writing for a large reading public placed upon literary quality. For as authors tried to appeal to a large number of people, they found themselves addressing the lowest common denominator among those people. Nonetheless, one needs to remember that, except for the circumstances surrounding an extraordinary bestseller, early-nineteenth-century literary publishing practice closely resembled the recent modern academic publishing of literary criticism, since most books were published in editions of somewhere between 500 and 1,500 copies, and, especially in the case of novels, were sold to libraries. This meant that reactions to a work by a few influential individuals, particularly reviewers, were vitally important to a book's immediate reception and sale. It also meant that making much money from writing books was highly unusual.

Although from time to time I comment on social class, gender, and age as issues in English publishing history, it should be clear that I am not engaged in a sociological or political analysis of nineteenth-century publishing history and literature, and that I am primarily concerned with the relations between literary forms and publishing market conditions. It would appear, for example, that those authors who could best resist market pressures were the most likely to be formally innovative: Browning, who had independent means, may have been frustrated because no one understood him and few people read him, but he felt in no way constrained by a need to make money to subordinate his poetic forms to cultural expectations. On the other hand, a writer like Jane Austen, who was interested in making money from her writing,[3] and who by the standards of her time was moderately successful, was happy to write within the conventions of the circulating library novel.

I

Since paper for books was made from cotton and linen rags during the early nineteenth century,[4] the expansion of readership and of book production during the period depended upon the industrialization of textile manufacturing in the late eighteenth century and the availability of cheap clothes for all of England's and Europe's population. There had to be an industrialization of cloth manufacturing before books could be similarly mass produced from recycled cotton and linen rags, and then sold at an

---

3. Consider, for instance, her remarks in a letter to Francis Austen, of September 25, 1813, on the advent of the third edition of *Sense and Sensibility*: "I shall rather try to make all the Money than all the Mystery I can of it" (*Jane Austen's Letters*, 340).

4. Dard Hunter, *Papermaking*, 309. In 1840 Friedrich Gottlob Keller invented in Germany a machine for grinding wood into wood pulp; K. F. G. Kuehn mixed this wood pulp with rag fibers to make paper but could not produce a marketable product. In 1846 Heinrich Voelter, a German paper manufacturer, bought Keller's patent, further developed and refined the process to make it commercially viable and began to produce paper made from wood pulp with an admixture of rags as early as 1852. But the new technology did not become important for the paper industry until the 1860s and 1870s (376–81). The expansion of the late-nineteenth-century publishing market made possible by cheaper wood-pulp paper is thus outside the historical scope of my study.

The development of bleaching processes so that colored rags could be used for paper matters more for the period. Henry Mayhew suggests how far this process had been developed by around 1850: "A good many years ago—perhaps until 30 years back—*rags*, and especially white and good linen rags, were among the things most zealously inquired for by the street-buyers, and then 3d a pound was a price readily paid. Subsequently the paper-manufacturers brought to great and economical perfection the process of boiling rags in lye and chlorine, so that colour became less a desideratum" (*London Labour and the London Poor*, 2:104). However, the process was still evidently expensive, because Mayhew observes that while clean white linen rags brought two to three pence a pound, colored linen rags were worth only 20 percent of the white ones, bringing just two pence for five pounds (139).

affordable price to a large reading public. Because people became able to afford larger wardrobes, to accelerate their consumption of clothing with new fashions, and to discard old clothes and bedding long before they were unwearable or unusable, the supply of rags available for paper production increased greatly. The new mountain of rags on rubbish heaps thus allowed for an exponential growth in publishing and increased the availability of books and periodicals to the English common reader. Around 1785, following the expansion of the textile industry, the English publishing industry's growth began to take off. This is reflected during the late 1780s in the accelerated increase in the number of printed items coming from English publishers. Having risen gradually from roughly 1,800 printed items of all kinds in 1740 to around 3,000 items in 1780, English publications suddenly double to 6,000 by 1792.[5] The industrialization of the clothing industry not only permitted the manufacture of clothing to increase much faster than the rate of increase in the population but also allowed the cost of books and periodicals, half to two-thirds of which stemmed from the cost of paper at the beginning of the nineteenth century, to remain generally constant during the period despite a rising demand from readers.[6] So when individual incomes rose, readers found that books and periodicals were much less expensive and much more numerous in 1850 than they had been in 1800.

During these fifty years the periodical became the dominant publishing format because it was the most dependably profitable one, so it affected the development and relative cultural importance of poetry, the essay, and the novel. Poetry, which had prospered in books when prices were high during the Napoleonic Wars, soon became unprofitable once periodicals became the main source of publishers' profits. With the rise of the periodicals, the essay was for about twenty years the dominant literary form in the reviews and magazines and was the most readily marketable literary commodity. Soon, however, publishers found that the serialized novel attracted great interest and held the reader's attention better from issue to issue, so by 1850 installments from novels carried many literary periodicals, while cheap reprints of popular novels dominated a publisher's backlist.

My analysis of the economy of literary forms focuses not only on the

5. These are the estimates of Michael Crump, based upon the Eighteenth-Century Short Title Catalogue, which have been graphically represented in James Raven, *Judging New Wealth*, 32, fig. 1. Raven presents a smoothed curve of the five-year moving average of the number of titles published (partly to adjust for problems in dating much of the printed ephemera more closely than within a decade), but the take-off pattern of an exponential growth curve is evident.
6. For the cost of paper in the period, see D. C. Coleman, *The British Paper Industry*, 203, fig. 8.

authors' attempts to supply the market but also on the demands created by readers. Since readers read within a framework of desire, the economy of literary forms can be described from the perspective of reception as well as that of production. In this way, literary forms can be viewed as historical, aesthetic products of market forces reaching a momentary equilibrium between the aspirations of writers and the desires of their audiences. They can be seen as aesthetic interference patterns or feedback phenomena, mutually created, on the one hand, by authors seeking to anticipate their readers' responses, and, on the other, by readers reading a work within what Hans Robert Jauss calls their "horizon of expectations."[7] From this viewpoint the study of literary forms is concerned with literature's imitation of itself, and a theory of genre must focus on a history of mimetic production. It is precisely for this reason that any idealist defense of literature has found it necessary to oppose genre. Benedetto Croce, for example, holds that "a work of art is always *internal*; and what is *external* is no longer a work of art."[8] But because it is the history of literature's self-imitation, the history of literary forms demonstrates that literature is materially and economically embedded in the reality of the publishing marketplace. As Rosalie Colie notes in observing that Renaissance booksellers frequently bound works on the same subject or of the same type together,[9] literary form is as much a product of the marketers and the readers as it is of the authors.

II

My approach offers a historical and economic reformulation of an aesthetics of literary reception that analyzes the relative marginal utility for

---

7. *Toward an Aesthetic of Reception*, 25–28, 139–85.
Marilyn Butler would appear sympathetic to an aesthetic of reception, when she says, "A book is made by its public, the readers it literally finds and the people in the author's mind's eye" (*Romantics, Rebels, and Reactionaries*, 9). But without a working knowledge of publishing history and without more than a passing interest in the contemporary reception of individual works, she sees the Romantic authors largely as Aeolian harps for the period's shifting political winds.
My approach also differs from those of Marc Shell and Kenneth Burke, whose work the title of my study may seem to echo. I am not presenting a semiotic analysis of the history of ideas about money and exchange as Marc Shell does in both *The Economy of Literature* and in *Money, Language, and Thought: Literary and Philosophical Economies from the Medieval to the Modern Era*. I am also not analyzing the symbolic action of forms as Kenneth Burke does in *The Philosophy of Literary Form: Studies in Symbolic Action*.
8. *Aesthetics*, 45.
9. *The Resources of Kind*, 15–17.

readers of literary forms by investigating the publishing market. For there to be incentives for writers to write, readers must pay for their pleasure. An analysis of the marginal utility[10] of literary forms is therefore possible; that is, the historical conditions of literary production and reception can be described in terms of the literary market reflected in publishing history.

By examining the structure of the aggregate demand of individual readers for literary forms as reflected by the nineteenth-century publishing market, I have inferred the character of the changes in the relative marginal utility of reading and buying certain literary forms during the period. Thus, for an individual reader a literary work offers on the first reading a certain pleasure, which usually diminishes with each subsequent rereading. But there are also many other works one does not finish or even begin. The aggregate calculus of such individual desires is then reflected in the market by the demand both for individual literary works and for genres. The more a work or a genre provides intense immediate pleasure for readers, the more likely it is to be a bestseller; the more it can stand up to rereading without its reading pleasure being diminished, the more readers think of it as a classic and as part of the literary canon. A work that provides great pleasure upon rereading is also more likely to be bought than borrowed.

This literary economy is, of course, already built into the pedagogical canon by professional readers, and privileges, for example, the verbal and allusive density of poetry over prose in surveying the history of literature. It would appear that when the cost of books is high, readers will prefer a work in a literary form which will provide the most pleasure upon rereading and has the most satisfying verbal texture. Conversely, when the cost of books is low, readers will care less about the pleasure of prospective rereadings

---

10. I use the term *marginal utility* in its standard economic sense as defined by, for example, Paul A. Samuelson and William D. Nordhaus in *Economics*; that is, marginal utility is the satisfaction gained by an individual from an additional unit of a thing, or in other words from the particular choice of a single good at the margin. Will, for example, a second apple have as much value as the first for an individual, especially in the context of other available choices? Similarly, one may consider the *relative* marginal utility for an individual of a choice among an apple, orange, or banana. Each thing that an individual wants or may acquire in the realm of all possible acquisitions has some particular value for that individual. This value is its relative marginal utility. Now, in general, each additional unit of a thing will be worth less than the first unit to an individual; and each subsequent additional unit of the same thing will be worth less than the previous one. This is the definition of diminishing marginal utility. For most people most of the time, the second apple will be worth less than the first to them. Since there generally is a diminishing marginal utility in acquiring additional units of a thing, at some point the price that an individual is willing to pay for one more unit of a thing will fall below its existing market price so that the individual will be unwilling to pay for some quantity (whether it be one unit or one hundred units) of that thing. The aggregate demand in the market for a particular product will then be the sum of individual demands.

and prefer a work in a genre that gives the most immediate pleasure. As Cyril Connolly remarks in his *Enemies of Promise*, "books grew cheaper, and reading them ceased to be a luxury; the reading public multiplied and demanded less exacting entertainment; the struggle between literature and journalism began. Literature is the art of writing something that will be read twice; journalism what will be grasped at once, and they require separate techniques."[11] Most readers who like mysteries, for instance, find that once they know they have already read a story and know its outcome, the suspenseful pleasure and play of the form is so seriously diminished that they will not reread it and instead much prefer to read another. Since certain literary forms apparently stand up to rereading better than others, those genres will do and have done better in the publishing market under specific economic conditions.

An analysis of the marginal utility of literary forms can then be pursued by examining the reading public's taste and the kinds of literature that were produced and sold at particular moments in publishing history. As the writers of the time did, I will point to changes in the forms that occurred because early-nineteenth-century authors and their works did or did not appeal to the growing reading public; in doing so, I will show that literature is greatly influenced by market pressures, and that literary history is greatly affected by economic history. As my study shows, economic pressures on literature are particularly acute at moments of technological change such as that which occurred at the beginning of the nineteenth century. My account of these pressures will help to explain, for instance, why there was suddenly such a massive alienation of the greatest writers from the reading public at a time when more people were reading than ever before, something that would have seemed to promise for the best writers a greater power than they had ever had before to influence many, to persuade a few, and to enrich themselves.

This study also examines how writers respond to the demands placed upon them by the market. When nineteenth-century authors found themselves wedded to the publishing marketplace, they became ambivalent about its effect upon the artistic work of their production, while recognizing that they could not escape the publishing conditions of their times. Although Byron, Shelley, and Keats died in the 1820s, for example, more poets would have written more poetry in the 1830s had there been a demand and a market for poetry. Observing this phenomenon in 1836,

11. *Enemies of Promise*, 18–19.

Thomas Love Peacock asserted that the literary Zeitgeist and its authors depend upon the marketplace:

> Every variety of mind takes its station, or is ready to do so, at all times in the literary market; the public of the day stamp the currency of fashion on that which jumps with their humour. Milton would be forthcoming if he were wanted; but in our time Milton was not wanted, and Walter Scott was. We do not agree with the doctrine implied in Wordsworth's sonnet,
>
> > Milton! thou should'st be living at this hour:
> > England hath need of thee.
>
> England would have been the better for him, but England would not have attended to him if she had had him. There was no more market for him than for Cromwell. When Shakspeare was, Mozart and Rossini and Giulietta Grisi were not. The musical drama has struck down the legitimate. Shakspeare wrote plays, because it was the best thing he could do for himself. If he were now carrying a link before the Teatro alla Scala, he would probably limit his ambition to writing libretti for the next Gran Maestro.[12]

As Peacock observes, the prevailing aesthetic of reception largely determines the market for authors. Further, as the examples of Milton and Shakespeare imply, when the quality of demand falls, both the quality of literature declines as well as the cultural status of the writing produced. In the Italy of 1836 Shakespeare could only have hoped to be a librettist for Verdi.

Literary talent that is not economically insulated must address itself to the demands of the publishing market. For this reason, the appearance of essayists such as Lamb, Hazlitt, Carlyle, and Macaulay in the 1820s was not a cultural or historical accident but the product of the economic demand for discursive prose by a relatively elite audience. Later, in the 1860s, the great prose writing came as the public suddenly focused on a smaller number of periodicals. Although no one imagines that the tragedies of Aeschylus, Sophocles, and Euripides were created in a cultural vacuum, or that Greek theater was without an audience, such considerations have usually been systematically excluded from the analysis of nineteenth-century literature. Why the connections between production and cultural reception have not been investigated is in part a pragmatic function of certain pedagogical imperatives in teaching students who need to develop their reading and writing skills for professional vocations and who have little use for the historical baggage that accompanies those texts which employ the most sophisticated rhetoric and language. Yet we need to understand how those

12. "The Épicier," in *The Works of Thomas Love Peacock*, 9:294–95.

historical conditions are mirrored in the very themes and rhetoric of those texts, and also have to realize that the historical conditions for the production of literature need to be mediated critically in a new way.

I have focused upon the production of literary forms: how the publishing market mediated between authors and their audiences, and how the periodical format became the driving force behind literary production in the early nineteenth century. Today's critical view of early-nineteenth-century literature has been obscured by teaching from anthologies and by privileging the book format in discussing the production of literature, when, in fact, to this day intellectual discourse on all levels usually appears first within and is always mediated by a periodical context. One needs to remember that a book serialized today in, say, the *New Yorker* will, with the exception of the best of the bestsellers, have a larger circulation in periodical than book form. Further, book reviews usually have a wider readership than the books themselves. Observing this phenomenon, Tom Wolfe considers it a kind of intellectual prison: "The literary-intellectual mode that still survives in the United States and England today was fashioned more than 150 years ago in Regency England with the founding of magazines such as the *Edinburgh Review*, the *Quarterly*, *Blackwood's*, the *London Magazine*, the *Examiner*, and the *Westminster Review*"; and as he later says, "Remarkably, the literary-intellectual mode has remained locked for more than a century and a half in precisely that format: of books and moral protest by gentlemen-amateurs, in the British polite-essay form."[13]

Certainly the focus upon literature as an isolated artistic product has had the benefit of encouraging much formal and rhetorical analysis. Especially in America, this focus has also had the pedagogical advantage of detaching the most sophisticated linguistic and rhetorical texts in the language from an increasingly alien English history and so of saving them for the students who will benefit from addressing them. At the same time, purely formal approaches have fostered a remoteness of literature from the concerns of human life, not least by separating literature from the way it is produced, and so have created a need for a historical study of the relations between literary forms and their publication formats. To isolate literature as an autonomous object for formal study has become an even less satisfactory critical approach in the current literary and cultural environment because of the dominance of images and their technology. While the focus of new criticism has been upon the relations between language and form, the

13. *The Pump House Gang*, 160.

center of any economic analysis of literary form will be on the mediation between the desires of author and audience as reflected by the literary marketplace. Further, as writing has begun to enter the computer and information-processing age, analysis of literature in terms of its publishing history seems particularly necessary and vital. The economic urgency that views texts as changing information on a computer screen is clearly opposed to the leisurely contemplation of literature as fixed artistic objects. Indeed, the new information technologies are readjusting critical questions about literature, its format, and its publication. They are also threatening in large measure a decentralization of culture, not just through desktop publishing but through the transmission and reception of information that is mediated not so much by publishers as by telecommunications companies.

Moreover, since dominant technologies of the image have typically been evident in highly stratified cultures of power (most notably during the medieval period), it would seem that we are on the threshold of a major reorganization of world cultures. This seems especially true when we realize that writing today has come to be subordinate to the image and when we know that the image represents authority more effectively than does the word. Because the free expression of individual viewpoints in writing appears to be endangered by the presentation of today's authoritative, corporate images that seek the conformity of viewers to them, I believe that the changes and threats that new printing technology created for literature in the early nineteenth century deserve special critical attention.

III

The intellectual hierarchy of written formats—books, magazines, and newspapers—has not changed since it assumed its present form in the early nineteenth century. The stratification of humanist intellectual culture has remained the same, even though the rise of the technologies of the image has changed the status of literature within the marketplace and marginalized many forms of writing in much the same way that the industrialization of publishing quickly marginalized poetry in the 1820s. Such cultural prophets as Marshall McLuhan in *The Gutenberg Galaxy* have meditated and speculated upon the social consequences of transformations in the way culture is and has been transmitted, but attention in publishing history has typically focused on the early stages of the Gutenberg revolution as represented most recently by Elizabeth Eisenstein's *The Printing Press As an Agent of Change* (1979). Yet the full implications that print has for literary genres only became clear with the industrialization of printing that oc-curred in the early nineteenth century, when literary culture had long been fully embedded in the technology of print, something which did not occur until the middle of the eighteenth century, as Alvin Kernan has recently shown in *Printing Technology, Letters, and Samuel Johnson* (1987).

Ian Watt, in *The Rise of the Novel* (1957), argued that the novel was a cultural sign of the legitimation of the growing middle class in eighteenth-century England and that the form reflected the ideology of that class and its growing prosperity, evidenced by the conspicuous consumption of time that reading novels entails. More recently, James Raven, in *Judging New Wealth* (1992), studied the relationship between the publishing of English novels in the late eighteenth century and the ambivalent portrayal in those novels of the conspicuous consumption by the nouveau riche. Yet, as the satire of Pope's *Dunciad* suggests, in the early eighteenth century many kinds of writing proliferated that displayed no neoclassical sense of genre as literary model; and from this competition for an audience among em-bryonic and well-established forms, the novel emerged. One can view genre formation, then, as the creation of new products by publishers and authors designed to entertain a growing market. The resulting range of products tends to stratify the reading market and so target particular seg-ments of it more effectively than before. From this perspective, every literary work will be in some sense a mixed genre as writers seek to accom-modate their writing to the demands of the marketplace and to suit part of it. So while there certainly is room for a sociology of readership and litera-ture (what were the bestsellers during a certain period, who wrote what, who read what, what were the relations between publishing and distribu-tion), my aim here is to examine the relation between reader preferences and generic production as reflected by the market.

Ironically, as the scale and stratification of the publishing market grew, some authors felt they were being asked merely to produce entertainments rather than express their personal vision of the truth, and they worried that appealing to the English public at large would lead them to create work without any artistic merit. This authorial anxiety is evident in Browning and Tennyson, and perhaps nowhere more clearly and painfully than in Browning's *Sordello* (1840), where the poetry's unreadability was evidently a deliberate attempt to make readers understand how authors almost in-evitably supported the existing political order despite their own wishes. Browning felt that although the liberal poet should address all of his fellow men, the poet's work and forms unconsciously reduplicated the prevailing ideology for the consumption of the people and the satisfaction of the state.[14] In short, as nineteenth-century English publishing history reveals, the expansion of the publishing market precipitates a crisis for literature, because the most profitable work is no longer that which appeals to the most sophisticated and literary taste.

My analysis of the marginal utility of literary forms and my survey of their relative cultural status as reflected by the history of the publishing market suggest that literary forms compete economically for audiences. As Thomas Love Peacock long ago recognized, "demand regulates supply in the most abundant productions of nature, as well as in those of human industry."[15] This points to a Darwinian model of literary development, in which literary forms compete with one another for readers because of the economic pressure on literary production to appeal to the common denominator of aggregate demand.[16] Only when readers are faced with material restraints and have few books to read, something which in modern history has typically occurred in and around the time of wars, do we find phenomena such as that which Charles Edmund Carrington, later the authorized biographer of Rudyard Kipling, recounts in A Subaltern's War (1929): "I was mocked in the dugout as a highbrow for reading 'The Ring and the Book,' but saying nothing I waited until one of the scoffers idly picked it up. In ten minutes he was absorbed, and in three days we were fighting for turns to read it and talking of nothing else at meals."[17] In the absence of such enthusiasm among most readers, today's society has sought to protect many authors by installing them in academies and so insulating them from the rigors of the marketplace. However, such anecdotes of passionate reading suggest that a particular literary form will be more popular

14. Although one might be tempted, like Walter Benjamin, to see such alienation and self-consciousness in writers that focused on literary technique as having politically revolutionary tendencies, advances in nineteenth-century literary technique were not necessarily associated with a progressive politics; see, though, Benjamin's "The Author as Producer," in *Reflections*, 220–38. Since the political implications of changes in literary forms depend primarily on the specific and complex cultural and historical forces at play in a given time and place, theorizing about the *a priori* significance of literary forms and changes in them, as if they were not always cultural and historical constructions, seems to me at best an academic exercise.
15. Peacock, *Works*, 9:292.
16. This should be distinguished from the purely formal historical evolution proposed for literature by Jurij Tynjanov in "On Literary Evolution" (1929); see *Readings in Russian Poetics*, 66–78.
17. "Charles Edmonds" [Charles Edmund Carrington], *A Subaltern's War*, 127–28.

than another not just because it fits the contemporary aesthetic fashion, but also because it is embedded within a public economy of desire.

IV

Part of my analysis of the market for literary forms focuses on the growing importance of periodical formats for publishers during the early nineteenth century. Although the importance of the periodical for English literature during this period has long been recognized, there has been little or no comprehensive integration of formal analysis of genre with publishing history. Saintsbury, in *A History of Nineteenth Century Literature* (1896), saw that during the century the periodical gradually absorbed every department of literature. Yet, as noted in *Victorian Periodicals: A Guide to Research* (1978), the standard work on early-nineteenth-century periodicals and their contributions to literature remains Walter Graham's *English Literary Periodicals* (1930), which simply surveys the works and authors that appeared in reviews and magazines and lists who of note wrote when for what periodical. Individual periodicals were studied by scholars in the 1930s and by others who have preserved their methods and outlook: most notably in Edmund Blunden's *Leigh Hunt's "Examiner" Examined* (1928); Miriam Thrall's *Rebellious Fraser's* (1934); G. L. Nesbitt's *Benthamite Reviewing* (1934); Leslie Marchand's *The Athenaeum: A Mirror of Victorian Culture* (1944); Francis Mineka's *The Dissidence of Dissent: The Monthly Repository* (1944); and John Clive's *Scotch Reviewers* (1957). Most of these studies turn into group biographies of minor literary figures who were important and influential in their day; and perhaps the most poignant of the studies written in this scholarly style is Malcolm Elwin's *Victorian Wallflowers* (1934), which surveys the nineteenth-century periodicals by focusing on John Wilson, William Maginn, Richard Barham, William Harrison Ainsworth, John Forster, Wilkie Collins, Mrs. Henry Wood, R. D. Blackmore, and Ouida. This biographical approach has also been taken by John Gross in *The Rise and Fall of the Man of Letters* (1969).

The sociological extension of biographical techniques to publishing history and the history of literary reception has been especially productive in the work of Robert Darnton, most notably in his study of the responses of readers to Rousseau in *The Great Cat Massacre* (1984) and his examination of the late-eighteenth-century French publishing business in connection with the *Encyclopédie* in *The Business of Enlightenment* (1979). Alvin Kernan in *Printing Technology, Letters, and Samuel Johnson* has provided an allied history of consciousness showing that in the eighteenth century, when authors could no longer count on patronage and had to make their own way in the literary marketplace, Samuel Johnson was the epitome of the self-consciously professional writer. The ideological implications of nineteenth-century publishing circumstances have recently been explored by Jerome McGann in *The Beauty of Inflections* (1985). The flood of publications for the mass market has been surveyed by Richard D. Altick in *The English Common Reader* (1957); particular attention has been paid to the serialization of novels in periodicals, most notably by J. A. Sutherland in *Victorian Novelists and Publishers* (1976); and for over ten years there has been the *Victorian Periodicals Newsletter*, dedicated to historical and bibliographical studies. But the relations among genres remain unexplored by scholars. The need has become all the most pressing as the rhetorical analysis predominant in literary studies over the past thirty years has tended to ignore the accumulation of a large mass of bibliographical information, represented most monumentally by the *Wellesley Index to Victorian Periodicals* (1966–89). Moreover, there is the even greater scholarly difficulty that the two standard histories of English publishing, Marjorie Plant's *The English Book Trade* and Frank Mumby's *Publishing and Bookselling*, continue to hold the field in slightly updated editions while their historical outlook and most of the scholarship on which they are based is well over half a century old.

That the publishing history of the nineteenth century is being rewritten and is clearly in need of a new synthesis has inevitably complicated my procedure, particularly when straightforward generic and rhetorical analysis of texts could be done without engaging in historical research. Throughout my discussion, then, I have felt it necessary to provide an account of nineteenth-century publishing and economic history for literary critics and historians. Furthermore, it has been necessary to explain some basic economic terms, since literary critics, historians, and bibliographers often do not have much familiarity with economics. In particular, although the analysis of intertwined class, political, and economic interests outlined by Karl Marx has provided a powerful critical framework for those describing nineteenth-century social and historical developments, Marx's analytic framework has unfortunately also kept alive his wishful, almost Lamarckian misunderstandings of market economics. There are still many who refuse to read Adam Smith and believe in Marxist economics, in much the same way, I think, as there are still those who refuse to read Darwin and believe in creationism.

My general aim, however, is to examine how the publishing market affected both the production and the reception of literary forms at a time when the expansion of the publishing market was creating problems for authors regarding the relationships between publishing quantity and literary quality. Three of the chapters are devoted to a historical survey of the market conditions for poetry, the essay, and the novel. I also consider how changes in the publishing market affected authors' attitudes, themes, and forms, and, to illustrate them, I have a corresponding chapter for poetry, the essay, and the novel, each treating an individual author. These three chapters focus on Wordsworth, Carlyle, and Austen. I have sought to demonstrate that the conditions of the literary marketplace were very much on the author's mind. Even Shelley—who, one might have thought, was above such mundane matters—can be found urging his publisher to advertise his work vigorously, asking to see his publisher's accounts, and, even if somewhat disdainfully, saying, to one's surprise: "I am, all citizens of the world ought to be, especially curious respecting the article of money."[18]

My economic analysis makes a contribution to literary history by, among other things, explaining why poetry does well in times of economic scarcity, why readers prefer to borrow novels from libraries rather than buy them, and why the ideological focus of the quarterly reviews provided a real bargain for readers in a period of publishing expansion and rising prices. By providing a history of the relationship among literary forms in the early nineteenth century as the periodical became the dominant publishing format, this study attempts to provide the foundations for a formal analysis comparable in its focus on technological change to Walter Benjamin's discussion of the relations of painting to photography and film in "The Work of Art in the Age of Mechanical Reproduction." The aesthetic difficulties involved in writing for a wide readership with many new readers and for a publishing market dominated by periodical publication created strains in the articulation of early-nineteenth-century literary forms. This conflict underlies the difference between Romanticism and modernism and at the same time provides the continuity between them, for not only has early-nineteenth-century genre development had a great significance for succeeding generations of authors, but has also had a lasting impact upon modern ideas of literary form.

18. Shelley to John Gisborne, March 7, 1822, *The Letters of Percy Bysshe Shelley*, 2:375.

1

The Poets' Corner:
The Impact of Technological
Changes in Printing on English
Poetry

All the markets overflow.

—Tennyson, "Locksley Hall"

The invention and development of stereotyping and the Four-drinier papermaking machine in the early 1800s, followed by that of the power press, have long been recognized as the technological foundation for the flowering of nineteenth-century English publishing in all of its profusion and for the rise of the common reader, who was enlightened and entertained by this renaissance in printing. The advances in printing technology led inexorably to both a democratization and a stratification of literary culture in England, as books and periodicals became available to all classes of readers and an economy of scale came into being. The technological changes propelled the expansion of the publishing industry and forced a reordering of the relationships among literary forms. In particular, the rise of the periodical format created powerful competitors for poetry's audience in the forms of the short story and serialized fiction, which together were eventually to drive poetry from the marketplace. Cheaper printing stripped poetry of its cultural preeminence and its mnemonic force. As poetry became financially marginal for publishers and was forced to retreat to the gentlemanly and increasingly academic realm of art, the best poets became isolated and alienated from the reading public and developed the dramatic monologue as a form symbolic of their predicament. Since the cultural, political, and ideological consequences of this reorganization of the relationships among literary forms have been enormous, the underlying technological basis of this cultural shift has understandably been obscured. Little attention has been paid to the connections between the publishing conditions for poetry in England during the first half of the nineteenth century and the cultural status of poetry, the poets' attitudes toward their audience, and their relation to their work. The provisional archaeology that follows is an attempt to alter the formal and psychological focus upon nineteenth-century English poetry and to show how the marginalization of that poetry is representative of technological and economic forces at work in history and culture.

I

After the French Revolution and throughout the Napoleonic Wars, the importation of rags from France was curtailed. This reduction in the supply of the raw material for making paper, coupled with a gradually increasing demand for paper in England, caused the price of demy (the kind of paper most commonly used in printing books) to rise from twenty shillings a ream in 1797 to thirty-two shillings a ream in 1810, an increase of over 50 percent.[1] Because the cost of paper was one-half to two-thirds of the cost of printing a book, books became more expensive. The greater cost of books generally encouraged poetry at the expense of prose and made poetry a more important part of the publishing market by rewarding its concentrated language while discouraging diffusive prose.[2] The labor that is re-

1. Coleman, *The British Paper Industry*, 174 and 203. Marjorie Plant provides fragmentary evidence from the Report of the Committee on the Booksellers and Printers Petition (1801) that paper doubled in price between 1793 and 1801; see *The English Book Trade*, 327. This is somewhat misleading, however, and exaggerates the relative magnitude of the rise in paper prices, since 1792 was the bottom of a deflationary period in the British economy. For relative price indexes for this period, see Glenn Hueckel, "War and the British Economy," 388.
2. In contrast, the publishing expansion in the eighteenth century and the system of payment by the sheet had deleterious effects on poetry; see Watt, "Publishers and Sinners," 12. Although the material constraints that favor poetry over prose can be observed today, especially in Russia, they have recurred in England only during war. Writing to Marian Scott on November 21, 1917, and commenting on the good fortune of those who inherited Rupert Brooke's copyrights, Ivor Gurney remarks, "Poetry pays—it took a War to make it; but still, there you are" (quoted in Michael Hurd, *The Ordeal of Ivor Gurney*, 121). In his survey of English literature during World War II, Robert Hewison notes that "while the number of fiction titles published steadily declined, poetry publication fell far less sharply in the first three years (from 310 in 1940 to 249 in 1942), and actually increased to 329 in 1943, followed by 328 in 1944"; he observes that "one reason for the boom in verse publication was that poetry was the

quired by the constraints of meter and rhyme and that produces the greater local density of a line of poetry as opposed to one of prose was more than proportionately rewarded, apparently because readers, able to afford fewer books than before and forced to read those few more often, demanded a verbal texture that would provide more pleasure upon reading and re-reading than would prose. Observing this economy of aesthetic pleasure, Wordsworth in his Preface to *Lyrical Ballads* (1800) extravagantly asserts that "of two descriptions either of passions, manners, or characters, each of them equally well executed, the one in prose and the other in verse, the verse will be read a hundred times where the prose is read once."[3] Similarly, Coleridge remarks in his *Biographia Literaria* that "not the poem which we have *read*, but that to which we *return*, with the greatest pleasure, possesses the genuine power and claims the name of *essential poetry*."[4] Less prescriptive and more directly illustrative of the contemporary taste are the comments of Byron, who notes in "To Mr. Murray" that "as the opinion goes, / Verse hath a better sale than prose," and declares in *Beppo* (1817), "I've half a mind to tumble down to prose, / But verse is more in fashion— so here goes."[5]

Indeed, there was a poetry boom during the first two decades of the nineteenth century. In *English Bards and Scotch Reviewers* (1809) Byron observes that

> This truth at least let satire's self allow,
> No dearth of bards can be complain'd of now.

---

simplest way to satisfy the demand for new material, without using up too much paper" (*Under Siege: Literary Life in London, 1939–1945*, 97–98).

One should note that the same phenomenon has occurred under conditions of political oppression and censorship. In the seventeenth century, for instance, when Gustavus Adolphus invaded Germany and defeated the Hapsburgs, as Christopher Hill notes, "the government, far from sharing popular joy, issued an order forbidding gazettes to print news of Swedish success. Shortly afterwards newspapers were prohibited altogether: the news for which public opinion was hungry could only be spread by ballads, whose popularity increased rapidly" (*Puritanism and Revolution*, 129).

3. *The Prose Works of William Wordsworth*, 1:150. On the differing expectations when reading poetry and prose, James Sutherland has observed that "the first reading of a poem may leave us with only an imperfect realization of what it says or means; but because we have obtained some impression of its structure, and because it *is* and our whole approach to poetry is conditioned by a different sort of expectation, we are prepared to read it a second and a third time, and even, if the experience seems likely to be worth it, to go on reading until our understanding is complete. We will do this for prose only to a limited extent. Most of us are willing to reread a sentence if its full significance has escaped us; but we will not readily give it a third or fourth chance" (*On English Prose*, 49).

4. *Biographia Literaria*, 1:23.

5. *Poetical Works*, 109, 629.

The loaded press beneath her labour groans,
And printers' devils shake their weary bones.[6]

The copyrights of established poets' work were particularly valuable commodities for publishers. Cowper had published his *Poems* in 1800, the year that he died; and the copyright for them was due to run out in 1814. In 1812 Longman bought one-sixteenth of the copyright for Cowper's poems for £260.[7] At the height of the boom in the 1810s Scott received £2,000 in advance for *Rokeby* (1812) from Ballantyne so that he could buy Abbotsford; Byron was offered £1,000 by John Murray for minor poems such as his *Giaour* in 1813; Longman gave Thomas Moore £3,000 for *Lalla Rookh* (1817); and though he claimed to have lost money on the arrangement, Murray willingly paid £3,000 for Crabbe's *Tales of the Hall* and *Poems* in 1819.[8] The financial rewards mirrored the sales. Samuel Rogers, the banker poet, first published *The Pleasures of Memory* with Thomas Cadell in 1792. It went through eleven editions and sold approximately eight thousand copies by 1800; another eight editions and more than fifteen thousand

6. Ibid., 115. Byron was skeptical of the vogue for poetry in a letter to J. Thomson of September 27, 1813: "Poetry has always been so unprofitable a pursuit—& the fame of our present race of bards depends so much upon the caprice of ye. public & ye. fashion of ye. day—that I hardly know if it be not injurious to a young man to encourage him to proceed" (*Byron's Letters and Journals*, 3:121).

7. Norma Russell, *Bibliography of William Cowper to 1837*, 47–48. This copyright sale shared out one firm's literary property to the trade so that, while in law no publisher would have a monopoly on publishing Cowper, the London book publishers were effectively agreeing not to compete with one another in publishing Cowper beyond their agreed shares and so publishing him together as a cartel. On the share book system, see Graham Pollard, "The English Market for Printed Books," 32–34.

8. On Scott's *Rokeby*, see John G. Lockhart, *Memoirs of the Life of Sir Walter Scott*, 2:378; on Byron's *Giaour*, see Samuel Smiles, *A Publisher and His Friends*, 1:221–22; on Moore's *Lalla Rookh*, see Henry Curwen, *A History of Booksellers*, 97–98; on Crabbe, see Smiles, *A Publisher and His Friends*, 2:71–72.

Byron disputed Murray's claim about losing money on Crabbe's poetry that he published in 1819: "when Crabbe published with M[urray]—M showed Moore an account proving that he had lost two thousand pounds by Crabbe—now—I fancy it is pretty well understood that in fact he cleared a good deal by Crabbe" (Byron to Douglas Kinnaird, December 14, 1822, *Byron's Letters and Journals*, 10:59).

Robert Bloomfield was reportedly paid £4,000 by Vernor and Hood for the copyright for *The Farmer's Boy* (1800) (John Taylor to his father, March 26, 1804, quoted in Tim Chilcott, *A Publisher and His Circle*, 10–11). The volume had gone through seven editions, and sold well over 26,000 copies from 1800 to 1803, according to Raynor Unwin, *The Rural Muse*, 92. John Taylor in a letter to his father of May 8, 1804, said that Bloomfield's book was the second one to be stereotyped in England (Chilcott, 10). Bloomfield's vogue faded after 1803. But unlike Clare, whose expectations were raised much higher, he did not become disaffected when he was unable to repeat his first success. On Bloomfield, see Jonathan Lawson, *Robert Bloomfield*, and Unwin, *The Rural Muse*, 87–109.

copies were printed between 1800 and 1816.[9] In 1810 Scott's *Lady of the Lake*, perhaps the most popular poem of the period, sold over twenty thousand copies in six months alone, going through a quarto edition of 2,050 copies and four octavo editions of 3,000, 3,250, 6,000, and 6,000 copies.[10] Byron's *Corsair* sold ten thousand copies on its first day of publication in 1814 and twenty thousand in its first fortnight.[11] And even Wordsworth and Coleridge had a modest publishing success with *Lyrical Ballads*, first published by Cottle in 1798 and then by Longman (who had bought Cottle's firm) in three succeeding editions from 1800 to 1805.

Reading poetry was clearly something of a fad in genteel society at the beginning of the nineteenth century. In no other period of English literature is there a parallel to Marianne Dashwood's complaint, in Austen's *Sense and Sensibility* (1811), about Edward Ferrer's indifferent expression while reading Cowper aloud at an evening with her family. And it was not accidental that the most popular English poets of the age were Sir Walter Scott and Lord Byron, the latter born and the former made a member of the aristocracy. For books were not only expensive (a book of poetry costing five shillings in 1810 would be priced at roughly the equivalent of twenty-five dollars today)[12], but the cost of living was also higher in the early nineteenth century than now relative to the average person's income. Commenting in a letter on the prospects for his *Madoc* (1805), published in quarto by Longman, Robert Southey says:

> In fact, books are now so dear that they are becoming rather articles of fashionable furniture more than anything else; they who buy them do not read them, and they who read them do not buy them. I have seen a Wiltshire clothier, who gives his bookseller no other instructions than the width of his shelves; and have just heard of a Liverpool merchant who is fitting up a library, and has told his bibliopole to send him Shakspeare, and Milton, and Pope, and if any of these fellows should publish anything new, to let him have it immediately. If Madoc obtain any celebrity, its size and cost will recom-

9. Theodore Besterman, *The Publishing Firm of Cadell and Davies*, xxxi.
10. Lockhart, 2:292–93. On Scott's later attempt in the collected edition of his poetry to capitalize on his early popularity, see Jane Millgate, "Scott the Cunning Tailor."
11. On the first day's sale of *The Corsair*, see *Byron's Letters and Journals*, 4:44n; on the first fortnight's sale, see Byron's letter to John Hunt, April 29, 1823 (10:161). Byron may well have exaggerated the first two weeks' sales in this late letter, since he remembers the first day's sale as being 3,000 more copies than Murray had reported to him nine years earlier.
12. The equivalency is calculated on the basis of an ounce of gold's being worth $400. On that basis, a guinea at that time would be worth about $100 today.

mend it among these gentry—*libros consumeri nati*—born to buy quartos and help the revenue.[13]

In a country of eleven million people lacking many of our modern forms of instruction or entertainment, a book in great demand sold ten to twenty thousand copies in 1810. Almost all books were read and bought by the wealthy, even though book clubs and circulating libraries in the late eighteenth and early nineteenth centuries were bringing books to the middle classes—that is, the rest of the upper 10 percent of the population. By way of contrast, in 1850, after the technological revolution in printing and with the general rise in the standard of living, a very popular book would sell several hundred thousand copies.[14]

A few poets of genius were inevitably unfashionable and ignored by the genteel audience for poetry, while others found themselves seeking to rationalize the difference between their own public currency and that of Scott and Byron. Blake, who became his own publisher and found that he was almost his only reader, complains in *The Four Zoas* (1797) that "Wisdom is sold in the desolate market where none come to buy."[15] Later, in "Essay, Supplementary to the Preface" for his *Poems* of 1815, Wordsworth philosophizes, "If there be one conclusion more forcibly pressed upon us than another by the review which has been given of the fortune and fate of poetical works, it is this,—that every author, as far as he is great and at the same time *original*, has had the task of *creating* the taste by which he is to be enjoyed: so has it been, so will it continue to be."[16] Abandoning Pope's criterion of true wit in his *Essay on Criticism*—"What oft was *Thought*, but

---

13. Southey to C. W. W. Wynn, June 25, 1805, *The Life and Correspondence of Robert Southey*, 2:329–30. The rise in the price of newly published books affected the market for used and antiquarian books and encouraged the collection of fine and rare editions by the wealthy, thus making book auctions both profitable and fashionable. This cultural phenomenon is celebrated by Thomas Frognall Dibdin in his *Bibliomania; or Book Madness: A Bibliographical Romance in Six Parts* (1809) and in *The Bibliographical Decameron; or, Ten Days Pleasant Discourse upon Illuminated Manuscripts, and Subjects Connected with Early Engravings, Typography, and Bibliography* (1817). In the latter, a very curious collection of pastoral dialogues, the allusions to book auctions, recent publishing developments, and notable book collectors and sellers are copiously annotated in footnotes to the text. As books became more plentiful and less expensive, the collector's market suffered. Dibdin laments this state of affairs in his *Bibliophobia: Remarks on the Present Languid and Depressed State of Literature and the Book Trade* (1832).
14. Richard D. Altick gives a list of and figures for bestsellers, including poetry, in *The English Common Reader: A Social History of the Mass Reading Public, 1800–1900*, 381–90. Altick has since published two supplements to this list: "Nineteenth-Century English Best-Sellers: A Further List" and "Nineteenth-Century English Best-Sellers: A Third List."
15. *The Poetry and Prose of William Blake*, 318.
16. *Prose Works of William Wordsworth*, 3:80.

ne'er so well *Exprest*"[17]—both Blake and Wordsworth give voice to the feeling that contemporary poetry which appeals strongly to the taste of a large audience ornaments commonplace thinking instead of teaching original wisdom. They also instinctively feared the conclusions Thomas Peacock draws in "The Four Ages of Poetry," published in *Ollier's Literary Miscellany* (1820), that

> the progress of useful art and science, and of moral and political knowledge, will continue more and more to withdraw from frivolous and unconducive, to solid and conducive studies: that therefore the poetical audience will not only continually diminish in the proportion of its number to that of the rest of the reading public, but will also sink lower and lower in the comparison of intellectual acquirement: when we consider that the poet must still please his audience, and must therefore continue to sink to their level, while the rest of the community is rising above it: we may easily conceive that the day is not distant, when the degraded state of every species of poetry will be as generally recognized as that of dramatic poetry has been.[18]

Peacock's argument is clear enough: poetry in the pursuit of a wider audience will descend to its audience's intellectual level and so suffer from the insidious degradation of democratization, while being forced to abandon to science and technology the high ground of teaching the truth and so commanding a diminishing proportion of England's increasingly enlightened readers. His thinking does presuppose a rational utopia, but it was unconsciously prophetic of the dilemma poetry was to face: a choice between a vulgar popularity and an insubstantial isolation. Writing three years earlier in *Biographia Literaria*, Coleridge thinks that this moment has already come to pass, and that in the name of the people reviewers have usurped the authority of poets (particularly that of himself and Wordsworth):

> Poets and Philosophers, rendered diffident by their very number, addressed themselves to "*learned* readers"; then, aimed to conciliate the graces of "the *candid* reader"; till, the critic still rising as the author sunk, the amateurs of literature collectively were erected into a municipality of judges, and addressed THE TOWN! And now finally, all men being supposed able to read, and all readers able to judge, the multitudinous PUBLIC, shaped into personal unity by the magic of abstraction, sits nominal despot on the throne of criticism. But, alas! as in other despotisms, it but echoes the decision of its invisible ministers, whose intellectual claims to the guardianship of the muses seem,

17. *The Poems of Alexander Pope*, 153.
18. *The Four Ages of Poetry*, 20.

for the greater part, analogous to the physical qualifications which adapt their oriental brethren for the superintendence of the Harem.[19]

Although Coleridge insists upon the primacy of the imagination in a valiant effort to reclaim for poets a universal potency and dominion, for the best of them there was to be no choice. Insofar as they were writing in advance of the multitudinous poetry-reading public, poets were condemned, as Shelley was, to choose to be "unacknowledged legislators of the world" and so reconcile themselves to their fate.

I I

The financial bonanza in which almost every poetic rift was found to be laden with ore did not last out the 1820s. Despite an increase of 23 percent in the number of titles appearing annually between 1815 and 1828 (1,121 as compared to 1,377) and another 30 percent increase in titles between 1828 and 1832 (1,377 as compared to an estimated 1,789), by 1830 almost all publishers refused to publish poetry.[20] John Murray refused any manuscripts of poetry after Byron's death in 1824; Longman said "nobody wants poetry now" and encouraged authors to write cookbooks instead of volumes of verse; John Taylor wrote to John Clare in 1830 saying that his firm "was no longer a publisher of poetry"; and Smith, Elder told Clare in the same year that they would publish poetry only at the author's risk.[21] As Benjamin Disraeli said in *Vivian Grey* (1826–27), "the reign of Poesy is over, at least for half a century."[22]

What had happened? The answer, I suggest, lies in the great technological revolution that occurred in printing and the effects it had upon publishing and the reading public. The rise in the cost of paper during the Napoleonic Wars encouraged entrepreneurs to develop the fledgling tech-

19. *Biographia Literaria*, 2:59.
20. The figures are drawn from those given by Ian Jack in *English Literature, 1815–1832*, 38. For the period from 1815 to 1825 and for 1828, his figures come from the lists of books entered at Stationers' Hall that were sent to the Cambridge University librarian. For the period from 1826 to 1832, he takes his figures from the less complete lists provided by *Brent's Monthly Literary Advertiser*. I have adjusted the figures from *Brent's Monthly Literary Advertiser* in terms of the overlapping year of 1828 (1,377 titles as compared to 854), and estimated the number of titles for 1832 on that basis.
21. On John Murray, see Smiles, *A Publisher and His Friends*, 2:244–45, 374; on Longman, see Jack, *English Literature*, 423; John Taylor's letter of January 6, 1830, Egerton MS. 2248, fol. 208, quoted by Chilcott in *A Publisher and His Circle*, 190; on Smith, Elder, see Harold G. Merriam, *Edward Moxon: Publisher of Poets*, 23–24.
22. *Vivian Grey*, 2:161.

nologies of stereotyping and mechanical papermaking that would eventually reduce the costs of printing substantially. Stereotyping, the process of casting plates from plaster and, later, papier-maché molds of set type, was developed under the direction of Lord Stanhope by Andrew Wilson.[23] In 1804 Wilson printed the first stereotyped book in England—John Anastatious Freylinghausen's *Abstract of the Whole Doctrine of the Christian*—from a manuscript in the possession of Queen Charlotte. Stereotyping cut the costs of printing associated with typesetting and type forms and with the warehousing of books, largely by reducing the publishers' risk and capital requirements and by allowing them to respond more flexibly to the demand for books. Oxford University Press, which underwrote much of the cost of development, employed Wilson to print Bibles and prayer books in 1805.[24] Cambridge University was licensed by Stanhope to use stereotyping in 1809. By 1820 there were twelve printing firms in London that did stereotyping; by 1840 it was the standard printing practice.[25] The Fourdrinier continuous papermaking machine was in operation by 1807. It both reduced the cost and improved the quality of paper. The cost of demy dropped from thirty-two shillings a ream in 1810 to twenty shillings a ream in 1835, during a period in which both demand and production increased enormously.[26] Since handmade paper was both harder to work with and had a greater percentage of waste because of defects in individual sheets, machine-made paper not only provided an improvement in the quality of publishing materials but also reduced the costs of printing by about 40 percent.[27] By 1825 over half of all paper in England was made by machine.[28]

The effect of these improvements upon the mass market is clear from Richard Altick's survey in *The English Common Reader* of the great number and variety of nineteenth-century publications. One might note that the terms *stereotype* and *cliché* (French for the frame for the stereotype plate) have become synonymous with the conformity created by mass reproduction. In particular, there was a great increase in the number of periodicals, especially of newspapers. *Poole's Index to Periodical Literature*, which is not

23. Horace Hart, *Charles Earl Stanhope and the Oxford University Press*, 369–95.
24. Ibid., 382–95.
25. Thomas Hodgson, *An Essay on the Origin and Process of Stereotype Printing*, 121.
26. Coleman, 203, fig. 8.
27. *Parliamentary Papers. Fourdrinier's Patent Committee* (1837), 23. In addition, the introduction of the Stanhope press in 1810 seems to have led to a 25 percent reduction in the prices for press work between 1810 and 1816. For a list of prices, see T. C. Hansard, *Typographia: A Historical Sketch of the Origin and Progress of the Art of Printing*, 788–89. Also see his discussion of the application of the Napier printing machine to newspapers, 710–14.
28. Coleman, 206, fig. 9.

exhaustive, lists over twenty new journals that came into being between 1815 and 1832, among them *Blackwood's Magazine*, the *London Magazine*, *Colburn's New Monthly Magazine*, and *Fraser's Magazine*. Unlike the more intellectual and political *Edinburgh Review* and *Quarterly Review*, the new periodicals offered a smorgasbord of short stories, essays, reviews, and poetry. Their variety greatly changed the tastes of readers of the middle and upper classes. The new periodicals directly undercut the sales of poetry, especially by turning the interest of readers from narrative verse to short prose fiction. In *Revelations of the Dead-Alive* (1824) John Banim, a popular Irish novelist, makes this observation:

> A small volume of poetry costs five shillings, and it will contain the bad as well as the good of an author; and you thus purchase his errors and slips, which you don't exactly want, along with his brilliant bits and savoury passages. Behold, on the other hand, a grand army of reviews, of all shapes and prices, from five shillings down to fourpence, in many of which was to be had the cream of from five to five-and-twenty authors together, carefully skimmed for your sipping palate, and ready for use at your tea or coffee in the morning. Moreover, you bought ready-made opinion for your money, a few shillings or pence, as it might be, and so were saved the trouble of forming your own. And what man or miss in his or her senses might be expected to pay a great deal for so little, when, with a little, he or she could have the great deal?
>
> "No one did so" said Mr. Drudge: "the 'reading public' rested satisfied with periodicals alone, and the author was left on the publisher's shelf."[29]

For the same price or less the periodicals more fully satisfied the elegant, sipping palate of the reader.

The English poetry market peaked in 1820, when more than 320 volumes of poetry were published, of which a little more than 200 were original publications.[30] The year 1820 was an extraordinary political year; not only did George IV ascend to the throne but he also immediately sought to divorce Queen Caroline. Panegyrics and satires flooded the market. In the five years preceding (1815–19), there had been an average of more than 225 volumes of poetry a year published, of which about 155 were first editions. This publication rate dropped off slightly in the succeeding four years (1821–24), during which a little more than 205 volumes a year were printed and around 145 of those for the first time. In 1825 the number of poetry volumes published remained about the same, but the number of original publications declined sharply, to 110. In 1826, the year of the bank panic,

---

29. *Revelations of the Dead-Alive*, 114.
30. Figures for annual production of poetry have been compiled from J. R. de J. Jackson, *Annals of English Verse, 1770–1835*.

which occurred early in the year, the volumes of poetry published dropped to 127, of which 91 were first editions. And although the general market for books quickly recovered and began to expand rapidly again, the market for individual volumes of poetry never did, gradually falling off to a low of 110 volumes in 1832, of which 77 were first editions.

In the meantime, the literary Annuals appeared and competed directly for most of the poetry readership. The eclectic character of the magazines and the weekly literary papers inspired the lighter and more fashionable potpourri of album verse, essays, travelogues, and short stories in the richly bound and lavishly illustrated literary Annuals and gift books, which began in the 1820s and were designed for sale as presents to women during the Christmas season, just as books of poetry were.[31] The *Forget Me Not*, the first of them, appeared in 1823. Its success soon attracted many competing publications, which also flourished. The Annuals dominated the market for poetry from 1825 to 1835 and were enormously popular: *The Literary Souvenir* sold six thousand copies in 1825 and by 1829 its editor anticipated eight to nine thousand; the *Forget Me Not* for 1826 had a sale of almost ten thousand copies; and in its first year *The Keepsake* of 1828 sold fifteen thousand.[32]

If one remembers that these Annuals sold for twelve shillings versus the average poetry volume's five, one realizes that the Annuals were clearly siphoning off whatever growth there was in the poetry-reading public and were significantly cutting into the market for volumes of verse written by individual authors. Indeed, if one generously assumes that the average volume of published poetry sold 300 of 500 copies at five shillings a copy, then the combined sales of the *Forget Me Not* and *The Literary Souvenir* in 1826 of around sixteen thousand copies at twelve shillings apiece would be the equivalent of the sales of 125 individual books of poetry. In fact the sales of just these two Annuals by themselves in 1826 could be said to account for the decline in poetry publication, although it is clear that the Annuals appealed to a wider audience than just those who regularly read poetry.

In 1828 Southey observed that "the Annuals are now the only books

31. On the Annuals, see [Leigh Hunt], "Pocket-Books and Keepsakes," 1–28; Bradford Allen Booth, *A Cabinet of Gems: Short Stories from the English Annuals*, 1–19; A. Bose, "The Verse of the English 'Annuals,'" 38–51; Jack, *English Literature*, 173–75; Anne Renier, *Friendship's Offering: An Essay on the Annuals and Gift Books of the 19th Century*; and Andrew Boyle, *An Index to the Annuals, 1820–1850*.
32. On *The Literary Souvenir*, see Alaric A. Watt, *The Literary Souvenir*, 1826 ed., v, and 1829 ed., vii. On the *Forget Me Not*, see Frederic Shoberl, *Forget Me Not*, vi. On *The Keepsake*, see Robert Southey to Caroline Bowles, February 22, 1828, *New Letters of Robert Southey*, 2:324.

bought for presents to young ladies, in which way poems formerly had their chief vent."[33] The Annuals were intimately connected with the social phenomenon of the young lady's album (made more popular by cheaper paper), which the famous were asked to autograph and to add their verse to. Lamb, whose *Album Verses* (1830) collects poems he wrote for and about albums and often published in Annuals, complained, "there is no other reading. They haunt me. I die of Albo-phobia!"[34] *The Keepsake* for 1829, the most notable of the Annuals, had Wordsworth, Coleridge, Southey, Scott, and, posthumously, Shelley contributing available bits and pieces. Near the end of his literary career, Coleridge also had poems appearing in *The Amulet, The Bijou,* and *The Literary Souvenir,* while at the beginning of his, Tennyson published lyrics in *The Gem, The Tribute, Friendship's Offering,* and *The Keepsake.*

But the left-handed work of great authors cost editors more than it was worth,[35] and it did not attract as much attention as the fine steel engravings of famous paintings and fashionable people. "The Annuals are picture-books for grown children," said Southey, who had himself discovered how true this was.[36] The editors of *The Keepsake* had refused his narrative poem "All for Love, or the Sinner Well-Saved," asking him to write instead a light lyric of his own choice (which was not printed) and two poems (which did

33. Southey to G. D. Bedford, December 8, 1828, *Life and Correspondence,* 5:336. In a letter of December 21, 1828, to Allan Cunningham, the editor of *The Anniversary* for 1829, Southey remarked that "having no less than seven females in family, you will not wonder that as yet I have seen little more than the prints in your book and its table of contents" (*Life and Correspondence,* 5:338).

Competing with and largely replacing the Annuals after 1850 were the gift-book poetry anthologies, which presented a collection of fine standard poems. Henry Viztelly's *Christmas with the Poets* (1851) is an early example of the genre, of which F. T. Palgrave's *Golden Treasury* (1861) is the most famous exemplar; see Sabine Haas, "Victorian Poetry Anthologies," 51–64.
34. Lamb to Bernard Barton, end of 1827, *The Letters of Charles Lamb,* ed. Lucas, 3:148.
35. In 1828 Charles Heath offered Scott £500 and Southey fifty guineas for contributions to *The Keepsake* of 1829. See the entry for February 29, 1828, in *The Journal of Sir Walter Scott,* 435; and Southey to Allan Cunningham, February 24, 1828, *Life and Correspondence,* 5:322.
36. Southey to Cunningham, December 21, 1828, in *Life and Correspondence,* 5:339. Alaric A. Watt, editor of *The Literary Souvenir,* noted that "tolerable single impressions of several of its plates are now selling for more than twice the price of the original volumes containing the entire set" (*The Literary Souvenir* [1829], vii). The Annuals acquired an international reputation for their fine engravings. In 1830 *The Keepsake* was published by Giraldon Bovinet in Paris, and in 1833, by Rittner and Goupil in Paris and by Charles Jügil in Frankfurt. Their widespread dissemination of paintings through the new process of steel engraving caused Stendahl to remark in *Promenades dans Rome* (1829), almost in anticipation of Malraux's comments on the "museum without walls" created by photography, that "most of the foreigners who come to Rome prefer to all Raphael's figures the pretty illuminated lithographs that are sold in Paris on the boulevards or the delicate and carefully executed small engravings of the *Keepsake* and other English almanacs" (*A Roman Journal,* 110). On the importance of the engravings, see also Renier, *Friendship's Offering,* 12–13.

appear) about drawings by J. M. Wright and J. M. W. Turner.[37] The editorial arrangements for engravings had to be made six months or more in advance and cost large sums of money. Frederic Mansel Reynolds, for instance, said that £11,000 had been invested in the plates for the 1829 edition of *The Keepsake*.[38] This put a great premium on the pictures and meant that editors solicited poets to write poems about pictures that were being engraved instead of commissioning engravings to provide illustrations for existing poems. In Thackeray's *History of Pendennis* the spring Annual of the publisher Bacon is described as "daintily illustrated with pictures of reigning beauties, or other prints of a tender and voluptuous character; and, as these plates were prepared long beforehand, requiring much time in engraving, it was the eminent poets who had to write to the plates, and not the painters who illustrated the poems."[39] Since editors rapidly discovered that eminent poets were not needed for such taskwork, one finds, for instance, that Pendennis's first literary work is a poem called "The Church Porch," which he writes to illustrate a plate for which sixty pounds has already been spent.[40] A few years later as the editor of and sole contributor to *Fisher's Drawing-Room Scrap-Book*, L. E. L. (Letitia Elizabeth Landon) was reduced to writing poems as commentary upon pictures.[41] It is no wonder that the quality of and the payment for poetry in the Annuals soon declined.

The Annuals lowered poetic standards and provided an inadequate shelter for poetry against the ever-rising tide of the periodicals. Thomas Cadell,

37. Southey to Cunningham, November 13, 1828, *Selections from the Letters of Robert Southey*, 4:124. Southey's poems were "Lucy and Her Bird" and "Stanzas, Addressed to J. M. W. Turner, Esq. R. A., on His View of the Lago Maggiore from the Town of Arona," in *The Keepsake*, 157–60, 238–39.
38. *The Keepsake*, iii. Samuel Carter Hall, who was an editor of Annuals, said that payments for engravings varied "from 100 to 150 guineas" (*A Book of Memories of Great Men and Women of the Age*, 94). For a brief account of steel engraving, see John Feather, "Technology and the Book in the Nineteenth Century," 5–13; for more thorough discussions, see Basil Hunnisett, *Steel-engraved Book Illustration in England*; Anthony Dyson, *Pictures to Print: The Nineteenth-Century Engraving Trade*; and Geoffrey Waterman, *Victorian Book Illustration: The Technical Revolution*.
39. *The History of Pendennis*, 1:313.
40. Ibid., 1:315. The title of Pendennis's poem indicates the religious character of much of the poetry in the Annuals. And although much of the poetry was really versified religion as opposed to religious verse, the early nineteenth century saw a vogue for devotional poetry. In particular, *The Christian Year* (1827) by John Keble sold 65,500 copies in the first twenty years of publication (Altick, "Nineteenth-Century English Best-Sellers: A Further List" 203). Rosemary Scott has surveyed the market for devotional poetry in "Pious Verse in the Mid-Victorian Market Place," 37–58. For the best study of this phenomenon that treats the poetry as poetry, see G. B. Tennyson, *Victorian Devotional Poetry*.
41. Renier, 20. Bose estimates that three-fourths of the poems in the Annuals were illustrative of engravings (39).

writing to William Blackwood in 1827, says, "I hope that the sale of Books is more favourable with you than it is here; the sort of reading most sought after at present is that contained in Periodicals & Newspapers."[42] In a letter to Wordsworth of 1842, Edward Moxon attributes the poor sale of books to "the immense number of weekly and Monthly publications—chiefly illustrated" and notes that Simpkin, Marshall and Co., a firm of wholesale booksellers, were paying £10,000 a month for periodicals.[43] The journals became the mainstays of publishing firms: Archibald Constable had the *Edinburgh Review* and the *Scots Magazine*; Longman, the London agency of the *Edinburgh Review*; John Murray, the *Quarterly Review*; Blackwood, *Blackwood's Magazine*; Taylor and Hessey, the *London Magazine*; and Colburn, *Colburn's New Monthly Magazine*. The London agency of *Blackwood's Magazine*, for instance, was estimated to account for one-third of Cadell and Davies's profits in 1833.[44] Their circulation may be gauged by that of the *Edinburgh Review*, which had a peak sale of 13,500 copies in 1818 before the stiff competition of the monthly magazines began.[45]

Morse Peckham has suggested that in the nineteenth century "the more profit depended on exploitation of the mass market, the more high-level cultural writing became economically marginal. A kind of Gresham's law took over: inferior culture drives out superior."[46] And there is a good deal of contemporary complaint from alienated poets to support this view. Writing to Elizabeth Barrett in 1845, Robert Browning says,

> I do know that for a dozen cabbages, if I pleased to grow them in the garden here, I might demand, say a dozen pence at Covent Garden Market,—and that a dozen pages of verse, brought to the Rialto where verse-makers most do congregate, ought to bring me a fair proportion of the Reviewers' gold-currency, seeing the other traders pouch their winnings, as I do see: well, when they won't pay me for my cabbages, nor praise me for my poems, I may, if I please, say "more's the shame," and bid both parties "decamp to the crows."[47]

As Browning suggests, book publishing came more and more to resemble marketing. There was a stratification of the public according to form and class, a demand for the old and familiar instead of the new and unfamiliar

---

42. Besterman, 78.
43. Merriam, 137–38.
44. Besterman, xvii.
45. Harold Cox and John E. Chandler, *The House of Longman*, 19.
46. *Beyond the Tragic Vision: The Quest for Identity in the Nineteenth Century*, 28.
47. *The Letters of Robert Browning and Elizabeth Barrett Browning, 1845–1846*, 1:18.

writer, and a preference for prose over poetry. The literary Annuals, in particular, revealed that the readership of poetry had become increasingly young and female and that this new market could be successfully segmented from the old with a new format and packaging. The Annuals effectively divided poetry into one kind for a limited audience made up largely of artistic gentlemen and scholars, and another for a much larger audience composed primarily of women and children.[48]

The declining sales of poetry, despite an expanding publishing market in the late 1820s, led publishers to change their financial arrangements for printing poetry. Many publishers, most notably John Murray, soon refused to publish new poetry because they found it to be an unprofitable business, and those that did asked the poets to share the risks of publication. New poets and their publishers felt the shifting taste of the expanding readership first. Although Keats received £100 from Taylor and Hessey for the copyright of *Endymion* in 1818 and another £100 from them for *Lamia, Isabella, and Other Poems*, together with his *Poems* of 1817, which were taken over from C. and J. Ollier,[49] none of his volumes went into a second edition. Similarly, none of Shelley's poems published with C. and J. Ollier went into a second edition, and all lost money.

The best-known poet most affected by this alteration in poetry publishing was John Clare. In the early 1820s Clare had had significant publishing successes: his first volume of poems, *Poems Descriptive of Rural Life and Scenery*, published in 1820, had gone to four editions by 1821; and his second volume, *The Village Minstrel*, published in 1821, had gone to a second edition. But *The Shepherd's Calendar*, published in 1827, had not sold more than four hundred copies by 1829, so that, according to Taylor's accounting in 1829, Clare actually owed Taylor money. Indeed, if any English poets of the period correspond to Carl Spitzweg's 1839 portrait of the poor poet, *Der arme Poet* (fig. 1), they are Thomas Hood and John Clare. The closest

48. As a harbinger of this trend, it is worth considering the vogue for Letitia Landon (L. E. L.), who was first published by William Jerdan, in the mid-1820s. In 1824 she published her first volume of poetry, *The Improvisatrice*, which reached its sixth edition in 1825 and for which she received £300. She then was paid £600 for her next volume of poems, *The Troubadour*, which went to three editions in 1825. There followed *The Golden Violet* in 1827 and *The Venetian Bracelet* in 1828, for which she received £200 and £150 respectively, as the public taste for her work was being satisfied by the Annuals. And while Landon tried her hand at writing novels with *Romance and Reality* in 1831 and *Francesca Carrera* in 1834 (for both of which she was paid £300), she returned to poetry as an editor and writer for the Annuals, particularly *Fisher's Drawing-Room Scrap-Book* and *Heath's Book of Beauty*. For the sums received for copyrights by Landon, see William Jerdan, *The Autobiography of William Jerdan*, 3:185.
49. *The Letters of John Keats, 1814–1821*, 2:334n.

English parallel to Spitzweg's poet is probably Hood, who, unable to make enough money from his poetry after the bankruptcy of his publisher in 1834, served as a mercenary soldier in Koblenz, Germany from 1835 to 1836, and may well have lived in a room much like that seen in the painting. An even poorer man than Hood, Clare for several years could find no one who would publish his poetry without the financial guarantee that he felt he could not afford to offer: "I would rather take a small sum for the volume altogether than a large promise in 'half profits' because I have been disappointed at that game already with Messrs Taylor & Hessey."[50] He was not able to publish his poetry again until 1835, when How and Whitaker gave him a small sum for the copyright of *The Rural Muse*. Clare's first publishers, Taylor and Hessey, dissolved their partnership in 1825 because of financial difficulties connected with their *London Magazine*. Hessey went bankrupt in 1829, while in 1831 Taylor gave up publishing to start a school in Hampstead.[51] Similarly, the indifferent response to *Ollier's Literary Miscellany*, which concentrated on poetry and literary criticism, not only delayed until 1840 the publication of Shelley's *Defence of Poetry*, which had been intended for the journal's second number, but also contributed to the eventual bankruptcy of the Olliers' firm in 1822.[52]

Established poets fared better. Rogers' poetry continued to sell well. Wordsworth had enough faith in his poetry to agree to take on the financial risk of underwriting two-thirds of publication costs in return for two-thirds of the profits,[53] and, as he slowly rose in the general public's estimation, made more money from his poetry. Scott gradually shifted from writing poetry to writing novels: his Waverley novels, the first of which was published in 1814, mark the beginning of an enormous resurgence in the novel.

50. Clare to William Sharpe of October 1829, *The Letters of John Clare*, 230. It is thus the financial circumstances of the poetry market which ruled out working-class poets, since they could not afford to provide their publishers with a subvention for publication. Ignorant of the realities of the publishing market for poetry, Nigel Cross waxes indignant about the social class prejudice that he sees accounting for Thomas Cooper's being unable to get either Moxon or Colburn to publish *The Purgatory of Suicides* (1845). It seems clear, however, they were just exercising good financial sense, since Jeremiah How, who was Clare's last publisher and who finally did publish Cooper's poetry, went bankrupt in 1846. See Nigel Cross, *The Common Writer: Life in Nineteenth-Century Grub Street*, 154–55.
51. Chilcott, *A Publisher and His Circle*, 188.
52. His son said about the firm and Charles Ollier that "the causes of its want of success were insufficient capital, the unpopular nature of the literature issues, and, perhaps it must be added, a certain commercial ineptitude on the part of the chief conductor" ([Edmund Ollier], "A Literary Publisher," 248).
53. Merriam, 138–40. Moxon, for instance, targeted the growing market for school texts with his edition of Wordsworth's *Selections* (1831), as indicated by the subtitle, "Chiefly for the Use of Schools and Young Persons." On Wordsworth's publishing strategy, see chapter 2 below.

The end of his poetic career—*The Lord of the Isles* (1815) and *Harold the Dauntless* (1817)—may be associated with the beginning of the end of the poetry boom, for no writer in all of English literature responded more readily to his public or could better create a taste in his audience than Scott. In retrospect, his declining the poet-laureateship in 1813 and his recommendation of Southey for the honor in his stead were sure signs of the coming shift in the readership's tastes.

Although the technological improvements in printing made the competition of literary magazines and novels possible, they still made publishing poetry cheaper. In 1810 there was an octavo edition of Cowper's *Poems* in two volumes on foolscap paper published for twenty-one shillings, while the same edition on the same paper stereotyped but without the engraved plates or titles cost only twelve shillings.[54] Yet despite lower printing costs, publishers found that most poetry appealed to an increasingly smaller portion of the reading public and so kept its price high. Prices of volumes of poetry in octavo editions remained relatively constant for well over a hundred years. Burns' first edition of his *Poems* in 1786 sold for three shillings and the first Edinburgh edition of 1787 sold for five shillings. Matthew Arnold's *Strayed Reveller and Other Poems* was sold by B. Fellowes for four shillings sixpence in 1849. Thomas Hardy's *Satires of Circumstance* was sold by Macmillan for the same price in 1914. There were, of course, great ranges in price. At the height of the poetry boom and at the peak of the cost of paper in 1810, Constable sold the quarto of Scott's *Lady of the Lake* at two guineas or forty-two shillings and the cheapest volume for twenty-one shillings. Later in 1841, a year of economic depression, Robert Browning attempted to gain the ear of the working man at the suggestion of his publisher, Edward Moxon, by selling *Pippa Passes*, the first number of *Bells and Pomegranates*, for a sixpence. And Richard Henry Horne, the Gigadibs of "Bishop Blougram's Apology," outrageously had his epic, *Orion*, which was published in 1843 and went through three editions that year, sold for a farthing in its first edition—though once readers rushed to buy the novelty, the price was raised to a shilling for the second and to two and a half shillings for the fifth.[55]

54. Russell, 78–79.
55. On Burns, see J. W. Egerer, *A Bibliography of Robert Burns* 3, 9; on Arnold, see Thomas Burnett Smart, *The Bibliography of Matthew Arnold*, 2; on Hardy, see Richard Little Purdy, *Thomas Hardy: A Bibliographical Study*, 172; on Scott, see Merriam, 19; on Browning, see Leslie Nathan Broughton et al., *Robert Browning: A Bibliography*, 4; on Horne, see Leonard Huxley, *The House of Smith Elder*, 34n.

After the rise of the periodicals and the Annuals, publishers required poets to underwrite the costs of publishing. Edward Moxon, who was almost the only one to publish serious poetry in the 1830s and 1840s, began his business with the help of Samuel Rogers. Rogers had published his *Pleasures of Memory* in 1792 with Cadell, his *Poems* with Cadell and Davies in 1812, *Italy* with Longman in 1822, and the second and third editions of it with John Murray in 1823. Moxon, who had worked for Longman and for Hurst, Chance, and Company, got Rogers to lend him £500 to set up as a seller of fine books. He first printed a collection of Lamb's *Album Verses* and distributed them for free in 1830, and then in the same year got Rogers to underwrite at the cost of £7,000 his illustrated edition of *Italy*, the volume that introduced J. M. W. Turner to the young Ruskin. Moxon printed 10,000 copies. Two years later he had sold almost seven thousand and needed to sell another seven hundred to break even. Moxon survived and flourished as a publisher of poetry at the beginning largely because so many of his authors were men of means and could afford to guarantee the costs.[56] This was important, because as "unacknowledged legislators" writing avant-garde work, poets found that their poetry would sell very slowly at first and only begin to pay for itself when their reputation was established and their place within English literary tradition almost set. For example, Tennyson's *Poems* of 1833 was published by Moxon in an edition of 800; and when Browning tried to offer *Paracelsus* to him two years later, Moxon refused it, saying that only 300 copies of Tennyson's poems had been sold in the last two years.[57] Poets who were not as fortunate as Tennyson and Browning to be gentlemen with independent incomes were unable to support themselves by writing poetry and were forced to abort promising careers. Hood became a journalist and was for a while a soldier; Darley became a journalist and later a mathematician; and Beddoes practiced medicine in Germany and Switzerland.[58]

Ironically, then, poets gained greater control over their poetry because it sold so slowly. In the days of the extended patronage of subscription publishing, poets were forced to solicit for subscribers (often for payment in advance) and then to show their list to a publisher, who would buy their

---

56. Merriam, 56; on Rogers' *Italy*, see 27–29. On the elegance of Moxon's list, see Leigh Hunt, "Mr. Moxon's Publications," *Tatler* (June 4, 1831); rpt. in *Leigh Hunt's Literary Criticism*, 389–93.
57. Mrs. Sutherland Orr, *Life and Letters of Robert Browning*, 69.
58. John Heath-Stubbs, *The Darkling Plain: A Study of the Later Fortunes of Romanticism in English Poetry from George Darley to W. B. Yeats*, 23.

copyright on that basis and who would own their work.[59] For example, Burns' first Edinburgh edition of *Poems; Chiefly in the Scottish Dialect*, published in 1787, had 1,300 subscribers who promised to pay five shillings for 2,900 copies.[60] That Burns' heirs made anything more at all from the enormous popularity of the volume, which saw an average of five editions a year (both pirated and authorized) throughout the nineteenth century, was due to the calculated generosity of Cadell and Davies, who were publishing a memorial edition of Burns' poetry in 1800.[61]

Circa 1840 Moxon's standard contract for 2,000 copies of a volume of poems stipulated that the author would have equal shares of the profits and losses and so retain copyright.[62] For new and unknown poets Moxon would print 500 copies in an edition, and for the popular, 2,000. His break-even point was generally around 70 to 80 percent of the copies of the first edition. Any work that went into a second edition was deemed a success. But since most volumes of poetry (and this was true of novels as well)[63] never went into a second edition (none of Browning's volumes did until his *Selections* in 1863, to take an extreme example), the publisher of poetry had to be cautious. Unlike Murray, Constable, Longman, and Cadell and Davies, Moxon advertised very little.[64] But this caution translated into profit for the poet who sold well, and particularly for Tennyson, whose half shares in his poetry were the makings of a veritable fortune. For those who could still sell their copyrights and who wrote poetry that caught the fancy of the general reading public, the financial returns were ironically disappointing. Richard Barham was able to sell his *Ingoldsby Legends*, which had originally appeared in *Bentley's Miscellany*, to Bentley in 1840 for a hundred pounds. Bentley sold 20,000 copies by 1856, and between 1857 and 1895 sold 425,000 copies.[65] The volume was one of the pillars of Bentley's house when Macmillan later purchased the firm; but Barham never saw a penny beyond his original hundred pounds.

Barham's success should remind us that the Romantic and Victorian readership wanted easy, versified narrative and sentimental melodrama in

59. F. E. Compton, "Subscription Books," in *Bowker Lectures on Book Publishing* (New York, 1957) 56–78. Compton notes that these lists "were a kind of Who's Who—social register" (63).
60. Egerer, 9, 12.
61. Besterman, xxi.
62. Merriam, 100.
63. See Royal A. Gettmann, *A Victorian Publisher: A Study of the Bentley Papers*, 125–27; also see J. A. Sutherland, *Victorian Novelists and Publishers*, 14–16.
64. Merriam, 77–80. Cadell and Davies' advertising was about 20 percent of a book's publishing cost (Besterman, xxxii).
65. Gettmann, 80.

their poetry. The most popular poems of the age were Scott's *Marmion* and *The Lady of the Lake*, Byron's *Childe Harold* and *Don Juan*, Barham's *Ingoldsby Legends*, Elizabeth Barrett Browning's *Aurora Leigh* (1856), and Tennyson's *Enoch Arden* (1864). Such poetry moved beyond the bounds of the intellectual and largely upper-class readership that the publishers of poetry normally catered to. Most publishers of poetry had begun as booksellers of fine and rare books to gentlemen and had moved into publishing without giving up their bookselling. As one might expect under such circumstances, there were relatively few publishers of poetry in the century of any note: Archibald Constable and John Murray from the turn of the century to 1826, Longman from 1800 to 1835, Taylor and Hessey from 1815 to 1825, C. and J. Ollier from 1817 to 1822, Edward Moxon from 1830 to 1858, and Macmillan in the later years of the century. One could also mention among others Smith, Elder and Chapman and Hall. But the seven houses mentioned published the bulk of the age's significant poetry. And, besides being a reminder that Edinburgh was the second largest market for books in Great Britain in the early nineteenth century, it is perhaps a sociological fact of some significance that of these seven publishers all but Longman and the Olliers were either Scottish or of Scottish descent. Longman had Wordsworth and Coleridge; Constable published Scott; John Murray issued Byron; Taylor and Hessey brought out Keats, Clare, and Darley; the Olliers printed Shelley and Keats.

In the middle of the century there was almost no one but Edward Moxon. He published Wordsworth's poetry after 1835, Shelley's *Masque of Anarchy* in 1832 and *Works* of 1839–40 (edited by Mary Shelley), Tennyson's work from the *Poems* of 1833 on, Browning's *Sordello* and *Bells and Pomegranates* in the 1840s, Milne's edition of Keats' *Life, Letters, and Literary Remains* in 1848, Swinburne's early poems, and those of a host of minor poets. Later Macmillan published Arnold, Tennyson, Hardy, and Yeats. Since they were both booksellers and publishers, they retained much of the servility of the former. They ordered and sent books to their authors, paid their debts in town, and acted as their literary agents. Wordsworth, for instance, when he was named poet laureate in 1843, sent Moxon around to Buckingham Palace to accept the honor for him and collect his stipend, so that it wasn't until 1845 when the young Queen Victoria summoned him to an audience that Wordsworth fulfilled a single duty of his post.[66] In short,

---

66. Merriam, 142, 146. Moxon was also once entrusted with Wordsworth's dentures to have them repaired by a dentist: see Mary Moorman, *William Wordsworth: A Biography*, 2:593n.

the publishing of poetry in the nineteenth century recalled in many ways the earlier days of Tonson and Dodsley.

III

Although the publishing of thin volumes of poetry had an anachronistic, gentlemanly air after 1830, it did so because publishers had obeyed market conditions and forced poets to underwrite the risks and costs of publication. Since poets retained copyright to their work, they tended to revise their texts in print instead of in manuscript before publication. This put less pressure on the poet to arrive at a final text and made poetic and artistic closure more problematic than it had already been. Poets gradually ceased to circulate poems in manuscript, began to revise in print, and to regret, like Arnold, that they couldn't selectively repress what they had rushed to print. Further, since it was easier and more profitable to appear in print as often as possible in different forms, poets were encouraged to adopt an additive strategy to publishing poems and volumes of poetry, and to market selections from their work, while letting their corpus grow and evolve through gradually enlarged editions of complete works.

In the 1820s pirates like William Benbowes had brought out selections of Byron and Shelley. But legitimate publishers soon licensed such operations. Indeed, as Arnold later stressed in his essay on Wordsworth,[67] the printing of selections from a poet's work was critical to establishing a poet's literary stature and worth. In 1831 Moxon bought the right from Longman to bring out a selection of Wordsworth's poetry, and Moxon gradually wooed Wordsworth into his fold. Moxon's marketing of selections and volumes of poetry between editions of collected works made Wordsworth both wealthy and famous[68]—and contributed to his being named poet laureate in 1843. Similarly, Browning's *Selections* published in 1863 was the first profitable volume of his verse.

It was to the publisher's advantage to present the public with many editions, largely because they brought the poet to the attention of the reviews more often; being reviewed favorably was one of the keys to, if not a guarantee of, success. Much care was taken by some authors or friends of authors to arrange for good reviews. Leigh Hunt, John Reynolds, and G. F. Matthews reviewed Keats's *Endymion* for him in 1818.[69] And Tennyson's

---

67. *The Complete Prose Works of Matthew Arnold*, 9:41–44.
68. Merriam, 130–49.
69. Walter Jackson Bate, *John Keats*, 220–23.

friends arranged to write glowing notices in the Edinburgh and Westminster reviews of the edition of his *Poems* published in 1842.[70] Lesser writers were often to be found in publishers' back rooms writing notices for newspaper reviewers who were paid too little to read what they had to review and were only too happy to accept copy provided for them.

Poets had earlier taken advantage of the serial nature of print to revise and add to their work (Spenser in *The Faerie Queene*, Milton in *Paradise Lost*, Thomson in *The Seasons*, for example). The great expansion of the publishing industry in the nineteenth century allowed poets even more flexibility in completing poems and also the freedom to revise, expand, and extend them in response to the demands of readers. The popular success of the first two cantos of *Childe Harold's Pilgrimage* in 1812 led Byron to write a third canto in 1816 and a fourth in 1818. Tennyson's *Idylls of the King* had but five romances in the original edition of 1859. Tennyson added four in 1869 (including *The Passing of Arthur*, which had been published in 1842), one in 1871, another in 1872, and the twelfth and last in 1885. One should note the American parallel of Whitman's *Leaves of Grass*. Among lesser poets, there was the gradual swelling of Philip Bailey's *Festus*, first published in 1839. Tennyson virtually rewrote many of his *Poems* of 1833 for his 1842 edition, most notably "The Lotus Eaters." At Elizabeth Barrett's suggestion, Browning published his "Saul" as a fragment in *Dramatic Romances and Lyrics* in 1845, and the finished version appeared in *Men and Women* in 1855. Once poets could do this, they would no longer retain manuscripts in gestation as Wordsworth did with *The Prelude*—unless, of course, they died young. Since they no longer sold their copyright to the publishers but retained it as their own, poets could maintain control over their text in a way that earlier generations of poets could not—hence the Browning, Yeats, and Hardy variorum editions.

I V

Even though our biographically centered memories may still find the death of Byron in 1824 a more convenient and conventional date, it would seem that with the end of the reign of poetry in the literary marketplace in 1825 also came the real end of Romanticism. If one looks closely at the poetry market, one finds that the literary Annuals were coming to dominate the gift-book market that poetry had previously dominated and that much

70. Hallam Tennyson, *Alfred, Lord Tennyson: A Memoir*, 1:188.

of the Annuals' popularity stemmed from their steel-engraved pictures of famous paintings and fashionable people. Further, much of the poetry in the Annuals simply described the engraved plates. One crucial aspect, then, of the shift from a Romantic to a Victorian poetic stemmed directly from the popular pressure exerted by the publishing market on poetry to conform to a purely pictorial aesthetic. Further, as serious early Victorian poets found that they had no popular audience, they thematized their poetic predicament in the dramatic monologue, as the work of Tennyson and Browning shows.

In making poetry subordinate to painting and pictures, the Annuals tied Victorian poets firmly to a descriptive, pictorial aesthetic. Tennyson, for instance, had written many poems for the Annuals. Writing in 1831 to William Henry Brookfield, who had asked him to contribute a poem to the *Yorkshire Literary Annual,* Tennyson replied, "Now, how have you the conscience to ask me to annualize for Yorkshire? Have I not forsworn all annuals provincial or metropolitan? I have been so beGemmed and beAmuletted and be-forget-me-not-ted that I have given all these things up."[71] Nonetheless, Tennyson contributed a poem to Brookfield's Annual. As one would expect, his early poetry reflects the Annuals' emphasis on descriptive pictorialism. The beginnings of "Mariana" and "The Lady of Shalott," to take two famous examples, are purely descriptive. Consider these lines from "Mariana":

> With blackest moss the flower-plots
>   Were thickly crusted, one and all;
> The rusted nails fell from the knots
>   That held the pear to the gable-wall.
> The broken sheds look'd sad and strange:
>   Unlifted was the clinking latch;
>   Weeded and worn the ancient thatch
> Upon the lonely moated grange. (1–8)[72]

The details of the neglected garden are meant to prepare the reader for Mariana's unhappiness. Moreover, while Tennyson's exterior description is provided by a narrator rather than, as in a dramatic monologue, by Mariana, the pictured landscape provides a symbolic parallel to Mariana's feelings. John Stuart Mill, writing in the *London Review*, was the first to praise Tenny-

71. Tennyson to Brookfield, August 3, 1831, *The Letters of Alfred Lord Tennyson*, 1:13.
72. Citations of Tennyson's poetry refer to line numbers in *Poems of Tennyson*, 2d ed., ed. Christopher Ricks.

son's creative "scene-painting" because it was, he says, "in keeping with some state of human feeling; so fitted to it as to be the embodied symbol of it, and summon up the state of feeling itself."[73] There is, of course, the further testimony to the pictorial suggestiveness of Tennyson's poem in Millais's later painting of Mariana.

Browning only once contributed to a literary Annual ("Ben Karshook's Wisdom" to *The Keepsake* of 1856), but he did recognize that pictorial poetry was popular and so he tried, as best he could, to appeal to his readers' eyes. Browning, however, from the very beginning of his poetic career incorporates any pictorial description within the perspective of a speaker's voice and thus colors any landscape with that person's character. Take, for instance, the opening lines of "Porphyria's Lover":

> The rain set early in to-night,
>   The sullen wind was soon awake,
> It tore the elm-tops down for spite,
>   And did its worst to vex the lake. (1–4)[74]

After reading the poem, one realizes that this description is in keeping with the speaker's violent inclinations and that in his ascription of a malevolence to the wind there is a foreshadowing of his murder of Porphyria. Unlike Tennyson, who paints a landscape appropriate to a particular mood in his early poems, Browning has clearly incorporated the pictorial within the dramatic monologue's poetics of character. The beginning of "Porphyria's Lover" nonetheless can be seen as an attempt to accommodate the contemporary reader's appetite for poetic description. This aim of appealing to the popular reading public may partly explain why Browning introduces the man in the booth in *Sordello* who presents the story of the troubadour poet through his diorama of historical scenes. Further, the idea Browning presents in *Sordello* that the poet should be a "Maker-see" ultimately derives from a visual and painterly model of poetic creation. A simpler version of this visual poetics certainly accounts for the success of "The Pied Piper of Hamelin," which Browning wrote for the nine-year-old William Macready to illustrate while the boy was convalescing from an illness. Later, in commenting to Joseph Milsand in 1853 on his plans for *Men and Women*, Browning says "I am writing a sort of first step toward popularity . . . with

73. "Tennyson's Poems," 404–5.
74. Citations of Browning's poetry refer to line numbers in *Robert Browning: The Poems*, ed. John Pettigrew and Thomas J. Collins.

more music and painting than before so as to get people to hear and see."[75] And it would seem that he was thinking in particular of such poems as "Andrea del Sarto" and "Fra Lippo Lippi."

After the market for serious contemporary poetry virtually disappeared with the advent of the literary Annuals, the new poetic form that most fully expressed the alienation of the poets from the reading public was the dramatic monologue. In the dramatic monologue the speakers seek to establish their sense of self in terms of their possible audiences.[76] Tennyson's Ulysses, for example, who feels that he has become just a name, rejects Penelope and Telemachus and sets out to the Happy Isles with his mariners. In Browning's "My Last Duchess" the Duke of Ferrara, who had found the generous eyes of his late wife such a threat to his nine-hundred-year-old name, has had her killed and, one realizes with horror, is much happier with her curtained portrait whose gaze he now controls. The speakers meditate on their lack of others to recognize their vocations and their very beings, and speculate upon or demonstrate unconsciously the spiritual emptiness of the autonomous self. The dramatic monologue, then, becomes a vehicle for the expression of such spiritual alienation, and, more concretely, it is the form in which the disappearance of the audience for poetry becomes both explicitly thematized and symbolically represented.

In Tennyson's "St. Simeon Stylites" (1832), the first dramatic monologue, the speaker is physically separated from the adoring but suspiciously regarded crowd of admirers below him and is also psychologically isolated from God by his guilt. His isolation has been a progressive one: he lived for three years on a pillar of six cubits, another three on one of twelve cubits, for six years on one of twenty, and for the last twenty years has lived on one of forty cubits. This distance is symbolic of his withdrawal from all audiences. He feels "Unfit for earth, unfit for heaven, scarce meet / For troops of devils" (3–4). The saint has sought to establish his spiritual worthiness but cannot be sure of it because he abjures any self based upon pride. He speaks of "those lead-like tons of sin" that have crushed his spirit (25). He desperately wants to be a saint and so be saved, but feels that those who worship him as a saint are "silly" (125), and may endanger his receiving

75. Browning to Milsand, February 24, 1853, "Deux lettres inédites de Robert Browning à Joseph Milsand," 251.
76. I have discussed this relationship between speakers of dramatic monologues and their audiences and its connections with the reception of Browning's poetry; see my *Robert Browning: His Poetry and His Audiences*, esp. 155–90.

God's grace. The hyperbole of the saint's self-renunciation and the rhetorical self-flagellation of his prayer were evidently intended to have a satiric point,[77] but, more generally, they indicate the generic decentering of the self implicit within the dramatic monologue as the speakers attempt to establish their identity by having others recognize them. The genre is thus symbolic of the lack of an audience for and the consequent alienation and self-doubt of the poets who were beginning their careers in the 1830s.

The self-consciousness of the dramatic monologue allows for an explicit thematizing of the poet's alienation from the publishing market. This is clear in Tennyson's "Will Waterproof's Lyrical Monologue" (1842). One sees that Will Waterproof's sole audience at the Cock Tavern is the head-waiter to whom he addresses his "random rhymes / Ere they be half-forgotten" (13–14). Inspired by the muse of alcohol, he proudly declares that "tho' all the world forsake, / Tho' fortune clip my wings, / I will not cramp my heart, nor take / Half-views of men and things" (49–52). He has asserted his independence from the market, which demands much less than he feels he can deliver. But he finds that his idealism has been costly, for he now sadly contemplates his faded poetic dreams: "For I had hope, by something rare / To prove myself a poet: / But, while I plan and plan, my hair / Is gray before I know it" (165–68). While he realizes that a poet must be devoted to the production of aesthetic rarity, he has had to define himself in terms of the popular audience for poetry. He has been dragged down into "the common day" by the "weight of that half-crown" (154–55) and has evidently amused others at the tavern by singing for his liquid supper. His rarefied hopes have dwindled because he needs half-crowns to pay for his pints. One clearly should not sympathize with Waterproof's self-pity or see a great poet in him, but one should understand that the lack of an audience for poetry was a condition of the age.

The alienation of the poet from his audience is evident also in the ironic complaint of Tennyson's "Amphion." The speaker recalls the myth of the poet Amphion, who could make the forests dance, and laments that now such ecstatic audiences are no longer available:

> in such a brassy age
> I could not move a thistle;
> The very sparrows in the hedge
> Scarce answer to my whistle;

77. See Jerome Buckley, *Tennyson: The Growth of a Poet*, 25–26; and A. Dwight Culler, *The Poetry of Tennyson*, 24.

Or at the most, when three-parts-sick
  With strumming and with scraping,
A jackass heehaws from the rick,
  The passive oxen gaping. (65–72)

Unlike the mythological poet who could control his audience's response and had great power over it, the speaker in this "brassy age" hears only the heehaws of jackasses in response to his verses. When not indifferent to his work, nature seems derisive. He has no audience because readers like his next-door neighbors, the "wither'd Misses," now prefer practical books on gardening, and "prose / O'er books of travell'd seamen" (81–82). The contemporary poet has no one who recognizes him as a poet and so, as the closing image of his growing a "little garden blossom" suggests (104), he must think of himself as cultivating his poetic blooms for his private pleasure.

Although Browning had struggled and failed in *Sordello* (1840) to represent the impossibility of Sordello's making a radical poetics a popular politics, perhaps the most memorable figure of the alienated poet is that of his "Pied Piper of Hamelin" (1842). The piper is unappreciated by the tight-fisted burghers of the city who refuse to pay him for the service he has rendered them in ridding their town of rats. Then, in a fancy of poetic revenge, the piper pipes the town's children away, too. The resonances of the tale are many,[78] but one should recognize in its mythopoeia the claim that the poet makes on future generations in the absence of being properly remunerated by his contemporaries. Although the moralizing narrative and its comic rhymes lead one to overlook the poem's underlying seriousness, it seems clear that in creating the Pied Piper Browning has successfully transcended the oppressive circumstances of the poetic marketplace which give the poem much of its subterranean energy.

In Browning's monologues, the poet who is psychologically alienated by the realities of the marketplace is perhaps best represented in a displaced form by the speaker of Browning's "Pictor Ignotus" (1845). Browning imposes the nineteenth-century distinction between a public and private market for art upon sixteenth-century Italian painting and imagines that painting portraits would bring more fame and fortune than working away at church frescoes. Pictor Ignotus has

    dreamed (how well!)
  Of going—I, in each new picture,—forth,

---

78. See my discussion of the poem in *Robert Browning*, 91–93.

As, making new hearts beat and bosoms swell,
   To Pope or Kaiser, East, West, South, or North. (25–28)

He has imagined how famous he would have become if he had dissemi-
nated his work in the new medium of easel painting.[79] He exclaims "Oh,
thus to live, I and my picture, linked / With love about, and praise" (36–37)
and declares he could have painted pictures like those that are so much
praised. He feels, though, that the art market is like "some strange house of
idols at its rites" (43), where he would be threatened by unsparing critics,
and he comforts himself with a certain spiritual disdain for those who might
have bought his work:

> These buy and sell our pictures, take and give,
> Count them for garniture and household-stuff,
>   And where they live needs must our pictures live
> And see their faces, listen to their prate,
>   Partakers of their daily pettiness. (50–54)

This less than sacramental appreciation of his pictures reconciles him to his
"endless cloisters and eternal aisles with the same series, / Virgin, Babe and
Saint" (59–60), because, he says, "At least no merchant traffics in my heart"
(62). Yet there seems to be much ambivalence in his attitude toward the
youthful painter that "men praise so" (70) when he asks, "Tastes sweet the
water with such specks of earth?" (72). This seems to be a real and not a
rhetorical question that he wishes he knew the answer to. Although the
unknown painter feels unable to descend from his artistic standards to
please the public taste, he seems to wish that he, too, could taste the
rewards of fame. And while his spiritual pride has kept him from trafficking
in his heart, his lack of any energizing recognition from others has condemned him to less than inspired art.

For Browning's artists, as well as for himself, the enabling audience is to
be found in the love of another or of God and not in the public marketplace.
The special private audience is preferred because it gives the artist access
to spiritual insight and a sense of identity obtainable nowhere else. In
"Rudel to the Lady of Tripoli" (1842), for example, Rudel, the French
troubadour poet, has constructed an allegory of his relations to the men
who, he says, "feed / On songs I sing" (30–31) and to the Lady whom he

---

79. Loy D. Martin considers the painter's disdain for the new market as artistic cowardice in
the light of the parable of the talents; see *Browning's Dramatic Monologues and the Post-Romantic
Subject*, 123. See also my discussion in *Robert Browning*, 100–101.

loves from afar but who does not recognize him. The allegorical device, however, is inadequate to his love while expressive of his need for an audience, because, as Rudel says, " 'tis a woman's skill / Indeed" (28–29) that is required to complete and fulfill him. Rudel's poetry gives voice to his feeling caught between the unsatisfying demands of a public audience and his desire for a particular private one. Similarly, in "One Word More: To E.B.B." (1855), Browning distinguishes between those audiences he hopes will read and buy his poetry and his wife, who sustains his being. Unable to find a public that can appreciate his poetry, Browning retreats to an introspective mode and form in the dramatic monologue that allows him to explore both subjectively and objectively the relation between artistic psychology and artistic success.

Although the dramatic monologue became expressive both of the alienation of speakers from their audiences and also of the need for the recognition and love of others in order for speakers to have a sense of self, the form arises from the historical decline of the market for poetry in the 1820s and 1830s and the attendant alienation of poets from the reading public as they sought to maintain their artistic integrity. The dramatic monologue as developed by Tennyson and Browning allowed poets a means of objectifying their own distance from and quest for an audience that would provide them with recognition and a sense of self, and it also provided them a vehicle for the subjective introspection that their artistic isolation had occasioned. In this way, the form reflects both in symbolic and literal terms the tension between aesthetic ideals and the realities of the early-nineteenth-century publishing marketplace. Although the form is complicated further by the age's predilection for seeking historical and mythological parallels to serve as allegories of the modern condition, the dramatic monologue nonetheless is testimony to the imaginative resources of Tennyson and Browning in articulating the predicament of poetry that they had to face, and still retains much of its aesthetic flexibility for contemporary poets.

V

Because they made cheaper books possible, stereotyping and the Fourdrinier papermaking machine were the driving forces during the early nineteenth century behind the shift in England from a literature written for an elite, wealthy audience to one written for the reading public at large. Once the materials and means of printing became cheaper, diffuse prose was no longer at a comparative economic disadvantage with compressed poetry. The periodical format, in particular, gave rise to a variety of shorter prose forms that competed for and largely won over the audience for poetry. The literary Annuals of the 1820s and 1830s further divided the market for poetry into a large one for light lyrics and a small one for self-consciously serious art. Although I believe it is possible to make too much of the literary Annuals, I think their popularity influences a shift from Romantic to Victorian poetics, one aspect of which is an emphasis upon purely pictorial description in poetry. It is certain, however, that the popularity of the Annuals radically changed the publishing marketplace for poetry and thus inevitably the place of the poet in early Victorian literary culture. Indeed, the division between Romantic and Victorian poetry rests in part upon underlying changes in the literary marketplace. Yet long before poetry lost its cultural preeminence, the best poets realized that, given an expansion of the readership in England, poetry was condemned to move in advance of the popular taste and to become an avant-garde art in order to retain its formal and artistic integrity. The most significant formal expression of this aesthetic evolution in poetry was the development of the dramatic monologue by Tennyson and Browning as the market for serious poetry disappeared. The marginalization of poetry during this period provides a useful index of the technological and market forces at work in the dissemination of culture in England; it also reminds us that literary genres and forms are themselves intimately connected with the history of society, both reflecting and anticipating changes in the conditions of literary production.

2

The Egoism of Authorship: Wordsworth's Poetic Career

━━━━━━━━

It is a difficult piece of Antiquarianism to decypher the Hieroglyphic of a publisher's balance— pro—con—or otherwise—or anywise.
—Byron to Douglas Kinnaird, December 19, 1822

O f the Romantic poets, William Wordsworth was the most concerned about his poetry as property, the most tenacious in retaining his copyrights, and, perhaps, the most disappointed in his expectations for the sales of his work. Even though he lamented how, in "getting and spending, we lay waste our powers," Wordsworth did not think of his work as transcending the world but as intimately involved in its daily business and as belonging to the literary marketplace. Yet as the poetry boom of the first two decades of the nineteenth century began, Wordsworth found himself largely unread in comparison with other poets of the day; and although he is now considered the greatest of the Romantic poets, most of his contemporaries would not have agreed. He nonetheless persisted in believing that his poetry would appeal to more readers as their taste improved; and when his poetic powers declined, he served as the editorial custodian of his early inspirations. Wordsworth sought to keep his poetry in print in the 1820s and 1830s but sacrificed circulation for profit. In the 1830s Edward Moxon replaced Thomas Longman as his publisher and by shrewdly marketing his works and exploiting the rise in Wordsworth's reputation greatly increased the sales of his poetry, which reached their height after Wordsworth became poet laureate in 1843. As the readership rapidly expanded in early-nineteenth-century England and as the popular

49

appreciation of great contemporary literature and especially of great poetry began to lag behind its production, Wordsworth was forced to develop a modern idea of authorship.

I

Although in 1793 he published two small books of poetry (*An Evening Walk* and *Descriptive Sketches*), Wordsworth did not take up authorship seriously until 1798, when together with Coleridge he wrote and published *Lyrical Ballads*. Coleridge had earlier collaborated with Robert Southey on *The Fall of Robespierre* (1794) and with Charles Lamb and Charles Lloyd in *Poems on Various Subjects* (1796). In order to help finance his planned trip with the Wordsworths to Germany in 1798–99, Coleridge suggested that he and Wordsworth co-author a volume of poems, assigning himself the task of writing poems illustrating "supernatural naturalism" and having Wordsworth attempt to illustrate "natural supernaturalism."[1] Joseph Cottle published *Lyrical Ballads* in an octavo edition of probably five hundred copies at five shillings each, and paid Wordsworth and Coleridge thirty guineas.[2]

Once Coleridge had received his money, he seems to have cared little about the future of the work. But Wordsworth found himself caring very much indeed, perhaps in part because until the death of Lord Lonsdale in 1802 the estate of Wordsworth's father was tied up and Wordsworth and his sister were living in expectation of their inheritance.[3] In 1800 Cottle sold

1. "Natural supernaturalism," denoting the sacralizing of all nature, is Thomas Carlyle's phrase from *Sartor Resartus*; see the Charles Frederick Harrold edition, 254. Meyer H. Abrams associates Wordsworth's project with secularized forms of religious experience and sees an analogy between it and the Russian formalist aesthetic of "defamiliarization" in *Natural Supernaturalism: Tradition and Revolution in Romantic Literature*, 65–66, 378–79. A study is still needed of the relation between the secularization of religion through making nature sacred and the bureaucratic centralization of power through sponsoring a rhetoric of terror or "secret ministry" of fear that seems to inform Coleridge's "supernatural naturalism." For Coleridge's account of the genesis of *Lyrical Ballads*, see *Biographia Literaria*, 2:6–7. On the connection with Germany, see the letter of Coleridge to Joseph Cottle of April 1798, *Collected Letters of Samuel Taylor Coleridge*, 1:402–03.
2. Thomas Raysor points out that in his *Early Recollections* Cottle claims an edition of 500 copies; see "The Establishment of Wordsworth's Reputation," 62. See also Robert Southey to S. T. Coleridge, July 25, 1801, *Life and Correspondence of Robert Southey*, 2:153. Southey speaks of 750 copies, but he could be referring either to the 1798 edition or to the first volume of the 1800 edition. Cottle was generous with Wordsworth and Coleridge in paying for their poetry, since on the basis of its gold content, a guinea would be worth about $100 today (see chap. 1, n. 12 above). Coleridge and Wordsworth, then, were paid the equivalent of $3,000 for the right to print the first edition of *Lyrical Ballads*.
3. Dorothy and William received over £3,800 as their share: see *The Letters of William and Dorothy Wordsworth*, 1:398, n.1. (Hereafter *Letters*.) Wallace W. Douglas has surveyed Wordsworth's complicated personal finances in "Wordsworth as Business Man."

his publishing firm along with his copyrights to Longman. When Longman and Rees were bringing out the second edition of *Lyrical Ballads* in 1800, Wordsworth wrote that copyright had never been transferred to Cottle and that he retained his rights to all subsequent editions of the volume.[4] Longman agreed to pay Wordsworth eighty pounds for the second edition of *Lyrical Ballads*, which was published in two volumes. There were 750 copies of the first volume and 1,000 of the second, the extra copies of the second volume being intended for those who had already purchased the first edition, which, substantially unchanged, comprised the first volume of the second edition. A third edition of 500 copies was called for in 1802 and a fourth of the same number in 1805.[5]

The modest success of *Lyrical Ballads* was encouraging and seemed to augur well for the future. In 1807 Longman agreed to pay Wordsworth a hundred guineas to publish his *Poems in Two Volumes* in an edition of 1,000 copies. But unlike *Lyrical Ballads*, this collection languished. Seven years later when Wordsworth was beginning to see proof for *The Excursion* and arranging for the publication of his *Poems* of 1815, 230 copies remained unsold.[6] This decline in Wordsworth's readership has been attributed to the hostility of reviewers and especially to the most influential of them, Francis Jeffrey, who objected to Wordsworth's diction, disliked Wordsworth's "connecting his most lofty, tender, or impassioned conceptions, with objects and incidents, which the greater part of his readers will probably persist in thinking low, silly, or uninteresting," and generally decried "the lamentable consequences which have resulted from Mr Wordsworth's open violation of the established laws of poetry."[7] Although these comments certainly were not calculated to advance the sale of his poetry, they had called attention to his work and had evidently also given voice to what other readers felt. The obvious conclusion, which Longman quickly drew, was that the success of *Lyrical Ballads* was primarily due to Coleridge's poems instead of Wordsworth's, and, one would guess, was attributable largely to "The Rime of the Ancient Mariner," which was the first poem in

4. Wordsworth to Longman and Rees, December 18, 1800 (*Letters*, 1:310). The confusion concerning the copyrights would seem attributable to the fact that Coleridge had handled the business affairs with Cottle.
5. W.J.B. Owen, "Costs, Sales, and Profits of Longman's Editions of Wordsworth," 94–95.
6. Letter to Wordsworth of May 20, 1814, in W. J. B. Owen, "Letters of Longman & Co. to Wordsworth, 1814–36," 26. The small extent of Wordsworth's sales seems to have been well known among the literati, for Byron in a letter to John Murray, July 15, 1817, asks for the literary news and whether there is now "no city Wordsworth more admired than read" (*Byron's Letters and Journals*, 5:252).
7. [Francis Jeffrey], "*Poems* by W. Wordsworth," 218, 231.

the collection. Coleridge's nightmare narrative was more accessible and enjoyable than Wordsworth's lyric broodings and ruminations.

It is against Wordsworth's introspective psychology and not his subjects that Jeffrey inveighs in his comparison of Wordsworth with Crabbe: "instead of the men and women of ordinary humanity, we have certain moody and capricious personages, made after the poet's own heart and fancy,—acting upon principles, and speaking in a language of their own." In his commentary on "The Boy of Winander," Jeffrey expands on this theme: "The sports of childhood, and the untimely death of promising youth, is . . . a common topic of poetry. Mr Wordsworth has made some blank verse about it; but, instead of the delightful and picturesque sketches with which so many authors of moderate talents have presented us on this inviting subject, all that he is pleased to communicate of the rustic child, is, that he used to amuse himself with shouting to the owls, and hearing them answer. . . . This is all we hear of him; and for the sake of this one accomplishment, we are told, that the author has frequently stood mute, and gazed on his grave for half an hour together!"[8] Whatever one may feel today about the relative merits of Wordsworth's projective psychology versus Crabbe's psychology of types, Jeffrey no doubt mirrored the tastes of English readers. While Wordsworth's *Poems* of 1807 lingered on the booksellers' shelves, Crabbe's *Poems* of the same year went through three editions by 1808 and eight editions by 1816.

The success achieved by almost every poet of some talent in the first two decades of the nineteenth century eluded Wordsworth when his poetry was published by itself and not with others as in *Lyrical Ballads*. So when Longman printed only 500 copies of *The Excursion* in 1814 and charged two guineas for the quarto edition and twenty-eight shillings for the octavo to make sure of a profit, Wordsworth inevitably felt frustrated both by the small size of his audience and the implication that it was a very wealthy one. This is evident in his "Essay, Supplementary to the Preface" of his *Poems* of 1815, where he says that every great and original author "has had the task of *creating* the taste by which he is to be enjoyed."[9] Since the *Poems* of 1815 were printed in a small edition of 500 and priced at twenty-eight shillings for the two volumes, there is something of sour grapes in Wordsworth's consoling of himself in his prefatory essay. And there is more than a hint of self-deluding sophistry when he draws a distinction between the

8. "Crabbe's Poems," 134–36.
9. *Prose Works of Wordsworth*, 3:80.

public and the people: "Still more lamentable is his error who can believe that there is any thing of divine infallibility in the clamour of that small though loud portion of the community, ever governed by factitious influence, which, under the name of the PUBLIC, passes itself, upon the unthinking, for the PEOPLE."[10] Wordsworth suggests to himself that there is a larger audience outside the realm of the reading public, namely the people, which will take him to heart once it learns of him and is no longer distracted by the clamor and the reviews of the day. Two years later Coleridge makes a similar distinction in *Biographia Literaria*, saying that "the multitudinous PUBLIC, shaped into personal unity by the magic of abstraction, sits nominal despot on the throne of criticism," but only "echoes the decision of its invisible ministers."[11] Both Wordsworth and Coleridge feel that the anonymous critics of the *Edinburgh* and *Quarterly* reviews are usurping the people's right to make their own literary judgments. But perhaps more important, the mediation of the "invisible ministers" between poets and their readers points to the preeminence prose had acquired over poetry and was prophetic of the decline in the sales of poetry that occurred in the next decade.

II

The popularity of poetry and the great sums paid to poets in the 1810s soon made everyone a would-be poet. Poets like Wordsworth who appealed to refined aesthetic and academic tastes sold relatively better than they did at first, but they never came close to the sales of Byron and Scott. Publishers were flooded with submissions from the hopeful. John Murray said in 1817 that he had "waded through seven hundred rejected poems in the course of a year"; writing to Byron in January of the same year, he complains, "I am continually harassed by shoals of MSS. poems—two, three, or four a day. I require a porter to carry, an author to read, and a secretary to answer them."[12] Loath to alienate potential readers, Murray had adopted a generous and far more polite policy toward potential authors than any present-day publisher. But as readers turned to prose in the periodicals and the sales of poetry declined, Murray took on fewer and fewer poets; and after the death of Byron, he declared that he no longer published

10. Ibid., 3:84.
11. *Biographia Literaria*, 1:59.
12. Smiles, *A Publisher and His Friends*, 1:342, 370.

poetry.[13] The rising tide of mediocrity in verse and the advent of the young lady's Annuals soon ended the enormous sales of poetry. As Robert Montgomery notes in *The Age Reviewed* (1827), "survey e'en Longman's mildew'd shelves, / What rhyme-drug moulders in forgotten twelves!"[14] In *Vivian Grey* (1826–27) Benjamin Disraeli analyzes the passing of the rage for poetry as a phenomenon connected to the effects of recent economic events upon the fashionable women who were a large part of its readership:

> There is nothing like a fall of stocks to affect what it is the fashion to style the Literature of the present day—a fungus production, which has flourished from the artificial state of our society—the mere creature of our imaginary wealth. Every body being very rich, has afforded to be very literary—books being considered a luxury almost as elegant and necessary as Ottomans, bonbons, and pier-glasses. Consols at 100 were the origin of all book societies. The Stockbrokers' ladies took off the quarto travels and the hot-pressed poetry. They were the patronesses of your patent ink, and your wire wove paper. That is all passed.

As Disraeli later says, "the reign of Poesy is over, at least for half a century."[15]

Although *The Excursion* and the *Poems* of 1815 were published in small editions of 500 copies, both made money for Wordsworth. By 1823 he had made almost £130 from his half-profits of the 1814 edition of *The Excursion*, which sold more than 400 of its 500 copies; and from the *Poems* of 1815, which were exhausted in 1820, Wordsworth received a little more than seventy pounds.[16] In 1820 Wordsworth collected his poems in a four-volume duodecimo edition, entitled *Miscellaneous Poems*, which was printed in 500 copies. The public's interest in poetry had also inspired him to issue a number of individual volumes of verse in the space of seven years: *The White Doe of Rylstone* (1815), *Thanksgiving Ode* (1816), *Peter Bell* (1819), *The Waggoner* (1819), *The River Duddon* (1820), *Memorials of a Tour on the Continent* (1822), and *Ecclesiastical Sketches* (1822). Except for *Peter Bell*, which went to a second edition in 1819 because of the ridicule it inspired (most memorably Shelley's *Peter Bell the Third*), none of the volumes did well. As Hartley Coleridge pointedly observed in "He Lived Amidst th' Untrodden Ways,"

13. Ibid., 2:375.
14. *The Age Reviewed: A Satire in Two Parts*, 35.
15. *Vivian Grey*, 2:160–61, 178.
16. Owen, "Costs, Sales, and Profits of Longman's Editions of Wordsworth," 97–98.

Unread his works—his 'Milk White Doe'
   With dust is dark and dim;
It's still in Longman's shop, and oh!
   The difference to him![17]

Writing in 1833, Wordsworth remarks to Thomas Forbes Kelsall: "My 4 or 5 last *separate* publications in verse, were a losing concern to the Trade."[18]

Wordsworth nevertheless maintained his sense of his own worth apart from his value in the market. Coleridge invokes Wordsworth's attitude in attempting to establish a negotiating position with William Blackwood in 1819 regarding how much he should be paid for contributing to *Blackwood's*: "I may adopt the words which Mr. Wordsworth once used to Longman: 'You pay others, Sir! for what they write; but you must pay *me* for what I do *not* write, for it is this [i.e., the omissions, erasures, &c.] that costs me most both Time and toil."[19] Wordsworth felt that his poetic care led to a stylistic excellence that deserved remuneration for intrinsically aesthetic reasons. In the late 1820s, when the literary Annuals flourished, for example, Wordsworth proved to be one of the hardest bargainers and agreed to write twelve to fifteen pages of verse for *The Keepsake* only after he was promised £100.[20] This professionalism, however, was not considered gentlemanly. Contrasting the poetic preoccupation of Wordsworth's egotistical sublime with the easy manners of Thomas Moore's fashionable sociability, Benjamin Haydon is reminded of the following anecdote, the first in a series showing a remarkably recalcitrant Wordsworth: "One day Wordsworth in a large Party, at a moment of silence, leaned forward & said, '*Davy,* do you know the reason I published *my* White Doe in *Quarto?*' 'No,' said Davy, rather blushing. 'To express my own opinion of it,' he replied."[21] Not only was Wordsworth unafraid of introducing his own poetry as a subject for general conversation (something which, as Haydon suggests, was evidently the source of some embarrassment to his friends), but he obviously thought when he issued *The White Doe of Rylstone* in a sumptuous edition at the price

17. *New Poems, Including a Selection from His Published Poetry,* 98.
18. Wordsworth to Thomas Forbes Kelsall, October 30, 1833, *Letters,* 5:656.
19. Coleridge to William Blackwood, April 12, 1819, *Collected Letters,* 4:933.
20. Wordsworth to Allan Cunningham, December 1828 (*Letters,* 4:680). For the comparison of Wordsworth as a bargainer with other writers, see Andrew Boyle, *An Index to the Annuals, 1820–1850,* vii.
21. Entry for March 29, 1824, *The Diary of Benjamin Robert Haydon,* 2:470. For an earlier account given by Lady Davy to Thomas Moore, see the entry for October 27, 1820, *The Journal of Thomas Moore,* 1:356.

of a guinea that he showed even his slightest poetry was worth what the wealthiest in their conspicuous consumption of books paid for a volume of poetry.[22]

When in 1825 the four-volume edition of his *Miscellaneous Poems* had finally been sold off, Wordsworth found himself in conflict with his publisher. Longman had profited from Wordsworth's collected works but had lost money on a number of individual volumes and was very cautious about overextending himself with a slow-selling poet, especially when the market conditions for poetry were much worse than they had been a decade earlier. Wordsworth wanted to issue a new edition of his poems in six volumes and to increase the size of the edition to 1,000 from his usual 500, but Longman resisted.[23] Wordsworth was dissatisfied with this response and spent well over a year trying to come to terms with either John Murray or Hurst and Robinson, before returning to Longman. In December of 1826 he agreed to a new edition of his poems, which was to consist of 750 copies. Most notably, however, Wordsworth was "paying two thirds the expenses, & receiving two thirds the profits" and so bearing most of the cost of publication, which came to well over £300.[24]

These terms represented a change both in Wordsworth's and Longman's attitudes. Wordsworth felt that his poetry would do well and was more than willing (and, perhaps most important, able) to shoulder the financial burden of publication in return for an increased share of the profits. Longman, on the other hand, was even less inclined to take any financial risk with Wordsworth's poetry. He had paid for the right to print *Lyrical Ballads*, the *Poems* of 1807, and *The White Doe of Rylstone*, but he had insisted on merely offering Wordsworth a half share of the profits for *The Excursion*, the *Poems* of 1815, and for works subsequent to them. The *Poems* of 1827 found him trying to cut his exposure to any loss and to shift the risk from himself to the poet. Indeed, as the major publishers abandoned poetry to Edward Moxon in the 1830s, writing poetry became a gentleman's avocation, for Moxon demanded that a poet agree to share in profits and losses and so ruled out

---

22. For the price, see Thomas J. Wise, *A Bibliography of Wordsworth*, 100. Publishing in quarto limited readership to a wealthy few. Byron, for instance, advised Leigh Hunt on printing *The Story of Rimini* (1816): "Don't let your bookseller publish in *Quarto* it is the worst size possible for circulation—I say this on Bibliopolical authority" (October 30, 1815, *Byron's Letters and Journals*, 4:326). Jerome McGann observes that Murray published the first two cantos of *Don Juan* (1819) in quarto deliberately to restrict the poem's audience, something which Byron clearly didn't want; see *The Beauty of Inflections: Literary Investigations in Historical Method and Theory*, 115–17.
23. Longman to Wordsworth, October 10, 1825, in Owen, "Letters of Longman," 29.
24. Longman to Wordsworth, December 27, 1826, and April 28, 1827, ibid., 30–31.

anyone without substantial means from trying their hand at turning out slim volumes of verse. Poets like John Clare who lacked independent means were shut out altogether from publishing their work because they had to make money upon publication in order to justify their having written anything at all. Longman's treatment of Wordsworth was a harbinger of the future and good evidence of Disraeli's claim that the fashion for reading poetry had passed.

While the *Poems* of 1827 were to sell slowly and steadily and to be exhausted by 1832, two significant publications of Wordsworth's poetry made their appearance during these five years. The first was Galignani's pirated edition in one volume of Wordsworth's works, which was published in Paris in 1828 in an edition of 3,000 and sold at the cost of forty francs or roughly a third or a fourth of the cost of the *Poems* of 1827.[25] The second was the publication by Edward Moxon in 1831 of *Selections from the Poems of William Wordsworth: Chiefly for the Use of Schools and Young Persons.* This volume was priced at five shillings and went to a second edition in 1834. Its success was twofold: it brought Moxon to the attention of Wordsworth, and it made Wordsworth's poetry reasonable in price for the first time since *Lyrical Ballads*—that is, if one grants that five shillings sixpence for *Peter Bell* and four shillings sixpence for *The Waggoner* were far from being bargains. As Matthew Arnold suggests in the preface to his selection of Wordsworth's poetry, the prolific poet gained from such pruning and framed presentation.[26] The volume also formed the taste of children in schools, where it was intended to be used as a textbook. Wordsworth seems to have benefited immediately from the reprinting of the cheap edition and the selections, for in 1832 his *Poems* of 1827 were reprinted by Longman in an edition of 2,000, the largest edition yet (excepting the pirated Paris edition) of any of Wordsworth's works.[27]

Still, Wordsworth was restive. He felt that his reputation was growing but that he was not profiting by it. As he said in a letter to Kelsall, "Even the Sale of my collected works, tho' regular, is but trifling—this perhaps will surprize you—and, the state of my reputation considered, is altogether inexplicable, except on the supposition of the interference of the Paris Ed[ition]: of which I know the sale has been great."[28] *Yarrow Revisited,* the

25. Wordsworth to Edward Quillinan, November 11, 1828, and to Isabella Fenwick, March 24, 1837, *Letters*, 3:656 and 6:384.
26. "William Wordsworth," in *The Complete Prose Works of Matthew Arnold*, 9:41–44.
27. Longman to Wordsworth, July 15, 1834, in Owen, "Letters of Longman," 32.
28. Wordsworth to Thomas Forbes Kelsall, October 30, 1833, *Letters*, 5:656.

last volume of Wordsworth's published by Longman, appeared in 1835, went through one edition of 1,500 copies, and entered a second within a year. Something of a groundswell for Wordsworth was developing, for in 1835 the edition of his *Poems* of 1832 was exhausted and negotiations for another collected edition started. W. J. B. Owen has speculated that Longman's proposal was merely to print a stereotype of the edition of 1832 together with a stereotyped second edition of *Yarrow Revisited* for the next edition of Wordsworth's poetry.[29] But Wordsworth's rejection of Longman's proposal and acceptance of Edward Moxon's seems to have been expressive instead of a long-standing dissatisfaction with Longman, and, more important, a personal triumph in negotiating with his publishers which had long eluded him.

After 1827 Wordsworth had agreed with Longman to pay two-thirds of the publishing costs in return for two-thirds of the profits. This meant that Wordsworth had to wait a long time before realizing a handsome profit on the 1832 edition of his poetry. In 1836 he received his account from Longman for the previous year and wrote to his family: "The profits of my last edition have been 687 [pounds]—received or to be received at midsummer, which will be about 370 [pounds] for this year in addition to the Yarrow."[30] Although the edition had been in print for four years, over half of his profit came in the last year, as most of the edition had to be sold before his costs were met. Still, Wordsworth's faith and investment in himself were paying off. Then in May of 1836, according to Wordsworth, Moxon offered to print a six-volume edition of 3,000 copies and "to give two thirds of the profits, amounting to 771 [pounds] to be paid in advance immediately after the publication of the 6th Vol[ume]; that is 771 [pounds] for eighteen thousand volumes, miserable pay! The stereotype plates remaining mine or my heirs. I like this not at all."[31] Wordsworth recognized that Moxon was proposing to sell the books for a relatively low price and a smaller profit margin than Longman did, roughly about 25 percent less. Wordsworth apparently accounted the risk as little or nothing and preferred a higher margin of profit even if it meant reduced sales. But Moxon's eagerness to add Wordsworth to his list led him to offer this second proposal a month later, which Wordsworth includes in a letter to his family and comments on:

29. "Letters of Longman," 32.
30. Wordsworth to his family, June 4, 1836, *Letters*, 6:241.
31. Wordsworth to his family, late May 1836, *Letters*, 6:233. For an account of Wordsworth's relations with Moxon, see Merriam, *Edward Moxon*, 130–49.

Mr. M[oxon] to print stereotype and pay all the expenses of an Edition of 3000 copies of Mr. W[ordsworth]'s P[oetical] works in 6 vols similar to the Edit[ion] in 5 vol 1827.

Mr. M[oxon] for the same to give Mr. W[ordsworth] 1000 pounds the whole to be paid in cash immediately after the Publication of the 6th vol. . . .

Mr. M[oxon] to give Mr. W[ordsworth] for every future edit[ion] of 1000 copies 400 [pounds], to be paid in Cash within 6 months of the day of publication.

The Copyright and stereotype plates to be Mr Wordsworth's—

So you see dearest Friends there is nothing like standing up for one's self, and one's own legitimate interest.[32]

These terms were not to Moxon's advantage. When in 1842 Wordsworth learned of Moxon's losses on his poetry, Wordsworth magisterially replies: "I am very sorry indeed to learn that your connection with me, at least considered in its direct bearings has been so unprofitable to you." He also seems to have interpreted Moxon's remarks as an attempt to renegotiate the terms of his *Poems, Chiefly of Early and Late Years,* which was issued in 1842 by Moxon at the price of nine shillings a copy; for later in the same letter he says, "the labour which from [the] first I have bestowed on the forth-coming volume is not likely to earn for me the wages of two shillings a day. Take that, ye Men of the Trade and make the best of it. I wish you may be right in charging the book so high."[33] But once Wordsworth became poet laureate in 1843, the collected edition of his works went through four editions in six years—1843, 1845, 1846, and 1849. *The Prelude* was published posthumously in an edition of 2,000 copies in 1850, and then reissued in its second edition in the 1851 edition of Wordsworth's poetry. It would appear that while Moxon may have continued to publish Wordsworth on a razor-thin margin for himself, the turnover and the reprinting of stereotyped texts made the poet profitable to him in the long run.

Commenting on the close of Wordsworth's career, Herbert Lindenberger has felt that the reception of *The Prelude* was uncharacteristically lukewarm, that it was remarkable that the *Edinburgh Review, Blackwood's,* and the *Quarterly Review* did not see fit to notice it, and that "whereas the first edition of *The Prelude,* which numbered 2,000 copies, was not exhausted until almost a year after its appearance, the first edition of *In Memoriam,* consisting of 5,000 copies, was exhausted within weeks, and by the end of

32. Wordsworth to his family, early June 1836, *Letters,* 6:239.
33. Wordsworth to Moxon, February 3, 1842, *Letters,* 7:289–90.

1851 Tennyson's poem had gone through five editions in contrast to only two for Wordsworth's."[34] Yet, as this survey has shown, no single work previous to *The Prelude* had been printed in as large an edition as 2,000 copies nor sold as quickly. Moreover, because he felt that no review had ever helped him, Wordsworth had requested "that no Copies be sent to any Reviewer or Editor of Magazines or Periodicals whatever";[35] given this reluctance to distribute review copies, it is not surprising that the reviews in question didn't notice him. (One might also note that poetry was relatively unfashionable in the 1840s and 1850s and that Browning, for example, was not reviewed by the *Quarterly Review* until 1864, some thirty-two years and a dozen volumes of poetry into his career.) Indeed, rather than the reception of *The Prelude* being an anticlimax, it seems characteristic of Wordsworth's poetic career.

III

Wordsworth strongly believed that literature would be better and that authorship would necessarily become more gentlemanly and more respectable if copyrights were inheritable. The profits from an author's legacy, he felt, ought to go not to booksellers but to the author's family. However, Wordsworth didn't realize that in supporting Sergeant Thomas Noon Talfourd's parliamentary campaign to reform copyright from 1837 to 1841 he had ironically allied himself with the major publishing houses that held almost all copyrights and had long argued that copyright was assigned to them in perpetuity by authors.

While writers might occasionally make as much money as gentlemen, their social status in Britain was something less than that of gentlemen in the early nineteenth century. But it was not so much income as property that made the gentleman, so we find Wordsworth saying to Talfourd in 1838 that if copyright were perpetual, "Authors as a Class could not but be in some degree put upon exertions that would raise them in public estimation—And say what you will, the possession of Property tends to make any body of men more respectable, however high may be their claims to respect upon other considerations."[36] Since their income was uncertain and not inheritable, Wordsworth felt authors had no incentive to create properties that would make them gentlemen or would have a gentlemanly character.

34. "The Reception of *The Prelude*," 197, 204.
35. Wordsworth to Moxon, March 23, 1842, *Letters*, 7:308.
36. Wordsworth to Thomas Noon Talfourd, October 25, 1838, *Letters*, 6:636.

Writing to Sir Robert Peel in April of the same year, Wordsworth declares that because of the current copyright law, "the literary talent of the country is in a great measure wasted upon productions of light character and transitory interest, and upon periodicals."[37] If copyright is lengthened and made inheritable, he says in a letter to the editor of the *Kendal Mercury*, "a conscientious author, who had a family to maintain, and a prospect of descendants, would regard the additional labour bestowed upon any considerable work he might have in hand, in the light of an insurance of money upon his own life for the benefit of his issue; and he would be animated in his efforts accordingly, and would cheerfully undergo present privations for such future recompense."[38] Inheritable copyright would thus create better literature and make gentlemen of authors.

Wordsworth's first meditations on copyright seem to date from the disappointing reception and sale of his *Poems* of 1807. Having not profited immediately from that publication, he becomes conscious that his work might well be fated to become alienated labor instead of productive property. In response to a request in 1808 to make a contribution to build a monument to Burns, he unexpectedly launches into the following discussion of copyright:

> I am told that it is proposed to extend the right from 14 years, as it now stands, after the decease of authors, till 28, this I think far too short a period; at least I am sure that it requires much more than that length of time to establish the reputation of original productions, both in Philosophy and Poetry, and to bring them consequently into such circulation that the authors, in the Persons of their Heirs or posterity, can in any degree be benefited, I mean in a pecuniary point of view, for the trouble they must have taken to produce the works.—The law as it now stands merely consults the interest of the useful drudges in Literature, or of flimsy and shallow writers, whose works are upon a level with the taste and knowledge of the age; while men of real power, who go before their age, are deprived of all hope of their families being benefited by their exertions. Take for instance in philosophy, Hartley's book upon Man, how many years did it sleep in almost entire oblivion! What sale had Collins' Poems during his lifetime, or during the fourteen years after his death, and how great has been the sale since! the product of it if secured to his family, would have been an independence to them.—Take a still stronger instance, but this you may say proves too much, I mean Milton's minor Poems; it is nearly 200 years since they were published, yet they were utterly neglected till within these last 30 years, notwithstanding they had, since the beginning

37. Wordsworth to Sir Robert Peel, April 18, 1838, *Letters*, 6:558.
38. Letter to the Editor of the *Kendal Mercury*, April 12, 1838, *Prose Works*, 3:312.

of the last century, the reputation of the Paradise Lost to draw attention towards them. Suppose that Burns or Cowper had left at their deaths each a child a few months old, a daughter for example, is it reasonable that those children, at the age of 28, should cease to derive benefit from their Father's works, when every Bookseller in the Country is profiting by them?[39]

Wordsworth's connection of copyright with children also occurs in a letter to J. Forbes Mitchell in 1819. He complains that the restricted length of copyright "is tantamount almost to an exclusion of all pecuniary recompense for the Author, and even where Works of imagination and manners are so constituted as to be adapted to immediate demand, as in the case of those of Burns, justly may it be asked what reason can be assigned that an Author who dies young should have the prospect before him of his Children being left to languish in Poverty and Dependence, while Booksellers are revelling in luxury upon gains derived from Works which are the delight of many Nations."[40] One rightly feels, I think, that in place of Burns and the hypothetical Cowper with children, Wordsworth is really thinking of himself and his own family.

As Wordsworth grew older, his concern over the inheritability of copyright grew. After turning sixty in 1830, he writes to John Gardner of his intention "to secure some especial value to any collection of my Works that might be printed after my decease, to reserve a certain number of new pieces to be intermixed with that collection" and tells of another author he knows who is saving any additions and corrections for posthumous publication "for the express purpose of benefiting his heirs."[41] Later in the same year, he writes to Sir Walter Scott asking him if he knows precisely what the law says about the length of copyright after an author's death.[42] In 1835 Wordsworth petitions Lord Lonsdale and Sir Robert Peel, asking that he

39. Letter to Richard Sharp, September 27, 1808, *Letters*, 2:266. At the heart of Wordsworth's poetic concern about money, then, is the issue of inheritance. But instead of a patient study of the Wordsworths' family history and the period's inheritance law in relation to his poetry, there has been a critical rush to mediate between Wordsworth's poetry and larger economic and ideological patterns of the Romantic period. Kurt Heinzelman sees "Michael" in terms of "alienated and unalienated labor" created by England's industrialization, in *The Economics of the Imagination*, 69. In an attack upon the ideology implicit in Wordsworth's poetic treatment of economics, Marjorie Levinson speaks of "Michael's emancipation from material concerns" in *Wordsworth's Great Period Poems*, 60. And although pointing to the indebtedness of the English laboring poor and linking it to the Wordsworth family's finances, Alan Liu ends up declaring that Wordsworth's poetry transcends its material conditions ("The Economy of Lyric: The Ruined Cottage," in *Wordsworth: The Sense of History*, 311–58).
40. Wordsworth to J. Forbes Mitchell, April 21, 1819, *Letters*, 3:534–35.
41. Wordsworth to John Gardner, May 19, 1830, *Letters*, 5:265.
42. Wordsworth to Sir Walter Scott, July 20, 1830, *Letters*, 5:306.

be allowed to resign his stamp distributorship so that his son Willy could assume the position, citing the injustice of the copyright law with regard to inheritance.[43] When his request is refused, he begins to think more and more about the need for copyright reform, especially since under law the copyright of the most popular of his poems, *The Excursion*, would expire in 1842 if he died before then.[44] His concern became particularly acute when in 1836 Moxon agreed to pay him a thousand pounds to publish a collected edition of his poetic works. It thus became evident that his determined retention of his copyrights and investment in his work was finally paying off. In 1836 he writes to Sergeant Talfourd, complaining that the Copyright Bill of 1814 "has refused to admit the doctrine of independent perpetuity of Copyright in literature."[45] Indeed, it seems possible that Wordsworth's remarks may have served as part of the impetus behind Sergeant Talfourd's campaign for copyright reform from 1837 to 1841; and it is certain that Wordsworth strongly encouraged Talfourd in his parliamentary efforts and wrote over fifty letters to members of Parliament.[46]

Wordsworth even mounted a minor literary campaign for longer copyright in his *Sonnets* of 1838. "A Plea for Authors" argues that there should be a "lengthened privilege, a lineal tie" for books; and in "A Poet to his Grandchild," a sequel to "A Plea for Authors, May 1838," Wordsworth strikes his most bathetic note in lamenting the poet's poor and illiterate great-grandchildren:

"Son of my buried Son, while thus thy hand
Is clasping mine, it saddens me to think
How Want may press thee down, and with thee sink
Thy Children left unfit, through vain demand
Of culture, even to feel or understand
My simplest Lay that to their memory
May cling;—hard fate! which haply need not be
Did Justice mould the Statutes of the Land.
A Book time-cherished and an honoured name
Are high rewards; but bound they Nature's claim

43. Wordsworth to Lord Lonsdale, January 24, 1835, and to Sir Robert Peel, February 5, 1835, *Letters*, 6:15–16, 20–22.
44. See the letter to his family, June 27, 1836, *Letters*, 6:266.
45. Wordsworth to Thomas Noon Talfourd, November 16, 1836, *Letters*, 6:322. There is reason to believe that this letter may have moved Talfourd to campaign for copyright reform, especially since Talfourd consults Wordsworth throughout his parliamentary maneuvering.
46. For a survey of his support of Talfourd's bill, see Paul M. Zall, "Wordsworth and the Copyright Act of 1842," and Russell Noyes, "Wordsworth and the Copyright Act of 1842."

Or Reason's? No—hopes spun in timid line
From out the bosom of a modest home
Extend through unambitious years to come,
My careless Little-one, for thee and thine!"[47]

It is worth pointing out that Wordsworth had the good taste not to republish the poem after the 1842 Copyright Act was passed.

Despite his public support for a bill that would obviously benefit him, Wordsworth felt strongly that his reward should come from the reading public in the marketplace. His principled adherence to laissez-faire capitalism was especially evident during the 1838 campaign for copyright reform. In the debate the Attorney General, Sir John Campbell, suggested that extending copyright be made a matter for the Judicial Committee of the Privy Council and be granted in special cases. In response to Robert Southey, who supported this compromise, Wordsworth said, "I should both dislike and dread such a tribunal.—Besides, such a distinction would put those Authors on whom it was conferred in an invidious position. Let the remuneration come from [the] public who would chearfully bestow it.—We want no pensions and reversions for our heirs, and no monuments by public or private Subscription.—We shall have a monument in our own works if they survive and if they do not we should not deserve it."[48] He believed that in the long run fame and economic rewards would coincide.

In championing a longer copyright, Wordsworth ironically didn't realize that, unlike him, only a few enterprising authors held onto their copyrights. Indeed, when Talfourd asked Wordsworth for a petition from notable authors in 1838, only a handful of others (Dickens, Thomas Arnold, and Carlyle, in particular) supported the bill, because only a very few authors thought it worth their while to sacrifice the certainty of present gain for the favor of future readers. The major publishers held almost all copyrights, so what any copyright bill threatened to do was to rearrange the existing economic arrangements within the book trade. Talfourd's bill particularly threatened the cheap reprint trade. As books were going out of copyright, shares in them were auctioned to all London booksellers, which allowed them to reprint the author's work being auctioned so long as the profits from reprinting were allocated according to the shares held. This meant that although by law after their copyright expired books passed into the

---

47. *Poetical Works of William Wordsworth*, 3:410–11. For "A Plea for Authors, May 1838," see 3:58.
48. Wordsworth to Robert Southey, April 30, 1838, *Letters*, 6:566.

public domain, the London book trade acted as a cartel and shared out profits from long-lived copyrights among themselves and enforced adherence to this profit-sharing by boycotting the books of, and by refusing a trade discount of their own books to, any publisher who violated this agreement. The most famous such sale in English publishing history was the sale of shares in Cowper's copyrights that occurred in 1812, two years before they were due to expire.[49] At the auction the trade valued Cowper's poetry as being worth over four thousand pounds, and, assuming a 5 percent return on investment, it thus expected his poetry to yield two hundred pounds a year.

By 1838 Wordsworth had become aware of this arrangement, but he rightly notes that the expansion of the publishing market was breaking down the cartel:

> There has been and still continues to be a conventional arrangement among Publishers who have purchased Copy-rights, not to interfere with each other's exclusive claims, after their rights by law have expired. This convention is breaking down under the force of the rapidly increasing demand for books, the consequence of extending education and an increase in the wealth of the community. Booksellers, while they enjoy exclusive right by law, are every year finding it more and more their interest to sell an increased number of Copies at a low price rather than a few at a high one. The same considerations would operate in the same way upon the heirs and descendants of Authors— as it is already doing among themselves—with a further motive in both cases of increased honour and distinction to the name and family. Besides, it would be of greater consequence to *them*, than to Publishers who have each the works of *many* to profit by, and they would naturally take more care to give to the public correct Editions. Nothing can be more detestable and injurious to knowledge and taste than the inaccuracies in the low priced Editions, that are thrown out upon the world by Tegg, and others of his stamp.[50]

However much couched in the moral terms of his utilitarian opponents and their arguments that the greater common good of mass education and rational pleasure should limit authors' enjoyment of monetary return from their work, Wordsworth's economic analysis is impeccable.

As Wordsworth indicates, by the 1830s it was no longer possible to bar

49. Norma Russell, *Bibliography of William Cowper to 1837*, 47–48. On the share book system, see Graham Pollard, "The English Market for Printed Books," 32–34; also see chapter 1, note 7 above.
50. Wordsworth to Thomas Wyse of May 3, 1838, *Letters*, 6:575–76. On the Booksellers' Regulations of 1829, see James J. Barnes, *Free Trade in Books: A Study of the London Book Trade since 1800*, 1–18.

entry to the publishing business by denying a reprinter access to the trade's distribution network and reciprocal discounting. The demand for books in London had evidently grown large enough by then that a fringe publisher could reprint works no longer in copyright and make a living selling his books directly to customers at his London bookstore. Indeed, the first such respectable publisher to maintain himself in this manner outside the book-sellers' cartel without resorting to piracy of contemporary works was the publisher of Coleridge's late works, William Pickering.[51] And within the cartel, reprinting was a profitable business. Thomas Tegg, the largest re-printer and the trade's chief dealer in remaindered books, was said by Talfourd to have a stock worth £170,000 in 1838.[52]

What Wordsworth didn't understand was that the big publishing houses had every interest in having the length of copyright extended, while only a very few gentleman authors like himself would benefit directly from it. Since most books never made money and most authors having invested their time could not afford to risk discovering the worthlessness of their labor, copyrights were sold to publishers who could spread the financial risks of publication over many such properties and profit from the one or two books in ten that sold well, as well as the very rare book in several hundred that would still be selling thirty years after its first publication. In fact, Wordsworth's desire that Parliament declare that authors had a common-law right to their literary property in perpetuity was exactly what the booksellers had claimed ever since the days of the Stationers' Com-pany and had lost by a single vote when the House of Lords had decided the case of *Donaldson vs. Beckett* in 1774.[53] (It is, by the way, no accident that this landmark case involved the reprinting of Thomson's *Seasons,* since few books that were not poetry were worth reprinting after their copyright had expired.)

Talfourd's bill, then, was directly aimed at the London publishing houses specializing in reprinting and, in particular, at the largest such firm, Thomas Tegg's. By lengthening copyright from twenty-eight to sixty years, reprint-ers would have had to suffer through a thirty-two year drought before any new works would become general property of booksellers. It comes as no

51. See Geoffrey Keynes, *William Pickering, Publisher: A Memoir and a Check-list of His Publica-tions.* Pickering's publishing interests were, however, not profitable in the long run and led his firm into bankruptcy; see Bernard Warrington, "The Bankruptcy of William Pickering in 1853."
52. *Parliamentary Debates* (May 9, 1838), 42:1072.
53. See the account in J. J. Barnes, *Authors, Publishers, and Politicians: The Quest for an Anglo-American Copyright Agreement, 1815–1854,* 122–26.

surprise, then, that Tegg used every argument possible in his 1837 pamphlet, *Remarks on the Speech of Sergeant Talfourd on the Laws relating to Copyright,* to oppose Talfourd's bill. He argued that "ninety-nine out of the hundred writers know that sixty days, instead of sixty years, is the natural term of their intellectual progeny."[54] In particular, he directed his return fire at Coleridge and Wordsworth:

> Mr. Coleridge and Mr. Wordsworth may probably deserve the encomiums of the learned Sergeant, but I, like the public at large, have not arrived at that maturity of poetical taste, to be fully sensible of their beauties; and I rather think Mr. Talfourd's publisher, Mr. Moxon would tell him that the admiration of that style of poetry is still confined to the gifted, or initiated, or enlightened few: the fault may not be in the poetry, but they who write for profit (and that is the question in debate, though, probably these poets despised it) should remember, that Moliere, who charmed, and still charms, all the world, always tried the effect of what he wrote on the old woman. And I cannot help suspecting, that the heirs of Mr. Wordsworth will not find his admiring minority, or section of the public, increase very fast for some generations to come; at any rate, it is not worth while to alter the law for the chance of it.[55]

Tegg distributed his remarks as widely as possible among the printing and distributive tradesmen who were dependent on selling cheap books. These small tradesmen vigorously petitioned Parliament so that the bill's third reading was prevented in 1838.

Since Tegg was the chief purchaser of remainders in the trade, the major houses didn't dare to support Talfourd's bill openly for fear of losing Tegg's business. Although Talfourd submitted his private bill every year as long as he remained a member, Lord Mahon, who consulted the interests of Longman and Murray rather than those of the authors, managed in 1842 to push through an extension of copyright to the length of forty-two years or the author's life plus seven years. This came at the bottom of the century's worst deflation in 1842, when only the wealthy had the money to buy books, when most small publishing firms had gone bankrupt, and when those reprinters like Tegg who were still in business could no longer afford to mount a strong lobby in Parliament.

While this obviously wasn't as much as Wordsworth had hoped for, it seems to have been enough. Besides, he had apparently decided long ago to keep *The Prelude* in reserve for posthumous publication so as to give his

---

54. *Remarks on the Speech of Sergeant Talfourd*, 8.
55. Ibid., 17–18.

heirs the strongest possible claim on his literary estate for as long as possible. He had come to feel that he had triumphed over his critics and the moralizing utilitarian of "A Poet's Epitaph,"[56] who scorns the dead poet's "unprofitable dust" by living long enough to enjoy the financial fruits of his poetic labor and to give his heirs the posthumous benefit of the returns from his collected works for another forty-two years.

Wordsworth was admired and respected as a poet but never really loved. As Hartley Coleridge remarked, he was "a bard whom there were none to praise, / And very few to read."[57] As one surveys Wordsworth's poetic career, the success of *Lyrical Ballads* is a signal anomaly, and it is to be attributed, I think, to the popularity of Coleridge's poems.[58] This success created false expectations on the part of Wordsworth and his publishers and also gave rise to a certain bitterness in Wordsworth's attitude toward the reading public. His books sold steadily to a few who could afford them. Wordsworth wanted to be read by more people, but he felt that while it would be better if the prices of his books could be lower, he would rather have a good return from those books he sold than reduce the percentage of his returns. In his correspondence with Edward Moxon, for example, regarding the collected volume of his *Sonnets* published in 1838, he says, "You somewhat surprize me in purposing to print *one* Son[net] on a page, the whole number being I believe 415. Your plan and consequent price would make it a book of luxury, and tho' I have no objection to that, yet still my wish is, to be read as widely as is consistent with reasonable pecuniary return."[59] Wordsworth recognizes a trade-off between the price of a volume and its circulation but clearly considers "reasonable pecuniary return" as his final publishing criterion.

Similarly, in 1838 Moxon proposed to Wordsworth the idea of issuing the whole of his poems in one volume after the pattern of the pirated Galignani edition of 1828 and of the pirated American edition by Henry Reed in 1837. Wordsworth particularly admired the width of the page in the cheap

56. Commenting on this poem, which compares the poet to other professionals, Clifford Siskin considers Wordsworth's view of the poet in the light of the period's idea of professionalism, but he focuses only upon Wordsworth's revitalization of the Virgilian georgic tradition; see "Wordsworth's Prescriptions: Romanticism and Professional Power," in *The Romantics and Us: Essays on Literature and Culture*, ed. Gene W. Ruoff, 303–21.
57. *New Poems*, 98.
58. In comparison, Coleridge's *Christabel; Kubla Khan, a Vision; The Pains of Sleep* (1816) went to a third edition in the year of its publication; *Remorse* went to three editions in 1813; and his *Poetical Works* in three volumes saw editions in 1828, 1829, 1834, 1836, 1837, 1840, 1844, and 1848.
59. Wordsworth to Moxon, February 3, 1838, *Letters*, 6:518.

American edition, which allowed all of the lines to fit without having them run over even though the volume was printed in double columns. But as Alan Hill notes, the proposed volume which would have been sold at one pound was deemed to interfere with the sale of the six-volume edition of 1837 and so was dropped.[60] In fact, Wordsworth displays a fascinated horror in contemplating the American pirated version, as he wonders at "*the whole of my Poems being now sold in America for . . . something less than* 13*d* of our money," or about 5 percent of the proposed cost of his own one-volume edition.[61] In really cheap books he had no interest.

IV

So when Wordsworth speaks of the "PEOPLE" in the Essay, Supplementary to the Preface of his *Poems* of 1815, he is thinking of a relatively restricted class of people and not of the masses. The modern study of Wordsworth has tended to stress the early liberal sympathies and to value most the high seriousness and philosophical weightiness of his poetry. But even if his poetry was not remunerative enough to support him, his status and seriousness as a professional author deserve more attention than they have hitherto had. Further, the successive revisions of earlier poems in the collected editions (especially of 1827, 1836–37, 1845, and 1849–50) need to be examined in the light of Wordsworth's custodianship of his early work. For the modern idea of an author defining himself in terms of his oeuvre and identifying his own ego with it stems in no small part from Wordsworth's continuing attention to his work, from his careful revision of his earlier poems, and from his determination to control his final text. Although some may see this activity as obsessive behavior, it is ultimately the behavior of all writers who understand that in the future's eyes they will be what they have written. Even when his publishers were unwilling to take financial risks with his work, Wordsworth was always willing to take his chances with future readers, and for this egoism of authorship there is much yet to be said.

60. *Letters*, 6:647n. When Wordsworth finally did publish a one-volume edition of his works in 1845, it sold for the high price of a guinea, or twenty-one shillings, and did not, as Mary Moorman wrongly suggests, "bring his poems within the reach of persons of small means" (*William Wordsworth: A Biography*,) 2:595.
61. Wordsworth to Moxon, December 11, 1838, *Letters*, 6:648.

Daniel Maclise, "The Fraserians." Frontispiece of *A Gallery of Illustrious Literary Characters*, London, 1873.
Reproduced courtesy of the General Research Division, The New York Public Library, Astor, Lenox and Tilden Foundations.

3

Ideological Focus and
the Market for the Essay

This is the age of Criticism.

—Byron to John Murray, August 26, 1813

A t the beginning of his 1832 review of Ebenezer Elliott's *Corn-Law Rhymes,* Carlyle in the person of Smelfungus Redivivus declares the ascendancy of prose over poetry when he ironically asks, "Poetry having ceased to be read, or published, or written, how can it continue to be reviewed?"[1] Later, as a Victorian sage, Carlyle advised every poet to abandon poetry for prose. From his professional perspective he was giving good, practical advice. For although most magazine writers or reviewers wrote to supplement their income, a hard-working one could reasonably expect to make a middle-class income of £300 a year.[2] John Stuart Mill, for instance, notes that at the beginning of the nineteenth century his father, John Mill, who was supporting a large family, had "no resource but the precarious one of writing in periodicals."[3] This contrasted sharply with the financial circumstances of the typical Grub Street writer of Samuel Johnson's day. The rise in the market for prose writers in the early nineteenth

---

1. "Corn-Law Rhymes," in *The Collected Works of Thomas Carlyle,* 28:136. For the intellectual history informing Carlyle's view of poetry, see David J. DeLaura, "The Future of Poetry: A Context for Carlyle and Arnold," in *Carlyle and His Contemporaries: Essays in Honor of Charles Richard Sanders,* 148–80. Compare Macaulay from his "Milton" (1825): "We have seen in our own time great talents, intense labour, and long meditation, employed in this struggle against the spirit of the age, and employed, we will not say absolutely in vain, but with dubious success and feeble applause" (*Critical and Historical Essays,* 2:156).
2. On the largely middle-class origin of authors, see Altick, "The Sociology of Authorship: The Social Origins, Education, and Occupations of 1,000 British Writers, 1800–1935."
3. *Autobiography,* 1:7.

century reflected the wider readership for the literary reviews and magazines. Publishers had found that established magazines and reviews were the steadiest and most profitable sources of income, and so throughout the period they published a continually increasing number.

The most important literary periodicals introduced in the first half of the nineteenth century were the *Edinburgh Review*, the *Quarterly Review*, *Blackwood's Magazine*, the *London Magazine*, the *New Monthly Magazine*, the *Westminster Review*, the *London Review* (afterwards with the previous journal under J. S. Mill the *London and Westminster Review* and then again the *Westminster Review*), *Fraser's Magazine*, the *Metropolitan Magazine*, *Bentley's Miscellany*, the *Literary Gazette*, and the *Athenaeum*. Still important, particularly at the beginning of the century, were the *Gentlemen's Magazine*, the *Critical Review*, the *Monthly Review*, and the *Monthly Magazine*. Most authors wrote for these magazines because they paid higher prices for prose than ever before. The payments for essays and reviews rose from the beginning of the century until the 1820s and remained steady until the late 1830s. With the exception of a revival of the essay occurring in the early 1860s in the shilling magazines such as *Cornhill*, the *Fortnightly*, and *Macmillan's*, writers were best paid by periodicals between 1815 and 1835, when the reviews and magazines had not yet attracted the competition of a large number of other magazines and had not yet had their circulation undermined by the literary weeklies and newspapers. Young men seeking their fortune in London and Edinburgh soon could afford to become professional journalists and could make enough money to live as gentlemen. The improved system of distribution and publication meant that writers like Coleridge and Hunt who persisted in trying to write one-man periodicals soon found themselves both financially and intellectually exhausted by the better-organized competition. As long as the entry costs for publishing a magazine remained fairly low relative to the possible profits, no single literary monthly or quarterly was able to expand its readership above 15,000 readers, while the cheaper literary weeklies seem not to have had a circulation greater than 20,000 copies a week in the 1830s and 1840s.

Reviews and magazines in stiff competition with one another effectively segmented the reading public along existing political, religious, and class lines. Criticizing this phenomenon in 1864 as indicative of England's lack of cultural unity, Matthew Arnold observes in "The Function of Criticism at the Present Time" that

> we have the *Edinburgh Review*, existing as an organ of the old Whigs, and for as much play of the mind as may suit its being that; we have the *Quarterly Re-*

view, existing as an organ of the Tories, and for as much play of mind as may suit its being that; we have the *British Quarterly Review*, existing as an organ of the political Dissenters, and for as much play of mind as may suit its being that; we have the *Times*, existing as an organ of the common, satisfied, well-to-do Englishman, and for as much play of mind as may suit its being that. And so on through all the various fractions, political and religious, of our society; every fraction has, as such, its organ of criticism, but the notion of combining all fractions in the common pleasure of a free disinterested play of mind meets with no favour.[4]

So although the number of readers was increasing, the segmentation of the market meant that no literary magazine or review gained a readership large enough to dominate the market.

The cultural status and remuneration of the essayists were unsurpassed until the late 1830s, when the most popular of the novelists began to feel constrained by magazine serialization and felt they could have a larger readership and greater profits by issuing a novel in parts at a price lower than that of any single issue of a monthly magazine. But the popular focus on prose did have some associated aesthetic costs. The essay became a more perishable commodity with a shorter reading life; and because writers needed to appeal to a larger number of less educated readers, prose style changed from the prevailing balanced antithesis of the eighteenth century to familiar anticlimax, which reinforced received wisdom and illustrated axioms with a multitude of examples and parallels.

Within the periodical format, the essay of Montaigne, Bacon, Addison, and Johnson evolved into a new form. What had been a modest experiment in skepticism and judgment became the dominant form of intellectual discourse. Writers became involved more closely with political and historical ephemera and so less likely to write anything that would survive longer than the three-months' celebrity of the latest review. Indeed, most reviews were essentially summaries with lengthy extracts of the books being considered. Occasionally in the quarterlies, the reviews were pretexts for original essays; and in the magazines, familiar essays found an outlet.[5] But with the exception of the *London Magazine* and the *New Monthly Magazine* in the early 1820s, payment for original work was not competitive with the reviews. The Johnsonian essay of moral judgment was replaced by the familiar essay, which sought to please the reader. The familiar essay did not establish the author's authority but instead tried to give the reader a sense

4. *Complete Prose Works of Matthew Arnold*, 3:270–71.
5. For a survey of the familiar essay, see Marie Hamilton Law, *The English Familiar Essay in the Early Nineteenth Century*.

of being included within the realm of discourse. As new ideas and information were transmitted through the form to a less knowledgeable readership, the essay acquired a didactic or condescending tone. This accommodation also required the development of a slower intellectual pace characterized by repetitive amplification and lengthy quotation and by more easily accessible prose styles in which anticlimax was the rhetorical rule.

I

Samuel Johnson once remarked to Boswell that "no man but a blockhead ever wrote, except for money."[6] Before the eighteenth century professional authors had depended on patronage for their livelihood. As Macaulay details marvelously in his review of Croker's edition of Boswell's *Life of Johnson*, writers had once benefited from official patronage and been given administrative positions and sinecures:

> Congreve, when he had scarcely attained his majority, was rewarded for his first comedy with places which made him independent for life. Smith, though his *Hippolytus and Phoedra* failed, would have been consoled with three hundred a year but for his own folly. Rowe was not only Poet Laureate, but also land-surveyor of the customs in the port of London, clerk of the council to the Prince of Wales, and secretary of the Presentations to the Lord Chancellor. Hughes was secretary to the Commissions of the Peace. Ambrose Phillips was judge of the Prerogative Court in Ireland. Locke was Commissioner of Appeals and of the Board of Trade. Newton was Master of the Mint. Stepney and Prior were employed in embassies of high dignity and importance. Gay, who commenced life as apprentice to a silk mercer, became a secretary of legation at five-and-twenty. It was to a poem on the death of Charles the Second, and to the *City and the Country Mouse*, that Montague owed his introduction into public life, his earldom, his garter, and his Auditorship of the Exchequer. Swift, but for the unconquerable prejudice of the queen, would have been a bishop. Oxford, with his white staff in his hand, passed through the crowd of his suitors to welcome Parnell, when that ingenious writer deserted the Whigs. Steele was a commissioner of stamps and a member of Parliament. Arthur Mainwaring was a commissioner of the customs, and auditor of the imprest. Tickell was secretary to the Lords Justices of Ireland. Addison was Secretary of State.[7]

6. Entry for April 5, 1776, *Boswell's Life of Johnson*, 3:19. Note also Mary Russell Mitford's comment: "All my thoughts of writing are for hard money" (Mitford to Sir William Elford, April 25, 1823, *The Life of Mary Russell Mitford*, 2:162; and consider Sydney Smith's letter to Francis Jeffrey, November 18, 1807: "I have 3 motives for writing reviews: 1st the love of you; 2nd the habit of reviewing; 3rd the love of money—to which I may add a fourth, the love of punishing fraud or folly" (*The Letters of Sydney Smith*, 1:126).
7. *Critical and Historical Essays*, 2:544.

In Johnson's day, authors without patrons struggled on Grub Street; only at the beginning of the nineteenth century does the readership and thus the market for literature become large enough for a few writers to support themselves as gentlemen on the income from their work.

Since authors who are not fortunate enough to have independent means must somehow make enough money to live, they will be attracted to that form of writing which pays the best. In the 1780s, toward the end of Johnson's career, reviewers were thought to be paid liberally at six guineas a sheet. The *Critical Review* offered only two guineas a sheet, but the *Monthly Review* paid four.[8] In 1796, Southey was writing for the newly established *Monthly Magazine* at five guineas a sheet. So Francis Horner, Sydney Smith, Henry Brougham, and Francis Jeffrey were right when they were planning the *Edinburgh Review* in 1802 to think that payment of ten guineas a sheet would be considered munificent and that many would be eager to contribute to their new enterprise.

From its beginning the *Edinburgh Review* represented a radical revaluation of the importance of authors, but what made the review important was its intellectual economy. The foundation of the *Edinburgh* and *Quarterly* reviews occurred during a period of rising inflation and high paper prices that had reduced the size of the reading public and had more than halved the number of new magazines introduced in the first decade of the nineteenth century in comparison with the 1790s.[9] This meant that if a magazine or review were to succeed it must appeal to the wealthiest readers. The quarterlies triumphed over the *Critical* and *Monthly* reviews because they provided an ideological and political focus that economized on the reader's need to read about books. In contrast to the encyclopedic character of the *Critical* and *Monthly* reviews, the *Edinburgh Review* covered a much smaller number of the books published each year. In their "Advertisement" to the first number, the *Edinburgh* editors announced their wish that their journal "be distinguished, rather for the selection, than for the number of its articles"; moreover, they declared that "the Conductors of the *Edinburgh Review* propose to carry this principle of selection a good deal

8. Entry for April 28, 1783, *Boswell's Life of Johnson*, 4:214 and n. Johnson observed that the labor of reviewing deserved to be paid well because "a man will more easily write a sheet all his own, than read an octavo volume to get extracts" (4:214).
9. G. F. Barwick notes that from 1801 to 1810 about twenty new magazines were started (as opposed to more than forty in the previous decade), that thirty-five magazines began between 1811 and 1820, about one hundred from 1821 to 1830, and that the number of new magazines reached its highest point at 170 between 1861 and 1870 ("The Magazines of the Nineteenth Century," 238).

farther; to decline any attempt at exhibiting a complete view of modern literature; and to confine their notice, in a great degree, to works that either have attained, or deserve, a certain portion of celebrity."[10] When the *Edinburgh Review* first appeared in October 1802, it reviewed twenty-nine books in separate articles and appeared to be a limited provincial attempt to imitate the existing monthly reviews. That same month the *Monthly* reviewed forty-four books, the *Critical* sixty, and the *British Critic* seventy-seven.[11] Even in its first year, when it most resembled the monthly reviews, the *Edinburgh Review* covered less than one-fifth as many books as did the *Critical Review*. By 1809, when its policy of selective reviewing had clearly paid off and its format was settled, the *Edinburgh* had in each of its numbers an average of fourteen reviews covering as many as twenty books and pamphlets, and so was reviewing at most eighty books a year. Although the *Monthly* and *Critical* reviews considered many more books and were the first to review most books, they cost two shillings for each monthly issue and each of their three yearly appendices so that a yearly subscription amounted to thirty shillings. So while the *Edinburgh Review* cost five shillings a number, its yearly subscription at twenty shillings was cheaper by a third. It raised the price of a number to six shillings in 1809 because the price of paper had risen so much,[12] but by then the quarterly had effectively triumphed over its competition.

The *Edinburgh Review* thus effectively functioned as a relatively inexpensive review of reviews, noticing those books and treatises that had already excited critical attention. As Derek Roper notes, "of the important new writers who appeared between 1802 and 1820—Jane Austen, Byron, Hazlitt, Hunt, Keats, Scott, Shelley—none was first recognized in the *Edinburgh* or the *Quarterly*."[13] The value of a review of one's book whether favorable or unfavorable stemmed directly from the selective scope of its coverage. Byron observes this in a letter to the Reverend John Becher where he is anticipating the appearance of a review of his *Hours of Idleness* (1807): "It is however something to be noticed, as they profess to pass judgment only on works requiring the public attention."[14] The *Edinburgh Review* was not actively seeking out new ideas and fresh literary talent to enlighten its readers, but instead saving its readers both time and money by

10. "Advertisement," *Edinburgh Review* 1 (1802): iii.
11. Derek Roper, *Reviewing before the "Edinburgh," 1788–1802*, 40.
12. John Clive, *Scotch Reviewers: The "Edinburgh Review," 1802–1815*, 135.
13. *Reviewing before the "Edinburgh,"* 41.
14. Byron to the Reverend John Becher, February 26, 1808, *Byron's Letters and Journals*, 1:157.

focusing their attention on the most important books when they were able to afford fewer and fewer books.

By 1805 the *Edinburgh Review* was publishing 4,000 copies a number. Thanks largely to the brief interregnum of the Whig administration under Grenville from 1806 to 1807 which attracted more attention to the review's politics, Constable was publishing 7,000 copies of each issue by 1807.[15] It was in 1807, then, when its circulation exceeded the 5,000 copies a month[16] of the *Monthly Review* that the *Edinburgh Review* became of central cultural significance. Assisting its reputation was Byron's *English Bards and the Scotch Reviewers* (1808), which was written in reply to its review of his *Hours of Idleness*. Byron recalls the composition of his poetic revenge in his journal:

> I remember the effect of the *first* Edinburgh Review on me. I heard of it six weeks before,—read it the day of its denunciation,—dined and drank three bottles of claret, (with S. B. Davies, I think,) neither ate nor slept the less, but, nevertheless, was not easy till I had vented my wrath and my rhyme, in the same pages against every thing and every body.[17]

Despite his wide knowledge, which Byron's classmates attributed to his reading reviews, it had not been much earlier that Byron looked into his first number of a review at Harrow: "I remember when Hunter & Curzon in 1804—told me this opinion at Harrow—I made them laugh by my ludicrous astonishment in asking them '*what is* a review?'—to be sure they were then less common—In three years more I was better acquainted with that same—but the first I ever read was in 1806–7."[18]

With more objectivity and less self-interest than Byron, Coleridge began to read the *Edinburgh Review* seriously in 1809, as he recounts in his *Friend*:

> I immediately recognized the work [the *Edinburgh Review*] itself, which I had often heard discussed for evil and for good. I was therefore familiar with its general character, and extensive circulation, although partly from the seclusion in which I live, and my inability to purchase the luxuries of transitory literature on my own account, and partly too from the experience, that of all books I had derived the least improvement from those that were confined to the names and passions of my contemporaries: this was either the third or the fourth number which had come within my perusal.[19]

15. Clive, 133–34.
16. On the circulation of the *Monthly Review*, see C. H. Timperley, *Encyclopedia of Literary and Typographical Anecdote*, 795.
17. Journal entry, November 22, 1813, *Byron's Letters and Journals*, 3:213.
18. Detached Thought no. 87, *Byron's Letters and Journals*, 9:42.
19. *The Friend*, 2:40.

His interest aroused, Coleridge declares, "I now look forward to the perusal of the whole series of the work, as made a point of duty to me by knowledge of its unusual influence on the public opinion."[20]

When the founders of the *Edinburgh Review* commenced their journal, they had doubled the going rate by offering contributors ten guineas a sheet and the editor £300 a year.[21] This entailed a great financial risk and courted a spectacular failure. Assuming a normal profit margin of 20 percent, from which payments of 210 guineas for each number to the editor and contributors would come, Constable had to sell 4,700 copies of each sixteen-sheet issue to break even, something which did not happen until 1807, although reprinting of bound copies began much earlier. Similarly, when Sir Walter Scott in 1809 arranged with John Murray to begin the *Quarterly Review* in order to further the government's policy toward Spain in the Peninsular War against that advocated by the *Edinburgh Review*, contributors were promised ten guineas a sheet. This practice was at first a money-losing proposition, for by 1811 Murray still had not recovered his costs.[22] But both quarterlies rapidly increased their circulation: the *Edinburgh Review* reached its peak of 13,500 in 1818, and the *Quarterly Review* achieved its greatest sale of around fourteen thousand in 1817.[23]

During this period the *Edinburgh Review* raised its minimum pay for contributors from ten to sixteen guineas per sheet, at which level it remained as long as Jeffrey was editor. Jeffrey claimed that most of the articles were bought for more than the minimum rate and that on average the review paid twenty to twenty-five guineas per sheet for each number.[24] The high pay was designed not to attract scholars and writers who were already willing to contribute for much less, but active men of affairs whose time was worth a great deal and who needed considerable financial incentive to put pen to paper after having written their briefs and memoranda during the day. The quarterlies thus typically drew upon more gentlemanly writers than did the magazines. The gentlemanly character of many of the reviewers may be gathered from Richard Ford's account of how he

20. Ibid.
21. Henry Peter Brougham, *The Life and Times of Henry Lord Brougham*, 1:254–55.
22. John Murray to Gifford of about 1810, in Smiles, 1:182.
23. For the *Quarterly*, see Smiles, 2:39; on the *Edinburgh Review*, see Harold Cox and John E. Chandler, *The House of Longman, 1724–1924*, 19.
24. Clive, *Scotch Reviewers*, 34n. The source cited for Jeffrey's remark is *Chamber's Encyclopedia*, 2:385. These rates remain constant through 1850, as is shown by the list of payments for authors given by Cyprian Blagden, "*Edinburgh Review* Authors, 1830–49," 212–14. Macvey Napier's list gives rates that "vary from 16 guineas for G. H. Lewes to 25 guineas for Macaulay" (212).

spent the proceeds from his article on George Borrow's *Bible in Spain* for the *Edinburgh Review* in 1843: "I have invested my £44 in Châteaux Margaux."[25]

The lawyerly manner was also widely recognized. Carlyle's comments on Jeffrey's style reveal the origins of the *Edinburgh Review*'s rhetorical method: "I found that essentially he was always as if speaking to a jury; that the thing of which he could not convince fifteen clear-headed men, was to him a no-thing—good only to be flung over the lists, and left lying without notice farther. This seemed to me a very sad result of Law!"[26] Carlyle felt that the speculative discourse in which he himself specialized had received little editorial encouragement from Jeffrey. Indeed, to attract the attention of wealthy and powerful readers, the editors of the *Edinburgh* felt that they needed political gentlemen like themselves as contributors to examine the ideas of the day and to lay bare the organizing principles of society, events, and intellectual discourse. And to insure a commonly shared ideology for a review, the chief editor of a review not only contributed many essays himself but also often substantially cut and rewrote those of his contributors, thus both establishing a house style and enforcing a consistent political outlook.[27]

The reviews quickly attracted competition in the form of lighter monthly miscellanies, most notably *Blackwood's Magazine*, the *London Magazine*, and the *New Monthly Magazine*, which paid authors almost as well. *Blackwood's* soon was trumpeting, "OUR SALE IS PRODIGIOUS—AND WE ARE ABSO-LUTELY COINING MONEY."[28] Even Coleridge discovered that a miscellany appealed more to readers than the heavy articles of the quarterlies, whose political significance was more important than their intellectual appeal. In the eleventh number of the *Friend* in 1809, for example, Coleridge proposes

25. Richard Ford to Henry Unwin Addington, February 27, 1843, *The Letters of Richard Ford, 1797–1858*, 186.
26. *Reminiscences*, 328. Carlyle has identified the source of the new reviewing rhetoric accurately: it is coming from legal forensics. In this regard, I think that in looking for a discourse of rhetorical "master signs" Jon P. Klancher has missed the critical boat in *The Making the English Reading Audiences, 1790–1832*. The implied audience of the *Edinburgh Review* can thus be sociologically and juridically defined as those who were eligible to serve on a jury in Scotland. For a more promising start to analyzing the legal rhetoric implicit in the *Edinburgh Review*, see Mark Schoenfield, "Regulating Standards: *The Edinburgh Review* and the Circulations of Judgment."
27. William Gifford, editor of the *Quarterly Review*, was perhaps the most notorious for altering his contributors' articles. For instance, bitterly complaining of Gifford's treatment, Southey exclaims in a letter to the Reverend Herbert Hill, December 31, 1819: "*He has repeatedly promised me that he would not do it, and yet every one of my papers comes forth castrated from under his hands*" (*Selections from the Letters of Robert Southey*, 3:167).
28. "An Hour's Tete-a-Tete with the Public," 80.

Ideological Focus and the Market for the Essay   79

to "interpose one or more Numbers devoted to the rational *entertainment* of my various readers; and, partly from the desire of gratifying particular requests, and partly as a specimen of the subjects which will henceforward have a due proportion of THE FRIEND allotted to them, I shall fill up the present Paper with a miscellany."[29] In 1831 *Fraser's Magazine* joined the fray, and was particularly noted for its youthful Tory high spirits and for the quality of its writers, who included Carlyle and Thackeray and who are memorably portrayed sitting around a table by Daniel Maclise in "The Fraserians" (see fig. 2). Later in the same year it claimed "a *bona fide* sale of . . . 8,700."[30]

In the 1830s came the cheap weekly magazines. From a literary viewpoint the most important was the *Athenaeum*. This literary weekly soon replaced the *Literary Gazette* and became the first and sometimes the only source of literary notices. Its frequency and size enabled it to cover the significant literary work much more thoroughly than did the quarterlies and monthlies. In 1830 its price was reduced by C. W. Dilke from eight pence to four pence, and later in 1835 its size enlarged from sixteen to twenty-four pages.[31] Leslie Marchand estimates that as a result of the reduction in price the circulation of the *Athenaeum* rose from three to eighteen thousand.[32] Richard Ford observes in a diary entry of March 10, 1834, that "Penny Magazines are all the order of the day."[33] In 1835 the circulation of such weekly papers was estimated at more than half a million copies.[34] As one might expect, this meant that the overall quality of writing declined and that at least some readers who might have read the quarterlies turned to lighter fare.

Writing essays quickly became the most lucrative and steady writing for writers and so attracted much of the available literary talent. Many of the essayists who are still read today, in particular Hazlitt, Lamb, Hunt, and De Quincey, wrote much of their best work for the *London Magazine*, the *New Monthly Magazine*, and the *Examiner*. But these periodicals were at the margins and not the center of the publishing market. The *London Magazine*, for example, set a literary standard too high for the popular taste, never had

29. *The Friend*, 2:151.
30. "Symposiac the Second," 260.
31. On the original price reduction, see H. R. Fox Bourne, *John Frances, Publisher of "The Athenaeum,"* xxiv. On the increase in size, see letter from Allan Cunningham to C. W. Dilke, December 28, 1835, in Charles Wentworth Dilke, *The Papers of a Critic*, 1:33.
32. Leslie Alexis Marchand, *"The Athenaeum": A Mirror of Victorian Culture*, 45.
33. *The Letters of Richard Ford*, 138.
34. "Our Weekly Gossip on Literature and Art," *The Athenaeum*, 968.

more than two thousand readers, began to lose circulation and money in 1823, and was sold by Taylor and Hessey in 1824. Writers who might have written a long shelf of books contributed instead a large collection of miscellaneous essays to English letters. De Quincey, for instance, whose essays on political economy were blamed for the downfall of the *London Magazine*, never felt at ease within the form and was clearly much more comfortable writing autobiography.

The greater a writer's reputation was or the more valuable an author's contribution, the more generous was the financial reward paid by the periodicals. In the 1830s, for example, Macaulay says that Macvey Napier discovered from Longmans and other booksellers that the *Edinburgh Review* "sells or does not sell according as there are or are not articles by Mr. Macaulay," whereupon Napier raised Macaulay's rate from twenty-four guineas a sheet to about thirty-two guineas a sheet.[35] The highest rate of payment for an essay seems to have been the ninety guineas a sheet Sir Walter Scott received for his review of Byron's *Childe Harold* in the *Quarterly* in 1818, and the forty-five guineas a sheet Sydney Smith was paid in the same year for writing in the *Edinburgh Review*.[36] These extraordinary sums were paid when the circulation of the quarterlies had reached their peak. But when the number of literary magazines and reviews was increasing a decade later, the height of the market for the essay was reached. The *Westminster Review* had begun, the *Foreign Review* was starting up, and the Annuals, especially the *Keepsake*, were soliciting well-known authors for contributions at premium prices. The *Westminster Review* at first paid its writers ten to sixteen guineas a sheet but raised its payments to those offered by other reviews.[37] Francis Place, the radical Charing Cross tailor who wrote frequently for the *Westminster Review*, noted in 1826 that "twenty pounds a sheet would . . . be much below the price paid for either the *Quarterly*, *Edinburgh*, or *Westminster Review*, and not more than is paid by the *New Monthly Magazine*."[38] The competition caused editors of existing jour-

35. Macaulay to Hannah Macaulay, June 3, 1833, *The Letters of Thomas Babington Macaulay*, 2:249.
36. Scott received £100 for his review of Byron's *Childe Harold* (*Quarterly Review* 19 [1818]: 215–32); see Scott's letter to the Duke of Buccleuch, November 20, 1818, *The Letters of Sir Walter Scott*, 5:223; for Sydney Smith, see his letter to Francis Jeffrey, November 23, 1818, *The Letters of Sydney Smith*, 1:305.
37. George L. Nesbitt, *Benthamite Reviewing: The First Twelve Years of "The Westminster Review," 1824–1836*, 36.
38. British Museum Additional Manuscript 35146, f. 66v., quoted in Nesbitt, 36. It should be noted that even though the *Westminster Review* cost a full six shillings, its circulation of only 2,000 copies could not sustain such high payments. The review's reserve fund of £4,000 was

nals to increase their payments to their best writers in order to keep them. Southey, for instance, was surprised in 1828 to receive an extra fifty pounds over his usual hundred pounds for an article in the *Quarterly* on the Catholic question in Ireland. This amounted to a little more than thirty-six guineas a sheet, which was the highest rate of payment he ever received in his long career.[39]

In the early 1820s the market for essay writing grew as the number of periodicals increased and attracted many authors who would have otherwise never considered writing for periodical publication. They needed to be paid for their time and were often reluctant to contribute without sufficient compensation. Coleridge, for example, wrote to William Blackwood that he would be willing to contribute only if he were paid at a rate to justify the pains he took in composition.[40] In a letter to Francis Place, whose work appeared in the *Westminster Review,* John Thelwall objected that the review would not guarantee the acceptance of anything that he submitted and thus would not pledge itself to pay him for his work: "If such be their mode of management with their contributors they must look for communications from those whose time has not yet become valuable, and whose capabilities are yet unknown. I cannot afford to put my time and labor into such a lottery."[41] In 1821 Henry Francis Cary resisted writing for the *London Magazine* at the rate of ten guineas a sheet, but he agreed to write for sixteen guineas a sheet beginning retroactively with an article on William Collins which the journal had already accepted for publication.[42]

---

exhausted in 1828 after four years of publication (Nesbitt, 130). If one supposes that payments to authors were running close to twenty-five guineas a sheet for each of the some seventy-five sheets published in a year's time and if one attributes all of the review's losses to its overpayment of contributors, one finds that authors should have been receiving a little more than thirteen pounds less a sheet, or less than half of what they were getting, so that the journal could break even.

39. Southey to John Rickman, November 1, 1828, *Selections from the Letters of Robert Southey* 4:121. See "The Roman Catholic Question—Ireland." Taking into account where it begins and ends on the page, the article was sixty-three pages long. Since a sheet was sixteen pages, the article was thus 3.9375 sheets in length. To arrive at the number of pounds per sheet, one divides the number of sheets into the £150. Finally, one must convert pounds to guineas, and multiply by the ratio of 20/21, since there were twenty shillings in a pound and twenty-one in a guinea. Performing these calculations yields 36.28 guineas, or almost thirty-six guineas six shillings a sheet. I have made similar calculations to arrive at rates of payment throughout my text though I provide only this one example for readers.

40. Coleridge to William Blackwood, April 12, 1819, *Collected Letters of Samuel Taylor Coleridge,* 4:933.

41. John Thelwall to Francis Place, May 21, 1824, British Museum Addition Manuscript 37949, f. 142, quoted in Nesbitt, *Benthamite Reviewing,* 133.

42. Cary to Taylor and Hessey, May 21 and June 9, 1821, and Taylor to Cary, June 9, 1821, in R. W. King, *The Translator of Dante: The Life, Work, and Friendships of Henry Francis Cary,* 130–31.

Henry Colburn, who had acquired the *New Monthly Magazine* in 1820, was actively competing for magazine writers. Mary Russell Mitford remarks on the "magnificent offers" of twenty guineas a sheet that Colburn made to Horace Smith, when Hazlitt was getting only fifteen guineas a sheet for his Table Talk essays in the *London Magazine*.[43] In 1820 John Wilson and John Lockhart were together writing almost all of *Blackwood's Magazine* but were beginning to find producing the monthly publication too much for them, especially since Lockhart was planning to marry. They solicited for contributors, writing to De Quincey and offering him ten guineas a sheet.[44] By having double columns and paying only ten guineas a sheet, however, as Mitford observes, *Blackwood's* was not a high-paying magazine.[45] Although he considered the rate good payment and said that he could make six hundred guineas a year by writing for the magazine, Wilson, its chief editor and the "Christopher North" of *Noctes Ambrosianae*, was paid only sixteen guineas a sheet.[46]

II

The traditional picture of the literary magazines as an authorial collective is drawn from Maclise's famous sketch of the Fraserians as if gathered together for a literary dinner (fig. 2). But, in fact, writers attached themselves to periodicals as a matter of convenience. The magazines gave them steady work and an easy access to print. If that meant their writing focused too much on recent events in the publishing world, why, that was a price most were willing to pay. Since until the early 1840s editors or regular contributors made enough to live a fairly comfortable life, they rarely looked elsewhere for employment and remained loyal to one periodical as long as their journal remained afloat or their politics accorded with those of their editors or publishers. Beginning with the economic depression of the early 1840s, however, such loyalties became less important because payments to the average contributor were not as great as they had earlier been. The

43. Mitford to Sir William Elford, December 12, 1820, in *The Life of Mary Russell Mitford*, 2:119. Cyrus Redding says that the *New Monthly Magazine*, which he was editing in the middle of the 1820s, paid twelve guineas a sheet for original articles and refused to pay Mitford six guineas for any article regardless of its length, as she wanted; see *Fifty Years' Recollections, Literary and Personal*, 2:222. Bulwer-Lytton was offered twenty guineas a sheet in 1828 for the *New Monthly*; see Michael Sadleir, *Bulwer and His Wife*, 141.
44. Wilson to De Quincey, March 22, 1820, *De Quincey Memorials*, 2:42.
45. Mitford to the Rev. William Harness, March 4, 1826, *Life of Mary Russell Mitford*, 2:220.
46. Margaret Oliphant, *Annals of a Publishing House: William Blackwood and His Sons, Their Magazine and Friends*, 1:298 and 302.

professional author in that period would usually write for four or five periodicals rather than be tied to one.

Southey's career as an essayist spans more than thirty years of the period covered here. He began as a reviewer for the *Monthly Magazine* in 1796 at five guineas a sheet, and a little later wrote for the *Morning Post* and the *Courier*. In 1809 Scott asked him to contribute to the *Quarterly Review*. His first essay was on "The Baptist Mission in India," for which he received twenty-one pounds thirteen shillings, or exactly ten guineas a sheet.[47] Unlike the gentleman who occasionally contributed, Southey needed the money to support his family and could provide a substantial review essay for each issue. He soon became the review's main contributing writer. By 1815 when he wrote "The Life of Wellington," he was receiving £100 an article, which in the case of the Wellington review amounted to about twenty-five guineas a sheet.[48] For twenty years he contributed to the *Quarterly*, customarily receiving £100 for an essay. He wrote on the average one substantial article of at least three sheets for each number of the review. From all of his writing, Southey seems to have averaged between six and seven hundred pounds a year. He was considered remarkable by Lamb for being almost the only one he knew to have "made a fortune by book drudgery."[49]

In 1834 Southey resigned from his position as the review's main contributor, because he had suddenly received seventy rather than one hundred pounds for his "Corn Laws," discovered that his introduction concerning Ebenezer Elliott's *Corn Law Rhymes* had been cut, and was surprised that Lockhart had added an account by Croker of the House of Commons debate on the tariffs to the essay.[50] Southey's retirement seems to have been deliberately induced, for Murray had already negotiated with Croker in 1832 to contribute one article a number to the *Quarterly*. Thereafter, following the pattern of his most popular work, *The Life of Nelson* (1813), which had been an expansion of a review he had written for the *Quarterly* in 1810, Southey concentrated on writing biographies, often appended to

47. Southey to Thomas Southey, March 14, 1809, *New Letters of Robert Southey*, 1:503.
48. Southey to the Rev. Herbert Hill, June 27, 1815, *Selections*, 2:411.
49. Lamb to Bernard Barton, January 9, 1823, *The Letters of Charles Lamb*, ed. Lucas, 2:363.
50. Southey to Edith May Southey, April 3, 1834, *New Letters* 2:406; and Southey to C. W. W. Wynn, June 3, 1835, *New Letters* 2:423. One should note, however, that this occurred a little more than a year after the agreement with John Wilson Croker to contribute four sheets to each number for £150; see the letter of John Murray to Croker, September 22, 1832, in Smiles, *A Publisher and His Friends*, 2:430. It would seem that Murray wanted to cut costs and that since Scott (who was both Southey's champion and Lockhart's father-in-law) was now dead, Lockhart felt that he no longer had to put up with the too liberal Southey.

modern editions of his subjects' works, most notably Bunyan, Isaac Watts, the Reverend Andrew Bell, and William Cowper.

As the life-long nurse of an extravagant father, Mary Russell Mitford was driven to write for money and wrote for a number of magazines and journals. She had published her *Miscellaneous Poems* (which were reviewed by Scott in the *Quarterly*) in 1810, had issued a few more volumes of verse, and had achieved her first notable success with her play *Julian* (1823). In 1824 she started to write *Our Village* for six guineas a sheet in the *Lady's Magazine*, which was closely printed in double columns. After a favorable review in the *Quarterly Review* in 1825, she began to receive solicitations for contributions from a number of journals. One of them, the *Panoramic Miscellany*, founded by John Thelwall in 1825, offered her ten guineas a sheet, but Thelwall quickly stopped the publication and never paid her. She soon was able, however, to place all of her essays with the *New Monthly Magazine*, which paid her ten guineas a sheet. Although she never managed to keep ahead of her spendthrift father, she was able to establish enough of a rapport with her audience so that when she made an appeal in 1843 to pay off her father's debts after he died, she received over £1,300.[51] On the whole, her career reflects that of the average steady writer whose contributions were welcomed but were never paid for at the highest rates.

The array of magazines in the 1840s and the payment for them may be briefly surveyed by considering the career of G. H. Lewes. He began writing for the *Westminster Review* in 1841. He received ten guineas, or a little more than four guineas a sheet, for an article on modern French historians. Beginning in 1842 he wrote essays for the *British and Foreign Review* on Hegel's *Aesthetics*, Goethe, and French history and philosophy and made sixteen guineas a sheet. In 1843 he contributed essays on George Sand and on Spanish and European drama to the *Foreign Quarterly Review* and averaged about eleven guineas a sheet. For an 1843 essay on theater reform he made sixteen guineas a sheet from the *Edinburgh Review*, then in 1845 twenty guineas a sheet for one on Lessing, and in 1847 sixteen guineas a sheet for another on Algazzali and Arabian philosophy that appeared in the review. In 1846 he wrote for *Fraser's Magazine* on Bach for seven and a half guineas a sheet, on Morell's history of philosophy and

51. On the *Lady's Magazine* and the *Panoramic Miscellany*, see Mitford's letters to T. N. Talfourd, June 5, 1824, and December 21, 1825, in W. A. Coles, "Mary Russell Mitford," 44, 46. On the *New Monthly Magazine* and the public appeal, see Mitford's letters to Mrs. Hofland, September 20, 1826, and to Miss Harrison, March 26, 1843, *Letters of Mary Russell Mitford. Second Series*, 1:133; 2:5.

Leopardi for ten guineas a sheet; and in 1847 he contributed an original article on the condition of authors in England, France, and Germany for fourteen guineas a sheet. His essay on Thomas Reid, the Scottish philosopher, appeared in the *British Quarterly Review,* which paid him sixteen guineas a sheet in 1847. In that same year he wrote a series of articles on political reform for *Douglas Jerrold's Shilling Magazine* for twelve guineas a sheet at first and thereafter seven and a half guineas. And his biography of Bulwer-Lytton was published in *Bentley's Miscellany* for twelve guineas a sheet in 1848. Lewes contributed to many more periodicals and wrote more than Southey did, but although Lewes made between three and four hundred pounds a year during the 1840s from his writing, he made less and could not live as well as Southey even though he did not have to depend upon one periodical for his income.[52]

During the first half of the century, writers began to make a distinction between literature and journalism and also became more conscious of writing as a profession, especially when they were not men or women of independent means. Even the most romantic of poets, John Keats, resolved to turn his pen to profit and "fag on as others do" at periodical literature, thinking to apply for direction in supporting himself as a writer to Hazlitt, who, Keats thought, "knows the market as well as any one."[53] Later, while comparing Keats favorably with the other Romantic poets and, perhaps, thinking of his own literary career, Matthew Arnold praised Keats for his resolution.[54] Writers pragmatically wrote for those periodicals that paid well and had a wide readership. Harriet Martineau in her *Autobiography* says, "I have refused to write for Magazines by the score; but the wide circulation of 'Household Words' made it a peculiar case; and I agreed to try my hand."[55] In a similar fashion, Arnold remarks upon printing his essay on Heinrich Heine in a letter to his mother, "I have had two applications for the lecture from magazines, but I shall print it, if I can, in the *Cornhill,* because it both pays best and has much the largest circle of readers."[56]

In contrast, the one-man journal founded on the pattern of Steele's *Tatler* had run into extremely stiff competition from the existing monthly magazines at the beginning of the nineteenth century. In announcing his aban-

---

52. On the figures for Lewes's contributions, see "GHL's Literary Receipts," in *The George Eliot Letters,* 7:365–69. Rates per sheet have been calculated on the basis of the length of the articles in the journals.
53. *Letters of John Keats,* 2:177.
54. "John Keats," *Complete Prose Works,* 9:209.
55. *Harriet Martineau's Autobiography,* 2:25.
56. June 16, 1863, *Letters of Matthew Arnold,* 1:195.

donment of his periodical, Coleridge in his "Address to the Readers of the Watchman" of May 13, 1796, notes that "those . . . who expected from it much and varied original composition, have naturally relinquished it in favour of the New MONTHLY MAGAZINE; a Work, which has almost monopolized the talents of the Country, and with which I should have continued a course of literary rivalship with as much success, as might be supposed to attend a *young Recruit* who should oppose himself to a Phalanx of disciplined Warriors."[57] Later, in 1809 Coleridge had been inspired by William Cobbett's *Political Register* and by his first reading of the *Edinburgh Review* to start *The Friend* (1809–10). Instead of having Longman publish and distribute the journal through booksellers, Coleridge became his own publisher. He arranged to have paper shipped to his printer John Brown in Penrith from the Fourdriniers by Daniel Stuart, who was to have it stamped in London; his friends, particularly Southey, agreed to be his proofreaders, and he sent copy by coach from Keswick to Penrith.[58] Coleridge charged a shilling for each issue in comparison to the ten pence charged by Cobbett's journal. He optimistically assumed that he would have 500 subscribers for each number and calculated that he would profit by three and a half pence a copy after expenses.[59] The journal had a troubled history. After he ceased publishing it in 1810, Coleridge almost ended up in jail over his debt to the printer.[60]

Leigh Hunt was the last of the one-man journalists. He single-handedly wrote the weekly *Literary Examiner* for six months in 1823, the weekly *Companion* from January to July of 1828, the *Chat of the Week* for three months in 1830, the daily *Tatler* from September 1830 to March 1832, and the weekly *London Journal* from 1834 to 1835. When Hunt tried to produce the four-page *Tatler* by himself, he was competing with the literary weeklies and the newspapers: "It was a very little work, consisting but of four folio pages; but it was a daily publication: I did it all myself, except when too ill; and illness seldom hindered me either from supplying the review of a book, going every night to the play, or writing the notice of the play the same night at the printing-office. The consequence was, that the work, slight as it

---

57. *The Watchman*, 374.
58. *The Friend*, 1:xlvi–xlvii, lviii.
59. Ibid., 1:xlix and n.
60. Later, in 1816, Gale and Fenner agreed to advance Coleridge £150 for the copyrights of *The Friend*, *Biographia Literaria*, and his poems. A new three-volume edition of *The Friend* was published in 1818. Only 250 copies had sold of the 750 that had been printed, when in 1819 Fenner went bankrupt. Coleridge had to borrow money to buy his copyrights back; see *The Friend*, 1:lxxx and lxxxv.

looked, nearly killed me."[61] Hunt's dependency upon his brother John to handle the business side of the *Examiner* meant that he was virtually incompetent when it came to handling the financial questions of publishing the journal. He says of the *Indicator* that it was "published in a corner, owing to my want of funds for advertising it, and my ignorance of the best mode of circulating such things—an ignorance so profound, that I was not even aware of its very sale."[62] Its failure was clearly inevitable.

Both Coleridge and Hunt were financial and publishing innocents. Their desire to be independent of the dominant periodicals transcended their common sense. But their difficulties and struggles are indicative of how individual quality found competing with collective quantity in the periodical format an impossible task. Publishers with deep pockets, well-established distribution networks, and stables of eager, willing writers had no need to fear competition from the lone literary adventurer who, Quixote-like, sought to take on the giant machines of the quarterly reviews and magazines.

The number of outlets for writing soon made professional journalism a respectable profession and also made it necessary for the weekly and monthly magazines to hire full-time editors, subeditors, and staff writers who were salaried and who wrote when no one else would. Lockhart and Wilson were offered £500 a year between them to edit *Blackwood's*.[63] In *Paul Clifford* (1830), Bulwer-Lytton satirizes this turn of events in his comments on Paul Clifford, who has a choice between writing or picking pockets and who is introduced to "Mr. Peter Mac Grawler, the editor of a magnificent periodical, entitled the 'Asinaeum,' which was written to prove, that whatever is popular is necessarily bad,—a valuable and recondite truth, which the Asinaeum had satisfactorily demonstrated by ruining three printers and demolishing a publisher. We need not add that Mr. Mac Grawler was Scotch by birth, since we believe it is pretty well known that *all* the periodicals of this country have, from time immemorial, been monopolised by the gentlemen of the land of cakes."[64] Of the weekly reviews, the strongest was the *Athenaeum* under Dilke. George Darley, Henry Fothergill Chorley, and Charles Knight all worked as subeditors on the *Athenaeum*.[65]

61. *The Autobiography of Leigh Hunt*, 2:203.
62. Ibid., 2:49.
63. J. G. Lockhart to Rev. Williams of 1818, in Oliphant, *Annals*, 1:191.
64. *Paul Clifford*, 1:20–21.
65. The pay of a subeditor was low. Chorley records receiving fifty pounds for the first six months of 1834 and sixty-five pounds for the last six months, in his *Autobiography, Memoir, and Letters*, 1:92, 101.

Because periodicals were the most lucrative and stable of a publisher's properties in a business where typically 70 percent of all publications lost money, reviews and magazines quickly came to dominate literary production. At first this meant that the essay attracted young writers who were looking to make either their fortune or their reputation by writing. As the reading market expanded, competition intensified, raising both the literary and financial stakes. Outlets for writing multiplied at a faster rate than the readership expanded after 1820, which meant that while payment to writers rose, profits at the reviews and magazines were squeezed. No one magazine or review was able to dominate the literary marketplace. Since education had not yet become widespread and the supply of writers was thus correspondingly limited, writers became paid better for prose than they had been before or have ever since. Their social standing rose from that of the mere scribbler or hack to near professional status, that is, when the authors were not already gentlemen. The ultimate arbiter of this status in the industrialization of the publishing industry was money, for literature had come to live in "the realms of gold."

III

As the market for the form reflects, essay writers were at the center of public attention in the 1810s and 1820s in a way they never were before or have been since. While Hazlitt, Hunt, Lamb, DeQuincey, Carlyle, and Macaulay were writing, Newman, Arnold, Huxley, and Ruskin were growing up. Much of the younger generation's characteristic mode of thinking is understandable only in the context of the periodicals. John Henry Newman, for example, recalls how as a boy of fourteen he emulated the rivalry of the *Edinburgh* and *Quarterly* reviews: "In 1815 I wrote two periodicals—that is, papers called the 'Spy' and 'Anti-Spy.' They were written against each other."[66] At nineteen William Harrison Ainsworth brought out a literary periodical in Manchester called the *Boeotian*, which ran for six numbers in the spring of 1824. Winthrop Mackworth Praed, while at Eton, founded a manuscript periodical, *Apis matina*. He later called upon Charles Knight to publish the *Etonian* (1820–21), and then with Knight as publisher started *Knight's Quarterly Magazine* (1823–25), to which his Cambridge friends, including the young Macaulay, contributed. Gladstone, whose father had founded the *Liverpool Courier*, began his literary career as the editor of the

66. *Letters and Correspondence of John Henry Newman*, 1:19.

Eton Miscellany (1827) and in the 1840s contributed to the *Foreign and Colonial,* the *English,* the *New Quarterly,* and the *Quarterly* reviews.[67] Perhaps the high point for the essay came in 1825, when Macaulay wrote his review of Milton for the *Edinburgh Review* and became famous overnight.

In a more modest fashion Harriet Martineau began her literary career by entering an essay contest. In 1830 the Central Unitarian Association announced a contest for essays that presented Unitarianism to Catholics, Jews, and Mohammedans—the prizes being ten, fifteen, and twenty guineas respectively, and the winning essays to be published in the *Monthly Repository.* Martineau employed a poor schoolboy for a sovereign to copy her essays to disguise her hand, entered each of the contests, and won all of the prizes.[68] With this success, she determined to make her living as a writer and wrote *Illustrations of Political Economy,* a series of tales explaining economic principles, but she had difficulty finding a publisher and ultimately had to agree in 1832 to get 500 subscribers for the publication of the work in parts. To advertise her work, she had a prospectus printed and sent a copy to almost every member of Parliament. This had the intended effect. The first edition of 1,500 copies was quickly sold. A successive edition of 5,000 was then immediately called for.[69]

Despite the advantages in dissemination and remuneration, authors generally felt that writing for periodicals and especially for reviews required them to prostitute their talents. In 1825 Thomas Lovell Beddoes laments that "the state of literature now is painful & humiliating enough—every one will write for £15 a sheet;—Who for love of art, who for fame, who for the purpose of continuing the noble stream of English minds?"[70] In "Characteristics" (1831) Carlyle saw reviewing as one of the symptoms of the age's self-conscious disease that was stifling originality and feeding on itself. He complains that "all Literature has become one boundless self-devouring Review."[71] Even those authors who sought to keep away from periodicals were swallowed by their insatiable demand for copy. Southey and Coleridge, for example, who had been attacked in the *Anti-Jacobin* (1798–1800) and had criticized the periodicals, eventually came to write in them. The advantages of appearing in a periodical publication are explained by Coleridge in the prospectus to his *Friend*:

67. See M. R. D. Foot, "Mr Gladstone and His Publishers," 156–75.
68. Martineau, *Autobiography,* 1:114–19.
69. Ibid., 121–35.
70. Beddoes to Thomas Forbes Kelsall, March 25, 1825, *The Works of Thomas Lovell Beddoes,* 598.
71. "Characteristics," in *Works,* 28:25.

I perceived too in a periodical Essay the most likely Means of winning, instead of forcing my Way. Supposing Truth on my Side, the Shock of the first
Day might be so far lessened by Reflections of the succeeding Days, as to procure for my next Week's Essay a less hostile Reception, than it would have
met with, had it been only the next Chapter of a present volume.[72]

Coleridge supposes that the periodical essay involves one in an aesthetic of
reception whereby the reader's understanding is operated on over time.
This temporal osmosis allows the author's truth to win readers over slowly
rather than to take them in a single forceful assault. As Hazlitt said, speaking of Coleridge and Southey, "these very persons have, in the end, joined
that very pack of hunting-tigers that strove to harass them to death, and
now halloo longest and loudest in the chase of blood. Nor was the result,
after all, so unnatural as it might at first appear. They saw that there was but
one royal road to reputation."[73]

The reviews and periodicals made everyone who wrote subject to them
because of their financial and critical power. By the 1830s an essayist could
make a gentleman's living by writing for them but was unlikely to be able
to please his readers and also write anything of lasting worth. Commenting
on the career and work of Laman Blanchard, a minor essayist and poet,
Bulwer-Lytton declares that "in England, the author who would live on his
works can only live by the Public; in other words, by the desultory readers
of light literature; and hence the inevitable tendancy (sic) of our literary youth is towards the composition of works without learning and fore-
thought. Leisure is impossible, to him who must meet the exigencies of the
day; much information of a refining and original kind is not for the multitude. The more imaginative rush to novels, and the more reflective fritter
their lives away in articles for periodicals."[74] George Darley despised himself for working for the *Athenaeum*; he remarked, "I have to scribble every
second day for means to prolong this detestable headachy life, to criticate
and review, committing *literary fratricide*, which is an iron that enters into
my soul, and doing what disgusts me, not only with the day, but the remaining one."[75] Although he would have preferred to have made his living as a
poet, Darley found himself enslaved to criticism. Of such painful compro-
mises with the market were the careers of many authors made.

72. *The Friend*, 2:17. However, Coleridge makes the philosophical character of his work clear
when he declares that it is distinguished by "its avowed exclusion of the Events of the Day,
and of all personal Politics" (2:13).
73. "The Periodical Press," *The Complete Works of William Hazlitt*, 16:234.
74. "Memoir of Laman Blanchard," in *Sketches from Life; by the late Laman Blanchard*, 1:viii.
75. Darley to Mary Russell Mitford, August 22, 1836, *Life and Letters of George Darley*, 150.

As Darley's remark about "literary fratricide" suggests, the writing market had become not only lucrative but competitive. The struggle among the reviews for predominance led to fierce personal struggles among writers. *Blackwood's* launched a virulent attack upon Leigh Hunt and his friends in "The Cockney School of Poetry" (1817–18), while Croker's review of *Endymion* in the *Quarterly* (1818) was blamed for hastening the death of Keats.[76] In "The Flying Tailor" James Hogg hoped to survive "the impotent scorn of base Reviews, / Monthly or Quarterly, or that accursed / Journal, the Edinburgh Review, that lives / On tears, and sighs, and groans, and brains, and blood."[77] The most infamous incident among feuding magazines involved a trading of insults and led to the duel at Chalk Farm between John Christie (acting as deputy for John Lockhart of *Blackwood's*) and John Scott, editor of the *London Magazine*, in which Scott was mortally wounded.[78] As Darley's disgust with himself indicates, this competitive energy often became introjected, producing such results as the following peroration from Hazlitt's extraordinary "On the Pleasure of Hating":

> What chance is there of the success of real passion? What certainty of its continuance? Seeing all this as I do, and unravelling the web of human life into its various threads of meanness, spite, cowardice, want of feeling, and want of understanding, of indifference towards others and ignorance of ourselves— seeing custom prevail over all excellence, itself giving way to infamy— mistaken as I have been in my public and private hopes, calculating others from myself, and calculating wrong; always disappointed where I placed most reliance; the dupe of friendship, and the fool of love; have I not reason to hate and to despise myself? Indeed I do; and chiefly for not having hated and despised the world enough.[79]

This essay has at its heart a brooding self-hatred that seems to reflect how many authors felt about sacrificing future immortality for present worldly gain, a feeling that perhaps explains why his contemporaries found Keats so extraordinary.

IV

In the eighteenth century, booksellers published periodical essays serially as speculations, hoping to make money afterwards by gathering them

---

76. [John Wilson Croker], "Keats's *Endymion*." Edward Copleston advises a beginning reviewer to censure the work being reviewed because it "is both easier, and will sell better" ("Advice to a Young Reviewer, with a Specimen of the Art," in *Memoir of Edward Copleston*, 288). The specimen review attacks Milton's "L'Allegro" (289–97).
77. *Selected Poems*, 61.
78. On Scott, see P. G. Patmore, *My Friends and Acquaintance*, 2:283–87.
79. *Complete Works*, 12:136.

together in a book. For the *Rambler* (1750–52), which sold for two pence and had a circulation of about five hundred, Samuel Johnson was paid two guineas a paper or about eight guineas a sheet and received half profits of the collected edition. The booksellers accepted a negligible profit on the serial issue because they expected a large one on the collected edition.[80] But in the nineteenth century, with the increased sale of the reviews and magazines, the publishing strategy was reversed, since reprinted essays were unlikely to reach more readers in books than they had already done in periodicals. In *Peter's Letters to His Kinfolk* (1819), John Lockhart says that "the happy man who is permitted to fill a sheet, or a half-sheet, of a monthly or quarterly journal with his lucubrations, is sure of coming into the hands of a vast number of persons more than he has any strict or even feasible claim upon, either from the subject-matter or execution of his work," and he notes that "these works *pay* so much better than any others."[81] In "The Periodical Press" (1823) Hazlitt notes that "booksellers will often refuse to purchase in a volume, what they will give a handsome price for, if divided piecemeal, and fitted for occasional insertion in a newspaper or magazine; so that the only authors who, as a class, are not starving, are periodical essayists."[82] Henry Francis Cary excused himself in 1823 from working on Pindar to write for the *London Magazine,* saying that "Hessey and Taylor are good pay; and Pindar himself was too well aware of the advantage of ready money . . . to be angry with me for this temporary desertion."[83]

There is also evidence that readers enjoyed their essayists more in magazines than on their own. Writing in 1830 Ainsworth says, "How it occurs, I know not, but some people never read so well as in a magazine. Wilson, for example, and Lamb: who likes Elia represented even in the types of Thomas Davison, and where could the Professor write as he does in *Blackwood*—surely not in three hot-pressed volumes, to be published by Henry Colburn of Old Burlington Street?"[84] Although Lamb was paid twenty

80. Walter Graham, *English Literary Periodicals*, 119–20. The memory of this strategy survived among authors, for one finds Byron writing to John Hunt in a letter of April 14, 1823, about continuing the *Liberal*: "The profits of the work will probably be greater when its periodical continuation has ceased—as it will then form two volumes of a curious Miscellany" (*Byron's Letters and Journals*, 10:151). For the history of the individual essay serial and its decline in the early nineteenth century, see Melvin R. Watson, *Magazine Serials and the Essay Tradition, 1746–1820.*
81. Lockhart, 2:192–93.
82. *Complete Works*, 16:221.
83. Cary to the Rev. Thomas Price, January 3, 1822, in *Memoir of the Rev. Henry Francis Cary,* 2:92.
84. Ainsworth to James Crossley, April 21, 1830, in S. M. Ellis, *William Harrison Ainsworth and His Friends,* 1:189–90.

guineas a sheet for his contributions to the *London Magazine,* Taylor only offered him a third of the profits of *The Last Essays of Elia* (1833). Lamb was to have gotten thirty pounds on the sales of the volume, but received nothing from Taylor.[85] John Banim collected the essays he had written for the *Literary Register,* which had ceased publication after forty-four numbers in 1823, and sold them as *Revelations of the Dead-Alive* to Simpkin and Marshall for thirty guineas in 1824.[86] Southey's *Essays, Moral and Political* (1832), reprinted from the *Quarterly Review,* never repaid the expenses of publication.[87]

Carlyle and Macaulay were much more fortunate. Although Carlyle complained to Emerson that bookselling is a trade "in which the Devil has a large interest," he received £239 as his share from the profits from the first edition of his *Miscellanies* (1839).[88] Macaulay was reluctant to republish his essays in book form even though the third unauthorized American edition was being smuggled into England. In writing to Macvey Napier in June of 1842, he says,

> The public judges, and ought to judge, indulgently of periodical works. They are not expected to be highly finished. Their natural life is only six weeks. Sometimes their writer is at a distance from the books to which he wants to refer. Sometimes he is forced to hurry through his task in order to catch the post. He may blunder; he may contradict himself; he may break off in the middle of a story; he may give an immoderate extension to one part of his subject, and dismiss an equally important part in a few words. All this is readily forgiven if there be a certain spirit and vivacity in his style. But, as soon as he republishes, he challenges a comparison with the most symmetrical and polished of human compositions.[89]

85. Lamb to Edward Moxon, early 1833, *The Letters of Charles Lamb,* 3:357.
86. Patrick Joseph Murray, *The Life of John Banim, the Irish Novelist,* 117, 140.
87. Robert Southey, *The Life and Correspondence of Robert Southey,* 5:306n.
88. Carlyle to Emerson, April 1, 1840, *The Collected Letters of Thomas and Jane Welsh Carlyle,* 12:92; on the profit from the *Miscellanies,* see letter of Thomas Carlyle to John A. Carlyle, February 29, 1840, *Collected Letters,* 12:63.
89. *Letters,* 4:40–41. Compare Samuel Johnson's meditation on much the same subject from *Rambler* 208 of March 14, 1752: "I am willing to flatter myself with hopes, that, by collecting these papers, I am not preparing for my future life, either shame or repentence. That all are happily imagined, or accurately polished, that the same sentiments have not sometimes recurred, or the same expressions been too frequently repeated, I have not confidence in my abilities sufficient to warrant. He that condemns himself to compose on a stated day, will often bring to his task an attention dissipated, a memory embarrassed, an imagination overwhelmed, a mind distracted with anxieties, a body languishing with disease: He will labour on a barren topick, till it is too late to change it; or in the ardour of invention, diffuse his thoughts into wild exuberance, which the pressing hour of publication cannot suffer judgment to examine or reduce" (*The Rambler,* 3:318).

For Macaulay the reason for imperfect prose is that writers have to economize on time, they cannot polish their periods and achieve the balanced symmetry of eighteenth-century prose. They are hurried and so subject to error. Their time as writers is not their own but rather something done for the moment and so to be indulged by the reader.

Macaulay was nonetheless finally persuaded to issue his *Essays* in 1843.[90] For essays, they sold extremely well. From 1843 to 1853, the collected edition averaged 1,230 copies a year; in the next decade 4,700 copies a year; and an average of over 6,000 a year were sold after 1865 until the early decades of this century.[91] Yet until 1850 the total number of copies of his collected essays that had been sold was less than that of any single issue of the *Edinburgh Review* in which they had originally appeared. Since the periodicals with the largest circulation reached more readers than almost any book except the best of the bestsellers, it was in most cases more profitable to have a work published in parts in a magazine than to publish it as a whole.

As Carlyle commented in 1832 on the predominance of the periodicals in the writing market: "One *has* no right vehicle."[92] Carlyle's *Sartor Resartus*, for example, was published in eight installments in *Fraser's Magazine* from November of 1833 to August of 1834. The book was squeezed into 112 double-columned pages, for which Carlyle received eighty-two pounds plus fifty-eight bound copies of the work.[93] Once the book had been published in this manner, Carlyle had difficulty arranging for publication on favorable terms. Murray in 1834 would only publish it for half-profits, which meant that Carlyle would have had little prospect of making anything at all from the book publication. Even when the volume was republished in 1838, Saunders and Otley cautiously required a subscription of 300 to cover most of their costs and then printed only 500 copies.[94] Although writing for periodicals, Carlyle was not happy with them, saying to his brother John in 1830, "in the valley of the shadow of the Magazine Editors we shall not always linger."[95] Later in 1843, when Herbert Spencer tried to publish a series of letters that had originally appeared in the *Nonconformist* as a pamphlet entitled "The Proper Sphere of Government," he found that

90. *Letters of Thomas Babington Macaulay*, 4:40–41.
91. *The Life and Letters of Lord Macaulay*, 2:428.
92. Carlyle to John A. Carlyle, January 10, 1832, *Collected Letters*, 6:85.
93. Carlyle to John A. Carlyle, August 15, 1834, *Collected Letters*, 7:271.
94. *Sartor Resartus*, lxiii.
95. Carlyle to John A. Carlyle, December 19, 1830, *Collected Letters*, 5:202.

Utter ignorance of the book-trade . . . was shown in the idea that the sale of such a pamphlet would return the cost. This end is but rarely achieved even when the author is well-known and the topic popular: one reason being that, with a small publication, the cost of advertising bears to the total expenditure so much larger a ratio than with a publication of any size; and the other being that publishers will not take any trouble about pamphlets, which, as they say, are not worth "handling"—the trouble of selling is the same as for a larger book and the profit next to nothing. I experienced the effects of these causes. Perhaps a hundred copies were sold and less than a tenth of the cost repaid.[96]

Spencer had not realized that the days of the pamphleteers had disappeared long ago. As Gifford had earlier said in a letter to John Barrow in 1812 about the *Quarterly*, "Our sale is at least 6000, and I know of no pamphlet that would sell 100; besides, pamphlets are thrown aside, Reviews are permanent."[97]

Although the periodicals were vehicles for the essayists and reviewers, their survival depended upon their publishers' interests. As Lockhart noted concerning *Blackwood's*, "The history of this Magazine may be considered in quite a different point of view—as the struggle, namely, of two rival booksellers, striving for their respective shares in the profits of periodical publications."[98] As competition increased, the prostitution of the journals for their publishers' ends became notorious. The practice of reviewing favorably those books published by the firm was widespread, as was that of attacking those of other publishers. In a letter to Coleridge written in 1808, Southey thanks him for praising *Espriella* in the *Courier*: "Puff me, Coleridge! if you love me, puff me! Puff a couple of hundreds into my pocket!"[99] As Robert Montgomery notes in *The Age Reviewed* (1827), commenting on the importance of Colburn's *Literary Gazette*, "Let but the smile of Colburn suavity, illuminate the MS. and your forthcoming prodigy will meander through all the papers in the full tide of paragraphic celebrity."[100] This advertising in the papers and periodicals gave other publishers an interest in a particular work so that, as Cyrus Redding reports that Colburn told him, "a hundred pounds 'discreetly' laid out in advertising would make any book go down, because the advertisements toned the criticism."[101] Writing in 1833, Richard Horne deplores the fact that "some

96. *An Autobiography*, 1:264.
97. John Barrow, *An Auto-Biographical Memoir of Sir John Barrow*, 506–7.
98. *Peter's Letters to His Kinfolk*, 2:226.
99. Southey to Coleridge, February 12, 1808, *Life and Correspondence*, 3:134.
100. *The Age Reviewed*, 34n.
101. Redding, *Fifty Years' Recollections*, 3:239.

periodicals, called literary and critical, seldom deign to notice, unless as objects of attack, the works which proceed from other publishers, who have no share as proprietors, or no collateral interest with them."[102] Writers who held objectionable political views were simply not reviewed. Hazlitt and Campbell, for example, independently suggested that Bulwer-Lytton be reviewed in the *Edinburgh Review* but were told the subject was "an interdicted one."[103] In 1838 Hood notes that "the leading reviews, Whig and Tory, have carefully abstained from noticing me or my works."[104]

Later, as publishers abandoned poetry to Edward Moxon in the 1830s and 1840s, only those poets who were well known socially and considered politically sound were reviewed in the monthlies and quarterlies; or, as Montgomery put it, poetic genius "must wither—fanned by no Review."[105] The *Edinburgh Review* reviewed Browning's drama *Strafford* in 1837 but did not notice him again until *Dramatis Personae* in 1864 and managed to ignore his best poetry completely. More tellingly, the *Quarterly* didn't bother to review any one of Browning's works until 1864. Symptomatic of the period is Macaulay's review of Robert Montgomery's poems in 1831. It was primarily an attack upon puffing, not a critique that pointed to the promising contemporary poets who deserved the public's attention instead of Montgomery. As Peacock says in "An Essay on Fashionable Literature," "the *legatur* of corruption must be stamped upon a work before it can be admitted to fashionable circulation."[106]

When not promoting the publishers' interests, criticism all too often was purely destructive. The effect of praise or blame was not calculated with regard to a work's author or artistic standards but with regard to the reading public. As Macaulay observes in his review of Montgomery's poetry, "The public is now the patron, and a most liberal patron. All that the rich and powerful bestowed on authors from the time of Maecenas to that of Harley would not, we apprehend, make up a sum equal to that which has been paid by English booksellers to authors during the last fifty years. Men of letters have accordingly ceased to court individuals, and have begun to court the public. They formerly used flattery. They now use puffing."[107] Marketing and advertising had begun to dominate the public's taste and could for a moment gain the attention of readers, even if they could not

102. *Exposition of the False Medium and Barriers Excluding Men of Genius from the Public*, 255.
103. Patmore, *My Friends and Acquaintance*, 3:156–57.
104. Thomas Hood to Philip de Franck, January 1838, *The Letters of Thomas Hood*, 353.
105. *The Age Reviewed*, 131.
106. *Works of Thomas Love Peacock*, 8:273.
107. *Critical and Historical Essays*, 2:645.

make readers care deeply for what they read. For once publishing became a profitable and lucrative business, financial considerations began to influence the production of literary form.

One should also recognize that many reviews were subsidized. In his *Life of John Sterling* Thomas Carlyle notes that "money is the sinews of Periodical Literature almost as much as of war itself; without money, and under a constant drain of loss, Periodical Literature is one of the things that cannot be carried on."[108] At the inception of the *Westminster Review* in 1824 Jeremy Bentham provided a reserve fund of £4,000, which was exhausted by 1828.[109] Later, John Macrone, the first publisher of Dickens and Ainsworth, was £5,000 in debt when he died in 1837, apparently because he was also the publisher of the *Westminster Review*.[110] In 1826, lured by the profits of the *Times,* which were reputed to be £40,000 a year, John Murray with the backing of J. D. Powles and Benjamin Disraeli tried to start a newspaper called the *Representative.* He sought to hire John Lockhart as the chief editor at £1,000 a year and employed William Maginn as a subeditor for £700 a year. But he was forced to cease publication within six months and lost some £26,000.[111] It has recently been shown that the Society for the Diffusion of Useful Knowledge was unknowingly subsidizing the almost £25,000 a year in direct production costs of the *Penny Magazine* after the journal's first three years, when its circulation fell and stayed below its break-even point of 112,000 copies in 1835.[112] The *British and Foreign Review,* founded by Thomas Wentworth Beaumont in 1835, paid its contributors handsomely at the rate of a guinea a page.[113] But the review never acquired a large enough readership to justify its generous treatment of writers and ceased publication in 1844 after having cost Beaumont £3,000 a year in subsidies.[114] In 1836 John Henry Newman assumed for a short time the editorship of the struggling *British Critic* with the backing of friends

108. *The Life of John Sterling,* 60.
109. John Bowring, *The Works of Jeremy Bentham,* 10:540; and George L. Nesbitt, *Benthamite Reviewing,* 35, 130. It should be noted that, despite espousing radically democratic politics, the *Westminster Review* remained a journal for the upper-middle-class intelligentsia as reflected by its high price, its overly generous payments to contributors, and, as Nesbitt observes, its propensity for "quoting Latin, Greek, French, and Italian at length and in important context without translation" (126).
110. This is John Sutherland's persuasive surmise; see "John Macrone: Victorian Publisher," 249.
111. Smiles, *A Publisher and His Friends,* 2:186–215.
112. Scott Bennett, "Revolutions in Thought: Serial Publication and the Mass Market for Reading," 236–41, 256n.
113. Henry Reeve to E. H. Handley, September 13, 1835, *Memoirs of the Life and Correspondence of Henry Reeve,* 1:54.
114. See Hans B. de Groot, "Lord Brougham and the Founding of the *British and Foreign Review,*" 31.

who were willing to spend three or four hundred pounds a year to publish a theological journal that gave voice to their views. The review was selling about 1,100 copies and losing £100 a year so that if he and his friends would supply about a third of the copy for free, then the review would break even.[115] He wrote to prospective contributors, including Henry Wilberforce, saying, "I fear you will find the pay very bad, only 5£ or guineas a sheet."[116]

The market for essay writing in the quarterlies began to deteriorate in 1831. When Murray wrote to Southey in November of 1831 and attempted to extract a retroactive reduction in payment for his contributions to the *Quarterly*, Southey argued that the "injury which the *QR.* has sustained from Magazines and literary Newspapers is indeed likely to be of a permanent kind, but it cannot I think go farther than it has done, farther competition must be among themselves and not with you."[117] Nevertheless, the quarterlies continued to decline in the face of competition from the likes of *Fraser's Magazine*, founded in 1831 by Maginn of *Blackwood's*; and as their circulation slowly declined, payments from editors became uncertain. Thomas Moore in early 1833 writes to Macvey Napier, the editor of the *Edinburgh Review*, concerning the payment for his last article on German rationalism: "Nor will I deny that, though conscious of how little real worth was the article I sent you (the subject not being of a kind to attract many readers), I still looked for some return of *substance* for my *shadow*."[118] Later in the year, Moore writes again, saying, "I hate reviewing, you *know*—but money makes the author, as well as the mare to 'go.' "[119] The financial pressure on the reviews soon had Carlyle saying of his essay on Johnson that it was "to be given to the Editor that *behaves himself* best."[120] Similarly, Carlyle says in 1833 that he has had to wait for more than a year and has had to dun Napier, who was notoriously tight-fisted as an editor, several times before settling for less than he had expected for his "Characteristics" (1831).[121] In 1837 Henry Crabb Robinson recorded in his diary that "the *Edinburgh Review* does not now pay its expenses nor does it regularly pay its contributors."[122]

In the same year James Grant, an American newspaperman working in

---

115. Newman to Richard Hurrell Froude, February 1, 1836, *The Letters and Diaries of John Henry Newman*, 5:223.
116. Newman to Henry Wilberforce, March 15, 1838, ibid., 6:213.
117. Southey to John Murray, December 3, 1831, *New Letters*, 2:372.
118. February 15, 1833, *The Letters of Thomas Moore*, 2:763.
119. August 31, 1833, ibid., 2:769.
120. Carlyle to Alexander Carlyle, January 14, 1832, *Collected Letters*, 6:92.
121. Carlyle to John A. Carlyle, January 8–9, 1833, *Collected Letters*, 6:290.
122. October 27, 1837, *Henry Crabb Robinson on Books and Their Writers*, 2:541.

England, surveyed the English literary market as best he could for his American readers in *The Great Metropolis*. He found that the *Quarterly* and *Edinburgh* reviews were paying twenty guineas a sheet on average, the *Westminster Review* ten guineas a sheet, the *Foreign Quarterly* from ten to sixteen guineas a sheet, the *British and Foreign Review* twenty guineas a sheet, the *Monthly Magazine* from five to ten guineas a sheet, the *New Monthly Magazine* ten to sixteen guineas a sheet, *Fraser's* sixteen guineas a sheet, the *Metropolitan Magazine* from five to ten guineas a sheet, the *Monthly Repository* nothing at all, the *Literary Gazette* twenty-four guineas per sheet, the *Athenaeum* from ten to sixteen guineas a sheet, the *Saturday Magazine* sixteen guineas a sheet, and the *Penny Magazine* (which had large double-columned pages) twenty-eight guineas a sheet.[123] These were still substantial rates by comparison with those paid in Johnson's day, but they were much below those paid to writers in the 1820s.

In his "Condition of Authors in England, Germany, and France," G. H. Lewes declares that "in the present state of things a man who has health, courage, and ability, can earn by literature the income of a gentleman" (in Lewes's terms, £300 a year).[124] On the Continent, in comparison, he found that readers were far fewer and that the payment for writing in the best and most widely circulated intellectual journals was far from lucrative. In France the conditions for writers were bad, but they were worse yet in Germany. It would appear that the extent of the French reading public in 1850 was roughly comparable to England's in 1800. This uneven development of reading publics probably contributed to the relatively high standard of the French novel, as Bulwer-Lytton notes in *England and the English*,[125] and the disparity was probably exacerbated by France's relatively

123. *The Great Metropolis*, 2:273–353. It should be noted that Grant's information is limited. He declares, for example, that the rate paid by the *Penny Magazine* "is perhaps the highest in the history of periodical literature" (2:352). He was evidently ignorant of arrangements between principal contributors to the quarterlies and their reviews. For example, during this period Croker was being paid £150 for four sheets to the *Quarterly*, or thirty-seven and a half guineas a sheet; see the letter of John Murray to John Wilson Croker, September 22, 1832, in Smiles, *A Publisher and His Friends*, 2:430.
124. "The Condition of Authors in England, Germany, and France," 285–86. Other writers had much more expensive tastes. Macaulay, for instance, writing to Hannah Macaulay on August 17, 1833, contemplates writing for a living and declares, "In order to live like a gentleman, it would be necessary for me to write, not as I have hitherto, but regularly, and even daily. I have never made more than two hundred a year by my pen. I could not support myself in comfort on less than five hundred" (*Letters*, 2:300).
125. "In France, where the reading public is less numerous than in England, a more elevated and refining tone is more fashionable in literature; and in America, where it is infinitely larger, the tone of literature is infinitely more superficial" (*England and the English*, 2:120–21).

poor roads and water transportation, which the distribution of books depended on. Lewes observes that "while our Quarterlies were paying often 50 pounds and, in some cases, even 100 pounds for one article, and their ordinary contributors, sixteen and twenty guineas a sheet, the French Quarterlies were paying ordinary contributors at the following rate: —100 francs (4 pounds) a sheet, no more than 100 francs was due; an author's *article de début* was not paid for at all. Other contributors, whose names were an attraction, received of course higher prices; but the highest price ever paid by the *Revue des Deux Mondes* . . . was that paid to George Sand . . . 250 francs (10 pounds) a sheet."[126] Lewes notes that, in contrast to the large circulation of the English reviews, that of the *Revue des Deux Monds* "never exceeded 3000 copies."[127] And although the German reviews were renowned for their objectivity, Disraeli's observations about one in *Vivian Grey* provide a fair assessment: "It numbered among its writers some of the most celebrated names in Germany; its critiques and articles were as impartial as they were able—as sincere as they were sound; it never paid the expense of the first number."[128]

By the 1850s the market for articles in the magazines had fallen off sharply because of the expanding number of magazines and because of the competition from newspapers. Comparing the modern circumstances with those of the seventeenth century, in commenting on Milton's *Joannis Miltoni Pro Populo Anglicano Defensio*, Carlyle says that there were "no newspapers then & his work is like the concentration of fifty "Couriers" or "Chronicles."[129] John Stuart Mill in 1847 says, "It seems to me that reviews have had their day, & that nothing is now worth much except the two extremes, newspapers for diffusion & books for accurate thought. Every thinker should make a point of either publishing in his life if possible, or at any rate leaving behind him the most complete expression he can produce of his best thoughts, those which he has no chance of getting into any review."[130] In the early nineteenth century many writers who had literary careers wrote for newspapers: Coleridge wrote for the *Courier;* Southey for the *Courier* and the *Morning Post*; in 1807 Henry Crabb Robinson was made foreign correspondent for the *Times*. In the 1830s and 1840s Thackeray

126. Lewes, "The Condition of Authors," 286.
127. Ibid.
128. 4:352–53.
129. Entry for March 25–26, 1822, *Two Note Books of Thomas Carlyle*, 3.
130. Mill to John Austin, April 13, 1847, *The Collected Works of John Stuart Mill*, 13:711–12. On the relation of literature to newspapers in the period, see Harold A. Innis, "The English Press in the Nineteenth Century," and Louis Dudek, *Literature and the Press*.

contributed to the *Times*. But in the 1840s writers who contributed to newspapers and later published significant intellectual work tended to be political thinkers. Marx started his career as a writer for the *Rheinische Zeitung* in 1842, and from 1851 to 1862 he wrote many articles for the *New York Daily Tribune* as its European correspondent. Friedrich Engels wrote for Robert Owens' *New Moral World* from 1843 to 1844 and was a regular contributor to the *Northern Star* from 1845 to 1850. One should also note that Harriet Martineau wrote over fifteen hundred articles for the *Daily News* between 1851 and 1866. With the rise of the newspapers, essays in reviews and magazines lost their urgency but gained in intellectual refinement and polish as witnessed by the prose of Arnold, Newman, and Ruskin.

V

The essays reflected the needs of an educated public in the early nineteenth century for organized information delivered in a manageable length and pleasing variety. The periodical format was ideally suited to satisfy these needs and to provide an overview from a particular political viewpoint of the important works being published and read. Besides essays and reviews, the quarterlies and magazines also published the latest prices of stocks and bonds, the Navy and Army lists, and other information that one associates today with newspapers. The *Edinburgh* and the *Quarterly* reviews remained throughout the first half of the century the most profitable of the magazines per single issue, though they ceased to have the impact upon sales of books that they once had when the weekly literary reviews and especially the *Literary Gazette* and the *Athenaeum* came into being. Because the periodicals were so profitable for publishers, editors sought to attract the best available talent with relatively high remuneration and led the best young writers to turn their hands to nonfiction prose for a generation. The essay was transformed by this development. It no longer functioned as marginal moral comment on social and political development, but instead became the form in which culture was formed and established. Nothing could escape the reviews or magazines; and everyone had to read them. Only with the rise of the newspapers did the reviews and magazines begin to settle down to represent middle-brow culture in the way they do today. Prose styles became both frenetic and anticlimactic, as authors worried about the capacities of their audience to understand what they were saying and sought to accommodate the needs of a wide readership. The personal, subjective note predominated, as authors attempted to engage their readers' preconceptions and prejudices instead of their reason.

Only when the market for fiction began to offer greater rewards than the market for prose did the publishers and authors turn elsewhere. Dickens ceased to be a parliamentary reporter and began to write stories. George Eliot, who could easily have had a career like that of G. H. Lewes, turned instead to the more profitable novel. Once the audience for imaginative fiction began to dwarf that for critical and familiar prose, the market for the essay went into decline, only to rise again for a short time in the 1860s when the shilling monthlies garnered such a large readership because the relatively high cost of paper created by the American civil war had temporarily consolidated the readership of periodicals. During the 1810s and 1820s, almost everyone tried their hand at prose, but thereafter fiction became the most profitable literary form. Poetry had already retreated to the Annuals and the small presses, which could afford to indulge the vanity of gentlemanly and academic ambitions. Prose became the currency of the day. The world was filtered through the literary periodicals much in the way it was soon to become seen through the newspapers.

4

Carlyle's Old Clothes Philosophy: The Material Form of Literature

*Knowledge is no longer confined to the few:
the object therefore is, to make it accessible and
attractive to the many.*

—Hazlitt, "The Periodical Press"

E ver since Socrates lamented the invention of writing in the *Phaedrus,* philosophers have deplored the dependence of ideas on their material form. The industrialization of publishing in the nineteenth century and the creation of a mass market for books intensified this philosophic abhorrence and naturally pushed philosophy into an alliance with aesthetics. Thomas Carlyle was the most original and influential nineteenth-century writer in this field. Despite being a central figure in the transmission of German thought into nineteenth-century English and American culture and a seminal thinker on questions of mass culture, Carlyle was so worried about and so fixated upon the dependency of thought and literature upon materiality that those engaged in current critical and theoretical inquiry have found him unattractive. Nonetheless, Carlyle's consideration of the physical means of transmitting literature and ideas needs to be examined because it is one of the very first responses to the nineteenth-century technological transformation of literary production.

In the late eighteenth and early nineteenth centuries, art and literature became defined dialectically in relation to payment for them; they were defined in terms of their uselessness and their existence outside the economy and its politics.[1] Defined as limited market items, not available for general consumption, art and literature were imagined as being produced by those who have no monetary interest in them, as if all art were an emanation of the human spirit and outside the realm of material life. This idealist definition of art and literature separated the production from the product, as if artists and writers did not need to eat in order to live, and as if art and literature could be produced only by gentlemen who got pleasure solely from their production. This Romantic ideology is deeply rooted everywhere in the American universities and is reinforced by the extensive institutional subsidization of scholarly publication. It is thus no accident that the Romantic, idealist opposition to an aesthetic of reception was born when literature was transformed by the increased availability of books and periodicals that occurred at the start of the nineteenth century. Friedrich Schlegel, for example, defined Romantic poetry as a transcendence of genre.[2] From this perspective only a work that is one of a kind, a genre unto itself, is truly literary, and so transcends conventional literary form.

The most rigorous proponent of this position among modern theorists has been Theodor Adorno in "The Culture Industry: Enlightenment as Mass Deception" (1949) and *Ästhetische Theorie* (1970). For Adorno the artistic work must be separate from the realm of commodities and must embody in its form an austere cultural negativity; further, the aesthetic experience of the artistic work must also participate in this austerity.[3] Consider, for instance, his comments on the essay in "The Essay as Form": "Its self-relativization is inherent in its form: it has to be constructed as though it could always break off at any point. It thinks in fragments, just as reality is fragmentary, and finds its unity in and through the breaks and not by glossing them over."[4] The history of modern art and literature and their emphasis on formal innovation over and against an aesthetic of pleasure has reflected this negativity at work. That literature is literally manufactured and mass produced, however, became a matter for concerned meditation first in the early nineteenth century with the advent of the industrialization of publishing in England. Carlyle's response to the industrialization of

1. Kant's *Critique of Aesthetic Judgement* presents the classical formulation of this view of the aesthetic. For a thorough critique of Kant's presuppositions, see Jacques Derrida, "Economimesis."
2. Philippe Lacoue-Labarthe and Jean-Luc Nancy in their discussion of Schlegel's definition call this "L'Absolu littéraire" ("Genre," 10).
3. Theodor W. Adorno, "The Culture Industry: Enlightenment as Mass Deception."
4. *Notes to Literature*, 1:16.

publishing is a signal example of these technological and historical conditions of literary production coming to authorial self-consciousness and also is a forerunner of the continuing modern discomfort with the materiality of ideas and literature.

I

Carlyle was the first English writer to observe that industrialization had affected publishing and the literary marketplace. In "Signs of the Times" (1829) he points to the way that the modern production of literature has become mechanized: "Literature, too, has its Paternoster-row mechanism, its Trade-dinners, its Editorial conclaves, and huge subterranean, puffing bellows; so that books are not only printed, but, in great measure, written and sold, by machinery."[5] Publishers' sales dinners, editorial meetings, and advertising activities are evidence for Carlyle of the new methods of industrial organization being applied to literary production. In *Sartor Resartus* (1833–34) and elsewhere Carlyle observes that because of new industrial techniques the quality of literature has been affected by the quantity of publishing. For instance, in "Biography" (1832), which reviews Croker's edition of Boswell's *Life of Johnson,* Carlyle remarks upon the great production of ephemeral modern literature:

> Ship-loads of Fashionable Novels, Sentimental Rhymes, Tragedies, Farces, Diaries of Travel, Tales by flood and field, are swallowed monthly into the bottomless Pool: still does the Press toil; innumerable Paper-makers, Compositors, Printers' Devils, Book-binders, and Hawkers grown hoarse with loud proclaiming, rest not from their labour; and still, in torrents, rushes on the great array of Publications, unpausing, to their final home; and still Oblivion, like the Grave, cries, Give! Give! (28:58)

The flood of publication that Carlyle sees is headed straight toward oblivion and the grave, despite the incessant industry it has spawned. Responding to the commodification of his own work, Carlyle focuses on its disturbing materiality and on its being literally manufactured from rags. Hence in the very title of *Sartor Resartus,* "the tailor retailored," one sees his emphasis upon the need to address, however painfully, the consequences of the connection between literature and the material of its physical transmission.

5. *The Collected Works of Thomas Carlyle,* 27:62. Further citations of Carlyle's works, with the exception of *Sartor Resartus,* his *Note Books,* and his *Reminiscences,* refer to volume and page numbers in this edition.

The connection between the growth of the clothing industry and that of publishing is explicitly made in *Sartor Resartus* by Carlyle:

> If such supply of printed Paper should rise so far as to choke-up the highways and public thoroughfares, new means must of necessity be had recourse to. In a world existing by Industry, we grudge to employ fire as a destroying element, and not as a creating one. However, Heaven is omnipotent, and will find us an outlet. In the mean while, is it not beautiful to see five-million quintals of Rags picked annually from the Laystall; and annually, after being macerated, hot-pressed, printed-on, and sold,—returned thither; filling so many hungry mouths by the way? Thus is the Laystall, especially with its Rags or Clothes-rubbish, the grand Electric Battery, and Fountain-of-motion, from which and to which the Social Activities (like vitreous and resinous Electricities) circulate, in larger or smaller circles, through the mighty, billowy, stormtost Chaos of Life, which they keep alive![6]

As Carlyle points out, literature is literally a transformation and transmutation of old clothes. But his tone and comments on this phenomenon clearly indicate his opposition to the large supply of paper and of the rags for its production. He imagines that if the amount of printed paper were so mountainous as to block streets, the government would be forced to get rid of it; but he recognizes that industry will not respond to an overproduction of paper by burning it (as he evidently thinks it should), especially when the recycling of rags to make paper contributes economically to the feeding of "so many hungry mouths." Nonetheless, he believes that the overabundance of printed paper works as so much electrical agitation on society and keeps it in constant chaos. The passage suggests both Carlyle's wish that the political stimulation of society through print be controlled by restricting the raw materials supplying it and also his resignation to the existing productive forces in the market.

Accepting the impossibility of repressing the paper and publishing industries, Teufelsdröckh's clothes philosophy seeks to transcend the dandy's material consumption of fashions and so find the spiritual order of being and becoming that he believes to be present amidst the apparent "Chaos of Life," represented by the rags on the rubbish heap from which literature is created. "The Chaos of Life" to which the circulation of rags and paper contributes has both political and literary meanings in Carlyle's thinking. The years before the French Revolution Carlyle calls "the Paper Age," in which paper represents the worthlessness of French currency and liter-

6. *Sartor Resartus*, 45.

ature: "Bank-paper, wherewith you can still buy when there is no gold left; Book-paper, splendent with Theories, Philosophies, Sensibilities,—beautiful art, not only of revealing Thought, but also of so beautifully hiding from us the want of Thought! Paper is made from the *rags* of things that did once exist; there are endless excellences in Paper" (2:29). The French books that are devoid of thought are no better than the rags from which they are made. In a similar metaphoric and ironic vein, Carlyle later comments on Teufelsdröckh's tour of Monmouth Street's old clothes market: "Might we but fancy it to have been even in Monmouth Street, at the bottom of our own English 'ink-sea,' that this remarkable Volume first took being, and shot forth its salient point in his Soul,—as in Chaos did the Egg of Eros, one day to be hatched into a Universe!"[7] As Carlyle points out, the "ink-sea" of publishing has its chaotic source in the old clothes of Monmouth Street and the rags of the rubbish heap. Similarly, Teufelsdröckh's autobiography is contained in "six considerable PAPER-BAGS," which are filled with "miscellaneous masses of Sheets, and oftener Shreds and Snips."[8] In Carlyle's vision, literature is materially connected to and a phoenix-like reincarnation of the dandy's consumption.

II

Given the seductive possibility but great unlikelihood of large financial returns from writing, Carlyle became alienated from his own work. In his notebooks Carlyle observes that there are "plenty of Magazine Editors applying to me; indeed sometimes pestering me. Do not like to break with any; yet must not close with any. Strange state of Literature, periodical and other: A man must just lay out his manufacture in one of those Old-Clothes shops, and see whether any one will buy it. The Editor has little to do with the matter, except as Commercial Broker; he sells it and pays you for it."[9] Carlyle is bothered that his new ideas must be sold alongside worn ideas recycled by others. In his analysis he reduces periodicals literally to the old clothes from which they are made. Like the raw materials from which books are made, texts themselves are seen as discards from the author's desk and are nothing more than used garments in a resale shop. He did not feel that his own work was suited to the periodical format and foregrounds the problem of publishing original ideas serially in the second chapter of *Sartor Resartus*, "Editorial Difficulties":

7. *Sartor Resartus*, 243.
8. Ibid., 77–78.
9. Entry of January 13, 1832, *Two Note Books of Thomas Carlyle*, 231–32.

The first thought naturally was to publish Article after Article on this remark-able Volume, in such widely-circulating Critical Journals as the Editor might stand connected with, or by money or love procure access to. But, on the other hand, was it not clear that such matter as must here be revealed, and treated of, might endanger the circulation of any Journal extant? If, indeed, all party-divisions in the State, could have been abolished, Whig, Tory, and Radical, embracing in discrepant union; and all the Journals of the Nation could have been jumbled into one Journal, and the Philosophy of Clothes poured forth in incessant torrents therefrom, the attempt had seemed possible. But, alas, what vehicle of that sort have we, except *Fraser's Magazine?* A vehicle all strewed (figuratively speaking) with the maddest Waterloo-Crackers, explod-ing distractively and destructively, wheresoever the mystified passenger stands or sits; nay, in any case, understood to be, of late years, a vehicle full to overflowing, and inexorably shut![10]

This is ironic discourse, since, of course, *Sartor Resartus* was being first published serially in *Fraser's Magazine.* But Carlyle rightly points to the editorial risk involved in publishing so experimental and odd a work as Teufelsdröckh's biography, and to the difficulty in reception that such a serious work as his own necessarily had in the context of the firecrackers "exploding distractively and destructively" around the reader in the jour-nal. As he indicates, the reception of his work is further complicated since that response is focused by the existing ideological and political viewpoints that the periodical journals reflect and embody, and since he is seeking to transcend such divisions in his discourse.

As the passage reflects, Carlyle was bothered by the predominance of the periodicals in the writing market. He especially detested their demand for essays because they encouraged the author to chop up his thought into pieces: "One *has* no right vehicle: you must throw your ware into one of those dog's-meat carts, such as travel the public streets, and get it sold there, be it carrion or not."[11] In this system of publication, he feels, one's ideas become "dog's meat," reduced by the need to slice them into pieces so that they can be consumed. Carlyle displays here his intense distaste for the production of such mental hamburger and his obvious dislike of the reading public that willingly consumes its literature in periodical form. Typical of his feelings on the subject are his remarks on "The Signs of the Times," which he had published in 1829 in the *Edinburgh Review*: "Bad in general; but the best I could make it under such incubus influences."[12]

10. *Sartor Resartus*, 10–11.
11. Carlyle to John A. Carlyle, January 10, 1832, *Collected Letters of Thomas and Jane Welsh Carlyle*, 6:85.
12. *Two Note Books*, 140.

Later, in "The Hero as Man of Letters" (1841), he speaks of "that waste chaos of Authorship by trade" (5:184), implying that the production of books from rags also involves a wastage of the human spirit.

Indeed, once Carlyle thinks of writing solely for money, he thinks of trash, of literature reduced to material leftover. Writing in 1831, he declares, "I have said a thousand times, when you would not believe me, that the trade of Literature was worse as a trade than that of honest Street Sweeping," and further on in the same letter he adds that "I could also prove that a life of Scribbling is among the worst possible for cultivating Thought, what is noblest and the only noble thing in us: your ideas never get root, cannot be *sown* but are ground down from day to day."[13] The street sweeping and grinding grain to which he compares periodical writing signify the trivial character of ideas produced to earn one's daily bread. Speaking of poetry written for the popular market, in *Past and Present* (1843), he intones similarly: "Thy No-Thing of an Intended Poem, O Poet who hast looked merely to reviewers, copyrights, booksellers, popularities, behold it has not yet become a Thing; for the truth is not in it! Though printed, hotpressed, reviewed, celebrated, sold to the twentieth edition: what is all that? The Thing, in philosophical uncommercial language, is still a Nothing, mostly semblance and deception of the sight;—benign Oblivion incessantly gnawing at it, impatient till Chaos, to which it belongs, do reabsorb it!" (10:205). Momentary celebrity with the reading public is no protection against being forgotten by posterity. For Carlyle a work in accord with the demand of the publishing market is doomed to oblivion since he thinks it is a product of chaos, perhaps enjoying a brief vogue but ultimately made from nothing and returning to nothing. The recurring metaphor of the popular writer's work being eaten by time underlines his insistence upon truths that transcend the marketplace.

Given his view of the publishing market, it is understandable that as soon as he could afford to devote less time to periodical writing, Carlyle gave his full time to writing his *French Revolution* (1837). Once writers, like Carlyle, saw that some of their number were able to wrest a realm of freedom from the market and could make enough to live as gentlemen, they naturally aspired to transcend the conditions of literary production altogether; and, like Shelley, they envisioned themselves as the "unacknowledged legislators of the world," exempt from the demands of any particular audience and claiming that literary value could not be determined by the publishing market. But the great historical irony has been that Carlyle's

13. Carlyle to John A. Carlyle of February 26, 1831, *Collected Letters*, 5:237.

works most insulated from public pressure—his *French Revolution* and *Frederick the Great* (1858–65)—have proven to be among his least enduring, and are now more often cited as an index of his political views than read for their historical insight.

As one might expect, there are Continental parallels to Carlyle's feeling. While he was mortally ill, Beethoven threw aside one of Scott's novels in disgust and exclaimed, "Why the fellow writes for money."[14] In his "Debates on the Freedom of the Press" written in 1842 for the *Rheinische Zeitung*, Marx says that he believes "the writer must earn in order to be able to live and write, but he must by no means live and write to earn."[15] He feels that "the writer does not at all look on his work as a means. It is an end in itself; it is so little a means for him himself and for others that, if need be, he sacrifices his existence to its existence."[16] Similarly, Kierkegaard writing in 1846 says, "That there are publishers, that there are men whose entire existence expresses the fact that books are merchandise and an author a merchant, is a completely immoral state of affairs."[17] The alienation of such authors ultimately represents a desire to deny the dependence of ideas upon material form and thus upon the distributive economy of the marketplace.

The aesthetic costs associated with periodical publication stemmed from writing's having become a perishable commodity with a short reading life. Because it is tied to events of the moment and often as a review to the latest publications, periodical writing can rarely transcend its particular time. In *The French Revolution* Carlyle thinks about the brief vogue of revolutionary journalism and addresses the man of letters who hopes to find immortality in writing: "Nay what, O thou immortal Man of Letters, is Writing itself but Speech conserved for a time? The Placard Journal conserved it for one day; some Books conserve it for a matter of ten years; nay some for three thousand: but what then?" (3:28). As far as Carlyle is concerned, the writer has no chance against the long perspective of eternity. The author's hope for immortality is a vain one. Speaking, in contrast, of his father who had been a mason in Nithsdale, Scotland, Carlyle remarks in his *Reminiscences* that "a noble craft it is, that of a mason: a good Building will last longer than most Books, than one Book of a million."[18]

The small chance of writing anything that will live long makes Carlyle

14. Quoted in Max Horkheimer and Theodor W. Adorno, *Dialectic of Enlightenment*, 157.
15. "Debates on the Freedom of the Press," in Karl Marx and Friedrich Engels, *Collected Works*, 1:174.
16. Ibid., 175.
17. *Journals of Søren Kierkegaard*, 155.
18. *Reminiscences*, 24.

despair; and the journalistic mode of his own moment contributes to his feeling. Books are now written to have an immediate appeal, he believes, and writers have adopted a satiric mode that cannot last because it depends so much on the reader's knowledge of the moment. Commenting on the first numbers of *Fraser's Magazine*, he observes that they are "on the whole such a hurlyburly of rhodomontade, punch, loyalty, and Saturnalian Toryism as eye hath not seen."[19] The journal's chaotic style has originated, he thinks, from the modern means of production: "a certain quickness, fluency of banter, not excluding sharp insight, and Merry-Andrew Drollery, and even Humour, are available here; however, the grand requisite seems to be Impudence, and a fearless committing of yourself to talk in your Drink.—Literature has nothing to do with this, but printing has; and Printing is now no more the peculiar symbol and livery of Literature than writing was in Gutenberg's day."[20] The fashionable "livery" of modern printing has been forced upon literary talent in the periodicals, whose mode requires in his eyes a demeaning public servitude. Here Carlyle is clearly distancing himself from Maclise's fictional authorial collective of "The Fraserians" (fig. 2), of which he is portrayed as being a full member. Further, he notes that what passes for literary activity is really a record of fluent "banter" and drunken "talk," since what is demanded is not so much careful thought but filled sheets ready for the press.

But this fashionable straitjacket is not new, for he laments that the man of letters "from of old has had to cramp himself into strange shapes: the world knows not well at any time what to do with him, so foreign is his aspect in the world!" (5:155). Speaking of Samuel Johnson, for instance, Carlyle portrays him "in his poverty, in his dust and dimness, with the sick body and the rusty coat" and exults that "he made it do for him, like a brave man" (5:184). Johnson's rusty coat is emblematic for Carlyle of the author's trials in the service of booksellers. Since the real literary figure has always been so alien and has never been comfortable in any existing form, the modern periodical form is for Carlyle no less cramping and distorting than any in literary history.

III

Periodical reviewing in its self-conscious and critical reflection upon literary production becomes typical for Carlyle of the writer's modern disease. His diagnosis leads him to develop a prose style that seeks to inocu-

19. Entry of September 9, 1830, *Two Note Books*, 170.
20. Ibid., 170–71.

late readers against this disease and to get them to stop thinking and instead to start doing.[21] However, what exactly Carlyle is teaching readers to do as they read his writing has not been adequately described. As I will try to show through an analysis of how the reader is meant to respond to his syntax,[22] Carlyle's prose style is one of familiar anticlimax: readers find that they already know enough, that they have known what they need to know from the very beginning, and that consecutive reasoning leads to logically inconsequential outcomes and to the conviction that one's original spiritual intuitions were already sufficient to order one's actions.

In "Characteristics" (1831), he sees reviewing as a kind of self-conscious and inflationary cannibalizing in which literature feeds upon itself instead of producing original works, implicitly subjecting itself more to the criterion of the marketplace than to independent creators:

> Far be it from us to disparage our own craft, whereby we have our living! Only we must note these things: that Reviewing spreads with strange vigour; that such a man as Byron reckons the Reviewer and the Poet equal; that at the last Leipzig Fair, there was advertised a Review of Reviews. By and by it will be found that all Literature has become one boundless self-devouring Review; and, as in London routs, we have to *do* nothing, but only to *see* others do nothing.—Thus does Literature also, like a sick thing, superabundantly "listen to itself." (28:25)

The prospect of a review of reviews points to the reproductive multiplication of the publishing marketplace, which advertises and feeds upon itself in order to sell itself in an acceptable format to the reading public. The

21. Previous discussions of Carlyle's style and particularly of his syntax are largely impressionistic. John Holloway, for instance, says that "there is little of sustained or close-knit argument demanding concentrated, dispassionate study; the reader is hurried, as if by an all-pervading and irresistible violence, from one problem to another" (*Victorian Sage: Studies in Argument*, 27). Similarly, G. B. Tennyson observes that "his style has a tortuous syntax, one that breaks and alters course, one that seems to have suffered an inward explosion" (*Sartor Called Resartus: The Genesis, Structure, and Style of Thomas Carlyle's First Major Work*, 244). The tendency to reduce Carlyle's style to a feeling arising from it or to its content is perhaps best evidenced by George Levine, who says that Carlyle's "mannerism is a reflex of the substance" and that in Carlyle's prose there is an "insistence on *doing*, and on the difficulty of doing" ("Use and Abuse of Carlylese," 104).

22. My approach here is a modified version of the reader-response analysis first employed by Stanley Fish in *Self-Consuming Artifacts: The Experience of Seventeenth-Century Literature*. In general, I agree that Carlyle's familiar anticlimax is a species of ideological rhetoric, but I think that Carlyle's prose finds its audience instead of creating one, as Jon P. Klancher suggests in "Reading the Social Text: Power, Signs, and Audience in Early Nineteenth-Century Prose." After all, Carlyle goes unappreciated until the appearance of his *French Revolution* in 1837, and only with his series of lectures in London following the publication of that work does he acquire a devoted readership. The height of Carlyle's influence comes in the 1840s, not in the days of his *Edinburgh Review* articles. Klancher argues that the author creates his audience by means of projection (*The Making of English Reading Audiences, 1790–1832*).

review tends to mediate the reception of works so that many readers now "do nothing" and only read the review of a book instead of the book itself, which, as Carlyle ironically implies, the author will be lucky to have even his reviewer read. Worse, some authors like Byron are ready to grant the same literary status to the reviewer as the poet, when the reviewer merely feeds on the ideas and works of others. But Carlyle's indignation is also indicative of his being disturbed by the insight that the rise of the reviews is evidence of the material and economic character of modern literature, that modern literature not only represents nature but also literature itself. Carlyle's metaphor of self-cannibalizing texts points again to the voracious readers who were willing to read almost anything whether "it be carrion or not." Indeed, given the proliferation of works to be read, "now your Reviewer is a mere *taster*; who tastes, and says, by the evidence of such a palate, such tongue, as he has got, It is good, It is bad" (28:24). Finally, this self-consciousness of literature is not so much evidence of the imaginative capacity of man as proof of the imagination's reluctant relationship with the materiality of its production and its reception in the marketplace.

Moreover, every metaphysical worry stems from the repetition of print and its reinforcement of doubt through the multiplication of perspectives. For Carlyle, this self-consciousness feeding upon itself uses up the mountain of rags and results inevitably in too much inquiry and doubt:

> Never since the beginning of Time was there, that we hear or read of, so intensely self-conscious a Society. Our whole relations to the Universe and to our fellow-man have become an Inquiry, a Doubt; nothing will go on of its own accord, and do its function quietly; but all things must be probed into, the whole working of man's world be anatomically studied. Alas, anatomically studied, that it may be medically aided! (28:19)

Carlyle employs his skeptical, ironic anticlimax against inquiry, which is reduced by the appositive to "doubt." Instead of acting, of going on quietly, everything is now examined and paralyzed. Through scientific inquiry all things are reduced to dreary anatomy and, he believes, become diseased in the process.

Solutions are then prescribed for problems about which one would otherwise know nothing:

> The whole Life of Society must now be carried on by drugs: doctor after doctor appears with his nostrum, of Coöperative Societies, Universal Suffrage, Cottage-and-Cow systems, Repression of Population, Vote by Ballot. To such height has the dyspepsia of Society reached; as indeed the constant grinding internal pain, or from time to time the mad spasmodic throes, of all Society do otherwise too mournfully indicate. (28:20)

Intellectual constipation comes from having had too much to read and too many cures for the ills thus created. From the word "drugs," the reader anticipates the worthlessness of the subsequent catalogue of nostrums. The redundancy within the sentence thus reassures any reader who may doubt Carlyle's diagnosis. By the time one arrives at the passage's end, Carlyle's elaborate dyspeptic metaphor has already been confirmed by the preceding ill-digested series of proposed solutions to society's disease. Further, the self-conscious internalization of inquiry characteristic of metaphysics has also affected religion:

> Religion, like all else, is conscious of itself, listens to itself; it becomes less and less creative, vital; more and more mechanical. Considered as a whole, the Christian Religion of late ages has been continually dissipating itself into Metaphysics; and threatens now to disappear, as some rivers do, in deserts of barren sand. (28:23)

The metaphor of the river disappearing beneath the sands is a figure of anticlimax and dissipation, of Religion losing itself in thought, when it should not so much think as believe. At the same time the anticlimaxes ("it becomes less and less creative, vital; more and more mechanical"—each syntactic member losing energy and significance) are further evidence of the adequacy of faith and the aridity of metaphysics. Modern religion has gotten into difficulty, according to Carlyle, because it has been listening to reason instead of relying on faith.

Indeed, although metaphysical questions about the nature of things inevitably arise, Carlyle believes we need not trouble ourselves with pursuing the answers:

> The disease of Metaphysics, accordingly, is a perennial one. In all ages, those questions of Death and Immortality, Origin of Evil, Freedom and Necessity, must, under new forms, anew make their appearance; ever, from time to time, must the attempt to shape for ourselves some Theorem of the Universe be repeated. And ever unsuccessfully: for what Theorem of the Infinite can the Finite render complete? We, the whole species of Mankind, and our whole existence and history, are but a floating speck in the illimitable ocean of the All; yet *in* that ocean; indissoluble portion thereof, partaking of its infinite tendencies: borne this way and that by its deep-swelling tides, and grand ocean currents;—of which what faintest chance is there that we should ever exhaust the significance, ascertain the goings and comings? (28:25–26)

The opening declaration that the "disease of Metaphysics . . . is a perennial one" is immediately comforting. Carlyle declares that metaphysics is a disease of thought, something to be cured and not to be pursued and caught by the reader. Further, it is not new, so that we already know all we need to know about it from the very beginning of Carlyle's sentence. Everything else in the passage confirms readers in their initial response. Even the phrase "from time to time," while contributing nothing new to the thought, reassures us through its redundancy of our spiritual adequacy despite the failure of metaphysical investigation. Strikingly, our very inability to arrive at a "theorem of the Universe" is satisfying. Aware already of our finite nature, we cannot by definition include the infinite, and so, according to Carlyle, we thus already know everything we need to know. Indeed, we are already comfortably contained within the ocean of the "All."

This encompassing image thus makes repetition fathomable to belief while inexhaustible to reason and lets one ask the anticlimactic rhetorical question without having to worry. Resolutely unconscious of any irony, he believes we can take heart in our ignorance:

> About the grand Course of Providence, and his final Purposes with us, we can know nothing, or almost nothing: man begins in darkness, ends in darkness; mystery is everywhere around us and in us, under our feet, among our hands. Nevertheless so much has become evident to every one, that this wondrous Mankind is advancing somewhither; that at least all human things are, have been and forever will be, in Movement and Change;—as, indeed, for beings that exist in Time, by virtue of Time, and are made of Time, might have been long since understood. (28:37)

This passage seeks to assure us of the adequacy of our understanding even though we understand nothing. We are given in the opening prepositional phrase a sense of certainty that there is a "grand Course of Providence" and that God has for us "final Purposes." But beyond such knowledge, "we can know nothing, or almost nothing." The anticlimactic "or almost nothing" further underlines in its repetition our ignorance, for, Carlyle believes, our knowledge does not extend beyond the certainty that God has a plan for us. All of our experience (as well of our experience of the sentence) goes nowhere and ends where it begins, "in darkness."

Yet, the repetition of "nothing" and "darkness" paradoxically makes them palpable for "feet" and "hands." Carlyle suggests that even without looking into God's plans we already know enough since we exist and are conscious of our existence. We can know where we are and will be, and can know that we are going "somewhither" in "Time," as everyone should already understand. Where we are going does not matter, just that we are going. Our ignorance, then, is of no consequence and no cause for worry. For Carlyle the "truth" is a foregone conclusion: "Remarkable it is, truly, how everywhere the eternal fact begins again to be recognized, that there is a Godlike in human affairs; that God not only made us and beholds us, but is in us and around us; that the Age of Miracles, as it ever was, now is" (28:42). Since the "eternal fact" is already evident "everywhere," everything is anticlimax once one recognizes the "Godlike in human affairs." Divine intervention through miracles in the affairs of mankind is "as it ever was." But since we should have already known and believed that this has always been the case, the "now is" comes as an anticlimactic fulfillment. The repetition and redundancy serve to comfort and reassure those who might have worried from the elaborate appearance of the syntax and punctuation that they would be surprised to learn something new from Carlyle. All readers of Carlyle can rest easy here.

In the coda to "Characteristics" Carlyle tells us that we already have had revealed to us all that we need to know. For with God, says Carlyle, echoing the beginning of the Book of John, has come our light: "Light has come into the world; to such as love Light, so as Light must be loved, with a boundless all-doing, all-enduring love" (28:43). The purpose and task of mankind, Carlyle believes, is already clear: to love God as our revelation. In contrast, he underlines the anticlimactic nature of man's efforts to understand the Infinite: "For the rest, let that vain struggle to read the mystery of the Infinite cease to harass us. It is a mystery which, through all ages, we shall only read here a line of, there another line of" (28:43). Once we have understood that the Infinite is a mystery, nothing more is worth pursuing, for all our efforts will only yield "a line" here and there, the clauses further emphasizing the insignificance of this activity by ending with "of." Carlyle's subsequent question reinforces the adequacy of our belief: "Do we not already know that the name of the Infinite is GOOD, is GOD?" (28:43). Since we already know the answer to the question, we don't need to worry about understanding anything more than God's name, so far as Carlyle is concerned. In fact, it would appear that we are battling in an unfathomable psychomachia: "Here on Earth we are Soldiers, fighting in a foreign land; that understand not the plan of the campaign, and have no need to understand it; seeing well what is at our hand to be done. Let us do it like Soldiers; with submission, with courage, with a heroic joy" (28:43). Earth for us is "a foreign land," about which we need know nothing. As heavenly soldiers, we are fighting in a spiritual war in which faith and belief are everything. Although the "it" may seem mysterious, we need only to "do it," for we already know that we are to love God. For Carlyle the doing and dying of mankind has as its proper aim not understanding abstruse theological matters but fighting against evil in order to retain one's faith in God.

Toward the end of "Characteristics" Carlyle speaks of those whose hard fate it has been to struggle in the world without a divine vision and discovers Hazlitt in one of the lower circles of living hell: "In lower regions, how many a poor Hazlitt must wander on God's verdant earth, like the Unblest on burning deserts; passionately dig wells, and draw up only the dry quicksand; believe that he is seeking Truth, yet only wrestle among endless Sophisms, doing desperate battle as with specter-hosts; and die and make no sign" (28:32). Carlyle's anticlimactic antitheses shrewdly reproduce the disappointing experience of reading Hazlitt. For as "Unblest" suggests, Carlyle believes that the mark of Cain foredooms Hazlitt's efforts to unfruitfulness, to the constant discovery of his own ironic negativity. Like all of the thinkers whom Carlyle deplores, Hazlitt questions too much. Carlyle believes instead that "the healthy Understanding, we should say, is not the Logical, argumentative, but the Intuitive; for the end of Understanding is not to prove and find reasons, but to know and believe" (28:5). As with most Carlylean sentences, the climax of the thought is reached midsentence after the first antithesis, where we find that true understanding is intuitive. Readers should be able to anticipate and know because they already believe; hence, according to Carlyle, the revelation of reason is necessarily an anticlimax that brings us back to our beginnings. Indeed, he had earlier observed in "The Signs of the Times" that the mechanical character of the age is clear in the inordinate attention it gives to logic: "Intellect, the power man has of knowing and believing, is now nearly synonymous with Logic, or the mere power of arranging and communicating" (27:74). But the organization and development of thought matters less than its spiritual result, how one arrives at the truth less than the truth itself, how well one can convince others less than how well one intuitively understands oneself. Such an understanding is "healthy" because it illustrates the Physician's Aphorism with which Carlyle opens "Characteristics": "The healthy know not of their health, but only the sick" (28:1). Because it is blissfully secure in its grasp of its religious beliefs, intellectual health for Carlyle is an unconscious condition and will remain sound so long as it is not infected by self-doubt.

IV

Although the Man of Letters is the modern hero of *On Heroes, Hero-Worship, and the Heroic in the History of Mankind* (1841), he is himself a species of anticlimax, since he "from of old has had to cramp himself into strange shapes" (5:155). The writer represents the lack of direction of modern society: "He wanders like a wild Ishmaelite, in a world of which he is as the spiritual light, either the guidance or the misguidance" (5:159). The writer himself does not know where he is going. Often for Carlyle he is a blind man just exhibiting his intellectual strength like Samson fighting the Philistines. Consider Carlyle's thoughts on Bentham: "Benthamism is an *eyeless* Heroism: the Human Species, like a hapless blinded Samson grinding in the Philistine Mill, clasps convulsively the pillars of its Mill; brings huge ruin down, but ultimately deliverance withal" (5:173). The human species, inspired by a blind Bentham who cannot see the end of the political reforms he proposes, exerts itself to bring down the social structure. Carlyle employs the same figure again when he describes Samuel Johnson quitting his position as a school usher: "Young Samson will grind no more in the Philistine mill of Bosworth" (28:95). At the beginning of his long authorial struggle, Johnson cannot see his illustrious future.

From the beginning of his literary career, Carlyle recognized a social mobility of intellectual talent, of which he himself as the son of a stone mason was self-consciously representative. In his *Reminiscences* he gives this moving tribute to his father: "I can see my dear Father's Life in some measure as the sunk pillar on which mine was to rise and be built; the waters of Time have swelled up round his (as they will round mine); I can *see* it (all transfigured) though I *touch* it no longer. I might almost say his spirit seems to have entered into me (so clearly do I discern and love him); I seem to myself only the continuation, and *second volume* of my Father."[23] Built on the foundation of his father's life, Carlyle sees his own as an anticlimax, as only the "*second volume*" of his father's. The sinking of his father's pillar beneath the waters of time looks forward to the same thing happening to his own. In some sense he feels authored by his father. In earlier describing his father's presence in his family, Carlyle emphasizes the security of having been ruled by an iron will: "An inflexible element of Authority encircled us all; we felt from the first (a useful thing) that our own *wish* had often nothing to say in the matter."[24] From the beginning, Carlyle learned that his wishes would not be fulfilled. His intuitive knowledge of his father's authority thus parallels psychologically (not to say psychoanalytically) his assurance of God's. The effect of the anticlimactic rhetoric, however, whether in personal recollection or critical meditation, aims to reassure the reader that everything always has been settled "from the first."

Despite his social background, Carlyle adhered to a conservative social

23. *Reminiscences*, 33.
24. Ibid., 28.

philosophy which held that men of letters should seek to regulate the aspirations of the lower classes from which they came:

> There is clear truth in the idea that a struggle from the lower classes of society, towards the upper regions and rewards of society, must ever continue. Strong men are born there, who ought to stand elsewhere than there. The manifold, inextricably complex, universal struggle of these constitutes, and must constitute, what is called the progress of society. For Men of Letters, as for all other sorts of men. How to regulate that struggle? There is the whole question. To leave it as it is, at the mercy of blind Chance; a whirl of distracted atoms, one cancelling the other; one of the thousand arriving saved, nine-hundred-and-ninety-nine lost by the way; your royal Johnson languishing inactive in garrets, or harnessed to the yoke of Printer Cave; your Burns dying broken-hearted as a Gauger; your Rousseau driven into mad exasperation, kindling French Revolutions by his paradoxes: this, as we said, is clearly enough the *worst* regulation. The *best*, alas, is far from us! (5:167–68)

While the great man of letters may rise above the chaos of blind chance as Johnson did, there is always the chance that he may not be adequately recognized and rewarded, as happened with Burns, or that he may come to resent the existing order, as Rousseau did. While, no doubt, his interpretation accords too much political power to intellectual activity, Carlyle makes it clear he feels that the progress of society depends on the healthy psychology of its men of letters. He wants to regulate the struggle of intellectuals from the lower to the upper regions of society, since blind chance is all that now governs this struggle and hence the progress of society itself.

By implication it would seem that he would like to organize a system of intellectual rewards that would free future Johnsons from their garrets and from servitude to booksellers like Cave. Yet, Carlyle's admiration of Johnson is based upon Johnson's ability to rise on his own above both his physical deformities and the literary marketplace: "That waste chaos of Authorship by trade; that waste chaos of Scepticism in religion and politics, in life-theory and life-practice; in his poverty, in his dust and dimness, with the sick body and the rusty coat: he made it do for him, like a brave man" (5:184). Despite his indomitable spirit, authorship reduces Johnson to poverty, dust, dimness, and a rusty coat. Similarly, Carlyle observes that Burns' poetic work is disappointing: "His writings, all that he did under such obstructions, are only a poor fragment of him" (5:190). What might at first seem a triumph to the reader—"all that he *did* under such obstructions"— becomes anticlimactically "a poor fragment of him," as Burns is not adequately rewarded in the marketplace for his poetry.

The symbolic close of "The Hero as Man of Letters" suggests that however great the enlightenment provided by authors appears, it is ultimately short-lived and ornamental:

> Richter says, in the Island of Sumatra there is a kind of "Light-chafers," large Fire-flies, which people stick upon spits, and illuminate the ways with at night. Persons of condition can thus travel with a pleasant radiance, which they much admire. Great honour to the Fire-flies! But—!— (5:195)

Like the Sumatran fire-flies, men of letters are consumed by rich men who find their writings pleasant and admirable. But whatever honor gained from entertaining and enlightening a wealthy readership, the fire-flies have lost their independence and have been subjugated to the most trivial of purposes.

The self-conscious, antithetical, anticlimactic "But—" with which the chapter breaks off not only is symbolic generally of the inconsequence of the efforts of the man of letters but also, more particularly, represents for Carlyle the fate of Friedrich Schlegel. In his "Characteristics," which was ostensibly a review in part of Schlegel's *Philosophische Vorlesungen* (1830), he comments on the end of that volume:

> A solemn mournful feeling comes over us when we see this last Work of Friedrich Schlegel, the unwearied seeker, end abruptly in the middle; and, as if he *had not* yet found, as if emblematically of much, end with an "*Aber—*," with a "But—"! This was the last word that came from the Pen of Friedrich Schlegel: about eleven at night he wrote it down, and there paused sick; at one in the morning, Time for him had merged itself in Eternity; he was, as we say, no more" (28:35).[25]

As seen by Carlyle, Schlegel's inquiry has led him nowhere, inasmuch as it has ended in the middle and has found nothing. Although Schlegel has been "unwearied" in his search for truth, he has not rested, as Carlyle believes he should have done, in the Bible's "Seek, and ye shall find," in the comfort of Christian faith. The anticlimactic "but" is thus symbolic of Schlegel's physical and metaphysical disease, when at his inquiry's unwitting end, he "there paused sick." The "but" is only ironically emblematical "of much," for Schlegel himself had not been able to finish his search, has

---

25. For the influence of Friedrich Schlegel on Carlyle, see Elizabeth M. Vida, *Romantic Affinities: German Authors and Carlyle,* 9–22. Chris R. Vanden Bossche emphasizes how Carlyle did not portray the man of letters "as the savior of the modern era" but "as a symptom of its problems" (*Carlyle and the Search for Authority,* 99).

ended with an original, unhappy contrariness, and is now "no more." This biographical example sadly underlines Carlyle's general proposition about all metaphysics: "Metaphysical Speculation, as it begins in No or Nothingness, so it must needs end in Nothingness; circulates and must circulate in endless vortices; creating, swallowing—itself" (28:27). By beginning with "No," metaphysics condemns itself to a circular negativity and ends where it began. For Carlyle, thought cannot go beyond its presuppositions; and those who seek to do so end in failure. Hence the great significance of Schlegel's final "but—," which takes Schlegel back at the end to his beginning negativity.

V

Carlyle's anticlimactic style clearly addresses a reading public that wishes to understand from reading what it already believes to be true. It reassures them that if they recognize the existence and omnipotence of God they will understand enough to live properly; and it constantly reinforces Carlyle's doctrine that religious belief is more important than skeptical inquiry. Moreover, it illustrates the truth of Bulwer-Lytton's comments in *England and the English* about how writers adapted their prose styles to the level of understanding they expected of their audiences: "It is natural that writers should be ambitious of creating a sensation: a sensation is produced by gaining the ear, not of the few, but the many; the style most frequently aimed at: hence the profusion of amusing, familiar, and superficial writings. People complain of it, as if it were a proof of degeneracy in the knowledge of authors—it is a proof of the increased number of readers." As he later observes, "the temper of the popular meeting is unavoidably caught by the mind that addresses it."[26] For Bulwer-Lytton, too, as for Carlyle, style has become a function of scale and of audience. The larger the public one wished to address, the more accommodating the style had to be. By 1850 this meant that the newspaper style was the most popular, that the reviews and magazines were rapidly becoming middle brow, and that soon scholarly journals would assume the high intellectual ground. One observes, for instance, that the brevity of Macaulay was more popular than the complications of Carlyle. Still, as long as the essay remained a popular form, essay writers modified their styles and adopted an anticipatory rhetoric, which could allow them to retain the syntactical complexity stemming from the

26. *England and the English*, 2:119.

balanced antithesis of Johnsonian and late-eighteenth-century prose. They also employed the strategy of anticlimactic redundancy, as Carlyle did, to underline their points. That few traces of this style appear in the prose of Arnold, Newman, and Ruskin suggests that the initial era of accommodation, occasioned by the expansion of the market for the essay and by an intellectual anxiety about the political and intellectual dangers of a much enlarged reading public, had ended long before the 1860s.

Thomas Malton after Georgiana Keate, *Hall's Library at Margate* (1789). Hand-colored etching and aquatint.
Reproduced courtesy of the Yale Center for British Art, Paul Mellon Collection.

5

The Economy of Novel Reading: Jane Austen and the Circulating Library

---

The author is already known to the public by the two novels announced in her title-page, and both, the last especially [Pride and Prejudice], *attracted, with justice, an attention from the public far superior to what is granted to the ephemeral productions which supply the regular demand of watering-places and circulating libraries.*

—Sir Walter Scott, Review of *Emma*

Many readers will have first learned of the circulating library from the scene in *Pride and Prejudice* during which Mr. Collins is asked to read to the Bennet family after dinner:

> Mr. Collins readily assented, and a book was produced; but on beholding it, (for every thing announced it to be from a circulating library,) he started back, and begging pardon, protested that he never read novels.—Kitty stared at him, and Lydia exclaimed.—Other books were produced and after some deliberation he chose Fordyce's Sermons.[1]

Lydia soon interrupts this solemnity and offends Mr. Collins sufficiently so that he abandons his reading. This passage suggests that books from a

---

1. *The Novels of Jane Austen*, ed. Chapman, 2:68. Further citations of Austen's novels in my text refer to volume and page numbers in this edition.

125

circulating library were identifiable from a distance, that such books were likely to be novels, and that stuffy clergymen did not read them, while young ladies read little else. Moreover, it is evident that this scene of reading and, indeed, the novel itself are embedded within a system of book distribution centering on the circulating library.

As is clear elsewhere in Austen's novels and especially in *Sanditon,* the circulating libraries made reading fashionable when books were very expensive. By 1800 most copies of a novel's edition were sold to the libraries, which were flourishing businesses to be found in every major English city and town, and which promoted the sale of books during a period when their price rose relative to the cost of living. The libraries created a market for the publishers' product and encouraged readers to read more by charging them an annual subscription fee that would entitle them to check out a specified number of volumes at one time. The very existence of the libraries, though, reflected the relatively low marginal utility of rereading novels for contemporary readers, the general view that novel reading was a luxury, and the social subordination of reading to the concerns of everyday life. An investigation of the history of circulating libraries and a contextual analysis of the references made to the libraries in Austen's works and letters will reveal the underlying economy of novel reading, buying, and selling during the early nineteenth century.[2]

I

A circulating library was a private business that rented books. There are records of booksellers renting books in the late seventeenth century, and

---

2. This approach has certain affinities with Robert Darnton's synthesis of publishing history and contemporary reception that reconstructs the consciousness of late-eighteenth-century French readers in "Readers Respond to Rousseau: The Fabrication of Romantic Sensitivity," in *The Great Cat Massacre and Other Episodes in French Cultural History,* 215–56; and with that of Alvin B. Kernan, who considers the formation of the professional writer's self-consciousness in terms of the "social construction" of literature in *Printing Technology, Letters, and Samuel Johnson.* My method is more oriented toward questions of form as articulated by the publishing market than is that of Jerome McGann, who considers the context of literary publication as ideological staging and who analyzes the history of literary reception as a register of ideological differences in *The Beauty of Inflections: Literary Investigations in Historical Method and Theory.* The use of publishing history as a basis for or a supplement to literary investigation has been variously labeled as "sociology of literature" and a species of "new historicism"; see John Sutherland, "Publishing History: A Hole at the Centre of Literary Sociology," and David Simpson, "Literary Criticism and the Return to 'History.'" Interested in larger realms outside literature, both Sutherland and Simpson seek to subsume recent literary studies making use of publishing history within their own theoretical frameworks and agenda, but only Simpson, it seems to me, sees this kind of criticism as worth pursuing in itself and accurately portrays

the practice of renting out books goes back to medieval times in university towns. But the circulating library as a separate establishment run by a bookseller or entrepreneur does not make its appearance until the early eighteenth century.[3] In 1740 Dr. Samuel Fancourt, a dissenting divine, was among the first to use the term when he advertised a circulating library in Salisbury that had begun in 1735 and that consisted primarily of religious books and pamphlets. In 1742 he moved his enterprise to London, where it flourished until his death. There were apparently established booksellers in London already renting books who took Fancourt's business as a model and soon were calling their firms circulating libraries.[4] By 1775 many such libraries were doing business in Bath and London, while others were to be found in the larger towns and in all the watering places and seaside resorts where the wealthy and fashionable congregated. In 1801 there were said to be one thousand circulating libraries in England.[5] The circulating libraries were at first natural outgrowths of bookselling, but by the beginning of the nineteenth century had often become enterprises in their own right. They were ultimately driven out by the rise of public libraries in England, but they dominated the market for fiction throughout the nineteenth century and were important until the 1930s, when Mudie's, the largest and most famous, closed.[6]

The circulating libraries were associated with leisure and were to be found in the resorts for the wealthy, where the characters of Austen's rural gentry usually encounter them. In the new resort of Sanditon, for example, there is Mrs. Whitby's. At Brighton, Lydia Bennet visits one of the town's

the origins of the recent critical use of publishing history in attempts to ground historically reception theory and literary self-consciousness.

3. For the history of the circulating library, see Alan Dugald McKillop, "English Circulating Libraries, 1725–50"; Hilda M. Hamlyn, "Eighteenth-Century Circulating Libraries in England"; Philip Kaufman, "The Community Library: A Chapter in English Social History"; Devendra P. Varma, *The Evergreen Tree of Diabolical Knowledge*; Guinevere L. Griest, *Mudie's Circulating Library and the Victorian Novel*; and Q. D. Leavis, *Fiction and the Reading Public*, 3–18. Since Varma's and Kaufman's histories end at 1800 and Griest's begins with the founding of Mudie's in the 1840s, there is a gap in the accounts of some forty years during the industrialization of book publishing. The only attempt to place Austen's novels within the context of the circulating libraries is R. W. Chapman's sketch "Reading and Writing" in his edition of her works (1:422).

4. On Fancourt, see Varma, 26–28; M. J. Crump and R. J. Goulden describe a printed catalogue of Fancourt's Salisbury library and print the library's rules of 1739 in "Four Library Catalogues of Note"; and see Elizabeth A. Swaim, "Circulating Library: Antedatings of the O.E.D." Under combinations of *circulating* the OED cites Fancourt's 1742 advertisement for his London library as the term's first appearance.

5. *Monthly Magazine* 11 (1801): 238.

6. Griest, 17–27. It is interesting to note, as Griest points out, that both Boots and Harrod's originally began as circulating libraries before moving into their present lines of business.

circulating libraries, which the contemporary *Guide to All the Watering and Sea-Bathing Places* says "are frequented by all fashionable people."[7] Indeed, the *Guide* tells us that "the taste and character of individuals may be better learned in a library than in a ball-room; and they who frequent the former in preference to the latter, frequently enjoy the most rational and the most permanent pleasure."[8] The *Guide* carefully describes the circulating libraries of the watering places and the amusements they can supply, lamenting, for instance, the location of the library at Lyme Regis that Mrs. Musgrove patronizes in *Persuasion*: "*Lyme* has a small Assembly-room, Card-room, and Billiard-table, conveniently arranged under one roof; and had the Library been joined to it, all the amusement which the place can furnish would have been comprised in one building."[9] The influence of such guidebook accounts is evident in Austen's description of the buildings of Sanditon close to the sea:

> Trafalgar House, on the most elevated spot on the Down was a light elegant Building, standing in a small Lawn with a very young plantation round it, about an hundred yards from the brow of a steep, but not very lofty Cliff—and the nearest to it, of every Building, excepting one short row of smart-looking Houses, called the Terrace, with a broad walk in front, aspiring to be the Mall of the Place. In this row were the best Milliner's shop & the Library—a little detached from it, the Hotel & Billiard Room—Here began the Descent to the Beach, & to the Bathing Machines—& this was therefore the favourite spot for Beauty & Fashion.[10]

As this social map of Sanditon suggests, the circulating library was expected to be centrally located in a resort's organization of pleasure.

The elegance of real seaside resorts in Austen's novels can be measured by descriptions in contemporary guides of their libraries. Cromer, which Mr. Woodhouse particularly recommends, has a nondescript circulating library, while Southend, where Mr. and Mrs. John Knightley went in the autumn for the sea air and bathing, not only has the virtue of being closer to London but also has a library in "an elegant building, somewhat in the gothic stile . . . beautifully situated on the brow of the hill."[11] The attractions of Ramsgate, where Mr. Wickham attempted to seduce Georgiana

---

7. [John Feltham], *A Guide to All the Watering and Sea-Bathing Places* (1803), 78.
8. Ibid.
9. [Feltham] (1806), 264.
10. *Minor Works*, ed. Chapman, 384.
11. [Feltham] (1806), 199 and 384. These descriptions remain the same throughout the *Guide*'s many subsequent editions; see, for example, the 1824 edition, 169 and 106.

Darcy, include Mrs. Witherden's library and Burgess's library, the latter having "a good stationery and toyshop attached to it."[12] And one learns that if Frank Churchill and Jane Fairfax felt forced to communicate while in public by playing with jumbled letters at Weymouth, they might have done so in the card room above Hervey's library in the Esplanade, which is "large, and elegantly furnished."[13] Austen herself is known to have seen the inside of several of them. In 1807 she tells Cassandra about changing books at one of Southampton's circulating libraries.[14] Writing in 1814 to her niece about a story the young lady had written, she comments, "I am not sensible of any Blunders about Dawlish. The Library was particularly pitiful & wretched 12 years ago, & is not likely to have anybody's publications."[15] The *Guide* evidently concurs, for it mentions no library and considers the place a disappointing resort, perhaps because it specialized in "all the long train of complaints known under the vulgar name of declines."[16]

In the resorts the circulating libraries became fashionable daytime lounges where ladies could see others and be seen, where raffles were held and games were played, and where expensive merchandise could be purchased. Perhaps Thomas Malton's 1789 print of *Hall's Library at Margate* after a drawing by Georgiana Keate gives the best contemporary picture of such a library (fig. 3). The library's reading room in the foreground has only two gentlemen reading newspapers, but has many other patrons strolling about and talking to one another, while one child plays with a dog, a young boy practices dance steps, and a young girl twirls a toy windmill on a bench. On the far right, one can see books arranged on open shelves, from which one lady is selecting a volume. More important, evidently, are the two glass-covered cases of silverware next to the bookshelves, which have a counter in front of them at which an attendant is standing to take orders. In the background at the picture's center is a window display of toys, from which a model boat is being taken down to be given to the outstretched arms of a child. The books are only one of several kinds of merchandise available in the library, and are clearly minor attractions compared to the patrons themselves, most of whom are enjoying one another's company.

12. [Feltham] (1815), 415.
13. Ibid., 493. This card room is later noted as regularly being used as a ballroom in the winter months; see [Feltham] (1824), 362.
14. January 7, 1807, *Jane Austen's Letters to Her Sister Cassandra and Others*, 173. (Hereafter *Letters.*)
15. August 10, 1814, *Letters*, 393.
16. [Feltham] (1803), 197.

Even in Meryton the local library is quite a social attraction. Not only are the novels that Mr. Collins never reads to be found there, but, as Lydia notes, Colonel Forster and Captain Carter are seen "very often standing in Clarke's library" (2:30).

Since it was the custom to subscribe to the libraries immediately upon arrival in the watering places and resorts, their subscription books became a useful guide to who was in town. In *Sanditon* the subscription book is used this way. Mr. Parker and Charlotte Heywood go to Mrs. Whitby's circulating library after dinner to examine the subscription book. When they look into it, Mr. Parker "could not but feel that the List was not only without Distinction, but less numerous than he had hoped."[17] The subsequent reference in *Sanditon* to Fanny Burney's *Camilla* recalls the fashionable circulating libraries in that novel: Camilla and Edgar go to a raffle for a locket at the library in Northwick; and later Camilla and Mrs. Arblay visit the bookseller's shop in Tunbridge Wells to subscribe to its circulating library in order to announce that they are in town. While they are there, Sir Sedley asks for the shop's subscription books, which are seized from him by Lord Newford, and, as the narrator acidly comments, "with some right as they were the only books in the shop he ever read."[18] In many respects, then, both books and an apparent interest in them were signs of gentility, and both were often displayed only for their social utility.

As the phenomenon of wealthy people borrowing books suggests, the circulating library made books available to readers, and especially to women, when books were very expensive. James Lackington, who made his fortune selling remaindered editions, says in the 1794 edition of his *Memoirs* that "when circulating libraries were first opened, the booksellers were much alarmed, and their rapid increase, added to their fears, had led them to think that the sale of books would be much diminished by such libraries. But experience has proved that the sale of books, so far from being diminished by them, has been greatly promoted, . . . and thousands of books are purchased every year, by such as have first borrowed them at those librar-

17. *Minor Works*, 389. Unfortunately, only one such subscription book from the period has survived, that of James Marshall in Bath from 1793 to 1799, but one notes that the signatures of the Prince of Wales and Mrs. Piozzi grace its pages. Philip Kaufman reproduces the page from this list that has the Prince of Wales' signature in "The Community Library," 21.
18. Frances Burney, *Camilla; or a Picture of Youth*, 402. Elaine Bander considers the allusion to *Camilla* as a comparison of Charlotte Heywood's financial prudence with Camilla's extravagance in Tunbridge Wells; see "The Significance of Jane Austen's Reference to 'Camilla' in 'Sanditon.' "

ies."[19] The libraries effectively pooled the demand of many people for books that only a few could afford. In the last decade of the eighteenth century and the first two decades of the nineteenth century, books were not only luxuries but also rising in price so that to have an extensive library was a sign of great wealth. The average three-volume novel cost a guinea in 1815, or, based on the current worth of a guinea's gold content, roughly the equivalent of $100 today; and that does not take into account how much lower the standard of living of the average person was then and so how many fewer people could afford to buy books.[20]

When Mr. Darcy says that he "cannot comprehend the neglect of a family library in such days as these" (2:38), he is not only asserting his belief in the importance of the age's literature but also implicitly declaring that the high cost of books does not concern him. For readers who did not own great estates and who had incomes much smaller than £10,000 a year, however, the high cost of books was important. Edward Ferrars teases Marianne Dashwood for having such a great love of reading that, if she had money, "the bulk of [her] fortune would be laid out in annuities on the authors or their heirs" (1:93). It is perhaps fortunate then that she marries Colonel Brandon, whose library, as Marianne observes, is particularly well-stocked with works of "modern production" (1:343). For those readers who, unlike Marianne, did not have access to private libraries, the circulating libraries made books accessible at a reasonable cost. Fanny Price, for instance, after returning home to Portsmouth from Mansfield Park, immediately notices the lack of books in her father's house and subscribes to a circulating library:

> Fanny found it impossible not to try for books again. There were none in her father's house; but wealth is luxurious and daring—and some of hers found its way to a circulating library. She became a subscriber—amazed at being any thing *in propria persona*, amazed at her own doings in every way; to be a renter,

19. *Memoirs of the First Forty-Five Years of the Life of James Lackington*, 247–48. More than one hundred years later, F. R. Richardson makes the same observation: "Surely the circulating library has met a demand, not created it. Surely the majority of its borrowers are people who would never pay seven shillings and sixpence for a new novel, who would very rarely buy books in any case, and who would simply read far fewer books, instead of buying more, if the libraries were swept out of existence" ("The Circulating Library," 196).

20. A guinea contained a quarter of an ounce of gold, while an ounce of gold sells for about $400 today. This rough comparison still understates the relative cost of books. For relative price indexes for this period, see Glenn Hueckel, "War and the British Economy, 1793–1815," 388.

a chuser of books! And to be having any one's improvement in view in her choice! But so it was. Susan had read nothing, and Fanny longed to give her a share in her own first pleasures, and inspire a taste for the biography and poetry which she delighted in herself. (3:398)

As Austen suggests, circulating libraries could ideally be, and certainly were in Fanny's eyes, a means for the intellectual liberation of women of small means.

I I

In practice the circulating libraries provided women with entertainment in the form of novels. Some men, of course, read novels. But although Henry Tilney in *Northanger Abbey* declares that "the person, be it gentleman or lady, who has not pleasure in a good novel, must be intolerably stupid" and says that he has "read all Mrs. Radcliffe's works," his views and knowledge of circulating library fiction seem to have been unusual for a man (5:106). More usual, apparently, is Mr. Thorpe, who, when asked if he has read *The Mysteries of Udolpho*, replies, "I never read novels; I have something else to do" and asserts that "there has not been a tolerably decent one come out since Tom Jones, except The Monk" (5:48).[21] The libraries became particularly associated with reading novels because of the low marginal utility of rereading them; that is, in comparison with other books, most novels were (and still are) disposable pleasures to be read once and forgotten. Writing in 1935, F. R. Richardson of Mudie's remarks that "even books by authors of substantial reputation rarely circulate for more than six or eight months, and those by unknown or comparatively unknown

21. Philip Kaufman has argued that the subscription list of James Marshall's library in Bath, 70 percent of which were men, "decisively dispels the traditional belief that women were the main support of the nefarious traffic in flashy novels" ("In Defense of Fair Readers," 75). But it is hard to see how this is so, based on the evidence. He fails to take into account that James Marshall's library had a relatively small percentage of fiction in its stock compared to other such establishments in Bath, and so was less likely to have women subscribers, given the competitive market. In 1808 the library (then run by his son, C. H. Marshall) had only 8 percent fiction versus the average library's 20 percent ("The Community Library," 12; Varma, 173–74). Further, since the records of individual borrowings have not survived, one cannot assume that the men were borrowing the library's fiction.

In agreement with Mr. Thorpe and seemingly reflecting the period's taste accurately is Lord Byron: "It is odd that when I do read, I can only bear the chicken broth of—*any thing* but Novels. It is many a year since I looked into one, (though they are sometimes ordered, by way of experiment, but never taken) till I looked yesterday at the worst parts of the *Monk*" (Journal entry, December 6, 1813, *Byron's Letters and Journals*, 3:234).

writers we do not expect to last more than four months, or three."[22] This meant that while among a large number of readers in the aggregate there might well be an appreciable demand for reading a novel once, the pleasure to be gained from rereading what one had just finished was relatively minimal—hence people were quite willing to rent a novel they were unwilling to buy.

Thus publishers of novels found that rental libraries were purchasing a large and gradually increasing part of an edition. As early as 1770 Richard Griffith observes that of 1,000 copies of a novel, 400 would be sold to circulating libraries.[23] When book prices rose, this became true for almost all books. In *Letters from England* (1809), Robert Southey states that the demand for books largely comes from "the main libraries, or from private societies instituted to supply their place, books being now so inordinately expensive that they are chiefly purchased as furniture by the rich. It is not a mere antithesis to say they who buy books do not read them, and that they who read them do not buy them."[24] Commenting on the prospects of a second edition of *Mansfield Park* in 1814, Austen says, "People are more ready to borrow & praise, than to buy—which I cannot wonder at."[25] She was right to worry, since of the 750 copies John Murray printed, only 252 were sold by 1820, when the leftover stock was remaindered.[26] It is likely, for example, that when Robert Martin says he will get *The Romance of the Forest* on Harriet's recommendation when he next goes to market in Kingston, he intends not to buy it but to obtain it from a circulating library as Harriet probably did previously.

Austen herself was a subscriber to Mrs. Martin's circulating library in

22. Richardson, 201.
23. [Richard Griffith], *A Series of Genuine Letters between Henry and Frances*, 5:15.
24. *Letters from England*, 349. Mrs. Catherine Gore observes that novels rose from two shillings sixpence a volume in 1780 to seven shillings a volume in 1810 ("The Monster-Misery of Literature," 557). Unaware of the general inflation in that period and of the economy of novel reading reflected by the existence of the circulating libraries, she blames the increase in prices on the libraries themselves, which as a whole are "the monster-misery of literature." Mrs. Gore's complaint that the libraries prevented authors from selling directly to their readers has long appealed to historians and critics of the novel, who have remained blissfully innocent of economics and economic history. See, for example, Michael Sadleir's comments in his Sanders Lectures of 1937, "Aspects of the Victorian Novel," 8; and, referring to Sadleir's lectures (existing then in typescript), Kathleen Tillotson in *Novels of the Eighteen-Forties*, 22.
25. Letter to Fanny Knight, November 30, 1814, *Letters*, 419.
26. David Gilson, *A Bibliography of Jane Austen*, 59–60. The largest edition of any novel printed during her life was the 2,000 copies of *Emma* published by John Murray in 1816. Although 1,248 copies were sold by October 1816, 539 were on hand in 1820 when the edition was remaindered (Gilson, 69).

Basingstoke and later lamented its demise. In a letter of December 18, 1798, she writes to Cassandra:

> I have received a very civil note from Mrs. Martin requesting my name as a Subscriber to her Library which opens the 14th of January, & my name, or rather Yours is accordingly given. My Mother finds the Money.— Mary subscribes too, which I am glad of, but hardly expected.— As an inducement to subscribe Mrs. Martin tells us that her Collection is not to consist only of Novels, but of every kind of Literature, &c. &c.— She might have spared this pretention to *our* family who are great Novel-readers & not ashamed of being so;—but it was necessary I suppose to the self-consequence of half her subscribers.[27]

By 1814, one would typically subscribe to a circulating library like Mrs. Martin's for two guineas a year and be entitled to have two volumes out; by paying more, one could have more volumes.[28] Assuming a moderate reader and three volumes per novel, this would mean that one could read twenty-six novels a year for a little more than the price of one. In *The Use of Circulating Libraries Considered; With Instructions for Opening and Conducting a Library* (1797), Thomas Wilson hyperbolically claims that "the yearly subscriber may read as many books for one guinea, which, to purchase, would cost ONE HUNDRED."[29]

The natural consequence of this economics of reading was that by Austen's time most copies of a novel's first edition were sold not to individuals but to circulating libraries. Since the libraries found that the vogue for a novel was usually limited to a few months, they bound their books in cheap marble-colored bindings that were distinguishable at a distance, as Mr. Collins' remark suggests, and that wore out quickly in the hands of their many readers. Thinking about the state of such volumes in "Detached Thoughts

---

27. *Letters*, 38–39.
28. Dorothy Blakey, *The Minerva Press, 1790–1820*, 116. This is the subscription price for John Lane's library, which had risen from a guinea in 1798 and which reflected the rising price of books.
29. In Varma, 196. D. H. Knott has identified the author as Thomas Wilson, a bookseller who during the 1790s operated a circulating library in Bromley, Kent; see D. H. Knott, "Thomas Wilson and *The Use of the Circulating Library*." Later, Wilson offers this fanciful calculation of the savings available to the most voracious of the circulating library's readers: "The subscriber for three months has seventy-eight clear days (Sundays excepted) to read in; he is entitled to two books at a time, and changes every day, which gives him the perusal of one hundred and fifty-six volumes, that at the low average of three shillings per volume, will cost twenty-three pounds eight shillings. Thus the subscriber at three shillings and six pence per quarter, will pay only one farthing per volume for reading, as one hundred and fifty-six farthings is three shillings and three-pence, leaving only the small difference of three pence in the calculation of a quarter's subscription" (Varma, 197).

on Books and Reading," Lamb rhapsodizes, "How beautiful to a genuine lover of reading are the sullied leaves, and worn-out appearance, nay the very odour . . . of an old 'Circulating Library' Tom Jones or Vicar of Wakefield!—How they speak of the thousand thumbs that have turned over their pages with delight!"[30] This hard use has meant that, with the exception of novels which were particularly valued and purchased by their readers, surviving copies of the period's novels are very rare. Witness, for example, Michael Sadleir's account in "Passages from the Autobiography of a Bibliomaniac" of his long quest to collect the seven gothic novels that made up Isabella Thorpe's list in *Northanger Abbey*.[31]

The general economy of novel reading is reflected in the catalogues of the period's circulating libraries. By contemporary accounts the largest circulating library of the period, and the largest from which a catalogue survives, was John Lane's library in London. Lane's catalogue advertises more than twenty thousand titles, while the smallest surviving catalogue from James Sander's library in Derby (circa 1770) lists just over two hundred titles.[32] The average circulating library issuing a catalogue had around five thousand titles, of which about one thousand were fiction, or roughly 20 percent. This figure probably understates somewhat the libraries' emphasis upon novels, since large enterprises would stock multiple copies of recent fiction. John Lane, for example, advertised that he had as many as twenty-five copies of a popular novel.[33] Further, since it is probable that catalogues have tended to survive from the larger and longer-lived businesses and that small libraries often may not have issued printed catalogues for their subscribers, one perhaps gets a better view of the great demand for novels by examining the figures from the catalogues of the small circulating libraries. These libraries averaged 430 titles, of which 70 percent were fiction.[34] The libraries' short lending period of two to six days for new

---

30. *The Works of Charles and Mary Lamb*, 2:173.
31. Sadleir, *XIX Century Fiction: A Bibliographical Record*, 1:xvi–xvii. See also Michael Sadleir, *The Northanger Novels: A Footnote to Jane Austen*.
32. Kaufman, "The Community Library," 11–13.
33. Advertisement in *The Oracle*, January 25, 1798, quoted in Varma, 53.
34. Kaufman, "The Community Library," 12. See also Hamlyn, 218. John Feather estimates that 40 percent of a bookseller's stockholding was fiction (*The Provincial Book Trade in Eighteenth-Century England*, 385). Q. D. Leavis cites figures from *The Report on Public Libraries* (1927) which, if taken as the direction that readers' tastes were headed, further suggest that the percentage of fiction titles in the stock of the large circulating libraries is likely to be misleading about what was borrowed. She notes that while urban libraries "had 63 per cent. of non-fiction works on an average to 37 per cent. of fiction, only 22 per cent. of non-fiction was issued in comparison with 78 per cent. of fiction, while in the county libraries, which stocked 38 per cent. of non-fiction to 62 per cent. of fiction, issued only 25 per cent. non-fiction" (*Fiction and the Reading Public*, 4, 274n).

books and their heavy fines (which required one to buy the book) also point to the concentrated demand for the latest publications.

In rural areas circulating libraries did not exist, since a bookseller needed an urban population of about two thousand to make a living.[35] Meryton has Clarke's, but the villages of Highbury and Uppercross are without this civilized amenity. While there were special arrangements for country subscribers that for the same price usually offered more books than a town subscription did (perhaps in the rational expectation that the wealthy would ultimately buy what they liked), the country patrons still had to provide or pay for carriage. In *Sanditon* one observes, for example, "a young Whitby running off with 5 vols. under his arm to Sir Edward's Gig" so that the books can be conveyed to Denham Park.[36] Those less well off either had to have access to the library of a country house or to belong to a book club or book society as Jane Austen did at Chawton. These clubs and societies, however, were unlikely to cater to the taste of women, composed as they were primarily of upper-middle-class men interested in political and economic subjects.[37] In 1813 Austen writes that she is reading her book society's latest acquisition, Captain Pasley's *Essay on the Military Policy and the Institutions of the British Empire,* and professing to find it "delightfully written & highly entertaining."[38] Yet despite the male preference for such heavy reading, Austen reports that "the Miss Sibleys want to establish a Book Society in their side of the country like ours."[39] There can be little doubt, then, that when isolated country readers of modest means like Mrs. Musgrove visited market towns and seaside resorts, they found the circulating libraries like the one at Lyme Regis to be significant attractions.

Most circulating libraries evidently had such a small stock that they could not rely solely upon renting books to support their proprietors and so usually sold a supplementary line of luxury items or offered some other form of entertainment in addition to their reading rooms. In *The Use of Circulating Libraries* Thomas Wilson remarks that "not one Circulating Library in twenty is, by its profits enabled to give support to a family, or even pay for the trouble and expence attending it; therefore the bookselling and stationary business should always be annexed, and in country towns, some other may be added, the following in particular, are suitable for this pur-

35. Feather, 148n.
36. *Minor Works*, 403.
37. See Philip Kaufman, "English Book Clubs and Their Role in Social History."
38. Letter to Cassandra, January 24, 1813, *Letters*, 292.
39. Ibid., 294.

pose. Haberdashery, Hosiery, Hats, Tea, Tobacco and Snuffs; or Perfumery, and the sale of Patent Medicines."[40] When she is in Brighton, Lydia Bennet reports that officers had accompanied her to the library, "where she had seen such beautiful ornaments as made her quite wild" (2:238)—as if Lydia needed any assistance. Charlotte Heywood in *Sanditon* turns away from the drawers of rings and brooches in Mrs. Whitby's library so that she won't spend "all of her Money the very first Evening."[41] In one of Hannah More's *Cheap Repository Tracts, The Two Wealthy Farmers; or, the History of Mr. Bragwell* (1796), the local circulating library is said to "sell paper with all manner of colours on the edges, and gim-cracks, and powder-puffs, and wash-balls, and cards without any pips, and every thing in the world that's genteel and of no use."[42] Alluding to More's dour utilitarian view of the circulating library, Austen's narrator in *Sanditon* cheerfully remarks of Mrs. Whitby's establishment that "the Library of course, afforded every thing; all the useless things in the World that could not be done without."[43] And in saying this as in much else, Austen displays her understanding of how necessary luxuries and books are for a civilized society, how many genteel and apparently useless things really cannot be done without.

III

As *Northanger Abbey* demonstrates, Austen not only appreciated the limits of an imagination formed solely by reading fiction and, in particular, gothic novels, but also recognized how they were being manufactured to order. Henry Tilney explains that his sister's misapprehension of what Catherine Morland means by new horrors coming from London stems from her not

---

40. Quoted in Varma, 199 (*sic*). Even for a bookseller, running a circulating library was apparently a difficult business, especially since the value of books for the enterprise rapidly depreciated. This meant that a substantial portion of the subscriptions and fines received was a return of capital which had to be reinvested constantly to maintain an attractive stock. It certainly was no business for the unsophisticated businessman or woman, particularly at the beginning of the nineteenth century when book prices were rising and thus forcing owners to increase their investment to keep the same number of new titles on their shelves. As one might expect, the relatively easy entry into the business and the necessity of reinvesting an increasing portion of receipts when book prices rose led to many bankruptcies. John Feather notes that almost half of the bankruptcies in the provincial book trade from 1732 to 1799 occurred from 1790 to 1799 (*The Provincial Book Trade*, 30). For instance, Mrs. Martin's circulating library in Basingstoke, which had begun in 1798, went bankrupt in 1800: "Our whole Neighbourhood is at present very busy greiving over poor Mrs. Martin, who has totally failed in her business, & had very lately an execution in her house" (Letter to Cassandra, October 25, 1800, *Letters*, 76).
41. *Minor Works*, 390.
42. *The Two Wealthy Farmers*, 12.
43. *Minor Works*, 390.

having appreciated Catherine's mixing of fact and fiction and not having foremost in mind the pleasures of reading the novels emanating from Paternoster Row:

> Miss Morland has been talking of nothing more dreadful than a new publication which is shortly to come out, in three duodecimo volumes, two hundred and seventy-six pages in each, with a frontispiece to the first, of two tombstones and a lantern—do you understand?—And you, Miss Morland—my stupid sister has mistaken all your clearest expressions. You talked of expected horrors in London—and instead of instantly conceiving, as any rational creature would have done, that such words could relate only to a circulating library, she immediately pictured to herself a mob of three thousand men assembling in St. George's Fields; the Bank attacked, the Tower threatened, the streets of London flowing with blood, a detachment of the 12th Light Dragoons, (the hopes of the nation,) called up from Northampton to quell the insurgents, and the gallant Capt. Frederick Tilney, in the moment of charging at the head of his troop, knocked off his horse by a brickbat from an upper window. (5:113)

Such novels were especially associated with the circulating library, not only because that is where most readers obtained them but also because John Lane, the proprietor of the Minerva Press, was both the leading publisher of gothic fiction in England and the principal wholesaler of complete, packaged circulating libraries to new entrepreneurs.[44] Consider the seven gothic novels on the list that Isabella Thorpe gave Catherine, for example: Mrs. Eliza Parsons' *Castle of Wolfenbach* (1793) and her *Mysterious Warning* (1796), Regina Maria Roche's *Clermont* (1798), Peter Teuthold's translation of Lawrence Flammenberg's *Necromancer of the Black Forest* (1794), Francis Lathom's *Midnight Bell* (1798), Eleanor Sleath's *Orphan of the Rhine* (1798), and Peter Will's translation of the Marquis of Grosse's *Horrid Mysteries* (1796). The Minerva Press issued all of them, with the exception of the novel by Lathom, who later published several novels with the press.[45] Lane's position as the leading publisher of gothic fiction and as a wholesaler of com-

---

44. See Blakey, 3–4, 111–24. In the *Star* for October 26, 1791, Lane advertised for sale complete libraries, ranging from 100 to 10,000 volumes (Blakey, 121).

45. For the publishers, see Sadleir, *The Northanger Novels*, 26–32; on Lathom, see Andrew Block, *The English Novel, 1740–1850: A Catalogue Including Prose Romances, Short Stories, and Translations of Foreign Fiction*, 133–34.

Of Austen's personal acquaintance with these particular novels, we only know that Austen's father read *The Midnight Bell*, which he had borrowed from the inn's library, when the family was staying at the Bull and George in Dartford; see Austen's letter to Cassandra, October 24, 1798, *Letters*, 21.

plete circulating libraries points to the large number of readers like Isabella Thorpe and Catherine Morland and to the substantial profits to be made from catering to their reading tastes.

Many people opposed circulating libraries and especially their encouragement of young women in reading novels. In *Northanger Abbey*, Austen notes that even novelists had joined "with their greatest enemies in bestowing the harshest epithets on such works, and scarcely ever permitting them to be read by their own heroine, who, if she accidentally take up a novel, is sure to turn over its insipid pages with disgust" (5:37). The objections to novels and novel reading ranged from their dignifying idleness to their encouragement of immorality. Although Coleridge had been made a free member of a circulating library in King Street, Cheapside at age eight and claimed that he read every book in the catalogue,[46] he says in *Biographia Literaria* (1815), "For as to the devotees of the circulating libraries, I dare not compliment their *pass-time*, or rather *kill-time* with the name of reading"; he declares that novel reading reconciles "indulgence of sloth and hatred of vacancy," and he considers it no better than "gaming, swinging or swaying on a chair or gate; spitting over a bridge; smoking; snuff-taking; [and] conning word by word all the advertisements of the daily advertizer in a public house on a rainy day."[47] In George Colman the Elder's *Polly Honeycombe* (1760), the father, after having just rescued his daughter from a disastrous engagement with the son of his maid, exclaims, "A man might as well turn his Daughter loose in Covent-garden, as trust the cultivation of her mind to A CIRCULATING LIBRARY."[48] Sir Anthony Absolute in Sheridan's *Rivals* (1775), having observed Lady Languish's maid returning from such a place, remarks to Mrs. Malaprop, "Madam, a circulating library in a town is, as an ever-green tree, of diabolical knowledge! It blossoms through the year!—And depend on it, Mrs. Malaprop, that they who are so fond of handling the leaves will long for the fruit at last."[49] In Hannah More's *Two Wealthy Farmers*, Mr. Bragwell, responding to Mr. Worthy's question as to whether his daughters read, says, "Read! I believe they do too. Why our Jack, the plough-boy, spends half his time in going to a shop

46. James Gillman, *The Life of Samuel Taylor Coleridge*, 17, 20.
47. *Biographia Literaria*, 1:48–49n. For a survey of objections to circulating libraries and to women reading novels, see John Tinnon Taylor, *Early Opposition to the English Novel*, 21–86. Robert W. Uphaus discusses the contemporary fear that novel reading aroused a young lady's "sensibility" in "Jane Austen and the Female Reader."
48. *Polly Honeycombe, A Dramatick Novel*, 43.
49. *The Dramatic Works of Richard Brinsley Sheridan*, 1:85.

in our Market-town, where they let out books to read with marble covers."[50] And Sir Edward Denham in *Sanditon* asserts, "I am no indiscriminate Novel-Reader. The mere Trash of the common Circulating Library, I hold in the highest contempt."[51] Although the English enjoyed reading novels, there was much prejudice against them, as Mr. Collins' disdain in *Pride and Prejudice* reflects.

Despite remaining a great reader of novels and vigorously defending the form, Austen in her own work depicts the age's great social ambivalence toward reading novels and its suspicion of anyone's finding pleasure in reading. In *Northanger Abbey* she defends the novel as a "work in which the greatest powers of the mind are displayed, in which the most thorough knowledge of human nature, the happiest delineation of its varieties, the liveliest effusions of wit and humour are conveyed to the world in the best chosen language" (5:38). But while Austen's own fiction certainly measures up to this high standard, the social context displayed within her work accurately reflects the low value placed on reading books in general and novels in particular. Reading can distract characters in her novels from performing their duty or indicate their incapacity. In *Persuasion* Mrs. Musgrove finds herself unable to care for Louisa after her fall at Lyme Regis and so, among other things, "had got books from the library and changed them so often, that the balance had certainly been much in favour of Lyme" (5:130). Isabella Thorpe, a great reader of gothic novels, is revealed to be an artificial coquette; and Catherine Morland is deceived by her fanciful expectation, gained from reading too many novels, that murder is to be discovered in every old country house. Harriet Smith, whose taste runs to Ann Radcliffe's *Romance of the Forest* (1791) and Regina Maria Roche's *Children of the Abbey* (1798), is a lightheaded young lady of little consequence, while Emma Woodhouse, who is not much of a reader and "has been meaning to read more ever since she was twelve years old" (4:37), not only has the greater social standing but also has so much else to do in attending to her father and managing everyone's affairs.

Reading was generally felt to represent a withdrawal from a woman's proper social concerns. Mary Bennet, whose interests are confined to reading sermons and moral essays, is the most limited and least marriageable of the family's sisters. This attitude informs both Miss Bingley's sneering comment about Elizabeth Bennet that "she is a great reader and has no

50. [More], 12.
51. *Minor Works*, 403.

pleasure in anything else," and also Elizabeth's spirited reply, "I am *not* a great reader, and I have pleasure in many things" (1:37). Later Elizabeth says to Darcy at the Netherfield ball, "I cannot talk of books in a ball-room; my head is always full of something else" (1:93). Very occasionally novels could even involve social embarrassment or immorality. Writing to Cassandra in 1798, Jane Austen announces, "We have got 'Fitz-Albini'; my father has bought it against my private wishes, for it does not quite satisfy my feelings that we should purchase the only one of Egerton's works of which his family are ashamed. That these scruples, however, do not at all interfere with my reading it, you will easily believe."[52] Later in 1804 she writes from Southampton, where she was borrowing books from a circulating library: " 'Alphonsine' [Madame de Genlis's novel] did not do. We were disgusted in twenty pages, as, independent of a bad translator, it has indelicacies which disgrace a pen hitherto so pure; and we changed it for the 'Female Quixote' " by Charlotte Lennox.[53] And in *Northanger Abbey* Austen convincingly depicts the social and moral dangers of taking fiction too seriously.

IV

Circulating libraries, then, were an important part of the social fabric in Austen's England and materially affected the conditions in which her own novels were produced. They helped to create an audience for the ephemeral novel when books were expensive and made reading a social activity in which women could usually properly participate. Nonetheless, one should also recognize that the circulating libraries institutionally represented the low social valuation of fiction, something that professional readers often forget. The existence of the libraries reveals both the ambivalence toward reading for pleasure and also the general aesthetic economy of novel reading. Still, despite the age's ambivalence toward novels and its suspicion of reading pleasure that informed its view of the circulating libraries, we should recognize that, if nothing else, the readers and their libraries encouraged and enabled Austen to write her novels. Among many others long forgotten, her works were to be found on the shelves of the circulating libraries and were to be numbered among their "useless things," useless and beautiful things that we still cannot do without.

52. *Letters*, 32.
53. Ibid., 173.

6

Marketing the Novel, 1820-1850

---

*Walter Scott has no business to write novels,
especially good ones.—It is not fair.—He has Fame
and Profit enough as a Poet, and should not be
taking bread out of other people's mouths.*

—Jane Austen to Anna Austen, September 28, 1814

The modern literary publisher's focus on fiction dates from the 1820s, when the reading public, following Scott, shifted its interest from poetry to fiction. By the beginning of the nineteenth century, publishing fiction had become fashionable and profitable if not entirely respectable. Until the 1820s publishers were content to publish novels in expensive editions bought largely by circulating libraries and occasionally by the wealthy. But in the late 1820s a few publishers came under financial pressure and sought to sell novels to readers who had only borrowed them before by marketing popular novelists in cheaper formats. As they experimented with formats, publishers discovered that there were distinct audiences for the expensive three-volume novel, the cheap one-volume reprint, the magazine serialization, and finally, fiction issued in parts. Most novels were issued originally in the expensive three-volume format; perhaps the bestselling tenth of those were reprinted in one-volume format; forthcoming novels by the five or six most popular novelists would be serialized by magazines; and, least important, in the 1830s and 1840s around twenty novels by these same novelists were issued in parts.

Although histories of the novel and the scholarship upon it has always taken notice of the sociology of readership, little attention has been paid to the economics of reading and publishing. Most readers of novels never read a work twice, so that given the cost of novels relative to their marginal utility (because they deliver all of their pleasure at once), few novels would be expected to sell widely. Until the advent of the circulating library, few could afford the cost of a novel in terms of the ephemeral pleasure to be gained from reading it. Throughout the late eighteenth century and the beginning of the nineteenth century, the high price of novels prohibited most individuals from purchasing them and, as shown in the last chapter, encouraged the establishment of circulating or subscription libraries that would lend books to a borrower for an annual fee of two guineas a year, which would allow a member of a library to borrow two volumes at a time. Supposing for the average reader, to whom a book was both family and individual entertainment, that a three-volume novel would last two weeks before it would be returned and the next one borrowed, then a reader might read twenty-six a year for a cost of reading each novel of about one shilling and eight pence. This would mean that, apart from the purposes of conspicuous consumption and displays of one's wealth, few readers for whom the expense of books mattered would want to purchase a book outright unless they planned to reread it a number of times. It is not surprising then that in a country of ten million people and with few of our modern forms of entertainment, the average novel from 1800 to 1850 was printed in an edition of between 500 and 1,000 copies. They were simply too expensive for even most of the financially comfortable people.

I

Proprietors of fashionable circulating libraries in London became publishers of novels. This phenomenon has a long history. The leading publishers of novels in the middle of the eighteenth century were John and Francis Noble. Francis Noble's business and library were located at Middle-Row, Holburn, while his brother's was at Dryden's Head, St. Martin's Court, near Leicester Square.[1] At the end of the century John Lane began the Minerva Press; and at the beginning of the nineteenth, Henry Colburn,

---

1. James Raven, "The Publication of Fiction in Britain and Ireland, 1750–70," 38–39. See also James Raven, "The Noble Brothers and Popular Publishing." For the most comprehensive background on novel publishing now available for the late eighteenth century, see James Raven, *Judging New Wealth: Popular Publishing and Responses to Commerce in England, 1750–1800*, 19–82. The bibliography in his book will prove particularly valuable for scholars in the field and is useful for those interested in nineteenth-century English publishing history as well.

James Boswell is known to have subscribed to one of the Nobles' libraries; see Alison Adburgham, *Women in Print: Writing Women and Women's Magazines from the Restoration to the Accession of Victoria*, 111.

the proprietor of a circulating library in Conduit Street located in the then newly fashionable Mayfair district, set up as a publisher of novels in New Burlington Street. As proprietors of libraries, such publishers were well placed to note the tastes of their subscribers, but were not inclined to risk publishing the unusual or the new work and instead followed their readers' tastes. The most striking examples of this practice were the gothic novels coming from John Lane's Minerva Press at the end of the eighteenth and the beginning of the nineteenth century and the silver-fork novels of the late 1820s and the early 1830s flowing from Colburn's house.[2]

The great economic irony of the literary market after the end of the Napoleonic Wars in 1815 was that, although the cost of book production and especially that of paper fell from the peak it had reached in 1810, the price of novels continued to rise by 50 percent from seven shillings a volume for Austen's *Emma* in 1816 to ten shillings sixpence a volume for Scott's *Kenilworth* in 1821. Scott's successful example established the standard for the three-decker novel and its guinea and a half price until 1894, when the circulating libraries were undercut by the publishing practice of rapidly issuing cheap reprints before the libraries could circulate novels long enough to cover their investment in stock and continue to satisfy their subscribers. The continuing rise in the price of novels during a period of declining publishing costs requires further explanation. As prices of books rose during the Napoleonic Wars, more readers borrowed their novels from libraries and naturally sought out from the libraries those novels that they could least afford, seeking the greatest value from their subscriptions. This, in turn, focused the libraries' demand on the most popular, high-priced form and helped to sustain the very high prices for original fiction. The circulating libraries, which articulated the aggregate demand of readers for fiction and the readers' collective appetite for new novels that they had not yet read, thus stimulated a market for the publication of many more novels than would have been the case had readers bought them directly from their booksellers. At the same time, the libraries restricted the number of copies that the average three-volume novel could be counted on to sell in the early nineteenth century to roughly seven hundred.[3] This meant that most nov-

2. On Lane, see Dorothy Blakey, *The Minerva Press*; on Colburn's novelists, see Matthew Whiting Rosa, *The Silver-Fork School: Novels of Fashion Preceding "Vanity Fair."*
3. It was, of course, possible to write something that no one would buy. Shelley, for instance, had *St. Irvyne* (1811) published on his own account with John Joseph Stockdale, believing that a novel was "a thing which almost *mechanically* sells to circulating libraries" (Letter to Stockdale, November 14, 1810, *The Letters of Percy Bysshe Shelley*, 1:20). He was later asking Stockdale, "Are there no expectations on the profits of its sale?" (Letter to Stockdale, August 1,

els were printed in editions of a thousand or fewer copies, that only works by popular novelists would be issued with a first printing of two thousand copies, and that only extraordinarily popular novelists such as Scott and Dickens had larger first printings.[4]

This phenomenon would seem at first to violate the law of supply and demand. One would expect that, given the reduction in the costs of book production, at least one publisher would have tried to maximize profits by lowering the price of novels and reaching a wider audience. But the high cost of novels during the wars with France had led readers to economize by borrowing more novels from circulating libraries and buying fewer from booksellers. Further, libraries had also become fashionable places to be seen, as Thomas Malton's print of Hall's Library at Margate shows (fig. 3). So unless a book was suddenly so much in vogue that it became almost impossible to borrow and thus forced those who wished to read it to buy a copy,[5] most readers had no reason to care about the high cost of books. Indeed, the reverse was the case. Once readers had paid for their subscription to a circulating library, they naturally wanted to get the most value for their money and sought to borrow the very high-priced novels they would not buy. If libraries wanted to remain competitive, they had to stock the most desirable and most expensive books. When the libraries ordered books from publishers, they reflected this demand and so made publishers aware that higher prices actually encouraged demand and fattened profits. Novelists understood that they had more readers than buyers, but did not understand the economics of book distribution and how it reflected the nature of readers' collective desire to maximize the number of novels they read rather than, as the popular novelist wished, to buy with the same money a much smaller number of novels.[6] One immediately realizes that

---

1811, *Letters*, 1:130). Finally, in 1827 Stockdale asserted that he had never received from Shelley the £300 that he was owed for the novel's publication (*Stockdale's Budget*, quoted in *Letters*, 1:130n).

4. Royal A. Gettmann, *A Victorian Publisher: A Study of the Bentley Papers*, 139. On Bentley's later practice and the variation in the size of editions, see Gettmann, 119–53. On the practice of other publishers, see J. A. Sutherland, *Victorian Novelists and Publishers*.

5. James Thin recalls being told that to meet the readers' demand for Scott's novels, William Wilson, a proprietor of a circulating library in Edinburgh in the 1810s, split in two each of the volumes of the three-volume Waverley novels, "and so made six volumes out of it," thus "increasing the cost of hire to the customers and doubling the profit of the librarian" (*Reminiscences of Booksellers and Bookselling in Edinburgh in the Time of William IV,* 28–29).

6. Mrs. Catherine Gore, writing at the end of a long economic depression in 1844, gave voice to authorial resentment of the libraries' practices and felt that it was perverse that "nearly the sole remaining customers of the modern bookseller are—the circulating libraries" ("The Monster-Misery of Literature," 557). As Guinevere L. Griest points out, the libraries "actually preferred nominally high prices as a kind of insurance that readers would be compelled to

almost all readers would prefer to pay an annual fee of two guineas that would allow them to read twenty-six borrowed books a year instead of paying the same amount to buy a little more than one three-volume novel. Further, even with significantly lower prices, only the most popular novels were likely to prove substantially profitable, because given the weak demand for rereading fiction, most readers would still rather borrow than buy the books.

I I

The history of the reprinting of novels and of the attempts to issue cheap original fiction during this period reflects the readers' calculus of supply and demand. Publishers sought to gain profits by selling novels directly to readers but found that, except for proven bestsellers, the price needed to sell the books was far below their break-even point. Original fiction simply could not be sold directly to readers in a cheap one-volume format, because most readers wanted to know that what they were buying was worth reading again and again.

Archibald Constable, Scott's publisher, was perhaps the first to envision selling cheap fiction to everyone and becoming wealthy in the process. John Lockhart reports that in his presence Constable said to Scott and the others there:

> I have now settled my outline of operations—a three shilling or half-crown volume every month, which must and shall sell, not by thousands or tens of thousands, but by hundreds of thousands—ay, by millions! Twelve volumes in the year, a half penny of profit upon every copy of which will make me richer than the possession of all the copyrights of all the quartos that ever were, or

---

borrow, and as an additional handicap to the retail bookseller, already at a disadvantage because of the extra discounts often allowed to libraries" (*Mudie's Circulating Library and the Victorian Novel*, 11).

By the end of the century the circulating libraries had become an index of respectability, since they had great power to determine public taste in novels because they ordered most of the copies printed. George Moore, who was really the first to succeed in publishing original fiction in a six-shilling book, constructs a myth of repression around the origins of the circulating library as he comments on its conservative social function in 1888: "Mother cannot keep a censor (it is as much as she can do to keep a cook, housemaid, and page-boy), besides the expense would be enormous, even if nothing but shilling and two-shilling novels were purchased. Out of such circumstances the circulating library was hatched.

The villa made known its want, and art fell on its knees. Pressure was put on the publishers, and books were published at 31s. 6d.; the dirty, outside public was got rid of, and the villa paid its yearly subscription, and had nice large handsome books that none but the *élite* could obtain, and with them a sense of being on a footing of equality with my Lady This and Lady That, and certainty that nothing would come into the hands of dear Kate and Mary and Maggie that they might not read, and all for two guineas a year" (*Confessions of a Young Man*, 144).

will be, hot-pressed! Twelve volumes, so good that millions must wish to have them, and so cheap that every butcher's callant may have them, if he pleases to let me tax him sixpence a-week![7]

This plan for Constable's *Miscellany*, which was to have begun with volumes reprinting *Waverley* and with Scott's *Life of Napoleon Bonaparte*, never quite worked out, since Constable went bankrupt in January 1826, taking Scott down with him.[8] The *Miscellany* started in 1826 at the price of three shillings sixpence and ran eighty volumes until 1835.

Only Robert Cadell made the fortune that Constable envisioned. As a junior member of the publishing house, he may well have heard Constable's remarks about the future of publishing fiction for the common man and resolved to try his hand in the matter. At any rate, Cadell somehow managed to convince the Edinburgh bankers not to declare him bankrupt in January 1826 and to allow him to manage the remaining assets of Constable's firm, which were largely Scott's future works and sense of honor.[9] And because Scott and his family were unable to live within their means and refused to cut back on their expenses, Cadell gradually was able to acquire Scott's copyrights in exchange for current living expenses, buying, for instance, half of Scott's interest in the novels after *Quentin Durward* for £10,000 in July 1831.[10] In the early 1820s Scott's novels had made their appearance in collected editions. There had been one at £15 for twenty-

7. J. G. Lockhart, *Memoirs of the Life of Sir Walter Scott*, 6:31.
8. Constable's debts amounted to £256,000 or roughly $25 million in today's money; Scott as a partner to James Ballantyne, Constable's printer, was legally responsible for £117,000; see Lockhart, 6:223.
9. Constable himself had tried to extricate himself from his debt by getting a loan of £100,000 to £200,000 from the Bank of England based largely on his control of Scott's copyrights and potential works; see Lockhart, 6:176.
10. On Cadell, see especially Jane Millgate, *Scott's Last Edition: A Study in Publishing History*, 41–52. Millgate makes Cadell out to be a grasping, self-seeking publisher who eagerly extorted an ever larger share of Scott's copyrights from Scott and his family in exchange for ready cash to pay off Scott's creditors. But while Cadell certainly profited from acquiring Scott's copyrights and ultimately published only Scott, he benefited from Scott's absurd denial of business realities in not immediately settling with the creditors of Ballantyne's firm and agreeing to pay off just 25 or 30 percent of the firm's debt, which would have been much more than the 2s. 9d. in the pound (or a little less than 13 percent) that the creditors of Constable received (Lockhart, 6:223). Scott might have had to give up Abbotsford, but he probably would have been out of debt by October of 1830, by which time he had in fact repaid fully half of the debt (Lockhart, 7:218). On the sale of half his interest in his copyrights in 1831, see *The Journal of Sir Walter Scott*, 611n.
   Despite his long experience with the publishing world as an editor of *Blackwood's Magazine*, Lockhart himself, as Scott's son-in-law, was hardly much better as a bargainer or a businessman and participated in the family's financial extravagance by agreeing to pay off all of Scott's debts after his death (when the custom was to repay much less and after a long time), and by selling the remainder of Scott's copyrights and promising Cadell to write a memoir of Scott for £30,000 (Lockhart, 7:421).

five octavo volumes, one at a little more than £12 for thirty-three duo-decimo volumes, and one for £8 and fifteen shillings for twenty-five 18mo volumes.[11] Although one did have to buy these editions all at once as a set, the last and cheapest of them cost only seven shillings a volume. But seeking to sell Scott to every willing buyer in order to rescue him from bankruptcy, Cadell began the cheap reprinting of novels for readers in earnest by reissuing the Waverley novels in a small format in June 1829. They appeared monthly in royal 18mo volumes costing five shillings each. This meant that most of Scott's novels were now available in a small, two-volume format for ten shillings as opposed to the original thirty-one shillings sixpence, or less than one-third of their original price.

The plan of monthly installment buying proved especially popular. To meet the anticipated demand and early orders, 20,000 copies of each volume were printed by Cadell. At the end of 1829, during the Christmas season, sales of the collected edition reportedly reached 35,000 copies a month.[12] In response to this great demand, Cadell began printing an additional 10,000 copies of each volume beginning in January 1830 with the first volume of *Waverley*.[13] Since Cadell was printing so much, he arranged for the expansion of Ballantyne's printing establishment by purchasing two new steam printing presses which were installed by April of 1830.[14] These presses were first used extensively in printing more than 27,000 copies of the first volume of *Ivanhoe*, which appeared in July 1830.[15] After eighteen months of publication, in January 1831 when the series had reached its twentieth of an eventual forty-eight volumes, Cadell began publishing a second parallel issue of the collected edition beginning with *Waverley*, the first novel in the series.[16] Advertising in the *Literary Gazette*, Scott's pub-

11. Millgate, 12.
12. Lockhart, 7:196.
13. Morgan Library MS 3556, pp. 152, 154, cited in Millgate, 125n.
14. Millgate, 35.
15. Ibid., 35–39.
16. Working from existing fragmentary account books of Cadell, Millgate has missed this subsequent reissue in her account of the publication of the cheap collected edition. My guess is that this reissue involved perhaps as many as 5,000 copies, and was probably adjusted downward in size within a few months. Enough capital was apparently tied up in paying for the initial printing costs for this parallel series to reduce the net profit for the first six months of 1831 to only £400 (*Journal*, 698n). This probably induced Scott to sell part of his interest in his copyrights to Cadell in July 1831; see note 10 above. I think that Cadell miscalculated, having been urged on by the impatience of the slowly dying Scott to see what the market would bear, and that Cadell didn't care much because he knew that in the long run he could only profit from Scott's thirst for funds to meet his living expenses.

I think that had Cadell stuck to publishing 30,000 copies of each volume in accord with his sales, Scott would have come close to paying off his creditors completely around the time of

lisher declared in December 1830 that "in order to meet the wishes of many who desire to possess the Waverley Novels, if they can procure the same in monthly vols., the Proprietors have resolved to commence a Re-Issue on the 1st of January next, beginning with Volume First, to be continued regularly on the 1st day of each month, till the whole is completed."[17] The great success of the cheap monthly issues of the Waverley novels had revealed to publishers the existence of an audience of over thirty thousand purchasers and also the possibility of appealing to them directly by encouraging monthly installment buying.

Soon many series modeled themselves after the cheap issue of Scott's novels. The first of them was John Murray's Family Library, which was published between 1829 and 1834, and began notably with Lockhart's abridged, two-volume version of Scott's *Life of Napoleon* in 1829, of which 19,950 of the 27,500 copies printed had been sold by November 1834, when the entire series was remaindered.[18] Shortly thereafter, Longmans inaugurated its long-lived, cheap monthly series *Lardner's Cabinet Cyclopaedia* with Scott's *History of Scotland*.[19] Beginning in 1832, Murray published Thomas Moore's edition of *The Works of Lord Byron, with His Letters* in fourteen volumes at five shillings a volume and advertised that the edition was "to correspond with the WAVERLEY NOVELS."[20] The advance publicity for the edition in the *Spectator* said that the copyrights had cost Murray £25,000 and that to break even at five shillings a volume he "must print thirty thousand copies."[21] This hyperbole must have included Murray's outlays on the first editions of Byron's various works on which Murray had already made substantial profits.

---

his death. Scott was apparently paying off his creditors at the rate of about £1,000 a month between January 1828 and December 1830 (largely due to the cheap edition), having retired about £23,000 of the debt in that period and leaving £54,000 to be paid (figures from Lockhart, 7:95, 245). Millgate calculates Scott's half share of the profits at £1,400 on the basis of 30,000 copies (Millgate, 49), which in the last eighteen months of his life would have produced a little over £25,000 had he not sold his copyrights. But £30,000 of debt was left when Scott died in June 1832 even after £22,000 in a life insurance payment was received (Lockhart, 7:421). This means that Scott's debts were reduced only by £2,000 from December 1830 to June 1832, although his novels were still selling at the rate of 30,000 copies a month in September 1831 (*Journal*, 659, 698n).

17. *Literary Gazette*, December 4, 1830: 791. As was typical with so many other such advertisements, the books had already been printed and were available at booksellers in time for Christmas.

18. See Scott Bennett, "John Murray's Family Library and the Cheapening of Books in Early Nineteenth Century Britain," 142, 144, 162. Bennett argues that the books in this series were "counter-revolutionary documents" of an effort "to publish across class lines" (141).

19. Gettmann, *A Victorian Publisher*, 31.

20. *Athenaeum*, January 7, 1832: 23.

21. "The Spectator's Library," *Spectator* 4 (October 8, 1831): 981.

In 1831 Cochrane and Pickersgill brought out Roscoe's Novelist's Library, which adopted the Waverley five-shilling format and also patterned itself after the more expensive octavo series, Ballantyne's Novelist's Library, which Scott had edited from 1821 to 1824. From 1831 to 1833 Cochrane and Pickersgill republished *Robinson Crusoe, Humphry Clinker, Roderick Random, Peregrine Pickle, Tom Jones, Joseph Andrews, Amelia, The Vicar of Wakefield, Sir Launcelot Greaves, Tristram Shandy, A Sentimental Journey, Don Quixote,* and *Gil Blas.*[22] In May of 1832 Baldwin and Craddock began publishing *The Tales and Novels of Maria Edgeworth* in eighteen volumes at five shillings a volume and advertised that they would be "uniform in size and appearance with the Waverley Novels and Lord Byron's Life and Works."[23]

When the August 1833 volume of Byron's works had just finished selling 19,000 copies in one month, John Murray was eager in September 1833 to make an arrangement to publish a collected edition of George Crabbe's life and poems.[24] Murray proposed an eight-volume edition at five shillings a volume with an initial printing of 5,000 copies.[25] After the initial orders from booksellers, it must have become clear to Murray that the demand for the first volume in the edition, which was to be an original life of Crabbe based on family letters and documents, was going to be greater than for the other volumes of the edition, for in February of 1834 a little more than 7,000 copies were printed of the first volume and were followed by the other volumes in printings of 5,000 copies at regular monthly intervals.[26] The edition was a success and small reprints of each volume were regularly required for more than ten years, totaling 9,500 copies of the first volume and over 7,000 of each of the others.[27]

I I I

The most successful series of cheap reprinted fiction was Colburn and Bentley's Standard Novels, which began in January 1831. Bentley's strategy in reprinting novels in the cheap Standard Novels format is intriguing. In selecting fiction for the series, Bentley had chosen from his bookselling

22. On Roscoe's Novelist's Library, see Michael Sadleir, *XIX Century Fiction: A Bibliographical Record,* 2:108–11.
23. *Athenaeum,* April 14, 1832: 247.
24. John Murray to George Crabbe Jr., February 28 and September 4, 1833, cited in Thomas C. Faulkner, "George Crabbe: Murray's 1834 Edition of the Life and Poems," 247.
25. John Murray to George Crabbe Jr., September 13, 1833, cited in Faulkner, 247.
26. Franklin P. Batdorf, "The Murray Reprints of George Crabbe: A Publisher's Record," 194.
27. Ibid., 195.

experience those of his recent bestsellers that had outlasted a single season's vogue, but he tried to restrict his losses, should the audience for any single author or novel prove not to extend beyond the taste of wealthy readers, by publishing editions that were smaller than would have seemed financially sound. Although his break-even point on a novel was around 3,300 copies sold, his first printing was just below that mark at 3,000 copies; he then ordered reprints from stereotyped plates as stock ran low, in runs of 1,000 copies.[28] He was willing to wait a year to receive a return of his capital and expected the risks to be much less than usual in a business accustomed to considering the remaining stock of a novel a dead loss if it didn't reach the break-even point after six months. In the agreement between the two partners to have Bentley buy out Colburn's share of the firm, the publishing house's accounts show that in August 1832 all but one of the first twelve volumes in the Standard Novels series published monthly in 1831 were showing a profit, while volumes thirteen through nineteen, published in 1832, were still in the red. Bentley's faith in the enterprise is further underlined by his agreeing to pay a little less than £2,800 for Colburn's 60 percent share of the series, which by August 1832 was showing a profit of only £221.[29] He obviously considered the series an almost risk-free proposition since his purchase price valued the series at a little more than £4,500 and so half of the firm's net worth, on which the rate of return in the previous year and a half had thus been a little more than 3 percent, or roughly the rate of interest available on the safest government bonds.

Bentley had little talent for spotting young novelists and giving them their initial start. Cooper, Marryat, Bulwer-Lytton, and Disraeli were first published by Colburn, while Ainsworth and Dickens, the chief pillars of Bentley's house in the late 1830s, were first published by Macrone.[30] Bentley was not an editor. Instead, he was an alert, sound businessman who could tell which authors were selling well and offer them more than their publishers were paying. He conducted his publishing business efficiently and drove hard bargains with his suppliers by demanding discounts as much as 10 percent for paying cash.[31] He was also willing to market proven fiction in cheap formats to see if additional money could be made from a title by appealing to a less affluent but larger reading public. He rightly judged that reprints of the authors on his list could not command the

28. Gettmann, *A Victorian Publisher*, 51.
29. Ibid., 52–53, 20n, 53.
30. On Macrone, see John Sutherland, "John Macrone: Victorian Publisher."
31. Gettmann, 23.

premium that those of Scott could. So while Scott's novels were being marketed in their cheap, popular format for five shillings a volume and thus in most cases for ten shillings a novel, Bentley reprinted his authors complete in one volume at six shillings.

In buying Colburn's share of the firm, Bentley shrewdly judged that his most dangerous competitor in novel publishing would be Colburn himself with a clean balance sheet, so he stipulated in the purchase agreement that Colburn could not publish books again within twenty miles of London without paying Bentley a large sum for the privilege. Although Colburn immediately set up as a book publisher in Windsor just outside the stipulated mileage limit, the transportation, communication, and distribution problems entailed in doing so had apparently been nicely judged by Bentley; for once the steady income from his remaining periodical investments had restored him to financial health, Colburn paid Bentley £3,500 in 1836 to be released from his agreement in order to become a London book publisher once again.[32]

In publishing history and the history of the novel Henry Colburn has acquired a reputation as an unscrupulous promotional genius who advertised widely and puffed his publishing firm's productions vigorously in his journals, especially the *Literary Gazette*, which he had founded in 1819. Certainly advertising books was nothing new, since many novels' publishers before Colburn, most notably William Lane of the Minerva Press, had owned newspapers and had puffed and advertised their newly published works in them. Colburn is said to have asserted "that with 200£ or 300£ spent in advertisements, he can *make* the public purchase an edition of any work that he pleases, however mediocre it may be."[33] His advertising technique extended to the distribution of and sometimes paid insertion of celebratory paragraphs in newspaper society gossip columns to the effect of "We hear that everybody who is anybody in town has been enjoying Mr. X's dashing new novel." Colburn recognized that demand for any new book had to be stimulated. He had in fact drawn up an internal "Memorandum on Paragraphing" for the firm's advertising managers. This practice was no secret, as Montgomery observes in *The Age Reviewed* (1827): "Let but the smile of Colburn suavity illuminate the MS. and your forthcoming prodigy will meander through all the papers in the full tide of paragraphic celebrity."[34] In "Publishing and Puffing," which appeared in the *Metro-*

32. Ibid., 21.
33. "Publishing and Puffing," 173.
34. [Robert Montgomery], *The Age Reviewed: A Satire in Two Parts*, 34n.

politan Magazine in 1833, the author (perhaps Marryat) traces the notices for *Alice Paulet* by the author of *Sydenham*. He lists announcements of the novel's imminent arrival beginning in April of 1831 and advertisements of its having been printed that October from Colburn's journals: the *New Monthly Magazine,* the *Literary Gazette,* the *Court Journal,* and the *Sunday Times.*[35]

Perhaps the best indication of the power of Colburn's advertising is the effective revenge he took upon Lady Morgan, who had published with Colburn since 1814 but who had decided in 1830 to publish her *France, 1829–1830* with Saunders and Otley because they were paying her a thousand pounds for the copyright.[36] On the appearance of *France,* Colburn put all of the copies of her works that he had on sale and advertised "LADY MORGAN AT HALF PRICE." This sharp practice effectively stopped the sale of *France.* Saunders and Otley then had to scramble to extricate themselves from what had turned out to be a losing proposition by giving up their copyright to Lady Morgan, taking back their bills for the second £500, and issuing on a half-profits basis a "second" edition of the 1,200 copies that had not yet sold.[37]

Leitch Ritchie in his preface to the first volume of the Library of Romance published by Smith, Elder attributes the emphasis upon marketing and advertising to the great financial risks involved with the publication of any single novel:

> Publications attended by such heavy expenses, and following so rapidly upon one another, could not be conducted in the usual manner. It was not enough to send them afloat upon the stream, and allow them to take their chance of being found by the world after few or after many days. As the moment of the launch approached, the owners became nervous; distrusting, sometimes with and sometimes without cause, the sea-worthiness of their argosie; distrusting the waves on which it was about to float, and the still skies that looked down upon it as calm as fate, they had recourse to every expedient which fear could invent. Steamers were sent out to marshal the way, puff-puff-puffing as they went; oil was cast, in plentiful libations, on the troubled waters, and fair winds bought from every old woman who sold them.
>
> But the rapidity with which such speculations followed each other, was not the cause of all this anxiety, but its consequence: for, otherwise, a very few losses would have wound up the affairs of the concern for ever. In the same way, when an author found favour with the public, the bookseller clung to

35. "Publishing and Puffing," 173–74.
36. Lady Sydney Morgan, *Lady Morgan's Memoirs: Autobiography, Diaries, and Correspondence,* 2:306.
37. Ibid., 2:307.

him, not from gratitude, but from nervous timidity; and when any particular class of novels became popular, it was persevered in *ad nauseum*.[38]

Ritchie clearly has Colburn in mind and rightly points to the editorial conservatism in appealing to popular taste once great financial risks were being undertaken. Given the potentially enormous profit margins on a three-decker novel sold at a guinea and a half, Colburn was right to try to create a demand among purchasers by making them aware of a new publication and may have succeeded somewhat in accelerating readers' requests for and hence circulating libraries' orders for individual novels. But he was unable to break the circulating library system or to discover a novelist like Scott whose works wealthy readers were eager both to read and to buy. By 1829, a year in which he published thirty-nine novels,[39] a number greater than that of any other single publisher, he had seriously overextended himself and had to begin a seven-year-long scramble to pay off his debts because his investment in his list of novels was not paying off.[40]

When one looks at the results of his advertising, one sees that for all of his efforts Colburn was unable to create a taste for his undesirable fiction. Of those authors on his list in 1829, only Frederick Marryat and James Fenimore Cooper could regularly sell more than a thousand copies of a three-decker novel.[41] By 1832 when Bentley took over his publishing house, Colburn was flirting with bankruptcy and was £1,800 in debt. Colburn's decisions to keep the *New Monthly Magazine* and, for a while, the *Literary Gazette*; to sell the *Sunday Times*, the *United Service Magazine*, and the *Court Journal*; and to force Bentley to buy out his senior partner's share of the book publishing firm show that Colburn's methods were unsuccessful.

But Colburn had realized that novels needed more and better advertising than they generally received. If one looks through the three monthly reviews of the first two decades of the nineteenth century (the *British Critic*, the *Critical Review*, and the *Monthly Review*), one sees that the average novel receives perhaps a condescending sentence or two. For instance, only the *British Critic*, the *Critical Review*, and the short-lived *New Review* noticed Austen's *Pride and Prejudice*. A review of a novel in the *Quarterly* or *Edinburgh* reviews was very rare. This made Scott's 1816 notice in the *Quarterly Review* of Austen's *Emma* all the more remarkable, even though Mur-

38. "Preface," in [Michael Banim], *The Ghost-Hunter and His Family*, vi–vii.
39. John Sutherland, "The British Book Trade and the Crash of 1826," 160.
40. On Colburn, see John Sutherland, "Henry Colburn Publisher."
41. Gettmann, 86 and 105.

ray was both proprietor of the review and the novel's publisher and even though the novel's publication had been carefully staged socially (one guesses by Murray) as an important event inasmuch as Austen had received permission to dedicate the work to the Prince Regent.

<h1 style="text-align:center">IV</h1>

It was certainly possible to make a reasonable living as a novelist in England by selling to the circulating libraries and a small number of individuals, provided one wrote enough. G. P. R. James, one of the century's most prolific minor novelists, is a case in point. He received £500 from Colburn in 1830 for his *Darnley, or The Field of Gold*, £600 in the same year for *De L'Orme*, and £600 in 1831 for *Philip Augustus, or The Brothers in Arms*.[42] Smith, Elder took James over from Colburn and Bentley in the early 1840s, paid James between £600 and £700 pounds for each novel, and issued them in printings of between 1,000 and 1,500 copies. James was remarkably prolific, though. George Smith reports that he "wrote so fast that I had the MSS. of three or four novels in my safe waiting for publication before the one last published moved off."[43] Despite fearing that they were saturating the market, Smith, Elder published nine novels by James between 1845 and 1848. Despite such remarkable Victorian industriousness on the part of authors and despite the enormous appetite of a larger reading public for fiction, even by the 1830s it was hard to emulate Scott's proven ability to sell more than two thousand copies of a three-volume novel.

G. P. R. James surveyed the book trade in England in 1843, trying to account for the difference in the cost of novels between England and France, and suggested that French novelists were better off than English novelists. James enviously notes, for example, that Balzac could make 30,000 francs (£1,200) for a work.[44] But he seems to have been unaware that there were English novelists who were paid more than Balzac, namely Frederick Marryat and Charles Dickens. Marryat, for instance, was paid £1,200 for *Midshipman Easy* by Saunders and Otley in 1835 after it had been serialized in the *Metropolitan Magazine*, and in 1837 he received £1,300 for *Snarley Yow*, which had appeared in the *New Monthly Magazine*.[45] In 1839 Bentley had agreed with Dickens to pay £2,000 for copyright in book form of *Barnaby*

42. S. M. Ellis, *The Solitary Horseman; or The Life & Adventures of G. P. R. James*, 47n, 57–58n.
43. [Leonard Huxley], *The House of Smith Elder*, 38.
44. "Some Observations on the Book Trade, as Connected with Literature, in England," 53.
45. Florence Marryat, *Life and Letters of Captain Marryat*, 1:213; 2:238.

Rudge (1840), to pay an additional £1,000 if more than 10,000 copies were printed, and to pay a final £1,000 for more than 15,000 copies.[46] Moreover, these figures do not include money made from serial publication. Contrary to James' assertion, then, the most popular English novelists were making more money than the most popular French novelists, even though they were selling novels that cost roughly 40 percent more a volume than did a French novel.

The sums available to successful writers began to attract many fashionable ladies and a handful of gentlemen to novel writing. Lady Morgan is generally given credit for being the first woman of fashion to devote herself to fiction. In 1814 she was paid £550 by Colburn for the copyright of *O'Donnel*. She was better paid for her accounts of her travels in *France* (1817) and *Italy* (1821), but returned to fiction with *O'Briens and the O'Flaherties* (1827), for which she received £1,300 for the first edition. Many others soon followed. Among later authors, perhaps the most noted is the Countess of Blessington, who received £600 for publishing *Strathern, or Life at Home and Abroad* (1845) first as a serial in the *Sunday Times* and afterwards as a book, with Henry Colburn. In 1831 Peacock parodies this phenomenon with his Lady Clarinda in *Crotchet Castle*:

> Yes, a novel. And I shall get a little finery by it: trinkets and fal-lals, which I cannot get from papa. You must know I have been reading several fashionable novels, the fashionable this, and the fashionable that; and I thought to myself, why I can do better than any of these myself. So I wrote a chapter or two, and sent them as a specimen to Mr. Puffall, the bookseller, telling him they were to be a part of the fashionable something or other, and he offered me, I will not say how much, to finish it in three volumes, and let him pay all the newspapers for recommending it as the work of a lady of quality, who had made very free with characters of her acquaintances.[47]

In a market hungry for such fashionable circulating-library fiction supplied by Colburn, it is no wonder that novelists with greater literary ambition and professionalism soon became alienated and sought to appeal directly to readers.

Efforts to issue original fiction in an inexpensive book format imitating that of the popular novelists' reprinted editions failed to find willing purchasers, however. The difficulty of getting the reading public to buy the

---

46. Agreement with Richard Bentley for *Barnaby Rudge*, February 27, 1839, in *The Letters of Charles Dickens*, 1:674.
47. *The Works of Thomas Love Peacock*, 4:68.

original work of authors in a five- or six-shilling format is illustrated by the fate of Leitch Ritchie's Library of Romance series published by Smith, Elder beginning in December of 1832 with *The Ghost-Hunter and His Family* by the O'Hara Family, the pseudonym of Michael Banim. The novels were advertised as being "uniform with the Waverley Novels" but were priced a shilling higher at six shillings a volume. Ritchie announced his series with a manifesto directed against the existing system of novel reading in his preface to the first volume, arguing that cheap novels that sold to more people could improve the quality of fiction: "It is *our* ambition to do away with *all* distinctions of price, by producing A SERIES OF NOVELS AND ROMANCES, GREATLY CHEAPER THAN THE CHEAPEST, AND FULLY AS GOOD AS THE BEST THAT HAVE PRECEDED THEM."[48]

The *Athenaeum*, which had assailed Henry Colburn's publishing and advertising of expensive novels, hailed Ritchie's new series with favorable reviews. Of *The Ghost-Hunter*, its reviewer declared that "the very graceful volume before us, well printed, on good paper, neatly, indeed elegantly, bound, must sell by thousands to repay the enterprising publishers for the cost of its production. With pleasure we add, that such extensive circulation the first volume of the series well merits; and if the succeeding even approach its excellence, Mr. Leitch Ritchie will well deserve canonization in the literary calendar."[49] The *Derbyshire Courier*'s reviewer declared that if the series did not succeed, then "the novel-readers deserve to be condemned, for the term of their natural lives, to continue to pay exorbitant prices for the trash of New Burlington Street."[50] And in response to the second volume in the series, Leitch Ritchie's *Schinderhannes, the Robber of the Rhine* (1833), the *Athenaeum* led with its review on the number's first page and again gave its ringing endorsement:

> The undertaking, besides being useful and agreeable in itself, has with us (as we have already acknowledged), additional merit, as one of the earliest visible manifestations of a spirit, whose office it is to destroy the monopoly so long exercised by a venal party in our literature;—a monopoly under whose strong, but illicit protection, persons have been enabled, for a time, to glut the market with their wretched compounds, covered with false labels, and forced, like the medicines of quacks by fictitious certificates, to an extent which has almost acted as a prohibition on dealers in more sound and wholesome wares. Like those same travelling quacks of old, the parties alluded to have ridden

48. Ritchie, "Preface" to *The Ghost-Hunter*, x.
49. Review of *The Ghost-Hunter*, *Athenaeum*, December 29, 1832: 836.
50. Review of *The Ghost-Hunter*, quoted in Huxley, 17.

into the marts and along the highways of our literature with a sound of trumpets and an energy of proclamation, which, at first, perfectly astonished the quiet and contemplative dwellers therein, and produced all the effect of a temporary mystification.[51]

By June 1833, however, the series was in financial trouble and its volumes were announced to be coming out only every other month. The Library of Romance ceased publication in 1835, having issued only fifteen volumes.[52]

V

Publishers resorted to two methods of serialization to reach a larger audience with their most popular authors: either regular monthly install-ments in established periodicals or, much less often, individual, usually monthly, part-issue publication. Since many of the best-known Victorian novels were published in one of these formats, one needs to be reminded that serialization involved great financial risk for a publisher, so that only a small percentage of the novels appearing in the nineteenth century were ever serialized, and that when any novel was serialized a weighty financial decision on its appeal to a relatively large readership had already been taken. Editorial experience had found that a serial's success or failure in either individual numbers or journal appearances could be determined after the fourth monthly installment. Ainsworth, for instance, stopped the serial publication in numbers of his own *Life and Adventures of Mervyn Clitheroe* after four numbers from December 1851 to March 1852, saying, "I could not go on at a loss, when that loss might be serious, if increased monthly."[53] Similarly, *Fraser's Magazine* began serializing Charles Kings-ley's *Yeast* in July 1848, but soon required Kingsley to abbreviate the ex-perimental novel and published only six installments through Decem-ber 1848 because the editor felt that the work was causing the periodical's circulation to fall.[54] No doubt Kingsley's emphasis in *Yeast* on presenting random thought instead of narrating a coherent plot found few willing readers.

Although the success of Dickens' *Pickwick Papers* in monthly shilling

51. *Athenaeum*, February 2, 1833: 65.
52. On the Library of Romance, see Sadleir, 2:170–75.
53. Ainsworth to James Crossley, March 4, 1852, in S. M. Ellis, *William Harrison Ainsworth and His Friends*, 2:182. Ainsworth's remarks seem to indicate that the numbers were being pub-lished on a half-profits basis and that the publisher was unwilling to bear all of the risk.
54. Una Pope-Hennessy, *Canon Charles Kingsley: A Biography*, 68. See also Alan Horsman, *The Victorian Novel*, 256–58.

parts foreshadowed the great triumph of prose fiction in the nineteenth century, part-issue was unpopular with publishers and generally unprofitable for writers, except, of course, for Dickens. *Pickwick* began with a printing of only 1,000 copies in April of 1836, but at its final number in November 1837 it was selling almost 40,000 copies.[55] Although the serialization was an enormous success, Dickens' agreement with Chapman and Hall called for a payment of nine guineas a sheet for the first three installments of a sheet and a half (twenty-four pages) and ten guineas a sheet for two sheets for the remaining numbers or £418 for the whole of the novel; and while the publishers paid Dickens a bonus of £500 in March 1837 and a further £2,000 in August 1837, they made £14,000 on the serial issue alone, while Dickens could only feel that he should have made much more money.[56] By 1841, when he was publishing *Martin Chuzzlewit* in shilling parts, Dickens had enormous financial leverage: he was guaranteed by Chapman and Hall £200 a number (or £100 a sheet) and three-fourths of any profits.[57] But only with the publication in parts of *Dombey and Son*, which began in October 1846 and ended in April 1848, did Dickens achieve financial security by making over £450 a number on sales of over 30,000 copies for each number; in contrast, *Vanity Fair*, which began publication in January 1847 and ended in July 1848, made a respectable £60 a number for Thackeray on sales of 4,500 copies and actually lost money for his publisher.[58]

Because booksellers were unwilling to stock pamphlet parts of unproven novels by unknown novelists, part-issue eventually became an occasional after-market strategy, employed only when the magazine serialization was over and sales of the three-volume format to libraries were coming to an end.[59] Further, although much is made of the cheapness of the one-shilling number, the cost of buying the complete twenty-issue set of monthly num-

55. Robert L. Patten, *Charles Dickens and His Publishers*, 64–68.
56. Ibid., 65, 68–70.
57. Memorandum of an Agreement with Chapman and Hall, September 7, 1841, in *Letters of Charles Dickens*, 2:478–80. It should be noted that with *Master Humphrey's Clock*, weekly numbers of which were sold for three pence, Dickens had tried to reach his largest audience. The first number sold 70,000 copies, but the circulation had dropped dangerously close to its break-even point of 26,000 copies in August 1841, when the latest sale was only 30,000, according to Dickens' letter to Thomas Minton of August 23, 1841 (*Letters*, 2:365); see also Patten, *Charles Dickens and His Publishers*, 106–20. Although his return on this format was a little over £5,400 by the end of 1841, Dickens was disappointed, for he could have made more by sticking to shilling numbers, selling perhaps only half the number of copies but making much more money.
58. Robert L. Patten, "The Fight at the Top of the Tree: *Vanity Fair* versus *Dombey and Son*."
59. J. Don Vann in his study of 192 serialized Victorian novels found that only twenty-five had appeared in part-issue; see *Victorian Novels in Serial*, 15.

bers of a Dickens novel added up to a guinea, which was exactly what Austen's *Emma* had cost in 1816. The price of a complete set of numbers was fully two-thirds the cost of a regular three-decker novel, was more than twice the cost of a Waverley novel in Cadell's cheap edition of 1830–34, and was more than three times as much as the six-shilling reprints of Marryat's novels in Bentley's Standard Novels series. The purchaser of one-shilling numbers, then, really saved because one didn't pay for a binding. In short, the cost of the shilling numbers priced them well above the pocketbooks of all but those of relatively well-to-do individual readers. There is evidence that there were some reading clubs of those who pooled their pennies and bought a number. But, more likely, most of the purchasers were middle-class adolescents spending their pocket money, for the great new audience for fiction in the 1830s and 1840s was composed largely of schoolboys and young clerks who consumed Marryat, Ainsworth, and Dickens.[60]

It should be further noted that part-issue serialization in one-shilling numbers also had to compete with cheap one-volume reprints of novels by other authors and so were even more expensive relatively speaking than a simple comparison with the cost of a three-volume novel suggests. The stiff competition in the market effectively confined the format to the most popular of contemporary authors. Serialization in numbers was even more risky after 1850, when Dickens' *Household Words*, which cost only two pence a number,[61] proceeded to undercut that market for novelists even further.

60. Dickens' readership clearly extended beyond this group, but one should note, to take a single example, the assortment of Dickens' works, including *Oliver Twist, Barnaby Rudge, Bleak House, Dombey and Son, Martin Chuzzlewit, Nicholas Nickleby, Little Dorrit, The Old Curiosity Shop, David Copperfield, Sketches by Boz,* and *A Tale of Two Cities,* given by Robert Browning to his son Pen on his fifteenth birthday, March 9, 1864; see Philip Kelley and Betty A. Coley, *The Browning Collections: A Reconstruction with Other Memorabilia,* 69–70. On Dickens' popularity among children, Thackeray offers especially persuasive testimony in "Charity and Humour," first published in the American edition of *The English Humourists of the Eighteenth Century* (1853): "All children ought to love him. I know two that do, and read his books ten times for once that they peruse the dismal preachments of their father. I know one who, when she is happy, reads 'Nicholas Nickleby;' when she is tired, reads 'Nicholas Nickleby;' when she is in bed, reads 'Nicholas Nickleby;' when she has nothing to do reads 'Nicholas Nickleby;' and when she has finished the book, reads 'Nicholas Nickleby' over again. This candid young critic at ten years of age, said, 'I like Mr. Dickens' books much better than your books, papa;' and frequently expressed her desire that the latter author should write a book like one of Mr. Dickens's books" (*The Oxford Thackeray,* 10:627).
    One should also note that the connection between novels, libraries, and education is further confirmed by the fact that W. H. Smith and Charles Mudie served on the first London school board; see Guinevere L. Griest, *Mudie's Circulating Library and the Victorian Novel,* 33.
61. Anne Lohrli, *Household Words: A Weekly Journal, 1850–1859, Conducted by Charles Dickens,* 4.

Nineteenth-century publishers were slow to serialize novels in their magazines. The practice had been employed in the eighteenth century, most notably with Smollett's *Life and Adventures of Sir Launcelot Greaves*, which was first published serially from January 1760 to December 1761 in the *British Magazine* and appeared in its collected form in 1762.[62] Looking back to Smollett and searching for a wider reading public, the comic novelists of the 1830s and 1840s, especially Marryat, Dickens, and Thackeray, revived the serialization of novels in literary magazines. Frederick Marryat is generally considered the first one, having published *Newton Forster* serially in the *Metropolitan Magazine* in 1832. He also established the precedent of having an eminent novelist serve as the editor of and chief contributor to a journal. But only after Dickens' success in issuing *Pickwick Papers* (1836–37) in parts did serialization of novels begin in earnest. From 1837 to 1839 *Oliver Twist* appeared in *Bentley's Miscellany*, which Dickens was editing, and fixed a form of publication that was to dominate the literary magazines for the next fifty years and beyond. Ainsworth's *Jack Sheppard* appears in *Bentley's Miscellany* from January 1839 to February 1840. It was issued in three volumes in October 1839 before completion in serial form, and also appeared in fifteen monthly parts beginning in 1840. It sold 12,000 copies in five years and had a greater sale than did *Oliver Twist*.[63] Beginning in the late 1830s, Thackeray wrote and illustrated for *Fraser's Magazine*, and Dickens, Ainsworth, and Bulwer-Lytton appeared in *Bentley's Miscellany*. In the early 1840s the payment for novel installments in literary periodicals began to exceed the payment for essays and soon became the most valuable literary form. Thackeray, for example, was receiving roughly £27 a sheet in February 1844 for publishing *The Luck of Barry Lyndon* in *Fraser's Magazine*.[64]

In 1839 Ainsworth replaced Dickens as the editor of *Bentley's Miscellany*. Although Bentley was afraid that the magazine might decline with the change of editors, the circulation rose about nine hundred copies to 8,500 during the run of Ainsworth's *Jack Sheppard*. But with the serialization of *Guy Fawkes* from 1841 to 1842, Bentley was selling only 5,000 copies a month and decided to edit the magazine himself, whereupon circulation plunged to about 2,800 copies a month.[65] This decline in sales probably had

62. Robert D. Mayo, *The English Novel in the Magazines, 1740–1815*, 276–88.
63. Ellis, *William Harrison Ainsworth*, 1:352, 358.
64. *The Letters and Private Papers of William Makepeace Thackeray*, 2:841. Since Thackeray was illustrating his own work, the payments he received were probably higher than they would have been for the story alone.
65. Gettmann, 143.

less to do with the relative merits of the editors, though, than with the severe economic depression that reached its nadir in 1843 and the resulting restraint of middle-class readers in spending money on entertainment. What one should notice instead is that the number of readers to be gained for a periodical by employing even the most popular of novelists was relatively small. As Dickens and Ainsworth discovered, their readership did not expand among the wealthy but among those less well to do, who were willing to read a novel in shilling monthly parts but loath to part with two shillings sixpence for an issue of a periodical. In fact, there seem to have been three audiences for the novels: one that read novels in magazines, one that read them in books, and yet another that did not have access to circulating libraries and read novels in individually issued parts. Once publishers discovered this, they exploited the market ruthlessly, none more so than Ainsworth himself, who reissued his earlier published novels such as *Crichton, Guy Fawkes,* and *Lancashire Witches* from 1848 to 1850 in *Ainsworth's Magazine* and then republished them in parts, thus recycling his old work while running two separate magazines.[66]

VI

The advent of serial publication of novels occasioned contemporary aesthetic and sociological doubts about what novelists were doing. Critics questioned how beneficial the pressure of serialization was for the art of the novel and feared that novelists were becoming journalists in both form and style. Further, when some popular novelists serialized their work in newspapers, critics felt that the authors had gone too far in addressing readers so clearly beneath them in social class.

Many thoughtful authors distrusted serialization because of the formal pressure that installments created for intermediate climaxes in order to attract interest and maintain the sale of the periodical. Harriet Martineau, for instance, says in her *Autobiography*:

> I could not conscientiously adopt any method so unprincipled in an artistic sense as piecemeal publication. Whatever other merits it may have, a work of fiction cannot possibly be good in an artistic sense which can be cut up into portions of an arbitrary length. The success of the portions requires that each should have some sort of effective close; and to provide a certain number of these at regular intervals, is like breaking up the broad lights and shadows of a

66. Ellis, *William Harrison Ainsworth*, 2:168.

great picture, and spoiling it as a composition. I might never do any thing to advance or sustain literary art; but I would do nothing to corrupt it, by adopting a false principle of composition.[67]

Martineau accurately presents one of the major problems in writing serialized novels, one which, for many readers, too often flaws the works of Dickens, since psychological development must be subordinated to questions of immediate narrative effect and episodic plot in the serialized form. To help his readers remember his characters from one monthly number to the next, Dickens often reduced his minor characters to caricatures by having them speak repeated tags.[68] The architectonics of the novel are sacrificed for local sensation. One has only to think, for example, of the spectacular spontaneous combustion of Krook in *Bleak House* (1852–53) to understand how the pressure to produce intermediate climaxes in serialization gives rise to some self-consciously dubious art.

Some authors, though, such as Charles Lever, an Irish novelist and editor of the *Dublin University Magazine* from 1842 to 1845, found serial publication an artistic advantage because from the responses of readers that he received to installments he could judge "what characters & incidents *tell* best with readers."[69] Yet, when serializing Lever's *A Day's Ride* in *All the Year Round*, Dickens writes to him about the first installment: "The only suggestion I have to make (and that rises solely out of the *manner* of publication) is, that we ought to get at the action of the story, in the first No. and that I therefore would, by a little condensation there, and a little enlargement of the quantity given in the first week, get at the invitation to the dinner, *as the end to the first weekly part*."[70] The pressure to "get at the action of the story" in the novel's first installment moves Dickens to suggest that Lever's novel needs revision if it is to hold the periodical reader's attention.

Early critics also complained that serialization encouraged novelists to adopt the style of newspaper writers who had to fill a set space regardless of the importance of the subjects being covered. A reviewer for *Fraser's*, for instance, complains of Dickens' procedure in *Oliver Twist* and *Nicholas Nickleby*:

> The necessity of filling a certain quantity of pages per month imposed upon the writer a great temptation to amplify trifling incidents, and to swell sen-

67. *Harriet Martineau's Autobiography*, 1:416.
68. Vann makes this point in *Victorian Novels in Serial*, 4.
69. Lever to Richard Bentley, December 11, 1839, quoted in Gettmann, 164.
70. Dickens to Charles Lever, June 21, 1860, in *Charles Dickens's Letters to Charles Lever*, 19.

tence after sentence with any sort of words that would occupy space. The very spirit of a penny-a-liner, for instance, breaks out in the prolix descriptions of the various walks through the streets of London, every turn in which is enumerated with the accuracy of a cabman.[71]

Although this left-handed verification of Dickens' descriptive accuracy should reassure modern historians who use his novels as a source of information for the period, one realizes that, while often locally attractive, his lengthy, unmotivated description reflected the English reader's great appetite for verbal pictures of the urban landscape. However, these narrative interpolations, which made the monthly installments enjoyable, detract from the collected whole, according to *Fraser's* critic: "Now, in the separate monthly essays this was no harm,—on the contrary, it was of positive good to the main object, viz. the sale; but when we find them collected, they do not improve the sequence of the story, or advance the fame of the writer."[72] If the aesthetic criteria of a novel's worth includes the relevance of its detail to the development of the story and its characters, the pleasure one has in reading a Dickens novel that has been elongated by descriptive passages may well be much diminished, if only locally, because reading such passages takes more time than readers may feel it is worth. Indeed, this particular aesthetic weakness stemming from the pressure of serialization may help to explain in part why the novels of Austen and the Brontës are evidently more appealing to modern readers.

In the 1830s when the cheap editions of novels began to sell well, a few observers realized that fiction would become the great popular literary form of the century. But when novelists began to serialize their work so that it was easily affordable from the beginning to less cultivated tastes, critics deplored the novelists' stooping to address those beneath them. In *England and the English* Bulwer-Lytton observed that "fiction, with its graphic delineations and its familiar emotions, is adapted to the crowd—for it is the oratory of literature."[73] Further, as a consequence, many novelists adopted a style designed to appeal to the new mass readership. Ainsworth, for instance, says, "The truth is, to write for the mob, we must not write too well. The newspaper level is the true line to take."[74] But when Ainsworth began to serialize his novels in newspapers as the French novelists had

71. "Charles Dickens and His Works," 400. On the attribution of this review, see note 75 below.
72. Ibid.
73. *England and the English*, 2:127.
74. Ainsworth to James Crossley, April 7, 1838, in Ellis, *Ainsworth*, 1: 336.

been doing, some readers abhorred the aesthetic consequences and the social implications of such publication. In a review of Ainsworth's *Tower of London* (1840) in *Fraser's Magazine*, the writer comments on Ainsworth's *Old Saint Paul's* (1841), which was appearing weekly in the *Sunday Times*, and on Captain Marryat's *Joseph Rushbrook* (1841), which appeared under the title of "The Poacher" in the *Era* in the style of the French feuilletons:

> If writing monthly fragments threatened to deteriorate Mr. Ainsworth's pro-
> ductions, what must be the result of this hebdomadal habit? Captain Marryat,
> we are sorry to see, has taken to the same line. Both these popular authors
> may rely upon our warning, that they will live to see their laurels fade, unless
> they more carefully cultivate a spirit of self-respect. That which was venial in
> a miserable starveling of Grub Street, is positively disgusting in the extrava-
> gantly paid novelists of these days—the caressed of generous publishers.
> Mr. Ainsworth and Captain Marryat ought to disdain such pitiful peddling—
> let them eschew it without delay.[75]

The reviewer excoriates Ainsworth and Marryat for risking their artistic reputations for more money by appealing to a newspaper's lowly readers.

The reviewer's admonishment occasioned a remarkable letter by Marryat defending newspaper serialization to one of the editors of *Fraser's*:

> If I understand rightly the term *pitiful peddling*, it would intimate that I have
> been induced by a larger sum than is usually offered for contributing to
> monthly periodicals to write for a weekly paper. If such is your impression,
> you are very much in error; . . . had I considered my own interests, I should
> have allowed "The Poacher" to have made its appearance in Mr. Bentley's
> "Miscellany" or Mr. Colburn's "New Monthly Magazine."[76]

Marryat's choice of the *Era* was deliberate and not as lucrative as magazine serialization would have been.[77] Publishing *Joseph Rushbrook* in the cheap weekly newspaper was a deliberate effort to entertain in a wholesome way poorer readers: "I have latterly given my aid to cheap literature, and I consider that the most decided step which I have taken is the insertion of this tale in a weekly newspaper—by which means it will be widely dissemi-

---

75. "The Tower of London," *Fraser's Magazine* 23 (1841): 169. While this review has been attributed to Thackeray, the attribution has been disputed. I am also doubtful that the reviewer is Thackeray, but am almost certain that the same author wrote both this review of Ainsworth and the review of Dickens' works in *Fraser's Magazine* that I cite above.
76. Quoted in Florence Marryat, *Life and Letters*, 2:102.
77. It should be noted that while Marryat might not have been well paid for his novel by the *Era*, the reviewer may well have been aware in 1841 that the *Sunday Times* paid Ainsworth £1,000 to serialize *Old Saint Paul's*; see Ellis, *Ainsworth*, 1:422.

nated among the lower classes, who, until lately (and the chief credit to the alteration is due to Mr. Dickens) had hardly an idea of such recreation."[78] Although he generously attributes to Dickens his own disinterested motives, in defending his choice of journals Marryat is obviously bristling at the reviewer's sneering at him for being so crassly ungentlemanly as to stoop to publish a novel in a newspaper and asserts that "if I do reach the mass and you do not, in spite of my inferiority I become the more useful of the two."[79] Entertaining the multitude in Marryat's eyes has more social utility than envious, high-minded criticism.

One can also point to the aesthetic tension stemming from the psychological difficulty of writing novels under the pressure of serialization. Commenting on this problem, Marryat remarks that "when every portion is severally presented to be analyzed and criticized for thirty days, the author dare not flag. He must keep up to his mark, or he can never encounter an ordeal so severe."[80] Minor novelists inevitably felt this pressure more because they did not know when or if they would get paid, since in the serial format they were participating much more in the publisher's risk. One may perhaps best imagine the difficulties of writing novels piecemeal through Leigh Hunt's description of his experience in writing *Sir Ralph Esher* for Henry Colburn in 1832:

> The reader may judge of the circumstances under which authors sometimes write, when I tell him that the publisher had entered into no regular agreement respecting this work; that he could decline receiving any more of it whenever it might please him to do so; that I had nothing else at the time to depend on for my family; that I was in very bad health, never writing a page that did not put my nerves into a state of excessive sensibility, starting at every sound; and that whenever I sent the copy up to London for payment, which I did every Saturday, I always expected, till I got a good way into the work, that he would send me word that he had had enough.[81]

As one might expect, *Sir Ralph Esher* was the last novel Leigh Hunt wrote. The intellectual and imaginative investment required of the novelist made it much too risky an occupation for Hunt, who had to worry from week to week about feeding his family. Worse, his uncertainty about the work's immediate editorial reception meant that he had to steel himself for the possibility that no payment would be forthcoming.

78. Quoted in Florence Marryat, 2:105–6.
79. Ibid., 2:104.
80. Quoted in Vann, *Victorian Novelists*, 3.
81. *The Autobiography of Leigh Hunt*, 2:201.

The attitude toward serialization of Bulwer-Lytton, who was a successful circulating-library novelist, illustrated the delicate considerations of class involved in appealing directly to a wide readership. Bulwer-Lytton's average novel had sold between 2,250 and 2,750 copies, while his most popular novel, *Eugene Aram,* had sold 3,000 copies.[82] But he recognized that his popularity could not sustain the same methods that Thackeray and Dickens employed. Suspicious of publication in parts after magazine serialization, which had been successful for the most popular novels in the 1840s, Bulwer-Lytton writes to Blackwood about plans for the publication of *The Caxtons* after its serialization in *Blackwood's Magazine*:

> I have to consider well your idea of the 5 shilling parts—I own I have great doubts therein it seems to me that there are 2 classes of readers—the one who like the serial form the other who prefer waiting till the whole is completed. Now the first will be taken off by the magazine—& the last will still wait till the whole is out— On the other hand—it is true that such a subdivision lightens the cost—to the purchasers. Many will pay 5s at a time who will not pay 30s at once. And the attempt may create a 3d class of readers & purchasers not existing here, but which does exist for the french novels—first published in newspapers & then in livraisons—before final completion— And lastly even if not very successful such an intermediary form might still take off from 5 to 700 copies—besides the ultimate reissue of the work completed & that would be all the difference between loss & gain—.[83]

The five-shilling parts, he feels, would sufficiently distinguish his format from Dickens' shilling numbers and would enable him "to throw over illustrations altogether, or at least restrict them to a single well executed woodcut on the title page of each vol."[84] Bulwer-Lytton clearly feels his audience is more select and discriminating than the one that reads Dickens; and, as his desire to cut down on illustrations indicates, he finds the addition of pictures to his text vulgar. He is clearly worried about maintaining his reputation with the socially conscious English reader and sensitive to the damage that could be done by appearing to stoop too low in pursuit of a large audience. In 1849 Bulwer-Lytton writes to Blackwood that "in the Magazine form—as in the Caxtons—the loss was [something] more than 100£—my reply to such overtures has been generally, that I must

82. Bulwer-Lytton to *Blackwood's Magazine,* November 12, 1849, in "The Letters of Sir Edward Bulwer-Lytton to the Editors of "Blackwood's Magazine," 1840–1873," 60. (Hereafter "Letters of Bulwer-Lytton.")
83. December 13, 1849, ibid., 64.
84. January 30, 1850, ibid., 67–68.

first see my way to such a form of publication as might sufficiently vary from those adopted by Dickens & Thackeray,—as not to trespass on their ground & appear directly to challenge comparison."[85] As with the illustrations, he was anxious to distinguish his work from those of his more successful competitors and to maintain his reputation.

Since he felt that the audience for the publication formats was very different, Bulwer-Lytton wanted to decide exactly what kind of readership he was addressing before beginning to write a novel:

> But I feel it would be desirable before getting on with the work—to decide pretty positively as to form, viz: according to the size & quality of the audience it addresses. What might be very attractive to the more lettered and Scholastic reader of the Magazine might be flat eno' to the purchasers of Shilling volumes. . . . Opinions too which I desire, irrespective of party politics, to convey—antidotal to those who desire to set class agst. class which might be pleasing expressed in the Magazine, must be very delicately & covertly insinuated when addressing the Multitude.[86]

Considering the different audiences for each serialized format, Bulwer-Lytton suggests that while he can directly address magazine readers who tolerate strongly expressed political views, he worries about inflaming the purchasers of shilling volumes whom he calls "the Multitude."

VII

Publishers of novels in England sought to sell fiction directly to a wider public in the late 1820s. Following the great success of Cadell's cheap edition of Scott's novels, which began publication in 1829, publishers issued inexpensive editions of established modern novelists. In particular, Colburn and Bentley initiated the Standard Novels series by reprinting James Fenimore Cooper's novels in a one-volume format costing just six shillings. In contrast, as the failure of the Library of Romance showed, cheap original fiction by unknown or second-rate authors found few willing buyers. While the potential readership was very large, its limited budget restricted its purchasing of fiction to a few popular authors. Nonetheless, beginning with Marryat, successful novelists enlarged their audience by serializing novels in literary magazines, which also employed them as their editors. Further, Dickens pioneered serialization in shilling numbers, which appealed to the

85. December 13, 1849, ibid., 63–64.
86. January 30, 1850, ibid., 68.

new adolescent readers and, as some reviewers lamented, to working-class readers. Finally, because selling cheap fiction directly to a large readership meant taking greater financial risks, sensible publishers marketed widely only the fiction written by those novelists who had already demonstrated their popularity.

Traffic in the Heart:
English Literature in the
Publishing Market

*Just think what a horrible condition of life it
is that any man of common vulgar wit, who knows
English grammar, can get, for a couple of sheets of
chatter in a magazine, two-thirds of what Milton
got altogether for* Paradise Lost*!*

—John Ruskin, *Fors Clavigera*

English publishing in the early nineteenth century expanded at
an even greater rate than it had in the eighteenth century and
followed the rise in the general standard of living and the growth of the
economy. As the audience for printed material increased, innovation in and
development of printing technology were encouraged and they brought
into being economies of scale that dramatically drove down the relative
cost of books despite a rising demand for them. Within a decade the technological developments lowered the cost of books by roughly half and
brought into being further economies of scale as a large number of readers
could suddenly afford more books so that bestsellers in the 1850s could sell
almost fifty times the number of copies that one in the 1810s could. They
especially encouraged the rise of literary reviews and magazines, which
were the foundations of the important publishing houses. Still, the publishing industry followed the development and expansion of the cotton and
textile industries and was dependent upon those industries throughout the
first half of the nineteenth century for its crucial raw material—cotton and
linen rags. Later, during the American civil war, when the Northern block-

ade of Southern ports effectively halted the export of cotton to textile mills in England, the price of paper rose, thus encouraging the development of new processes for making paper first from esparto grass and then from wood pulp, which effectively separated publishing from its link to the cotton and textile industries.[1] But what was good for the publishing industry during the early nineteenth century wasn't necessarily good for literature. As Bulwer-Lytton says in *England and the English* (1831), "Cheap publications of themselves are sufficient for the *diffusion* of knowledge, but not for its *advancement*."[2] In contrast to an "epoch of concentration" like that of the late sixteenth and early seventeenth centuries, in which rising demand encountered material constraints upon production, the diffusion rather than the advancement of knowledge was the general literary consequence of what Arnold in "The Function of Criticism at the Present Time" called an "epoch of expansion," a diffusion which flowed directly from the industrialization of publishing in the early nineteenth century.

As the market for literature expanded once technological developments in printing made books much cheaper, periodicals dominated the reading public's consumption of literature and tempted authors to write for the immediate moment instead of futurity and for the many instead of the few. Authors soon were delivered from the confinement of patronage and subscription into the maelstrom of the marketplace, while authorship itself became easier, more profitable, and more respectable. But the standards of style and tone inevitably suffered as authors sought to accommodate their greatly enlarged audience, while those concerned with creating new literary forms (especially the poets) quickly became alienated.[3] These changes made some of the politically conservative worry about the deleterious consequences of writers appealing to the democratic desires of a wide reading

1. For a history of papermaking, see Dard Hunter, *Papermaking: The History and Technique of an Ancient Craft*.
2. *England and the English*, 2:116. For comprehensive surveys of nineteenth-century publishing history, one must still rely on the slightly revised versions of work originally done in the 1930s and earlier. Still useful are Marjorie Plant, *The English Book Trade: An Economic History of the Making and Sale of Books*, 3d ed. (1974), and Frank Arthur Mumby and Ian Norrie, *Publishing and Bookselling*, 5th ed. (1974). For a good history of the modern technical developments in English printing, see Michael Twyman, *Printing 1770–1970: An Illustrated History of Its Development and Uses in England* (1970). For an overview of the expansion of the reading public and its effect upon literature, see Richard D. Altick, *The English Common Reader: A Social History of the Mass Reading Public, 1800–1900* (1957).
3. My discussion here roughly parallels Walter Benjamin's argument about the relation of painting to photography and film in "The Work of Art in the Age of Mechanical Reproduction," 219–53. It also broadly contradicts Peter Bürger's rash statement in his criticism of Benjamin that "in literature, there is no technical innovation that could have produced an effect comparable to that of photography in the fine arts" (*Theory of the Avant-Garde*, 32).

public and led them to propose that the best authors be insulated from the ideology of the market by being granted government pensions, thus establishing the English equivalent of the French Academy. But while many pensions were granted to maintain the living standard of a few writers, this was a haphazard process that reflected not so much any concerted political aim as a more general desire to institutionalize literature as a social construction.

I

Periodical publication made it easier for authors to write and publish. When their works were collected with others', writers did not have to negotiate directly with publishers but had the welcome mediation of an editor. This meant, in practice, that writing became more respectable and more popular. When the economies of scale were created in periodical publication, it became possible for authors to make large sums from their writing. As literature became fashionable instead of being patronized, it became both more profitable and more political insofar as its success depended upon reflecting prevailing ideologies rather than upon appealing to particular individual tastes. As Samuel Smiles says in *A Publisher and His Friends*, "Literature becomes fashionable; men of position are no longer ashamed to be known as authors, nor women of distinction afraid to welcome men of letters in their drawing-rooms. On all sides the excitement and curiosity of the times is reflected in the demand for poems, novels, essays, travels and every kind of imaginative production, under the name of *belles lettres*."[4] Of course, something must also be said for the relatively literary taste of George IV, who knew and cared enough about literature to make Theodore Hook accountant general and treasurer of Mauritius, to award Walter Scott a baronetcy, and to have Leigh Hunt imprisoned for saying in "The Prince on St. Patrick's Day" issue of the *Examiner*, "this *Adonis in Loveliness*, was a corpulent gentleman of fifty."[5] Byron, for instance, was once presented at a ball to the Prince Regent, who "professed a predilection for Poesy."[6]

Speaking of periodical publication, Bulwer-Lytton remarks that

4. *A Publisher and His Friends: Memoir and Correspondence of the Late John Murray*, 2:511. For authorship as a profession, see A. S. Collins, *The Profession of Letters: A Study of the Relation of Author to Patron, Publisher, and Public, 1780–1832*; also J. W. Saunders, *The Profession of English Letters*.
5. Edmund Blunden, *Leigh Hunt's "Examiner" Examined*, 22–23.
6. Byron to Lord Holland, June 25, 1812, *Byron's Letters and Journals*, 2:180.

the length of time intervening between the publication of its numbers was favourable to the habits and taste of the more elaborate and scholastic order of writers; what otherwise they would have published in a volume, they willingly condensed into an essay; and found for the first time in miscellaneous writings, that with a less risk of failure than in an isolated publication, they obtained, for the hour at least, an equal reputation. They enjoyed indeed a double sort of fame, for the article not only obtained praise for its own merit, but caught no feeble reflection from the general esteem conferred upon the Miscellany itself; add to this the high terms of pecuniary remuneration, till then unknown in periodicals, so tempting to the immediate wants of the younger order of writers, by which an author was sure of obtaining for an essay in the *belles lettres* a sum almost equal to that which he could have gleaned from a respectable degree of success if the essay had been given separately to the world; and this by a mode of publication which saved him from all the chances of loss, and the dread of responsibility;—the certain anxiety, the probable mortification.[7]

The ease of publication, the high rate of payment, the favorable notice to be gained from being known to write for a particular periodical, and, at the same time, the convenient shelter of anonymity which made it the author's choice to reveal whether or not his was the hand that had written a particular article—all this made the periodical format attractive to writers.

Bulwer-Lytton further remarks that "the consequence was unavoidable; instead of writing volumes, authors began pretty generally to write articles, and a literary excrescence monopolized the nourishment that should have extended to the whole body: hence talent, however great; taste, however exquisite; knowledge, however enlarged, were directed to fugitive purposes. Literary works, in the magnificent thought of Bacon, are the Ships of Time; precious was the cargo wasted upon vessels which sunk for ever in a three-months' voyage."[8] Writers wrote for the moment and most often bound their thoughts to a review of some currently fashionable book, something which soon made them all but unreadable. But there were celebrators of this phenomenon, too. In 1819 John G. Lockhart says about the habit of writing books that "there is reason to hope that people may become sensible of the absurdity of such ante-diluvian notions, and consent, for their own sakes, to keep up all their best things for the periodicals."[9] Yet, as Lockhart's association of periodical literature with the image of the flood suggests, writers were having to submit themselves to a destructive

7. *England and the English*, 2:64–65.
8. Ibid., 2:65.
9. *Peter's Letters to His Kinfolk*, 2:194.

element against which all their efforts would be required in order to avoid sinking forever from attention after a "three-months' voyage."

One might take as a specimen of advice to authors under the circumstances created by the periodical format that which was offered to Ebenezer Elliott, the "Corn-Laws" poet, by Robert Southey in 1808:

> Feel your way before you with the public, as Montgomery did. He sent his verses to the newspapers; and when they were copied from one to another it was a sure sign they had succeeded. He then communicated them, as they were copied from the papers, to the Poetical Register; the Reviews selected them for praise; and thus, when he published them in a collected form, he did nothing more than claim, in his own character, the praise which had been bestowed upon him under a fictitious name.[10]

Southey's step-by-step strategy points to the gentlemanly reserve in poetic production: the author is expected to write for the most unexacting market first and to hide behind his anonymity until it is safe to emerge from behind the mask. The system of publication and reception in periodicals allows the gentleman to test the publishing waters before assuming responsibility for his work.

So as writing became more profitable and drew gentlemen and the middle class to it, one finds a great self-consciousness about the gentility of writing. John Barrow was enlisted as a contributor to the *Quarterly* by Canning, who in answer to Barrow's doubts about the propriety of writing for money said, "I can assure you I myself have received pay for a short article I have already contributed, merely to set the example."[11] As Margaret Oliphant remarks of the first two decades of the nineteenth century, "these were the days . . . in which remuneration was suggested with delicacy, as beneath the exquisite feelings and purpose of a writer, notwithstanding the large sums which were paid to the great authors of the day."[12] This phenomenon would seem to reflect the gentlemanly aspirations of middle-class writers; it comes as no surprise, then, that Richard D. Altick in his sociological survey of the backgrounds of English authors from 1800 to 1935 should conclude that most English authors came from middle-class backgrounds.[13] Writers from a working-class background often found it difficult or humiliating to cross editorial barriers. Gerald Griffin, an Irish short story writer, found the fashionable journals particularly conscious of

10. Southey to Elliott, October 13, 1808, *The Life and Correspondence of Robert Southey,* 3:173–74.
11. *An Auto-Biographical Memoir of Sir John Barrow,* 500.
12. *Annals of a Publishing House: William Blackwood and His Sons, Their Magazine and Friends,* 1:145.
13. "The Sociology of Authorship."

the social standing of their writers and was shamed into other lines of writing: "I wrote for the great magazines. My articles were generally inserted; but on calling for payment—seeing that I was a poor, inexperienced devil, there was so much shuffling and shabby work that it disgusted me, and I gave up the idea of making money that way."[14] Although his talent gained him the acceptance of his work, Griffin's ungentlemanly appearance evidently bothered his editors so much that they sought to discourage him from submitting his manuscripts to them again.

Although writers might make as much as gentlemen, their status was something less than that. Typical of the social condescension shown to writers was the Duke of Gloucester's remark to Gibbon in 1781 upon receiving the second volume of *The History of the Decline and Fall of the Roman Empire*: "Another d-mn'd thick, square book! Always scribble, scribble, scribble! Eh! Mr. Gibbon?"[15] Writing to Augusta Leigh in 1811, Byron remarks that there is "nothing so fretful, so despicable as a Scribbler, see what *I* am, & what a parcel of Scoundrels I have brought about my ears, & what language I have been obliged to treat them with to deal with them in their own way;—all this comes of Authorship, but now I am in for it, & shall be at war with Grubstreet, till I find some better amusement."[16] Hazlitt was particularly sensitive to William Gifford's sneers in the *Quarterly* at those who were not gentlemen, and he lashed out at Gifford, the editor of the *Quarterly*, in *The Spirit of the Age*: "He stands at the door of Mr. Murray's shop, and will not let any body pass but the well-dressed mob, or some followers of the court. To edge into the *Quarterly* Temple of Fame the candidate must have a diploma from the Universities, a passport from the Treasury."[17]

In 1840 Francis Rivington, the publisher of the High Church *British Critic*, can be found writing with exquisite snobbery to its editor, John Henry Newman, about paying a contributor before publication: "Perhaps I ought to have said that it is not usual to prepay Contributors to Reviews: but it is no inconvenience to us where you think it desireable. I believe Mr. Price's case is but too common in the literary world. I observe he writes a commercial hand."[18] Reflecting on his editorship in the 1830s of the *New Monthly Magazine*, Bulwer-Lytton says to Robert Bell that "you hardly ever

14. *Life of Gerald Griffin*, quoted in Patrick Joseph Murray, *The Life of John Banim, the Irish Novelist*, 134.
15. [Henry Digby Beste], *Personal and Literary Memorials*, 68.
16. September 2, 1811, *Letters and Journals*, 2:88.
17. *Complete Works of Hazlitt*, 11:118.
18. February 19, 1840, in Lawrence N. Crumb, "Publishing the Oxford Movement: Francis Rivington's Letters to Newman," 27.

find a *Gentilhomme* writes for Magazines—When I undertook the New Monthly I was the first gentleman of birth who had done so, more followed my example. I only did it for bread & cheese & soon threw it up convinced how much it lowered me."[19] In the mid-nineteenth century G. H. Lewes gives this eloquent testimony upon his going to the Registrar of Children:

> "I believe, Sir, you are an author?"
> Assent was signified by a bow.
> "Humph!" said the registrar, deliberating. "We'll say *Gent.*"
> Accordingly he proceeded to inscribe "gent" in his best calligraphy; as he crossed the *t*, however, his mind misgave him, and looking up with puzzled ingenuousness, he blandly asked,—
> "I suppose, sir, *authors rank as gents?*"
> His look spoke volumes![20]

In the social order the author's status was uncertain and his position as a gentleman less than assured, for even a clerk at the children's registry was doubtful that Lewes deserved the rank despite recognizing the author's name.

One might compare the lordly condescension to Gigadibs, a writer for *Blackwood's Magazine*, shown by Browning's Bishop Blougram, who says

> the best you have to show being still
> That lively lightsome article we took
> Almost for the true Dickens,—what's its name?
> 'The Slum and Cellar, or Whitechapel life
> Limned after dark!' it made me laugh, I know,
> And pleased a month, and brought you in ten pounds.[21]

The respectability of writers who wrote for the reviews and magazines was always in question. Ruskin, for example, says in his preface to the *Academy Notes* of 1856, "Although I consented, some nine years ago, to review Lord Lindsay's *Christian Art* and Sir Charles Eastlake's *Essay on Oil Painting*, in the *Quarterly*, I have ever since steadily refused to write even for that once respectable periodical."[22] As an established writer, Ruskin had no need to stoop to reviewing and could better use his time writing original work. By Ruskin's day writing books had attained a gentlemanly dignity that made

19. September 15, 1853, quoted in Nigel Cross, *The Common Writer: Life in Nineteenth-Century Grub Street*, 123.
20. Lewes, "The Condition of Authors in England, Germany, and France," 294.
21. *Robert Browning: The Poems*, 1:641.
22. *The Works of John Ruskin*, 14:44.

writing for periodicals and money, in his mind at least, something beneath him.

As the bourgeoisie supplanted both the aristocracy and the court and became the patrons of literature en masse in the early nineteenth century, literature itself became subject all the more to the whims of fashion. This meant that the popular and fashionable author became wealthy, especially novelists, like Sir Walter Scott, who had a wide readership. I doubt that a publisher today, for example, would try to obtain a loan from the Bank of England, as Archibald Constable tried to do on the security of unwritten books from Scott.[23]

Although the money that could be made from writing in periodicals began to make such authorship socially respectable, it still made writers worry, especially since payment by the sheet tended to encourage the expansion of the slightest thought into a paragraph and so diminish the quality of prose. In 1805 Southey writes, "The abuses . . . of printing, spring from one evil,—it almost immediately makes authorship a trade. Per-sheeting was in use as early as Martin Luther's time, who mentions the price—a curious fact."[24] Still, the generous payment available for writing had made writing much more secure than it had been in Samuel Johnson's day, although Lamb could still lament, 'I have known many authors for bread, some repining, others envying the blessed security of a Counting House, all agreeing they had rather have been Taylors, Weavers, what not? rather than the things they were. I have known some starved, some to go mad, one dear friend literally dying in a workhouse."[25]

But writers who began their careers in the 1820s were concerned not so much with financial insecurity as with the formal constraints that writing in the periodical format placed upon their ideas. As soon as he could afford to devote less time to periodical writing, Carlyle moved to London to work on

23. Oliphant, *Annals*, 1:25–26; and John G. Lockhart, *Memoirs of the Life of Sir Walter Scott*, 6:176. The possibility of greater returns from writing novels seems to have gradually made writing novels more respectable and in the late nineteenth century apparently, at least so far as the Macmillan Archives indicate, seems to have encouraged more men to write novels and to submit them for publication, as Gaye Tuchman with Nina E. Fortin have shown in *Edging Women Out: Victorian Novelists, Publishers, and Social Change*. However, as John Sutherland rightly points out, the methodology of Tuchman and Fortin is badly flawed by beginning with and thus incorporating the male-oriented bias of the *Dictionary of National Biography* as the basis for the selection of the late-nineteenth-century novelists to be surveyed and by relying on material drawn from one publisher, Macmillan, which, as he says, was close to the male ethos of Cambridge. See his review of their book in *American Journal of Sociology*.
24. Southey to John Rickman, March 22, 1805, *Life and Correspondence*, 2:319.
25. Lamb to Bernard Barton, January 9, 1823, *Letters of Charles Lamb*, 2:363.

his *French Revolution*. Some authors remained opposed to having their work be paid by the sheet. In 1819 Coleridge wrote to William Blackwood wanting to be paid for his authorial care in revision.[26] To this Blackwood blandly replied, "I have it not in my power to say more than ten guineas per sheet; but . . . the Editor has it in his power to add to this allowance according to the value of the articles."[27] As one might expect, Coleridge never wrote for *Blackwood's*. In an 1826 letter to Bernard Barton, Charles Lamb catalogues "the miseries of subsisting by authorship": " 'Tis a pretty appendage to a situation like yours or mine, but a slavery worse than all slavery to be a bookseller's dependent, to drudge your brains for pots of ale and breasts of mutton, to change your free thoughts and voluntary numbers for ungracious TASK-WORK."[28] In 1827 Bulwer-Lytton writes to his mother that "at present, I must write for the many, or not at all. I cannot afford to write for the few. I do not write for writing's sake."[29] Like him, most authors could not afford the luxury of ignoring the popular taste and had to write what they knew they could sell.

Given this state of affairs, the writer typically became alienated from his own work. Carlyle asked himself: "Is the *form* of our literature an improvement intrinsically, or only a form better adapted to *our* actual condition? I often think, the latter."[30] Macaulay writing to Lord Lansdowne in 1833 notes that

> Hitherto, literature has been merely my relaxation,—the amusement of perhaps a month in the year. I have never considered it as the means of support. I have chosen my own topics, taken my own time, and dictated my own terms. The thought of becoming a bookseller's hack, of writing to relieve not the fulness of the mind but the emptiness of the pocket, of spurring a jaded fancy to reluctant exertion, of filling sheets with trash merely that the sheets may be filled, of bearing from publishers and editors what Dryden bore from Tonson and what, to my own knowledge, Mackintosh bore from Lardner is horrible to me. Yet thus it must be, if I should quit my office.[31]

Like Carlyle, once Macaulay thinks of writing solely for money, he thinks of trash, of literature reduced to material leftover.[32] Thomas Hood, who,

---

26. Quoted in Oliphant, *Annals*, 1:410. For the earlier portion of the letter see *Letters of Samuel Taylor Coleridge*, 4:931–33.
27. Quoted in Oliphant, *Annals*, 1:411.
28. January 9, 1823, *Letters of Charles Lamb*, 2:363.
29. June 17, 1827, in *The Life, Letters, and Literary Remains of Edward Bulwer, Lord Lytton*, 2:180.
30. *Two Note Books of Thomas Carlyle*, 69.
31. *The Letters of Thomas Babington Macaulay*, 2:353.
32. See Jacques Derrida for an analysis of this phenomenon in Kant's *Critique of Aesthetic Judgement*: in "Economimesis."

unlike Macaulay, did become a literary hack, notes that "Authorship has been treated like a slave ship, & a writer, as a black-&-white fellow somewhere between a buckra man & a nigger."[33] In 1843 Thackeray observes that writing is "a bad trade at best. The prizes in it are fewer and worse than in any other professional lottery."[34] Speaking of Scott in his *Memoirs*, Robert Pearse Gillies remarks that "no sooner has the notion of writing for pecuniary gain acquired *pre-eminence* in the mind of an author than his proper vocation is gone."[35] Perhaps most idealistically of all, G. H. Lewes writing in 1847 says that "literature should be a profession, not a trade. It should be a profession, just lucrative enough to furnish a decent subsistence to its members, but in no way lucrative enough to tempt speculators."[36] Throughout these remarks the writers emphasize gentlemanly leisure and free contemplation as ideals for authorship. They make a sharp contrast to the hard-headed Samuel Johnson who had written in a much smaller and much tougher market. Most early-nineteenth-century writers had come to authorship with middle-class expectations and with literary ideals that they saw threatened by the advent of popular literary forms and lucrative publishing formats; and they resisted the equation of market value with literary value, while also realizing that once literary concerns were subordinated to the market, authors would not slowly polish their work for posterity but instead quickly publish it for profit.

The greatest decline created by the enlarged market for literature was felt to be in the tone and civility of writing. Thomas Love Peacock in "An Essay on Fashionable Literature" says that "to any one who will compare the Reviews and Magazines of the present day with those of thirty years ago, it must be obvious that there is a much greater diffusion of general talent through them all, and more instances of great individual talent in the present than the former period: at the same time it must be equally obvious that there is much less literary honesty, much more illiberality and exclusiveness, much more subdivision into petty gangs and factions, much less classicality and very much less philosophy."[37] In an 1826 letter to his brother Derwent, Hartley Coleridge remarks, "I find great difficulty in acquiring the staid philosophic style required for the Essay on Poetry. Magazine writing is bitter bad practice, and utterly destroys the faculty of

33. Hood to Thomas Noon Talfourd, January 1841, *The Letters of Thomas Hood*, 445.
34. Thackeray to Richard Bedingfield of December 21, 1843, *The Letters and Private Papers of William Makepeace Thackeray*, 2:137.
35. *Memoirs of a Literary Veteran*, 3:81.
36. "The Condition of Authors in England, Germany, and France," 285.
37. *The Works of Thomas Love Peacock*, 8:266–67.

grave, unimpassioned composition."[38] Commenting on the first numbers of *Fraser's Magazine*, Carlyle says that they are "on the whole such a hurly-burly of rhodomontade, punch, loyalty, and Saturnalian Toryism as eye hath not seen. This out-Blackwoods Blackwood. Nevertheless the thing has its meaning: a kind of wild popular Lower-Comedy; of which John Wilson is the Inventor: it may perhaps, for it seems well adapted to the age, carry down his name to other times, as his most remarkable achievement."[39] Hartley Coleridge says to his brother about *Blackwood's*, "I cannot advise you to be a contributor. The book is always in hot water, and you may be answerable to public opinion for more than you write. This I set down among the casualties of trade, but it would much misbecome your profession."[40] In Bulwer-Lytton's *Paul Clifford* the hero writes for "The Asinaeum," a review that specialized in "the mangling of authors and the murder of grammar."[41]

The decline in style occasioned by periodical publication was created by the economic necessity of making an immediate appeal to the lowest common denominator of the common reader.[42] In his essay on Charles Lamb, De Quincey subtly analyzes this connection among writing in installments for the many, a hyperactive style, and reading periodicals: "To read therefore habitually by hurried instalments has this bad tendency—that it is likely to found a taste for modes of composition too artificially irritating, and to disturb the equilibrium of the judgment in relation to the colourings of style."[43] With a more pointed and aristocratic disdain, Byron returned a copy of the *Quarterly Review* to John Murray in 1822 uncut and unopened, saying "it is a kind of reading which I have some time disused, as I think the periodical style of writing hurtful to the habits of the mind, by presenting the superficies of too many things at once."[44] Similarly, Southey re-

---

38. *The Letters of Hartley Coleridge*, 92.
39. *Two Note Books*, 170.
40. *Letters of Hartley Coleridge*, 92.
41. *Paul Clifford*, 1:116.
42. In his lecture to the London Philosophical Society, "On Style," Coleridge describes the characteristic balanced-antithesis prose style of the eighteenth century as a result of economic pressure being placed upon writing: "After the Revolution, the spirit of the nation became much more commercial, than it had been before; a learned body, or clerisy, as such, gradually disappeared, and literature in general began to be addressed to the common miscellaneous public. That public had become accustomed to, and required, a strong stimulus; and to meet the requisitions of the public taste, a style was produced which by combining triteness of thought with singularity and excess of manner of expression, was calculated at once to soothe ignorance and to flatter vanity" (*Lectures 1808–1819 on Literature*, 2:236).
43. "Charles Lamb," *Collected Writings of Thomas De Quincey*, 5:234.
44. November 23, 1822, *Letters and Journals*, 10:40.

marks in his *Colloquies* (1829), "Even with the better part of the public that author will always obtain the most favourable reception, who keeps most upon a level with them in intellectuals, and puts them to the least trouble of thinking."[45] Given the pressure of the marketplace, it is not at all surprising that during the 1830s, the period of England's fastest growth in the nineteenth century,[46] the quality of literature should decline so noticeably.

I I

Once authors became fully aware of the market for writing, they recognized that it was organized for the publishers' benefit and not theirs. Poets, for example, after 1825 found their work unpublishable unless they were willing either to subsidize the publication or to assume the financial risks involved. What did pay from the publishers' perspective were periodicals, since their sale was rapid and predictable and so ensured a rapid turnover on capital. The reviews and magazines in the early nineteenth century became the most profitable part of almost every publisher's business and certainly of every one of note. This meant that publishers had great interest in anything that could be fitted piecemeal into their reviews and magazines, and further that their house periodicals naturally became vehicles for advertising and promoting the publisher's stock. Colburn, for instance, was notorious for having every one of his publications profusely praised in his *Literary Gazette* and for having everything else attacked, unless appropriate advertising were paid for. Further, since the reviews were serving as arbiters of taste for the reading public, publishers could delay the development of any rational critical judgment of a book for decades by arranging to have it attacked, or worse, simply by not reviewing it at all. And, to add one last stone to an already heavy burden, English authors discovered that they had an American audience overseas, which in some cases was larger than the one they had at home, but because of the lack of an international copyright agreement, they found themselves unprotected against the piracy of their work.

Since it was in the publishers' interests to maintain the readers' interest in the next issue of their periodical, they quickly discovered that running continuing series within their magazines was an effective means of attracting and sustaining the readers' attention. The first of these series was John

45. *Sir Thomas More; or, Colloquies on the Progress and Prospects of Society*, 2:394.
46. The rate of growth for the decade is estimated to have been 3.9 percent a year; see François Crouzet, *The Victorian Economy*, 49.

Wilson's *Noctes Ambrosianae*, which ran in *Blackwood's Magazine*. Speaking of it, Oliphant says that periodical literature "is never so powerful as when it can manage to prolong the interest of the reader from publication to publication, giving him as it were himself a part to play in the discussions which are there carried on."[47] Lockhart, in fact, says that the feature is the "best vehicle for discussing the Periodical Press."[48]

As the publishing market expanded in the early nineteenth century, the change in scale radically affected the development of literary reputations, since a writer could reach many more times the readers than were represented by the 14,000 quarterly copies of the *Edinburgh* and *Quarterly* reviews. Macaulay's essay on Milton in the *Edinburgh Review* of 1826 made him famous overnight. Once great fortunes were perceived to flow from Paternoster Row, many rushed to stake their claims on greatness and submitted manuscripts to the publishers for consideration. The novelty of this phenomenon and the interest in the sheer scale of the publishing industry are reflected in the 1818 letter of the engraver W. B. Cooke to John Murray: "When you have the twelve thousand *Quarterly Reviews* printed and heaped up at Albemarle Street, I shall be glad to bring some friends to have a look at such a prodigy of press work."[49] Similarly, after the first numbers of Harriet Martineau's *Illustrations of Political Economy* (1832–34) had sold thirteen thousand copies in 1832, she became the despair of her local postmaster, who, she says, "one day sent word that I must send for my own share of the mail, for it could not be carried without a barrow."[50] And the success of Dickens, beginning with *Pickwick Papers*, is virtually the stuff of legend.

Once the periodicals became the most profitable property of publishers, advertising became one of the primary aims of any periodical. Every publishing house sought to promote its own production in its house journal. So as Peacock observes, "The success of a new work is made to depend, in a great measure, not on the degree of its intrinsic merit, but on the degree of interest the publisher may have with the periodical press."[51] Carlyle records in his notebooks that Colburn and Bentley spend £10,000 annually on advertising.[52] The literary consequences of this practice were particularly great for poetry. Macaulay in his review of Robert Montgomery's poetry says,

47. *Annals*, 1:198.
48. Ibid., 1:202.
49. December 24, 1818, in Smiles, 2:50.
50. *Autobiography*, 1:136.
51. "An Essay on Fashionable Literature," *Works*, 8:272.
52. Entry for October 22, 1831, *Two Note Books*, 208–9.

Some of the well-puffed fashionable novels of eighteen hundred and twenty-nine hold the pastry of eighteen hundred and thirty; and others, which are now extolled in language almost too high-flown for the merits of *Don Quixote*, will, we have no doubt, line the trunks of eighteen hundred and thirty-one. But, though we have no apprehensions that puffing will ever confer permanent reputation on the undeserving, we still think its influence most pernicious. Men of real merit will, if they persevere, at last reach the station to which they are entitled, and intruders will be ejected with contempt and derision. But it is no small evil that the avenues to fame should be blocked up by a swarm of noisy pushing, elbowing pretenders, who, though they will not ultimately be able to make good their own entrance, hinder, in the mean time, those who have a right to enter. All who will not disgrace themselves by joining in the unseemly scuffle must expect to be at first hustled and shouldered back. Some men of talents, accordingly, turn away in dejection from pursuits in which success appears to bear no proportion to desert. Others employ in self-defence the means by which competitors, far inferior to themselves, appear for a time to obtain a decided advantage. There are few who have sufficient confidence in their own powers and sufficient elevation of mind, to wait with the secure and contemptuous patience, while dunce after dunce presses before them. Those who will not stoop to the baseness of the modern fashion are too often discouraged. Those who do stoop to it are always degraded.[53]

While Macaulay blames the advertising of the publishing industry for the decline of literature, the real aesthetic problem stems from the author's having to "stoop" in order to address a wide and profitable public. Advertising made authorship seem less than gentlemanly. Carlyle, for instance, in 1832 comments in his notebook that "last Friday, saw my name in large letters at the Athenaeum Office in Catherine street Strand; hurried on with downcast eyes, as if I had seen myself in the Pillory."[54] Further, to the extent that literary elites later self-consciously adopted the self-presentational tactics of the early nineteenth-century publishers in the service of uncommercial artistic enterprises, they entered into the domain of the avant-garde.[55] But for those like Tennyson and Browning the wait was to be a long one, and it required all of their gentlemanly reserve and patience to overcome.

Perhaps the greatest indignity English authors suffered, though, was at the hands of American publishers who freely pirated English works and paid them little or nothing at all. As Margaret Oliphant notes commenting on this practice in the early 1830s, "The literary market over the seas in

---

53. *Critical and Historical Essays*, 2:649–50.
54. Entry of January 13, 1832, *Two Note Books*, 233.
55. For a discussion of the avant-garde, see Renato Poggioli, *The Theory of the Avant-Garde*, esp. 103–28.

America was scarcely thought of in these days, when the pirates pirated freely, the authors were so surprised and gratified by any acknowledgment from across the Atlantic that they had scarcely awakened to the idea of having any right in the matter."[56] Southey remarked in 1836 about American publishers that "they reprint English works, because it pays them better than to buy native copyrights; and until men are paid, and paid well for writing, depend on it that writing well must be an exception rather than the rule."[57] Wordsworth admired the width of the page in the one-volume American pirated edition of his works, but was horrified by its cheapness; in fact, according to Southey, "Wordsworth could scarcely believe that of a three volume work, published here at a guinea and a half—the reprint was usually sold in New York for two shillings—in later days the price has been as low as sixpence, the great sale making a fraction of profit worth looking for."[58] Apparently by 1836 America, despite its having far fewer people than England, had both a more literate and wealthier per capita population than did England. For example, Martin Tupper is said to have made £10,000 from the sale of 250,000 copies of *Proverbial Philosophy* (1838–42), but only £80 on the sale of a purported 1,500,000 copies in America.[59] Carlyle was the first English author to arrange for separate American publication of his work and to profit from it. He notes, for example, that he received £150 from the first American edition as opposed to nothing from the English one of his *French Revolution* (1839).[60] Since the market for fiction in the United States was dominated by pirated fiction that had cost its publishers nothing,[61] Americans like Irving, Cooper, Melville, and James

---

56. *Annals*, 2:40.
57. Conversation recalled by Dr. Shelton Mackenzie, quoted in *Life and Correspondence*, 6:301.
58. Wordsworth to Moxon, December 11, 1838, *The Letters of William and Dorothy Wordsworth*, 6:648. Southey's remark recalled by Dr. Shelton Mackenzie, quoted in *Life and Correspondence*, 6:301. One of the great puzzles of nineteenth-century publishing that awaits the next historian of American publishing is why the cost of paper, and hence the cost of books, was so low in America relative to that in England. For the moment, I can only speculate that since cotton and linen rags for paper were imported in the form of ship's ballast and did not pay their way as freight, America apparently had an enormous abundance of rags as a consequence of its international trade, presumably because the country was importing light manufactured goods and exporting heavy bulk commodities. This would have meant that ships trading between Europe and America would have a great demand for ballast in the form of rags when sailing to America and little or none on the return voyage.
59. " 'Mr. Tupper and the Poets . . . ': A Victorian Best Seller," 137; the extent of the American sales because of many fewer editions is disputed by Jesse S. Reeves, "Martin Tupper," 252.
60. Carlyle to John A. Carlyle, February 4, 1839, *Letters* 11:16.
61. The scale of this piracy is made clear by John Sutherland, who notes that in 1856 the *American Literary Gazette and Publisher's Circular* listed for January only 37 new American titles (only two of which were novels) against 370 new English titles (twenty-four of which were novels); see "The Economics of the Victorian Three-Volume Novel," 29. On piracy in France,

were consequently forced to look to English publishers to realize their financial potential. Indeed, it was not until the International Copyright Law of 1891 (which, one should note, permitted the free publication of any work that had appeared earlier and had not been simultaneously printed in both England and America) that American authors could even begin to compete on equal ground with their English counterparts and that the English could expect fair treatment.

III

The expansion of the reading public and the subsequent undermining of the market for contemporary literature and especially for modern poetry led to attempts to preserve the status and income of authors through institutional means. Having himself been favored with the patronage of the Wedgwood brothers and having received a Privy Purse pension in 1824 of £100 in return for a yearly essay when he was made an associate in the Royal Society of Literature,[62] Coleridge regrets in *Table Talk* (1835) that under economic pressure first the professions have fallen away from the clerisy, then literature has been separated from the professions, and within his lifetime the press has been detached from literature.[63] To counter this decline of letters, in 1831 Southey proposed to Lord Brougham a Literary Academy for England:

> A yearly grant of 10,000 pounds would endow ten such appointments of 500 pounds each for the elder class, and twenty-five of 200 pounds each for younger men; these latter eligible of course, and preferably, but not necessarily to be elected to the higher benefices, as those fell vacant, and as they should have approved themselves.
> The good proposed by this as a political measure, is not that of retaining such persons to act as pamphleteers and journalists, but that of preventing them from becoming such, in hostility to the established order of things; and of giving men of letters, as a class, something to look for beyond the precarious gains of literature; thereby inducing in them a desire to support the

see Giles Barber, "Galignani's and the Publication of English Books in France from 1800 to 1852."

62. Coleridge to J. H. Green, February 16, 1824, and to Richard Cattermole, March 16, 1824, *Letters of Samuel Taylor Coleridge*, 5:328–29, 343–44. In addition, Lord Liverpool had promised a Civil List pension of £200 a year to Coleridge but had suffered a paralyzing stroke before arranging for it to be given; see the letter of Coleridge to John Hookham Frere, January 1826, *Letters*, 6:539 and n. 3.

63. *Table Talk*, 1:285.

existing institutions of their country, on the stability o. ...nich their own welfare would depend.[64]

Southey obviously envisions such an academy as a counterrevolutionary institution which would not so much make authors ideologues for the state as prevent them from becoming its active opponents. A more liberal argument for government patronage is put forward by Bulwer-Lytton in *England and the English*:

> The patronage of the State is advantageous, not in creating great ornaments in either [art or science], but in producing a general taste and a public respect for their cultivation: For the minds of great men in a civilized age are superior to the influence of laws and customs; they are not to be made by ribands and titles—their world is in themselves, and the only openings in that world look out upon immortality. But it is in the power of law and custom to bring those minds into more extensive operation—to give a wider and more ready sphere to their influence; not to create the orators, but to enlarge and still the assembly, and to conduct, as it were, through an invisible ether of popular esteem, the sound of the diviner voices amidst a listening and reverent audience.[65]

Although his comments might seem at first allied with Southey's plan by a phrase such as "still the assembly," Bulwer-Lytton seeks neither to repress great writers nor to avert a revolution, but instead to have those writers civilize and enlighten a public that has been encouraged to listen to them by the government.

Neither of these proposals seems to have been taken seriously by the government, which had in fact dispensed with the Royal Society of Literature on the death of George IV. In opposition to such plans, the *Spectator*, in "Rewards of Literature," declared its belief "that the ordinary doctrines of demand and supply are as applicable to literary productions as to any other" and "that public rewards, unless for public benefits, are improper; that no benefit is to be esteemed public in which all classes do not participate; that literature ought to look for compensation to those who receive enjoyment from its productions."[66] Still, many Civil List pensions were

---

64. February 1, 1831, *Life and Correspondence*, 6:135.
65. *England and the English*, 327. One should also note Richard Henry Horne's proposal for a Society of English Literature and Art that with £15,000 per annum would insure "a comfortable maintenance to thirty of the greatest men of the time" and "independence or encouragement" to "upwards of one hundred others" (*Exposition of the False Medium and Barriers Excluding Men of Genius from the Public* [1833], 296). The social class difference between Southey and Horne can be measured by Horne's proposing that the thirty great men receive together in salaries and annuities only £200, which would not raise them above the middle class.
66. "Rewards of Literature," 590–91.

given to once popular older writers and a few young writers who needed supplemental income to maintain a gentlemanly standard of living and who had politically powerful friends that were able to procure such pensions for them. Since the Civil List Act of 1782, which had been drawn up by Edmund Burke, the Civil List had given pensions largely to writers. In 1837 the Civil List Act devoted £1,200 a year to these pensions.[67] But this seems not to have been a systematic program and seems more to reflect a desire to institutionalize culture than to depoliticize literature. The creation of the Literary Fund and, while Peel was prime minister, the generous use of the pension list to support writers subsidized high culture to some extent. In 1835, for example, Peel added £300 to Southey's existing pension as poet laureate.[68] This supplement followed close on Southey's having been forced by Murray and Lockhart to retire as the main contributor of the *Quarterly*, and may well be considered a reward for his long service in promoting Tory politics.

In 1841 Harriet Martineau was offered a Civil List pension of £150 a year to compensate her for the inadequate protection afforded by the provisions of the copyright law, but she declined it.[69] In the same year Thomas Hood writes to the Literary Fund accepting £50 as a destitute author and later in 1844 accepts a Civil List pension of £100 settled on his wife.[70] Tennyson had foolishly sold his estate at Grasby in 1842 and invested the proceeds in the Patent Decorative Carving Company, which went bankrupt within a few months. Tennyson, whose poetry's sales were insufficient to support him, had to rely on his friends until Henry Hallam induced Peel to grant him a pension of £200 a year in 1845.[71] Before being named poet laureate in 1843, Wordsworth in 1842 was given a Civil List pension of £300 a year.[72] In 1844 Hood complains softly that the pension of £100 offered to him is the

67. Cross, *The Common Writer*, 82.
68. Peel to Southey of April 4, 1835, *Life and Correspondence*, 6:263.
69. Martineau, *Autobiography*, 1:589–92.
70. Hood to the Committee of Literary Fund, May 25 and June 1841, to Frederick Oldfield Ward, November 6, 1844, and to Robert Peel, November 9, 1844, *The Letters of Thomas Hood*, 463–65, 662–63, 664–65. On these awards, a posthumous grant of seventy-five pounds, and a subsequent subscription, see John Clubbe, *Victorian Forerunner: The Later Career of Thomas Hood*, 111–12, 180–83, 194–95.
71. Tennyson to Sir Robert Peel, September 29, 1845, *The Letters of Alfred Lord Tennyson*, 1:242–43. See Hallam Tennyson, *Alfred Lord Tennyson: A Memoir*, 1:225.
72. Wordsworth to his brother Christopher, October 17, 1842, *Letters of William and Dorothy Wordsworth*, 7:380; on Peel's earlier offer in 1835 to put Wordsworth's wife, Mary, on the Civil List, see Wordsworth's letter to Viscount Lowther, February 14, 1835, *Letters* 6:26–27; see also Victor Bonham-Carter, *Authors by Profession: From the Introduction of Printing until the Copyright Act 1911*, 1:42.

"lowest ever granted an author," and he enviously notes the recent deaths of Thomas Campbell, who had a pension of £200, of Henry F. Cary, the Dante translator, who had one of £200, and of the novelist John Banim, who had one of £150.[73] Leigh Hunt was granted a pension of £200 in 1847.[74]

The government's support of so many intellectuals left more liberal writers unhappy, as is reflected in Browning's "The Lost Leader," where the speaker expresses his disdain for those co-opted by the government—"just for a handful of silver he left us."[75] One should recognize, however, that the Civil List pensions represented in many cases individual campaigns for the support of an author. Henry Hallam, for instance, had put Tennyson's name in for a pension; and Richard Monckton Milnes personally recommended Tennyson to the prime minister when in 1845 Peel had to choose between Tennyson and Sheridan Knowles, the dramatist, for the available pension. The telling point is that Peel had heard of neither author and that Milnes gave him "Ulysses" to read and thus persuaded him that Tennyson deserved the pension.[76] For politicians, literature was at best a subsidiary concern.

IV

This institutionalization of literature as high culture was later reinforced by the inclusion of English literature as a subject of examination at Oxford and Cambridge. But in the early nineteenth century authors and society were just beginning to grasp the significance of the changes in the market for literature that had been created by the industrialization of publishing and were unlikely to understand the technological basis for those changes. This ignorance, together with the historical perception that things had

---

73. Hood to Frederick Oldfield Ward, November 6, 1844, *Letters of Thomas Hood*, 662–63.
74. Bonham-Carter, *Authors by Profession*, 1:54.
75. *Robert Browning: The Poems*, 1:410. Since Wordsworth's politics had long been known to be conservative and since he had received his stamp distributorship because of his family's long alliance with the Lords Lonsdale and their Tory interests, the real historical puzzle has been why the identification of Wordsworth with the "lost leader" ever arose and why Browning writing in the 1840s would have thought of Wordsworth as a leader. The answer, I would suggest, lies in Wordsworth's role in Sergeant Talfourd's parliamentary campaign to extend the length of copyright discussed above in chapter 2. Wordsworth had conducted a letter-writing campaign on behalf of Talfourd's bill, had gotten other authors to support the bill, and had been the target of Thomas Tegg's determined defense of the existing law. I think that Browning, who had dedicated his first play *Strafford* (1837) to Talfourd, had thought of Wordsworth as a voice of authorial independence despite his politics and had viewed him as a leader in behalf of the rights of authors.
76. Hallam Tennyson, 1:225.

been better for the production of literature earlier in England's history, led many authors to feel alienated both from their own work and also from the common reader. A few, like Peacock, thought that the democratization of ideas that the periodicals and the expansion of publishing represented was nothing short of an intellectual disaster. In *Crotchet Castle* (1830) he comments on these developments in the person of the Reverend Doctor Folliott: "I am out of all patience with this march of mind. Here has my house been nearly burned down, by my cook taking it into her head to study hydrostatics, in a sixpenny tract, published by the Steam Intellect Society, and written by a learned friend who is for doing all the world's business as well as his own, and is equally well qualified to handle every branch of human knowledge."[77] Some cheerfully addressed the public that they had, asking, like Hazlitt, "Why should we dismiss *the reading public* with contempt, when we have so little chance with the next generation?"[78] But, like Carlyle, most felt financially constrained to write within the periodical format and to fear rightly that their work was too much constricted by the format in which it appeared.

The great irony of the transformation in the conditions of literary production was that authors felt their influence upon society diminished even as they saw that the possibilities for it were enormously expanded—hence their ambivalence toward the publishing marketplace where a commodity value was placed on their work. From the tension between the possibility to succeed financially by writing for the common reader and the desire to preserve an artistic integrity are born the avant-garde movements of nineteenth-century literature. The estrangement that writers felt from the reception of their writing had its foundation in the economic changes in the publishing industry created by technological improvements in printing. In the correspondence and diaries of the age's authors, these changes are writ large upon their literary concerns. That few at the time could see the connections between writing and the industrialization of publishing points to a systematic ideological blindness to the relations between literary production and mechanical reproduction. The political fears implicit in this blindness are made explicit by Southey's proposal for a literary academy and later by Matthew Arnold in *Culture and Anarchy*. For if literature is viewed as a means of enlightenment, then it is essential that its production not fall to authors who must appeal to the common reader for their suste-

77. *Works*, 4:13.
78. "The Periodical Press," *Complete Works*, 16:219.

nance. It is not surprising, then, that as the publishing market expanded in England in the early nineteenth century, there was an institutional impulse to insulate the producers of high culture from the demands of the marketplace. Whether any institutional defense of literature still has a future in England, much less here in America, is a question the answer to which seems much less certain today.

Bibliography

Abrams, Meyer H. *Natural Supernaturalism: Tradition and Revolution in Romantic Literature*. New York: W. W. Norton, 1971.

Adburgham, Alison. *Women in Print: Writing Women and Women's Magazines from the Restoration to the Accession of Victoria*. London: George Allen and Unwin, 1972.

Adorno, Theodor W. *Ästhetische Theorie*. Ed. Rolf Tiedemann and Gretl Adorno. Frankfurt: Surkamp Verlag, 1971.

———. "The Culture Industry: Enlightenment as Mass Deception." In Max Horkheimer and Theodor W. Adorno, *Dialectic of Enlightenment*, 120–67. Trans. John Cumming. New York: Herder and Herder, 1972.

———. "The Essay as Form." *Notes to Literature*, 1:3–23. Ed. Rolf Tiedemann. Trans. Shierry Weber Nicholsen. 2 vols. New York: Columbia Univ. Press, 1991.

"Advertisement." *Edinburgh Review* 1 (1802):iii.

Altick, Richard D. *The English Common Reader: A Social History of the Mass Reading Public, 1800–1900*. Chicago: Univ. of Chicago Press, 1957.

———. "Nineteenth-Century English Best-Sellers: A Further List." *Studies in Bibliography* 22 (1969):197–206.

———. "Nineteenth-Century English Best-Sellers: A Third List." *Studies in Bibliography* 39 (1986):235–41.

———. "The Sociology of Authorship: The Social Origins, Education, and Occupations of 1,100 British Writers, 1800–1935." *Bulletin of the New York Public Library* 66 (1962):389–404.

Arnold, Matthew. *The Complete Prose Works of Matthew Arnold*. Ed. R. H. Super. 10 vols. Ann Arbor: Univ. of Michigan Press, 1960–77.

———. *The Letters of Matthew Arnold, 1848–1888*. Ed. George W. E. Russell. 2 vols. London: Macmillan, 1895.

Austen, Jane. *Jane Austen's Letters to Her Sister Cassandra and Others*. 2d ed. Ed. R. W. Chapman. Oxford: Oxford Univ. Press, 1952.

———. *Minor Works*. Ed. R. W. Chapman. Rev. B. C. Southam. London: Oxford Univ. Press, 1969.

———. *The Novels of Jane Austen*. 3d ed. Ed. R. W. Chapman. 5 vols. London: Oxford Univ. Press, 1932–34.

Babbage, Charles. *On the Economy of Machinery and Manufactures.* 2d ed. London: Charles Knight, 1832.

Bander, Elaine. "The Significance of Jane Austen's Reference to 'Camilla' in 'Sanditon': A Note." *Notes and Queries,* n.s., 25 (1978):214–16.

Banim, John. *Revelations of the Dead-Alive.* London: W. Simpkin and R. Marshall, 1824.

Barber, Giles. "Galignani's and the Publication of English Books in France from 1800 to 1852." *Library,* 5th ser., 16 (1961):267–86. ·

Barnes, J. J. *Authors, Publishers, and Politicians: The Quest for an Anglo-American Copyright Agreement, 1815–1854.* Columbus: Ohio State Univ. Press, 1974.

——. *Free Trade in Books: A Study of the London Book Trade since 1800.* London: Oxford Univ. Press, 1964.

Barrow, John. *An Auto-Biographical Memoir of Sir John Barrow.* London: John Murray, 1847.

Barwick, G. F. "The Magazines of the Nineteenth Century." *Transactions of the Bibliographical Society* 11 (1909–11):237–49.

Batdorf, Franklin P. "The Murray Reprints of George Crabbe: A Publisher's Record." *Studies in Bibliography* 4 (1951–52):192–99.

Bate, Walter Jackson. *John Keats.* Cambridge: Harvard Univ. Press, 1963.

Bauer, Josephine. *The London Magazine, 1820–29.* Copenhagen: Rosenkilde and Bagger, 1953.

Beddoes, Thomas Lovell. *The Works of Thomas Lovell Beddoes.* Ed. H. W. Donner. London: Oxford Univ. Press, 1935.

Benjamin, Walter. *Illuminations.* Ed. and trans. Hannah Arendt. New York: Harcourt Brace and World, 1968.

——. "The Author as Producer." In *Reflections: Essays, Aphorisms, Autobiographical Writings,* 220–38. Ed. Peter Demetz. New York: Harcourt Brace Jovanovich, 1978.

Bennett, Scott. "John Murray's Family Library and the Cheapening of Books in Early Nineteenth Century Britain." *Studies in Bibliography* 29 (1976):139–66.

——. "Revolutions in Thought: Serial Publication and the Mass Market for Reading." In *The Victorian Periodical Press: Samplings and Soundings,* 225–57. Ed. Joanne Shattock and Michael Wolff. Leicester: Leicester Univ. Press, 1982.

Beste, Henry Digby. *Personal and Literary Memorials.* London: Henry Colburn, 1829.

Besterman, Theodore. *The Publishing Firm of Cadell and Davies: Select Correspondence and Accounts, 1793–1836.* London: Oxford Univ. Press, 1938.

Beyle, Henri Marie. *A Roman Journal.* Trans. Haakon Chevalier. New York: Orion Press, 1957.

Blagden, Cyprian. "*Edinburgh Review* Authors, 1830–49." *The Library,* 5th ser., 7 (1952):212–14.

Blake, William. *The Poetry and Prose of William Blake.* Ed. David V. Erdman. Garden City, N.Y.: Doubleday, 1965.

Blakey, Dorothy. *The Minerva Press, 1790–1820.* London: Oxford Univ. Press, 1939.

Block, Andrew. *The English Novel, 1740–1850: A Catalogue Including Prose Romances, Short Stories, and Translations of Foreign Fiction.* 2d ed. London: William Dawson and Sons, 1961.

Blunden, Edmund. *Leigh Hunt's "Examiner" Examined*. London: Cobden-Sanderson, 1928.

Bonham-Carter, Victor. *Authors by Profession*. Vol. 1: *From the Introduction of Printing until the Copyright Act 1911*. London: The Society of Authors, 1978.

Booth, Bradford Allen. *A Cabinet of Gems: Short Stories from the English Annuals*. Berkeley: Univ. of California Press, 1938.

Bose, A. "The Verse of the English 'Annuals.'" *Review of English Studies*, n.s., 4 (1953):38–51.

Boswell, James. *Boswell's Life of Johnson*. Ed. George Birckbeck Hill and L. F. Powell. 6 vols. Oxford: Clarendon Press, 1934–1950.

Bourne, H. R. Fox. *John Frances, Publisher of "The Athenaeum": A Literary Chronicle of Half a Century*. London: Richard Bentley and Son, 1888.

Bowring, John. Ed. *The Works of Jeremy Bentham*. 11 vols. Edinburgh: William Tait, 1843.

Boyle, Andrew. *An Index to the Annuals, 1820–1850*. Worcester, Eng.: Andrew Boyle, 1967.

Brougham, Henry Peter. *The Life and Times of Henry Lord Brougham*. 2d ed. 3 vols. Edinburgh: William Blackwood and Sons, 1871.

Broughton, Leslie Nathan, et al. *Robert Browning: A Bibliography*. Cornell Studies in English, vol. 39. Ithaca: Cornell Univ. Press, 1953.

Browning, Robert. "Deux lettres inédites de Robert Browning à Joseph Milsand." Ed. W. Thomas. *Revue Germanique* 12 (1921):249–55.

——. *The Letters of Robert Browning and Elizabeth Barrett Browning, 1845–1846*. Ed. Elvan Kintner. 2 vols. Cambridge, Mass..: Harvard Univ. Press, 1969.

——. *Robert Browning: The Poems*. Ed. John Pettigrew and Thomas J. Collins. 2 vols. New Haven: Yale Univ. Press, 1981.

Buckley, Jerome. *Tennyson: The Growth of a Poet*. Boston: Houghton Mifflin, 1960.

Bulwer-Lytton. *England and the English*. 2d ed. 2 vols. London: Richard Bentley, 1833.

——. "The Letters of Sir Edward Bulwer-Lytton to the Editors of 'Blackwood's Magazine,' 1840–1873, in the National Library of Scotland." Ed. Malcolm Orthell Usrey. Ph.D. dissertation, Texas Technological College, 1963.

——. *The Life, Letters, and Literary Remains of Edward Bulwer, Lord Lytton*. Ed. Edward Robert Bulwer-Lytton. 2 vols. London: Kegan Paul, Trench, 1883.

——. "Memoir of Laman Blanchard." In *Sketches from Life: by the late Laman Blanchard*, 1:v–xliv. 3 vols. London: Henry Colburn, 1846.

——. *Paul Clifford*. 3 vols. London: Henry Colburn and Richard Bentley, 1830.

Bürger, Peter. *Theory of the Avant-Garde*. Trans. Michael Shaw. Minneapolis: Univ. of Minnesota Press, 1984.

Burke, Kenneth. *The Philosophy of Literary Form: Studies in Symbolic Action*. 2d ed. Baton Rouge: Louisiana State Univ. Press, 1967.

Burney, Frances. *Camilla; or a Picture of Youth*. Ed. Edward A. Bloom and Lillian D. Bloom. London: Oxford Univ. Press, 1972.

Butler, Marilyn. *Romantics, Rebels, and Reactionaries: English Literature and Its Background, 1760–1830*. Oxford: Oxford Univ. Press, 1982.

Byron, George Gordon, Lord. *Byron's Letters and Journals*. Ed. Leslie A. Marchand. 12 vols. London: John Murray, 1973–82.

——. *Poetical Works*. Ed. Frederick Page and John Jump. 3d ed. London: Oxford Univ. Press, 1970.

Carlyle, Thomas. *The Collected Letters of Thomas and Jane Welsh Carlyle*. Ed. Charles Richard Sanders and Kenneth J. Fielding. 21 vols. Durham, N.C.: Duke Univ. Press, 1970–.

——. *The Collected Works of Thomas Carlyle*. Ed. H. D. Traill. 30 vols. London: Chapman and Hall, 1896–99.

——. *The Life of John Sterling*. 2d ed. London: Chapman and Hall, 1852.

——. *Reminiscences*. Ed. Charles Eliot Norton. London: J. M. Dent and Sons, 1932; rpt. 1972.

——. *Sartor Resartus: The Life and Opinions of Herr Teufelsdröckh*. Ed. Charles Frederick Harrold. New York: Odyssey Press, 1937.

——. *Two Note Books of Thomas Carlyle from 23d March 1822 to 16th May 1832*. Ed. Charles Eliot Norton. New York: The Grolier Club, 1898.

Carrington, Charles Edmund. *A Subaltern's War: Being a Memoir of the Great War from the Point of View of a Romantic Young Man*. London: Peter Davies, 1929.

Cary, Rev. Henry. *Memoir of the Rev. Henry Francis Cary*. 2 vols. London: Edward Moxon, 1847.

"Charles Dickens and His Works." *Fraser's Magazine* 21 (1840):381–400.

Chilcott, Tim. *A Publisher and His Circle: The Life and Work of John Taylor, Keats's Publisher*. London: Routledge and Kegan Paul, 1972.

Chorley, Henry Fothergill. *Autobiography, Memoir, and Letters*. Comp. Henry G. Hewlett. 2 vols. London: Richard Bentley and Son, 1873.

Clare, John. *The Letters of John Clare*. Ed. J. W. and Anne Tibble. New York: Barnes and Noble, 1970.

Clive, John. *Scotch Reviewers: The "Edinburgh Review," 1802–1815*. Cambridge, Mass.: Harvard Univ. Press, 1957.

Clubbe, John. *Victorian Forerunner: The Later Career of Thomas Hood*. Durham, N.C.: Duke Univ. Press, 1968.

Coleman, D. C. *The British Paper Industry, 1495–1860: A Study in Industrial Growth*. Oxford: Clarendon Press, 1958.

Coleridge, Hartley. *The Letters of Hartley Coleridge*. Ed. Grace Evelyn and Earl Leslie Griggs. London: Oxford Univ. Press, 1936.

——. *New Poems, Including a Selection from His Published Poetry*. Ed. E. L. Griggs. London: Oxford Univ. Press, 1942.

Coleridge, Samuel Taylor. *Biographia Literaria*. Ed. James Engell and W. Jackson Bate. 2 vols. In *The Collected Works of Samuel Taylor Coleridge*. Princeton: Princeton Univ. Press, 1983.

——. *Collected Letters of Samuel Taylor Coleridge*. Ed. Earl Leslie Griggs. 6 vols. Oxford: Clarendon Press, 1956–71.

——. *The Friend*. Ed. Barbara E. Rooke. 2 vols. In *The Collected Works of Samuel Taylor Coleridge*. Princeton: Princeton Univ. Press, 1969.

——. *Lectures 1808–1819 on Literature*. Ed. R. A. Foakes. 2 vols. In *The Collected Works of Samuel Taylor Coleridge*. Princeton: Princeton Univ. Press, 1987.

——. *Table Talk*. Ed. Carl Woodring. 2 vols. In *The Collected Works of Samuel Taylor Coleridge*. Princeton: Princeton Univ. Press, 1990.

——. *The Watchman*. Ed. Lewis Patton. In *The Collected Works of Samuel Taylor Coleridge*. Princeton: Princeton Univ. Press, 1970.

Coles, W. A. "Mary Russell Mitford: The Inauguration of a Literary Career." *Bulletin of the John Rylands Library* 40 (1957):33–46.

Colie, Rosalie L. *The Resources of Kind: Genre Theory in the Renaissance*. Ed. Barbara K. Lewalski. Berkeley: Univ. of California Press, 1973.

Collins, A. S. *The Profession of Letters: A Study of the Relation of Author to Patron, Publisher, and Public, 1780–1832*. New York: E. P. Dutton, 1929.

Colman, George, the Elder. *Polly Honeycombe, A Dramatick Novel*. 4th ed. London: T. Becket, 1778.

Compton, F. E. "Subscription Books." In *Bowker Lectures on Book Publishing*, 56–78. New York: R. R. Bowker, 1957.

Connolly, Cyril. *Enemies of Promise*. Rev. ed. New York: Persea Books, 1983.

Constable, Thomas. *Archibald Constable and His Literary Correspondents*. 3 vols. Edinburgh: Edmonston and Douglas, 1873.

Copleston, Edward. "Advice to a Young Reviewer, with a Specimen of the Art." In William James Copleston, *Memoir of Edward Copleston*, 281–97. London: John W. Parker and Son, 1851.

Cox, Harold, and John E. Chandler. *The House of Longman, 1724–1924*. London: Longmans, Green, 1925.

Croce, Benedetto. *Aesthetics*. Trans. Douglas Ainslie. New York: Macmillan, 1922; rpt. Farrar, Straus, 1965.

Croker, John Wilson. "Keats's *Endymion*." *Quarterly Review* 19 (1818):204–8.

Cross, Nigel. *The Common Writer: Life in Nineteenth-Century Grub Street*. Cambridge: Cambridge Univ. Press, 1985.

Crouzet, François. *The Victorian Economy*. Trans. A. S. Forster. New York: Columbia Univ. Press, 1982.

Crumb, Lawrence N. "Publishing the Oxford Movement: Francis Rivington's Letters to Newman." *Publishing History* 28 (1990):5–53.

Crump, M. J., and R. J. Goulden. "Four Library Catalogues of Note." *Factotum* 1 (1978):9–13.

Culler, A. Dwight. *The Poetry of Tennyson*. New Haven: Yale Univ. Press, 1977.

Curwen, Henry. *A History of Booksellers: The Old and the New*. London: Chatto and Windus, 1873.

Darley, George. *Life and Letters of George Darley, Poet and Critic*. Ed. Claude Colleer Abbott. Oxford: Clarendon Press, 1928.

Darnton, Robert. *The Business of Enlightenment: A Publishing History of the "Encyclopédie," 1775–1800*. Cambridge, Mass.: Harvard Univ. Press, 1985.

——. *The Great Cat Massacre and Other Episodes in French Cultural History*. New York: Random House, 1985.

DeLaura, David J. "The Future of Poetry: A Context for Carlyle and Arnold." In *Carlyle and His Contemporaries: Essays in Honor of Charles Richard Sanders*, 148–80. Ed. John Clubbe. Durham, N.C.: Duke Univ. Press, 1976.

De Quincey, Thomas. "Charles Lamb." *The Collected Writings of Thomas De Quincey*, 5:215–58. Ed. David Masson. 14 vols. Edinburgh: Adam and Charles Black, 1889–90.

——. *De Quincey Memorials*. Ed. Alexander H. Japp. 2 vols. London: William Heine-
mann, 1891.

Derrida, Jacques. "Economimesis." *Diacritics* 11, no. 2 (Summer 1981):3–25.

Dibdin, Thomas Frognall. *The Bibliographical Decameron; or, Ten Days Pleasant Discourse upon Illuminated Manuscripts, and Subjects Connected with Early Engravings,
Typography, and Bibliography*. London: W. Bulmer; Shakespeare Press, 1817.

——. *Bibliomania; or Book Madness: A Bibliographical Romance in Six Parts*. London:
Longman, Hurst, Rees, Orme, and Brown, 1809.

——. *Bibliophobia: Remarks on the Present Languid and Depressed State of Literature and
the Book Trade*. London: Henry Bohn, 1832.

Dickens, Charles. *The Letters of Charles Dickens*. Ed. Madelaine House et al. 7 vols.
Oxford: Clarendon Press, 1965– .

——. *Charles Dickens's Letters to Charles Lever*. Ed. Flora V. Livingston. Cambridge,
Mass.: Harvard Univ. Press, 1933.

Dilke, Charles Wentworth. *The Papers of a Critic*. 2 vols. London: John Murray, 1875.

Disraeli, Benjamin. *Vivian Grey*. 5 vols. London: Henry Colburn, 1826–27.

Douglas, Wallace W. "Wordsworth as Business Man." *PMLA* 63 (1948):625–41.

Dudek, Louis. *Literature and the Press: A History of Printing, Printed Media, and Their
Relation to Literature*. Toronto: Ryerson Press, 1960.

Dyson, Anthony. *Pictures to Print: The Nineteenth-Century Engraving Trade*. London:
Farrand, 1984.

Edmonds, Charles. See Charles Edmund Carrington.

Egerer, J. W. *A Bibliography of Robert Burns*. Edinburgh: Oliver and Boyd, 1964.

Eisenstein, Elizabeth. *The Printing Press as an Agent of Change: Communication and
Cultural Transformations in the Early-Modern Era*. 2 vols. Cambridge: Cambridge Univ. Press, 1979.

Ellis, S. M. *The Solitary Horseman; or The Life & Adventures of G. P. R. James*. Ken-
sington, Eng.: Cayme Press, 1927.

——. *William Harrison Ainsworth and His Friends*. 2 vols. London: John Lane; Bodley
Head, 1911.

Elwin, Malcolm. *Victorian Wallflowers*. London: Jonathan Cape, 1934.

Erickson, Lee. *Robert Browning: His Poetry and His Audiences*. Ithaca, N.Y.: Cornell
Univ. Press, 1984.

Faulkner, Thomas C. "George Crabbe: Murray's 1834 Edition of the Life and
Poems." *Studies in Bibliography* 32 (1979):246–52.

Feather, John. *The Provincial Book Trade in Eighteenth-Century England*. Cambridge:
Cambridge Univ. Press, 1985.

——. "Publishers and Politicians: The Remaking of the Law of Copyright in Britain, 1775–1842. Part I: Legal Deposit and the Battle of the Library Tax."
Publishing History 24 (1988):49–76.

——. "Publishers and Politicians: The Remaking of the Law of Copyright in Britain, 1775–1842. Part II: The Rights of Authors." *Publishing History* 25 (1989):
45–72.

——. "Technology and the Book in the Nineteenth Century." *Critical Survey* 2, no. 1
(1990):5–13.

Feltham, John. *A Guide to All the Watering and Sea-Bathing Places*. London: Richard
Phillips, 1803.

——. *A Guide to All the Watering and Sea-Bathing Places.* London: Richard Phillips, 1806.

——. *A Guide to All the Watering and Sea-Bathing Places.* London: Longman, Hurst, Rees, Orme and Brown, 1815.

——. *A Guide to All the Watering and Sea-Bathing Places.* London: Longman, Hurst, Rees, Orme and Brown, [1824].

Fish, Stanley. *Self-Consuming Artifacts: The Experience of Seventeenth-Century Literature.* Berkeley: Univ. of California Press, 1972.

Foot, M. R. D. "Mr Gladstone and His Publishers." In *Author/Publisher Relations during the Eighteenth and Nineteenth Centuries,* 156–75. Ed. Robin Myers and Michael Harris. Oxford: Oxford Polytechnic Press, 1983.

Ford, Richard. *The Letters of Richard Ford, 1797–1858.* Ed. Rowland E. Prothero. New York: E. P. Dutton, 1905.

Francis, John C. *John Francis, Publisher of "The Athenaeum": A Literary Chronicle of Half a Century.* Intro. H. R. Fox Bourne. London: Richard Bentley and Son, 1888.

Gettmann, Royal A. *A Victorian Publisher: A Study of the Bentley Papers.* Cambridge: Cambridge Univ. Press, 1960.

Gillies, R. P. *Memoirs of a Literary Veteran.* 3 vols. London: Richard Bentley, 1851.

Gillman, James. *The Life of Samuel Taylor Coleridge.* London: William Pickering, 1838.

Gilson, David. *A Bibliography of Jane Austen.* Oxford: Clarendon Press, 1982.

Gore, Mrs. Catherine. "The Monster-Misery of Literature." *Blackwood's Magazine* 55 (1844):556–60.

Graham, Walter. *English Literary Periodicals.* New York: Thomas Nelson and Sons, 1930.

Grant, James. *The Great Metropolis.* 2 vols. in 1. New York: Saunders and Otley, 1837.

Griest, Guinevere L. *Mudie's Circulating Library and the Victorian Novel.* Bloomington: Indiana Univ. Press, 1970.

Griffith, Richard. *A Series of Genuine Letters between Henry and Frances.* 6 vols. London: W. Johnston; vols. 5 and 6, W. Richardson and L. Urquhart, 1766–70.

Groot, Hans B. de. "Lord Brougham and the Founding of the *British and Foreign Review.*" *Victorian Periodicals Newsletter* 8 (April 1970):22–32.

Gross, John. *The Rise and Fall of the Man of Letters: A Study of the Idiosyncratic and the Humane in Modern Literature.* New York: Macmillan, 1969.

Haas, Sabine. "Victorian Poetry Anthologies: Their Role and Success in the Nineteenth-Century Book Market." *Publishing History* 17 (1985):51–64.

Hall, S. C. *A Book of Memories of Great Men and Women of the Age, from Personal Acquaintance.* London: Virtue, 1871.

Hamlyn, Hilda M. "Eighteenth-Century Circulating Libraries in England." *Library,* 5th ser., 1 (1946–47):197–222.

Hansard, T. C. *Typographia: A Historical Sketch of the Origin and Progress of the Art of Printing.* London: Baldwin, Cradock, and Joy, 1825.

Hart, Horace. *Charles Earl Stanhope and the Oxford University Press.* Ed. James Mosley. London: Printing Historical Society, 1966.

Haydon, Benjamin Robert. *The Diary of Benjamin Robert Haydon.* Ed. Willard Bissell Pope. 5 vols. Cambridge, Mass.: Harvard Univ. Press, 1960–63.

Hazlitt, William. *The Complete Works of William Hazlitt.* Ed. P. P. Howe. 21 vols. London: J. M. Dent and Sons, 1930–34.

Heath-Stubbs, John. *The Darkling Plain: A Study of the Later Fortunes of Romanticism in English Poetry from George Darley to W. B. Yeats.* London: Eyre and Spottiswode, 1952.

Heinzelman, Kurt. *The Economics of the Imagination.* Amherst: Univ. of Massachusetts Press, 1980.

Hewison, Robert. *Under Siege: Literary Life in London, 1939–1945.* New York: Oxford Univ. Press, 1977.

Hill, Christopher. *Puritanism and Revolution: Studies in the Interpretation of the English Revolution of the 17th Century.* London: Secker and Warburg, 1958.

Hodgson, Thomas. *An Essay on the Origin and Process of Stereotype Printing.* Newcastle: S. Hodgson, 1820.

Hogg, James. *Selected Poems.* Ed. Douglas S. Mack. Oxford: Clarendon Press, 1970.

Holloway, John. *The Victorian Sage: Studies in Argument.* London: Macmillan, 1953.

Hood, Thomas. *The Letters of Thomas Hood.* Ed. Peter F. Morgan. University of Toronto Department of English Studies and Texts, no. 18. Toronto: Univ. of Toronto Press, 1973.

Horne, Richard Henry. *Exposition of the False Medium and Barriers Excluding Men of Genius from the Public.* London: Effingham Wilson, 1833.

Horsman, Alan. *The Victorian Novel.* Oxford: Clarendon Press, 1990.

"An Hour's Tête-à-Tête with the Public." *Blackwood's Magazine* 8 (1820):80.

Hueckel, Glenn. "War and the British Economy, 1793–1815: A General Equilibrium Analysis." *Explorations in Economic History* 10 (1973):365–96.

Hunnisett, Basil. *Steel-engraved Book Illustration in England.* London: Scolar Press, 1980.

Hunt, Leigh. *The Autobiography of Leigh Hunt; With Reminiscences of Friends and Contemporaries.* Ed. Roger Ingpen. 2 vols. Westminster: Archibald Constable, 1903.

——. "Mr. Moxon's Publications." *Tatler* (June 4, 1831). Rpt. in *Leigh Hunt's Literary Criticism,* 389–93. Ed. L. H. and C. W. Houtchens. New York: Columbia Univ. Press, 1956.

——. "Pocket-Books and Keepsakes." In *The Keepsake,* 1–28. London: Hurst, Chance, Robinson, 1828.

Hunter, Dard. *Papermaking: The History and Technique of an Ancient Craft.* 2d ed. New York: Alfred A. Knopf, 1947.

Hurd, Michael. *The Ordeal of Ivor Gurney.* Oxford: Oxford Univ. Press, 1984.

Huxley, Leonard. *The House of Smith Elder.* London: Privately Printed, 1923.

Innis, Harold A. "The English Press in the Nineteenth Century." *University of Toronto Quarterly* 15 (1945):337–46.

Jack, Ian. *English Literature, 1815–1832.* Oxford: Clarendon Press, 1963.

Jackson, J. R. de J. *Annals of English Verse, 1770–1835: A Preliminary Survey of the Volumes Published.* New York: Garland Press, 1985.

James, G. P. R. "Some Observations on the Book Trade, as Connected with Literature, in England." *Journal of the (Royal) Statistical Society of London* 6 (1843):50–60.

Jauss, Hans Robert. *Toward an Aesthetic of Reception.* Trans. Timothy Bahti. Theory and History of Literature, no. 2. Minneapolis: Univ. of Minnesota Press, 1982.

Jeffrey, Francis. "Crabbe's Poems." *Edinburgh Review* 12 (1808):131–51.
———. "*Poems* by W. Wordsworth." *Edinburgh Review* 11 (1807):214–31.
Jerdan, William. *The Autobiography of William Jerdan.* 4 vols. London: Arthur Hall, Virtue, 1852–53.
Johnson, Samuel. *The Rambler.* Ed. W. J. Bate and Albrecht B. Strauss. 3 vols. New Haven: Yale Univ. Press, 1969.
Kaufman, Philip. "The Community Library: A Chapter in English Social History." *Transactions of the American Philosophical Society*, n.s., 57, pt. 7 (1967).
———. "English Book Clubs and Their Role in Social History." *Libri* 14 (1964):1–31.
———. "In Defense of Fair Readers." *Review of English Literature* 8 (1967):68–76.
Keats, John. *The Letters of John Keats, 1814–1821.* Ed. Hyder E. Rollins. 2 vols. Cambridge, Mass.: Harvard Univ. Press, 1958.
Kelley, Philip, and Betty A. Coley. *The Browning Collections: A Reconstruction with Other Memorabilia.* Winfield, Kans.: Wedgestone Press, 1984.
Kernan, Alvin B. *Printing Technology, Letters, and Samuel Johnson.* Princeton: Princeton University Press, 1987.
Keynes, Geoffrey. *William Pickering, Publisher: A Memoir and a Check-List of His Publications.* Rev. ed. London: Galahad Press, 1969.
Kierkegaard, Søren. *The Journals of Søren Kierkegaard.* Ed. and trans. Alexander Dru. London: Oxford Univ. Press, 1938.
King, R. W. *The Translator of Dante: The Life, Work, and Friendships of Henry Francis Cary, (1772–1844).* London: Martin Secker, 1925.
Klancher, John P. *The Making of English Reading Audiences, 1790–1832.* Madison: Univ. of Wisconsin Press, 1987.
———. "Reading the Social Text: Power, Signs, and Audience in Early Nineteenth-Century Prose." *Studies in Romanticism* 23 (1984):183–204.
Knott, D. H. "Thomas Wilson and *The Use of the Circulating Library.*" *Library History* 4 (1976):2–10.
Lackington, James. *Memoirs of the First Forty-Five Years of the Life of James Lackington.* 7th ed. London: James Lackington, 1794.
Lacoue-Labarthe, Philippe, and Jean-Luc Nancy. "Genre." In *Glyph* 7. Baltimore: Johns Hopkins Univ. Press, 1980.
Lamb, Charles. *The Letters of Charles and Mary Anne Lamb.* Ed. Edwin W. Marrs Jr. 3 vols. Ithaca: Cornell Univ. Press, 1975– .
———. *The Letters of Charles Lamb to Which are Added Those of His Sister Mary Lamb.* Ed. E. V. Lucas. 3 vols. New Haven: Yale Univ. Press, 1935.
———. *The Works of Charles and Mary Lamb.* Ed. E. V. Lucas. 7 vols. London: Methuen, 1903–05.
Law, Marie Hamilton. *The English Familiar Essay in the Early Nineteenth Century.* New York: Russell and Russell, 1934.
Lawson, Jonathan. *Robert Bloomfield.* Twayne's English Authors Series 310. Boston: Twayne Publishers, 1980.
Leavis, Q. D. *Fiction and the Reading Public.* London: Chatto and Windus, 1932.
Levine, George. "Use and Abuse of Carlylese." In *The Art of Victorian Prose*, 101–26. Ed. George Levine and William Madden. London: Oxford Univ. Press, 1966.
Levinson, Marjorie. *Wordsworth's Great Period Poems: Four Essays.* Cambridge: Cambridge Univ. Press, 1986.

Lewes, G. H. "The Condition of Authors in England, Germany, and France." *Fraser's Magazine* 35 (1847):285–95.

——. "GHL's Literary Receipts." In *The George Eliot Letters*, 7:365–79. 9 vols. Ed. Gordon S. Haight. New Haven: Yale Univ. Press, 1954–78.

Lindenberger, Herbert. "The Reception of *The Prelude*." *Bulletin of the New York Public Library* 64 (1960):196–208.

Liu, Alan. *Wordsworth: The Sense of History*. Stanford, Calif.: Stanford Univ. Press, 1989.

Lockhart, John G. *Memoirs of the Life of Sir Walter Scott*. 7 vols. Edinburgh: Robert Cadell, 1837–38.

——. *Peter's Letters to His Kinfolk*. 2d ed. 3 vols. Edinburgh: William Blackwood, 1819.

Lohrli, Anne. *Household Words: A Weekly Journal, 1850–1859, Conducted by Charles Dickens*. Toronto: Univ. of Toronto Press, 1973.

Macaulay, Thomas Babington. *Critical and Historical Essays*. Ed. A. J. Grieve. 2 vols. London: J. M. Dent, 1907.

——. *The Letters of Thomas Babington Macaulay*. Ed. Thomas Pinney. 6 vols. Cambridge: Cambridge Univ. Press, 1974–81.

——. *The Life and Letters of Lord Macaulay*. Ed. Sir George Otto Trevelyan. 2 vols. London: Longmans, Green, 1923.

McGann, Jerome. *The Beauty of Inflections: Literary Investigations in Historical Method and Theory*. Oxford: Clarendon Press, 1985.

McKillop, Alan Dugald. "English Circulating Libraries, 1725–50." *Library*, 4th ser., 14 (1934):477–85.

McLuhan, Marshall. *The Gutenberg Galaxy: The Making of Typographic Man*. Toronto: Univ. of Toronto Press, 1962.

Madden, R. R. *The Literary Life and Correspondence of the Countess of Blessington*. 3 vols. London: T. C. Newley, 1855.

Marchand, Leslie Alexis. *"The Athenaeum": A Mirror of Victorian Culture*. Chapel Hill: Univ. of North Carolina Press, 1941.

Marryat, Florence. *Life and Letters of Captain Marryat*. 2 vols. London: Richard Bentley and Sons, 1872.

Martin, Loy D. *Browning's Dramatic Monologues and the Post-Romantic Subject*. Baltimore: Johns Hopkins Univ. Press, 1985.

Martineau, Harriet. *Harriet Martineau's Autobiography*. Ed. Maria Weston Chapman. 2 vols. Boston: James R. Osgood, 1877.

Marx, Karl. "Debates on the Freedom of the Press." In vol. 1 of Karl Marx, and Friedrich Engels, *Collected Works*. New York: International Publishers, 1975– .

Mayhew, Henry. *London Labour and the London Poor*. 4 vols. London: Griffin, Bohn, 1861–62.

Mayo, Robert D. *The English Novel in the Magazines, 1740–1815*. Evanston, Ill.: Northwestern Univ. Press, 1962.

Merriam, Harold G. *Edward Moxon: Publisher of Poets*. Columbia University Studies in English and Comparative Literature, no. 137. New York: Columbia Univ. Press, 1939.

Mill, J. S. *Autobiography*. Ed. John M. Robson and Jack Stillinger. Vol. 1 of *The Collected Works of John Stuart Mill*. Toronto: Univ. of Toronto Press, 1981.

——. *The Earlier Letters of John Stuart Mill, 1812–1848*. Ed. Francis E. Mineka. Vol. 13 of *The Collected Works of John Stuart Mill*. Toronto: Univ. of Toronto Press, 1963.

——. "Tennyson's Poems." *London Review* 1 (1835):402–24.

Millgate, Jane. "Scott the Cunning Tailor: Refurbishing the *Poetical Works*." *Library*, 6th ser., 11 (1989):336–51.

——. *Scott's Last Edition: A Study in Publishing History*. Edinburgh: Edinburgh Univ. Press, 1987.

Mineka, Francis E. *The Dissidence of Dissent: "The Monthly Repository," 1806–1838*. Chapel Hill: Univ. of North Carolina Press, 1944.

Mitford, Mary Russell. *Letters of Mary Russell Mitford. Second Series*. Ed. Henry Chorley. 2 vols. London: Richard Bentley and Son, 1872.

——. *The Life of Mary Russell Mitford*. Ed. A. G. L'Estrange. 3 vols. London: Richard Bentley, 1870.

Montgomery, Robert. *The Age Reviewed: A Satire in Two Parts*. London: William Carpenter, 1827.

Moore, George. *Confessions of a Young Man*. Ed. Susan Dick. Montreal: McGill-Queen's Univ. Press, 1972.

Moore, Thomas. *The Journal of Thomas Moore*. Ed. Wilfred S. Dowden. 6 vols. Newark: Univ. of Delaware Press, 1983– .

——. *The Letters of Thomas Moore*. Ed. Wilfred S. Dowden. 2 vols. Oxford: Clarendon Press, 1964.

Moorman, Mary. *William Wordsworth: A Biography*. 2 vols. Oxford: Clarendon Press, 1957–65.

More, Hannah. *The Two Wealthy Farmers; or the History of Mr. Bragwell*. London: Howard and Evans, [1800].

Morgan, Lady Sydney. *Lady Morgan's Memoirs: Autobiography, Diaries, and Correspondence*. 2 vols. London: William H. Allen, 1862.

Morgan, Peter F. "Taylor and Hessey: Aspects of Their Conduct of the *London Magazine*." *Keats-Shelley Journal* 7 (1958):61–68.

" 'Mr. Tupper and the Poets . . . ': A Victorian Best Seller." *TLS* (February 26, 1938):137.

Mumby, Frank Arthur, and Ian Norrie. *Publishing and Bookselling*. 5th ed. London: Jonathan Cape, 1974.

Murray, Patrick Joseph. *The Life of John Banim, the Irish Novelist*. London: William Lay, 1857.

Nesbitt, George L. *Benthamite Reviewing: The First Twelve Years of "The Westminster Review," 1824–1836*. New York: Columbia Univ. Press, 1934.

Newman, John Henry. *Letters and Correspondence of John Henry Newman: During His Life in the English Church; with a Brief Autobiography*. Ed. Anne Mozley. 2 vols. London: Longmans, Green, 1891.

——. *The Letters and Diaries of John Henry Newman*. Ed. Ian Ker, Thomas Gornall et al. 31 vols. Oxford: Clarendon Press, 1961– .

Noyes, Russell. "Wordsworth and the Copyright Act of 1842: Addendum." *PMLA* 76 (1961):380–83.

Oliphant, Margaret. *Annals of a Publishing House: William Blackwood and His Sons*,

Their Magazine and Friends. 2d ed. 2 vols. Edinburgh: William Blackwood and Sons, 1897–98.

Ollier, Edmund. "A Literary Publisher." *Temple Bar* 58 (1880):243–52.

Orr, Mrs. Sutherland. *Life and Letters of Robert Browning.* 2d ed. London: Smith, Elder, 1891.

"Our Weekly Gossip on Literature and Art." *Athenaeum*, December 26, 1835: 968–69.

Owen, W. J. B. "Costs, Sales, and Profits of Longman's Editions of Wordsworth." *Library*, 5th ser., 12 (1957):93–107.

——. "Letters of Longman & Co. to Wordsworth, 1814–36." *Library*, 5th ser., 9 (1954):25–34.

Parliamentary Papers. Fourdrinier's Patent Committee. 1837.

Patmore, P. G. *My Friends and Acquaintance: Being Memorials, Mind-Portraits, and Personal Recollections of Deceased Celebrities of the Nineteenth Century.* 3 vols. London: Saunders and Otley, 1855.

Patten, Robert L. *Charles Dickens and His Publishers.* Oxford: Clarendon Press, 1978.

——. "The Fight at the Top of the Tree: *Vanity Fair* versus *Dombey and Son.*" *Studies in English Literature, 1500–1900* 10 (1970):759–73.

Peacock, Thomas Love. *The Four Ages of Poetry.* Ed. John E. Jordan. Indianapolis: Bobbs-Merrill, 1965.

——. *Memoirs of Shelley and Other Essays and Reviews.* Ed. Howard Mills. London: Rupert Hart-Davis, 1970.

——. *The Works of Thomas Love Peacock.* Ed. H. F. B. Brett-Smith and C. E. Jones. 10 vols. London: Constable, 1926–34.

Peckham, Morse. *Beyond the Tragic Vision: The Quest for Identity in the Nineteenth Century.* New York: George Braziller, 1962.

Plant, Marjorie. *The English Book Trade: An Economic History of the Making and Sale of Books.* 3d ed. London: George Allen and Unwin, 1974.

Poggioli, Renato. *The Theory of the Avant-Garde.* Trans. Gerald Fitzgerald. Cambridge, Mass.: Harvard Univ. Press, 1968.

Pollard, Graham. "The English Market for Printed Books." *Publishing History* 4 (1978):7–48.

Pope, Alexander. *The Poems of Alexander Pope.* Ed. John Butt. New Haven: Yale Univ. Press, 1963.

Pope-Hennessy, Una. *Canon Charles Kingsley: A Biography.* London: Chatto and Windus, 1948.

"Publishing and Puffing." *Metropolitan Magazine* 8 (October 1833):171–78.

Purdy, Richard Little. *Thomas Hardy: A Bibliographical Study.* London: Oxford Univ. Press, 1954.

Raven, James. *Judging New Wealth: Popular Publishing and Responses to Commerce in England, 1750–1800.* Oxford: Clarendon Press, 1992.

——. "The Noble Brothers and Popular Publishing, 1745–1789." *Library*, 6th ser., 12 (1990):293–345.

——. "The Publication of Fiction in Britain and Ireland, 1750–70." *Publishing History* 24 (1988):31–47.

Raysor, Thomas. "The Establishment of Wordsworth's Reputation." *JEGP* 54 (1955):61–71.

Redding, Cyrus. *Fifty Years' Recollections, Literary and Personal.* 3 vols. London: Charles J. Skeet, 1858.

Reeve, Henry. *Memoirs of the Life and Correspondence of Henry Reeve.* 2d ed. Ed. John Knox Laughton. 2 vols. London: Longmans, Green, 1898.

Reeves, Jesse S. "Martin Tupper." *TLS* (April 9, 1938):252.

Renier, Anne. *Friendship's Offering: An Essay on the Annuals and Gift Books of the 19th Century.* London: Private Libraries Association, 1964.

Review of Leitch Ritchie's *Schinderhannes, the Robber of the Rhine.* *Athenaeum,* February 2, 1833:65.

Review of Michael Banim's *The Ghost-Hunter.* *Athenaeum,* December 29, 1832: 836.

"Rewards of Literature." *Spectator* 4 (June 18, 1831):590–91.

Reynolds, Frederic Mansel, ed. *The Keepsake.* London: Hurst, Chance, and Robert Jennings, 1829.

Richardson, F. R. "The Circulating Library." In *The Book World,* 195–202. Ed. John Hampden. London: Thomas Nelson and Sons, 1935.

Ritchie, Leitch. "Preface." In Michael Banim, *The Ghost-Hunter and His Family.* London: Smith, Elder, 1833.

Robinson, Henry Crabb. *Henry Crabb Robinson on Books and Their Writers.* Ed. Edith J. Morley. 3 vols. London: J. M. Dent and Sons, 1938.

Roper, Derek. *Reviewing before the "Edinburgh," 1788–1802.* Newark: Univ. of Delaware Press, 1978.

Rosa, Matthew Whiting. *The Silver-Fork School: Novels of Fashion Preceding "Vanity Fair".* Columbia University Studies in English and Comparative Literature, no. 123. New York: Columbia Univ. Press, 1936.

Ruskin, John. *The Works of John Ruskin.* Ed. E. T. Cook and Alexander Wedderburn. 39 vols. London: George Allen, 1903–12.

Russell, Norma. *Bibliography of William Cowper to 1837.* Oxford: Clarendon Press, 1963.

Sadleir, Michael. "Aspects of the Victorian Novel." *Publishing History* 5 (1979):7–47.

——. "Bentley's Standard Novel Series: Its History and Achievement." *The Colophon* 10 (May 1932):[45–60].

——. *Bulwer and His Wife: A Panorama, 1803–1836.* London: Constable, 1933.

——. *XIX Century Fiction: A Bibliographical Record.* 2 vols. Cambridge: Cambridge Univ. Press, 1951.

——. *The Northanger Novels: A Footnote to Jane Austen.* Engish Association Pamphlet no. 68. Oxford: [Oxford Univ. Press], 1927.

Saintsbury, George. *A History of Nineteenth Century Literature (1780–1895).* London: Macmillan, 1896.

Samuelson, Paul A. and William D. Nordhaus. *Economics.* 13th ed. New York: McGraw-Hill, 1989.

Saunders, J. W. *The Profession of English Letters.* London: Routledge and Kegan Paul, 1964.

Schoenfield, Mark. "Regulating Standards: *The Edinburgh Review* and Circulations of Judgment." *The Wordsworth Circle* 24 (Summer 1993):148–51.

Scott, Rosemary. "Pious Verse in the Mid-Victorian Market Place: Facts and Figures." *Publishing History* 33 (1993):37–58.

Scott, Sir Walter. *The Journal of Sir Walter Scott*. Ed. W. E. K. Anderson. Oxford: Clarendon Press, 1972.

———. *The Letters of Sir Walter Scott*. Ed. H. J. C. Grierson. 12 vols. London: Constable, 1932–37.

———. Review of Austen's *Emma*. *Quarterly Review* 15 (October 1815; published March 1816):188–201.

———. Review of Byron's *Childe Harold*. *Quarterly Review* 19 (1818):215–32.

Shell, Marc. *The Economy of Literature*. Baltimore: Johns Hopkins Univ. Press, 1978.

———. *Money, Language and Thought: Literary and Philosophical Economies from the Medieval to the Modern Era*. Berkeley: Univ. of California Press, 1982.

Shelley, Percy Bysshe. *The Letters of Percy Bysshe Shelley*. Ed. Frederick L. Jones. 2 vols. Oxford: Clarendon Press, 1964.

Sheridan, Richard Brinsley. *The Dramatic Works of Richard Brinsley Sheridan*. Ed. Cecil Price. 2 vols. Oxford: Clarendon Press, 1973.

Shoberl, Frederic, ed. *Forget Me Not*. London: R. Ackermann, 1827.

Simpson, David. "Literary Criticism and the Return to 'History.'" *Critical Inquiry* 14 (1988):721–47.

Siskin, Clifford. "Wordsworth's Prescriptions: Romanticism and Professional Power." In *The Romantics and Us: Essays on Literature and Culture*, 303–21. Ed. Gene W. Ruoff. New Brunswick, N.J.: Rutgers Univ. Press, 1990.

Smart, Thomas Burnett. *The Bibliography of Matthew Arnold*. London: J. Davy and Sons, 1892.

Smiles, Samuel. *A Publisher and His Friends: Memoir and Correspondence of the Late John Murray*. 2 vols. London: John Murray, 1891.

Smith, Sydney. *The Letters of Sydney Smith*. Ed. Nowell C. Smith. 2 vols. Oxford: Clarendon Press, 1953.

Southey, Robert. *Letters from England*. Ed. Jack Simmons. London: Cresset Press, 1951.

———. *The Life and Correspondence of Robert Southey*. 6 vols. Ed. Charles Cuthbert Southey. London: Longman, Brown, Green, and Longmans, 1849–50.

———. "Lucy and Her Bird." In *The Keepsake*, 157–60. London: Hurst, Chance and Robert Jennings, 1829.

———. *New Letters of Robert Southey*. Ed. Kenneth Curry. 2 vols. New York: Columbia Univ. Press, 1965.

———. "The Roman Catholic Question—Ireland." *Quarterly Review* 38 (1828):535–98.

———. *Selections from the Letters of Robert Southey*. Ed. John Wood Warter. 4 vols. London: Longman, Brown, Green, and Longmans, 1856.

———. *Sir Thomas More; or, Colloquies on the Progress and Prospects of Society*. 2 vols. London: John Murray, 1829.

———. "Stanzas, Addressed to J. M. W. Turner, Esq. R. A., on His View of the Lago Maggiore from the Town of Arona." In *The Keepsake*, 238–39. London: Hurst, Chance and Robert Jennings, 1829.

"The Spectator's Library." Spectator 4 (October 8, 1831):980–81.

Spencer, Herbert. *An Autobiography*. 2 vols. New York: D. Appleton, 1904.

Stendahl. See Beyle, Henri Marie.

Sullivan, Alvin, ed. *British Literary Magazines: The Romantic Age, 1789–1836*. Westport, Conn.: Greenwood Press, 1983.

——. *British Literary Magazines: The Victorian and Edwardian Age, 1837–1913*. Westport, Conn.: Greenwood Press, 1984.

Sutherland, James. *On English Prose*. Toronto: Univ. of Toronto Press, 1957.

Sutherland, John. "The British Book Trade and the Crash of 1826." *The Library*, 6th ser., 9 (1987):148–61.

——. "The Economics of the Victorian Three-Volume Novel." *Business Archives* 41 (1976):25–30.

——. "Henry Colburn Publisher." *Publishing History* 19 (1986):59–84.

——. "John Macrone: Victorian Publisher." *Dickens Studies Annual* 13 (1984):243–59.

——. "Publishing History: A Hole at the Centre of Literary Sociology." *Critical Inquiry* 14 (1988):574–89.

——. Review of Gaye Tuchman with Nina E. Fortin's *Edging Women Out. American Journal of Sociology* 95 (1989):814–16.

——. *Victorian Novelists and Publishers*. Chicago: Univ. of Chicago Press, 1976.

Swaim, Elizabeth A. "Circulating Library: Antedatings of the O.E.D." *Notes and Queries*, n.s., 25 (1978):14–15.

"Symposiac the Second." *Fraser's Magazine* 3 (1831):253–68.

Taylor, John Tinnon. *Early Opposition to the English Novel: The Popular Reaction from 1760 to 1830*. New York: King's Crown Press, 1943.

Taylor, Olive M. "John Taylor, Author and Publisher, 1781–1864." *London Mercury* 12 (1925):158–66, 258–67.

Tegg, Thomas. *Remarks on the Speech of Sergeant Talfourd, on Moving for Leave to Bring in a Bill to Consolidate the Laws relating to Copyright, and to Extend the Term of Its Duration*. London: Thomas Tegg and Son, 1837.

Tennyson, Alfred Lord. *The Letters of Alfred Lord Tennyson*. Ed. Cecil Y. Lang and Edgar F. Shannon Jr. 3 vols. Cambridge, Mass.: Harvard Univ. Press; vol. 3. Oxford: Clarendon Press, 1981–90.

——. *The Poems of Tennyson*. 2d ed. Ed. Christopher Ricks. 3 vols. Berkeley: Univ. of California Press, 1987.

Tennyson, G. B. *Sartor Called Resartus: The Genesis, Stucture, and Style of Thomas Carlyle's First Major Work*. Princeton: Princeton Univ. Press, 1965.

——. *Victorian Devotional Poetry: The Tractarian Mode*. Cambridge, Mass.: Harvard Univ. Press, 1981.

Tennyson, Hallam. *Alfred Lord Tennyson: A Memoir*. 2 vols. London: Macmillan, 1897.

Thackeray, William Makepeace. *The History of Pendennis*. 2 vols. London: Bradbury and Evans, 1849–50.

——. *The Letters and Private Papers of William Makepeace Thackeray*. Ed. Gordon N. Ray. 4 vols. Cambridge, Mass.: Harvard Univ. Press, 1945.

——. "Charity and Humour." In *The Oxford Thackeray*, 10:614–28. Ed. George Saintsbury. 17 vols. London: Oxford Univ. Press, 1908.

Thin, James. *Reminiscences of Booksellers and Bookselling in Edinburgh in the Time of William IV*. Edinburgh: Oliver and Boyd, 1905.

Thrall, Miriam M. H. *Rebellious "Fraser's": Nol Yorke's Magazine in the Days of Maginn,*

Thackeray, and Carlyle. Columbia Univ. Studies in English and Comparative Literature, no. 117. New York: Columbia Univ. Press, 1934.

Tillotson, Kathleen. *Novels of the Eighteen-Forties*. Oxford: Clarendon Press, 1954.

Timperley, C. H. *Encyclopedia of Literary and Typographical Anecdote*. London: Henry G. Bohn, 1842.

"The Tower of London." *Fraser's Magazine* 23 (1841):169–83.

Tuchman, Gaye, with Nina E. Fortin. *Edging Women Out: Victorian Novelists, Publishers, and Social Change*. New Haven: Yale Univ. Press, 1989.

Twyman, Michael. *Printing, 1770–1970: An Illustrated History of Its Development and Uses in England*. London: Eyre and Spottiswoode, 1970.

Tynjanov, Jurij. "On Literary Evolution." In *Readings in Russian Poetrics: Formalist and Structuralist Views*, 66–78. Ed. Ladislav Matejka and Krystyna Pomorska. Cambridge, Mass.: MIT Press, 1971.

Unwin, Raynor. *The Rural Muse: Studies in the Peasant Poetry of England*. London: George Allen and Unwin, 1954.

Uphaus, Robert W. "Jane Austen and the Female Reader." *Studies in the Novel* 19 (1987):334–45.

Vanden Bossche, Chris R. *Carlyle and the Search for Authority*. Columbus: Ohio State Univ. Press, 1991.

Vann, J. Don. "The Early Success of *Pickwick*." *Publishing History* 2 (1977): 51–55.

——. *Victorian Novels in Serial*. New York: Modern Language Association, 1985.

Vann, J. Don, and Rosemary T. VanArsdel, eds. *Victorian Periodicals: A Guide to Research*. New York: Modern Language Association, 1978.

Varma, Devendra P. *The Evergreen Tree of Diabolical Knowledge*. Washington, D.C.: Consortium Press, 1972.

Vida, Elizabeth M. *Romantic Affinites: German Authors and Carlyle*. Toronto: Univ. of Toronto Press, 1993.

Warrington, Bernard. "The Bankruptcy of William Pickering in 1853: The Hazards of Publishing and Bookselling in the First Half of the Nineteenth Century." *Publishing History* 27 (1990):1–25.

Waterman, Geoffrey. *Victorian Book Illustration: The Technical Revolution*. Newton Abbott, Eng.: David and Charles, 1973.

Watson, Melvin R. *Magazine Serials and the Essay Tradition, 1746–1820*. Louisiana State Univ. Studies, Humanities Series, no. 6. Baton Rouge: Louisiana State Univ. Press, 1956.

Watt, Alaric A., ed. *The Literary Souvenir*. London: Hurst Robinson, 1826.

——. *The Literary Souvenir*. London: Longman, Rees, Orme, Brown, and Green, 1829.

Watt, Ian. "Publishers and Sinners: An Augustan View." *Studies in Bibliography* 12 (1959):3–20.

——. *The Rise of the Novel*. Berkeley: Univ. of California Press, 1957.

The Wellesley Index to Periodical Literature. Ed. Walter E. Houghton et al. 5 vols. Toronto: Univ. of Toronto Press, 1966–89.

Wilson, Thomas. *The Use of Circulating Libraries Considered; With Instructions for Opening and Conducting a Library*. London: J. Hamilton, 1797. Rpt. in Devendra P. Varma, *The Evergreen Tree of Diabolical Knowledge*, 196–203. Washington, D.C.: Consortium Press, 1972.

Wise, Thomas J. *A Bibliography of Wordsworth: The Writings in Prose and Verse.* London: Richard Clay and Sons, 1916.

Wolfe, Tom. *The Pump House Gang.* New York: Farrar, Straus, and Giroux, 1968.

Wordsworth, William. *The Letters of William and Dorothy Wordsworth.* 2d ed. Ed. Ernest de Selincourt, Chester L. Shaver, Mary Moorman, and Alan G. Hill. 8 vols. Oxford: Clarendon Press, 1967–93.

——. *The Poetical Works of William Wordsworth.* Ed. E. de Selincourt and Helen Darbishire. 5 vols. Oxford: Clarendon Press, 1940–49.

——. *The Prose Works of William Wordsworth.* Ed. W. J. B. Owen and Jane Worthington Smyser. 3 vols. London: Oxford Univ. Press, 1974.

Zall, Paul M. "Wordsworth and the Copyright Act of 1842." *PMLA* 70 (1955):132–44.

Index

Barwick, G. F., 75n
Batdorf, Franklin P., 150n
Bate, Walter Jackson, 39n
Beaumont, Thomas Wentworth, 98
Becher, Reverend John, 76
Beddoes, Thomas, 36, 90
Bedford, G. D., 30n
Bedingfield, Richard, 179n
Beethoven, Ludwig von, 111
Bell, Reverend Andrew, 85
Bell, Robert, 175–6
Benbowes, William, 39
Benjamin, Walter, 15n, 18, 171n
Bennett, Scott, 98n, 149n
Bentham, Jeremy, 98, 119
Bentley, Richard, 37, 145n, 150–2, 154, 155–6, 160, 161–2, 163n, 168, 182
Bentley's Miscellany, 37, 72, 86, 161–2, 165
Beste, Henry Digby, 175n
Besterman, Theodore, 23n, 32n, 37n
Bijou, The, 30
Blackmore, Richard D., 16
Blackwood, William, 32, 55, 82, 167–8, 178
Blackwood's Magazine, 12, 28, 32, 55, 59, 72, 79, 83, 92, 93, 96, 99, 147n, 167, 176, 178, 180, 182; "The Cockney School of Poetry," 92
Blagden, Cyprian, 78n
Blake, William, *The Four Zoas*, 24–5
Blakey, Dorothy, 134n, 138n, 144n
Blanchard, Laman, 91
Blessington, Marguerite, Countess of, *Strathern*, 156
Block, Andrew, 138n
Bloomfield, Robert, *The Farmer's Boy*, 22n
Blunden, Edmund, 16, 172n
Boeotian, 89
Bonham-Carter, Victor, 187n, 188n
book societies and clubs, 24, 54, 136, 160
Booth, Bradford Allen, 29n
Borrow, George, *The Bible in Spain*, 79
Bose, A., 29n, 31n
Boswell, James, 143n; *Life of Johnson*, 3, 74, 75, 106
Bourne, H. R. Fox, 80n
Bovinet, Giraldon, 30n
Bowles, Caroline, 29n
Bowring, John, 98n
Boyle, Andrew, 29n, 55n
Brent's Monthly Literary Advertiser, 26n
British and Foreign Review, 85, 98, 100

British Critic, 76, 98–9, 154, 175
British Magazine, 161
British Quarterly Review, 73, 86
Brontë sisters (Anne, Charlotte, and Emily), 164
Brooke, Rupert, 20n
Brookfield, William Henry, 41
Brougham, Henry Peter, 75, 78n, 185
Broughton, Leslie Nathan, 35n
Brown, John, 87
Browning, Elizabeth Barrett, 32, 40, 47; *Aurora Leigh*, 38
Browning, Robert, 3, 6, 14–5, 32, 36, 39, 42–8, 60–1, 160n, 183; *Bells and Pomegranates*, 35, 38; "Ben Karshook's Wisdom," 42; "Bishop Blougram's Apology," 35, 176; *Dramatic Romances and Lyrics*, 40; *Dramatis Personae*, 97; *Men and Women*, 40, 42; "My Last Duchess," 43; "The Lost Leader," 188; "One Word More: To E. B. B.," 47; *Paracelsus*, 36; "Pictor Ignotus," 45–6; "The Pied Piper of Hamelin," 45; *Pippa Passes*, 35; "Porphyria's Lover," 42; *The Ring and the Book*, 15; "Rudel to the Lady of Tripoli," 46–7; "Saul," 40; *Selections* (1863), 37, 39; *Sordello*, 14–5, 38, 42, 45; *Strafford*, 97, 188n
Browning, Robert Weidemann (Pen), 160n
Brydges, Samuel Egerton, *Fitz-Albini*, 141
Buccleuch, 4th Duke of (Charles William Henry Scott), 81n
Buckley, Jerome, 44n
Bulwer-Lytton, Edward Lytton, 4, 83n, 86, 97, 151, 161, 167–8, 175–6, 178; *The Caxtons*, 167–8; *England and the English*, 100, 122, 164, 171, 172–3, 186; *Eugene Aram*, 167; "Memoir of Laman Blanchard," 91; *Paul Clifford*, 88, 180
Bunyan, John, 85
Bürger, Peter, 171n
Burke, Edmund, 187
Burke, Kenneth, 8n
Burney, Frances (Fanny), *Camilla*, 130
Burns, Robert, 62, 120; *Poems*, 35, 37
Butler, Marilyn, 8n
Byron, George Gordon, Lord, 3, 10, 23, 24, 26, 38, 39, 49, 51n, 53, 56n, 71, 76, 77, 81, 93n, 113–4, 132n, 149–50, 172, 175, 180; *Beppo*, 21; *Childe Harold's Pilgrimage*, 38, 40; *The Corsair*, 23; *Don Juan*, 38, 56n; *English Bards and Scotch Reviewers*, 21–2, 77;

The Giaour, 22; *Hours of Idleness*, 76, 77; "To Mr. Murray," 21; *The Works of Lord Byron*, 149–50

Cadell, Robert, 147–9, 160, 168
Cadell, Thomas, 22–3, 31–2, 36, 37
Cambridge University Press, 27
Campbell, Sir John, 64
Campbell, Thomas, 97, 188
Canning, George, 174
Carlyle, Alexander, 99 n
Carlyle, John A., 94 n, 95 n, 109 n, 110 n, 184 n
Carlyle, Thomas, 11, 18, 64, 71, 79, 80, 89, 90, 94–5, 98, 99, 104–23, 180, 182, 183, 184, 189; "Boswell's Life of Johnson," 3, 106; "Characteristics," 90, 113–8, 121–2; "Corn-Law Rhymes," 71; *Frederick the Great*, 111; *The French Revolution*, 110–1, 113 n, 177–8, 184; "The Hero as Man of Letters," 110, 112, 118–21; *On Heroes, Hero-Worship*, 118; *The Life of John Sterling*, 98; *Miscellanies*, 94; *Past and Present*, 110; *Reminiscences*, 111–2, 119; *Sartor Resartus*, 50 n, 95, 106–9; "Signs of the Times," 106, 109, 118
Caroline, Queen, 28
Carrington, Charles Edmund, *A Subaltern's War*, 15
Cary, Henry Francis, 82, 93, 188
Cattermole, Richard, 185 n
Cave, Edward, 120
Cervantes, Miguel de, *Don Quixote*, 150, 183
Chamber's Encyclopedia, 78 n
Chandler, John E., 32 n, 78 n
Chapman, R. W., 127 n, 128 n
Chapman and Hall, publishers, 38, 159
Charlotte, Queen, 27
Chilcott, Tim, 22 n, 26 n, 34 n
Chorley, Henry Fothergill, 88
Christie, John, 92
circulating library, 6, 24, 124–41, 142–6, 154, 162
Clare, John, 22 n, 26, 33–4, 38, 57; *Poems Descriptive of Rural Life and Scenery*, 33; *The Rural Muse*, 34; *The Shepherd's Calendar*, 33; *The Village Minstrel*, 33
Clive, John, 16, 76 n, 77 n, 78 n
Clubbe, John, 187 n
Cobbett, William, 87
Cochrane and Pickersgill, publishers, 150

Colburn, Henry, 32, 34 n, 83, 93, 96, 143–4, 150–5, 156, 166, 168, 181, 182
Coleman, D. C., 7 n, 20 n, 27 n
Coleridge, Derwent, 179–80
Coleridge, Hartley, 179–80; "He Lived Amidst th' Untrodden Ways," 54–5, 68
Coleridge, Samuel Taylor, 21, 23, 30, 38, 50, 51–2, 55, 66, 67, 68, 72, 77–8, 79–80, 82–3, 86–7, 90–1, 96, 178, 185; *Biographia Literaria*, 21, 25–6, 50 n, 53, 87 n, 139; *Christabel; Kubla Khan, a Vision; The Pains of Sleep*, 68 n; *The Fall of Robespierre*, 50; "On Style," 180 n; *Poems on Various Subjects*, 50; *Poetical Works*, 68 n; *Remorse*, 68 n; "The Rime of the Ancient Mariner," 51–2; *Table Talk*, 185. *See also* Wordsworth, William, *Lyrical Ballads*
Coles, W. A., 85 n
Coley, Betty A., 160 n
Colie, Rosalie, 8
Collins, A. S., x, 172 n
Collins, Wilkie, 16
Collins, William, 61, 82
Colman, George, the Elder, *Polly Honeycombe*, 139
Companion, 87
Compton, F. E., 37 n
Congreve, William, 74
Connolly, Cyril, 10
Constable, Archibald, 32, 35, 38, 77, 78, 146–7, 177
Constable's Miscellany, 147
Cooke, W. B., 182
Cooper, James Fenimore, 151, 154, 168, 184–5
Cooper, Thomas, *The Purgatory of Suicides*, 34 n
Copleston, Edward, "Advice to a Young Reviewer," 92 n
copyright: international, 185; reform of, 60–8
Cornhill, 72, 86
Cottle, Joseph, 23, 50–1; *Early Recollections*, 50 n
Courier, 84, 96, 101
Court Journal, 153, 154
Cowper, William, 22, 23, 62, 65, 85; *Poems* (1810), 35
Cox, Harold, 32 n, 78 n
Crabbe, George, 150; *Poems* (1807) 52; *Poems* (1819), 22; *Tales of the Hall*, 22

Fortin, Nina, 177 n
Fortnightly Review, 72
Fourdrinier papermaking machine, 5, 19, 27, 47
Fourdriniers, 87
Franck, Philip de, 97 n
Fraser's Magazine, 16, 28, 72, 80, 83, 85, 95, 99, 100, 103, 109, 112, 158, 161, 163, 165, 180
Frere, John Hookham, 185 n
Freylinghausen, John Anastatious, *Abstract of the Whole Doctrine of the Christian*, 27
Friend, The, 79–80, 87, 90–1
Friendship's Offering, 30
Froude, Richard Hurrell, 99 n

Gale and Fenner, publishers, 87 n
Galignani, Jean-Antoine and Guillaume, publishers, 57, 68
Gardner, John, 62 n
Gay, John, 74
Gem, The, 30, 41
Genlis, Madame de, *Alphonsine*, 141
Gentleman's Magazine, 72
George IV, 28, 130 n, 155, 172, 186
Gettmann, Royal A., 37 n, 145 n, 149 n, 151 n, 152 n, 154 n, 161 n, 163 n
Gibbon, Edward, *Decline and Fall of the Roman Empire*, 175
Gifford, William, 78 n, 79 n, 96, 175
Gillies, Robert Pearse, *Memoirs of a Literary Veteran*, 179
Gilson, David, 133 n
Gisborne, John, 18 n
Gladstone, William, 89–90
Gloucester, Duke of, 175
Goethe, J. W. von, 85
Goldsmith, Oliver, *The Vicar of Wakefield*, 135, 150
Gore, Mrs. Catherine, "The Monster-Misery of Literature," 133 n, 145 n
Goulden, R. J., 127 n
Graham, Walter, 16, 93 n
Grant, James, *The Great Metropolis*, 99–100
Green, J. H., 185 n
Grenville, William Wyndham, 77
Gresham, Sir Thomas, 32
Griest, Guinevere L., 127 n, 145–6 n, 160 n
Griffin, Gerald, 174–5
Griffith, Richard, *A Series of Genuine Letters between Henry and Frances*, 133

Grisi, Giulietta, 11
Groot, Hans B. de, 98 n
Gross, John, 16
Grosse, Marquis of, *Horrid Mysteries*, 138
Gurney, Ivor, 20 n
Gutenberg, Johannes, 13, 112

Haas, Sabine, 30 n
Hall, Samuel Carter, 31 n
Hallam, Henry, 187–8
Hamlyn, Hilda M., 127 n, 135 n
Handley, E. H., 98 n
Hansard, T. C., *Typographia*, 27 n
Hardy, Thomas, 38, 40; *Satires of Circumstance*, 35
Harness, Reverend William, 83 n
Harrison, Miss, 85 n
Harrold, Charles Frederick, 50 n
Hart, Horace, 23 n
Hartley, David, 61
Haydon, Benjamin, 55
Hazlitt, William, 11, 76, 80, 83, 86, 89, 97, 118; "On the Pleasure of Hating," 92; "The Periodical Press," 91, 93, 104, 189; *The Spirit of the Age*, 175
Heath, Charles, 30 n
Heath-Stubbs, John, 36 n
Hegel, Georg, 85
Heine, Heinrich, 86
Heinzelman, Kurt, 62 n
Hessey, James Augustus, 32, 33–4, 38, 81, 82 n, 93
Hewison, Robert, 20–1 n
Hill, Alan, 69
Hill, Christopher, 21 n
Hill, Reverend Herbert, 79 n, 84 n
Hodgson, Thomas, *An Essay on the Origin and Process of Stereotyping*, 25 n
Hofland, Mrs. Barbara, 85 n
Hogg, James, 92
Holland, Lord (Henry Richard Vassall Fox), 172 n
Holloway, John, 113 n
Hood, Thomas, 34, 36, 97, 178–9, 187–8
Hook, Theodore, 172
Horkheimer, Max, 111 n
Horne, Richard Henry (later Hengist): *Exposition of the False Medium and Barriers Excluding Men of Genius*, 96–7, 186 n; *Orion*, 35
Horner, Francis, 75

Radcliffe, Ann: *The Mysteries of Udolpho*, 132; *Romance of the Forest*, 133, 140
Rambler, 92–3, 94 n
Ramée, Maria Louise de la (Ouida), 16
Raphael, 30 n
Raven, James, 7 n, 14, 143 n
Raysor, Thomas, 50 n
Redding, Cyrus, 83 n, 96 n
Reed, Henry, 68
Rees, Owen, 51
Reeve, Henry, 98 n
Reeves, Jesse S., 184 n
Reid, Thomas, 86
Renier, Anne, 29 n, 30 n, 31 n
Representative, 98
Revue des Deux Monds, 101
Reynolds, Frederic Mansel, 31
Reynolds, G.W.M., *The Mysteries of London*, 4
Reynolds, John, 39
Rheinische Zeitung, 102, 111
Richardson, F. R., 131 n, 132–3
Rickman, John, 82 n, 177 n
Ritchie, Leitch, 153–4, 156–8; *Schinderhannes*, 157–8
Rittner and Goupil, publishers, 30 n
Rivington, Francis, 175
Robinson, Henry Crabb, 99
Roche, Regina Maria: *Children of the Abbey*, 140; *Clermont*, 138
Rogers, Samuel, 22–3, 34, 36
Roper, Derek, 76
Rosa, Matthew Whiting, 144 n
Roscoe, Thomas, 150
Roscoe's Novelist's Library (series), 150
Rossini, Gioachino, 11
Rousseau, Jean Jacques, 16, 120, 126 n
Rowe, Nicholas, 74
Ruskin, John, 36, 89, 102, 123; *Fors Clavigera*, 170; Preface to the *Academy Notes* (1856), 176
Russell, Norma, 22 n, 35 n, 65 n

Sadleir, Michael, 83 n, 133 n, 135, 138 n, 150 n, 158 n
Saintsbury, George, 16
Samuelson, Paul A., 9 n
Sander, James, 135
Saturday Magazine, 100
Saunders, J. W., 172 n

Saunders and Otley, publishers, 95, 153, 155
Schlegel, Friedrich, 105, 121–2
Schoenfield, Mark, 79 n
Scots Magazine, 32
Scott, John, 92
Scott, Marian, 20 n
Scott, Rosemary, 31 n
Scott, Sir Walter, 3, 11, 22, 23, 24, 30, 34–5, 38, 53, 62, 76, 78, 81, 84, 85, 111, 142, 144, 145, 146–50, 152, 154, 160, 168, 172, 177, 179; *Harold the Dauntless*, 35; *History of Scotland*, 149; *Ivanhoe*, 148; *Kenilworth*, 144; *The Lady of the Lake*, 23, 38; *Life of Napoleon*, 149; *Lord of the Isles*, 35; *Marmion*, 38; *Quentin Durward*, 147; review of *Emma*, 125; *Rokeby*, 22; *Waverley*, 148
Shakespeare, William, 11, 23
Sharp, Richard, 62 n
Sharpe, William, 34 n
Shell, Marc, 8 n
Shelley, Mary, 38
Shelley, Percy Bysshe, 10, 18, 30, 33, 39, 76, 144 n; *Defence of Poetry*, 34; *Masque of Anarchy*, 38; *Peter Bell the Third*, 54; *St. Irvyne*, 144 n; *Works*, 38
Sheridan, Richard Brinsley, *The Rivals*, 139
Shoberl, Frederic, 29 n
Simpkin, Marshall and Co., publishers and book wholesalers, 32, 94
Simpson, David, 126 n
Siskin, Clifford, 68 n
Sleath, Eleanor, *Orphan of the Rhine*, 138
Smart, Thomas Burnett, 35 n
Smiles, Samuel, 22 n, 53 n, 54 n, 78 n, 84 n, 98 n, 100 n, 172, 182 n
Smith, Adam, 17
Smith, Edmund, *Hippolytus and Phoedra*, 74
Smith, Elder, publishers, 26, 35 n, 38, 153, 155, 157
Smith, George, 155
Smith, Horace, 83
Smith, Sydney, 74 n, 81
Smith, W. H., 160 n
Smollett, Tobias: *Humphry Clinker*, 150; *Peregrine Pickle*, 150; *Roderick Random*, 150; *Sir Launcelot Greaves*, 150, 161
sociology, literary, 14, 16–7, 126 n
Sophocles, 11
Southey, Edith May, 84 n
Southey, Robert, 23–4, 29 n, 30, 35, 50, 64,

LIBRARY OF CONGRESS CATALOGING-IN-PUBLICATION DATA

Erickson, Lee.
   The economy of literary form : English literature and the
industrialization of publishing, 1800–1850 / Lee Erickson.
      p.   cm.
   Includes bibliographical references and index.
   ISBN 0-8018-5145-9 (hc : alk. paper)
   1. English literature—19th century—History and criticism.
2. Literature publishing—Economic aspects—Great Britain—
History—19th century.   3. Authors and publishers—Great
Britain—History—19th century.   4. Authors and readers—Great
Britain—History—19th century.   5. Authorship—Economic
apsects—Great Britain.   6. London (England)—Intellectual
life—19th century.   7. Literature and society—Great Britain—
History—19th century.   8. Printing—Great Britain—History—
19th century.   9. Literary form.   I. Title.
PR451.E75   1996
820.9′007—dc20   95-17054